A ZOOM
WITH A VIEW

A ZOOM *with a* VIEW

A Mystery

JESS CANNON

DUTTON

DUTTON
An imprint of Penguin Random House LLC
1745 Broadway, New York, NY 10019
penguinrandomhouse.com

Book design by Shannon Nicole Plunkett

LIBRARY OF CONGRESS CATALOGING-IN-PUBLICATION DATA

Names: Cannon, Jess author
Title: Zoom with a view: a mystery / Jess Cannon.
Description: New York, NY : Dutton, 2026.
Identifiers: LCCN 2025041523 (print) | LCCN 2025041524 (ebook) |
ISBN 9798217047444 hardcover | ISBN 9798217047468 ebook
Subjects: LCGFT: Cozy mysteries | Novels | Fiction
Classification: LCC PS3603.A548 Z43 2026 (print) |
LCC PS3603.A548 (ebook)
LC record available at https://lccn.loc.gov/2025041523
LC ebook record available at https://lccn.loc.gov/2025041524

Printed in the United States of America
1st Printing

The authorized representative in the EU for product safety and compliance is Penguin Random House Ireland, Morrison Chambers, 32 Nassau Street, Dublin D02 YH68, Ireland, https://eu-contact.penguin.ie.

To my mom, who is nothing like Karina,
except for the fierce way she loves
our family and community.

And to my sister, who is like Emily
in all the best ways—especially always
being there for me.

The well-known world had broken up, and there emerged Florence, a magic city where people thought and did the most extraordinary things. Murder, accusations of murder, a lady clinging to one man and being rude to another—were these the daily incidents of her streets? Was there more in her frank beauty than met the eye—the power, perhaps, to evoke passions, good and bad, and bring them speedily to a fulfillment?

—E. M. Forster, *A Room with a View*

A ZOOM WITH A VIEW

Prologue

10 p.m., July 4

The fights would begin as they did twice a year—every New Year's Eve and Independence Day—on social media. There would be the customary reminders (as if anyone had forgotten) about what was legal within the city limits of Blue Oak, Texas: you couldn't light anything bigger than a sparkler, so those full-grade fireworks going off down the block were certainly not permissible. Had no one read the city council's policies? Because if not, here's a link to those documents, highlighted and annotated in full.

There would be reminders about the childhood friend whose house burned down as a result of a wayward firecracker, possibly with photos of questionable origin showing burnt-out holes in the ground where a house used to stand.

There would be reminders about the fur-babies—those precious shaking pups cowering in terror beneath beds and under the weight of ThunderShirts. They suffered so, and would no one think of their needs?

There would be references to war zones, as if the town-turned-suburb of Blue Oak—once a tiny stop outside Austin and now a relatively wealthy commuter hub that had been economically developed within an inch of its communal life—had suddenly morphed into a made-for-TV movie with bombs exploding all around.

There would be pushback too. That one irascible neighbor who comments at least three times a day has fond memories of the bottle-rocket days of his youth. Yes, there was that one time when his childhood buddy Stan lost a finger. But once it healed, Stan drew a smiley face on it and made constant off-color jokes, and everyone loved Stan, so what was the big deal?

There would also be the people who—for the love of all that was holy—were deeply sick of this discussion. Every. Single. Year. Was anyone's mind *ever* changed on social media? they would ask, trying to change people's minds on social media.

The people who posted or commented would, of course, be a tiny margin of the overall population on the neighborhood Facebook group. Or, in this case, groups—the citizens of Blue Oak had two rival Facebook groups to choose from, another source of tension in the seemingly idyllic town. The debates about which was better and why they had to have two in the first place were constant. Many people wrote the same posts in both groups, giving an odd, alternate-universe quality to the discussions that played out into the night.

The vast majority of their neighbors would ignore them completely, because who bothered to watch the same tired online discussions every year when they could set off the fireworks they had just bought?

And there would be the handful of neighbors who loved other people's petty drama. They popped metaphorical—or maybe actual—popcorn, grabbed another beer or topped off their wine, and opened their app as the first bright lights burst outside their windows.

One person in Blue Oak, however, would be particularly grateful for the fireworks that night.

The neighborhood fireworks would make it easier to commit, and then cover up, the first murder in Blue Oak in more than a decade.

1

Five hours earlier, July 4

Leonora "Leo" Holloway squints at the fading Pepto-and-teal HAIR TODAY, DYE TOMORROW sign and sighs—she's home, unfortunately. She spent two days driving twenty-six hours and thirty-eight minutes from Scranton, Pennsylvania, to arrive exhausted and hot in downtown Blue Oak, Texas. The drive was only made bearable by her blue heeler mix, Derrida—named to irritate the theory bros from graduate school who loved to lecture others on the term *deconstruction*. Derrida's occasional whine and nuzzle would reminder her that not everyone had an ironclad bladder. Otherwise, Leo might have white-knuckled the wheel and kept her foot on the pedal until she calcified. The drive itself was mind-bendingly boring; the audiobooks and podcasts she'd downloaded could not distract her from the fact that she was fleeing a career in flames. But still—as she stands outside her mother's salon and looks around at the irritatingly twee downtown decorated in red, white, and blue—she knows in her bones this move is a mistake.

Back in May, Leo had finally called her mother in defeat as she faced the end of the job-seeking process: after her last rejection emails had all come in with their flowery "unfortunatelys," their pseudo-shocked "overwhelming responses," their anemic "best of lucks." Her mom had called her best friend. And together they called Leo within the hour. They proposed a job she couldn't refuse. Well, wouldn't, anyway—it was the only job offer she had.

The salary downright stunned her, after years of trying to survive on the dregs of English department budgets. Leo will now be a *photographer*, though not the kind she fantasized about when she imagined chucking her career as a professor and literary scholar to follow her art. Photography has always been her escape, a connection to happier days spent rambling with her dad. This job will likely involve much less creativity.

Leo takes her camera out for a few shots of her mother's salon sign, instinctively crouching down to change the angle to one she likes better—her father's daughter, always. She wants to view the town through her lens as a kitschy-quaint roadside stop, a place for a quick snack—like a slice of pecan pie and a glass of tea so sweet her spoon stands up in it from the diner across the street named I Spie—before continuing on her journey. If she can convince herself that she's just a tourist, perhaps this won't be as bad.

Around the town square in front of the shop, small groups are starting to gather, setting up chairs for the Fourth of July parade later that evening. Law enforcement officers and park workers string yellow tape that reads POLICE LINE: DO NOT CROSS through strategically placed traffic cones with circles on top to keep the crowd off the parade route. When Leo was young, the parade had been a few people in trucks with streamers throwing candy. But as with anything in Blue Oak, or anything that has Kay Schneider's hand on it, the parade has grown exponentially over the years.

The photography job that brought her back is exactly the kind of thing Leo's mother's best friend would cook up. The name on Leo's mother's birth certificate is Karen. And her mother's best friend is also named Karen. When she met Karen K. on the first day of kindergarten in Blue Oak, Leo's mother officially became Karen J.

As Karen K. likes to say, the two Karens have been thick as thieves since that day in kindergarten. To keep their names straight in school, Karen J. soon became Karina. And Karen K. just went by Kay.

Their favorite joke: They'd been smart to change their names years earlier; they might have been born Karens but weren't actually "Karens." Leo—along with Kay's two daughters, Beth and Emily—rolls her eyes every time they make that joke.

As adults, Kay and Karina settled four doors down from each other, just a few blocks over from where each of them had grown up. Leo calls Kay "Aunt Kay," and they tell everyone Kay is Leo's godmother, despite the fact that the Karens grew up Baptist. Leo has almost no memories from her childhood that do not include Kay's family, especially Emily, who is a year younger than Leo.

That day in May when Kay called to offer her a job, Leo could hear her mother whispering in the background, but Kay was the only one who spoke.

"Come back to Blue Oak, honey," Kay insisted, her tone warm but adamant. "I know you think I'm BS-ing you, but I'm really not. You've done great work freelancing for our social media for the last few years, and we need more. You know the real estate business is growing faster than we can keep up with. I need you to be my in-house photographer."

Leo tried to turn Kay down, she really did, but it was like Kay had cheated and seen Leo's list of reasons to say no.

Leo said she had no experience taking pictures of houses. "Shoot, sister, it's the easiest thing in the world—I'll show you what to do, we just need some decent lights and to make it look artsy. Our last guy couldn't even get things in focus! With all the Californians coming, we'd rather our photos be artistic than commercial. That's why we want you."

Leo had no place to live, and she wasn't moving in with her mother—they'd kill each other within a week. "Lucky you! We just finished fixin' up the pool house last fall! Emily said it's probably bigger than that closet you lived in in New York City anyway. You can stay as long as you need to."

By the time she started negotiating rent for the pool house ("Of course we won't charge family!"), Leo knew she'd lost. She'd had just enough wherewithal to say she wanted a couple of days to think about it. ("Honey, take your time! We know how to get ahold of you if we need to.") By the time they hung up, Leo had as good as moved.

That day, Leo had felt the beginnings of an anxiety spiral. Moving home could not be the answer. The last few years going from one yearlong postdoc to another had been deeply lonely, but she at least added lines to her CV, and honed her scholarly skills. Sure, she wanted marriage and kids and a full life, but those things would be waiting when she got a tenure-track job, when she had more publications, when she'd proven herself as a professor. She had no idea how Emily, younger than Leo but with a wife and three kids and a mortgage, had jumped feetfirst into life while Leo was still *preparing*. Contemplating the job offer from Kay, Leo felt a clawing sense of panic—was she just going to give up on everything she'd worked so hard for? The sacrifices she'd made over the years to achieve goals that now seemed to be moving farther and farther away? Had all those years been a waste?

After hanging up with Kay, Leo immediately called Emily, who answered without a greeting, as she always did.

"Whatever that mean voice in your head is telling you, it's a lie, you know."

Leo huffs out a rueful laugh. "Why do you know me so well?"

"Did my mom steamroll you?"

"Completely."

"Are you coming?"

"Do I have a choice?"

"You always have a choice. Hudson, *put that glitter down*. Just a sec." Emily set the phone down and Leo could hear her yell-talking, and then a bellow: “Tess! Can you help? Talking to Leo.”

Emily’s wife’s soothing voice was not quite quiet enough. “Did Kay convince her yet?” There was a beat of silence, so Leo guessed Emily was mouthing something. Then the sound of screaming faded as Emily walked to the back porch; Leo could hear the thwack of the screen door over the phone.

“Glitter, huh?”

Emily laughed. “Tess is the fun mom. If it were up to me, glitter would be banned within a five-mile radius of this house.”

Leo breathed in. “How many people know about this job?”

As always, Emily knew what she was asking. “First of all, it was my idea. It’s not a pity job. We genuinely need you, Lee. I’ve told you a million times that when you started managing our social media three years ago, we noticed an immediate uptick in business. We probably need at least two of you. And you need a job.”

Leo pursed her lips. “I need an academic job. I’ve worked too hard to give up now.”

“I’m not having this conversation again. You’re not giving up, you’re acknowledging the truth of the situation. No one has tried harder than you. It’s not a failure to recognize that a crumbling system is no longer worth devoting your life to.”

By the end of the phone call, Leo had agreed, but with a gnawing sense of wrongness in the pit of her stomach. She had never been as outspoken as Emily, Karina, and Kay. She preferred to withdraw and refuse to do what she didn’t want to do—Emily called it “turtling.” Except now she couldn’t even turtle; with no other options, her stubbornness would no longer help her.

That’s how Leo ended up here, back in her hometown, standing outside her mother’s salon. In the reflection in the salon window, she even looks essentially the same as she did when she lived here in high school. Her black tank top has a block of text that repeats *Read Banned Books* in rainbow colors; she has on ripped-up jean shorts and the Tevas she's owned for ten years. Leo has been in enough therapy to recognize that her unvarying wardrobe choices are a direct response to her mother's fussy "glamour shots" aesthetic. When Leo teaches, she's poetry-prof chic—black linen pants with cardigans paired with sensible shoes in funky colors. Otherwise, she looks like a high schooler at a summer job at the beach. She's already worried about what to wear at the realty office—Texas isn't exactly the place for a professionally bland all-black ensemble. Today, in the salon reflection, she feels a sense of déjà vu—as if she's morphed back into the angry, grieving senior who couldn't wait to get the hell out of town.

The building contributes to her feeling of having moved back in time. Everything at the salon is unchanged from when she lived in Blue Oak. A bedazzled, curlicued CLOSED sign is slightly askew in the window. The four pink haircut chairs are dim ghosts in the interior; the back of the teal velvet couch set against the window where customers wait for their appointments and peruse magazines—or, more likely these days, their phones—has faded in the sunlight.

Leo swallows. In the last few years, she has been focused on her own life and her career. But now, standing outside her mother's salon, it hits her—life has gone on here in Blue Oak. And her mother might not be doing so well.

It's not like her mother to let the shop go; she is always impeccably turned out, even if her flashy, sparkling version of well-dressed has nothing to do with Leo's taste. In fact, her mother's paranoia about how they look and act, how the community receives them, is one of the many reasons Leo couldn't wait to get out of town in the first place. Her mother, on the other hand, adores Blue Oak, leaving only for the cruises she always seems to be traveling on. Mother and daughter rarely FaceTime anymore; they tend to do better with phone calls that they keep short and sweet. And even if they had FaceTimed, Leo wouldn't have thought to ask about the exterior paint job on the salon.

Her throat catches at the memory of her father on a ladder slapping on the pink color her mother had chosen almost fifteen years ago.

After the first coat, Richard had called Karina and Leo out to look at it.

Teenage Leo hadn't been able to keep the horror out of her voice. "Mom, honestly, are you sure you don't want black and white? It'll be so tasteful."

"With a name like 'Hair Today, Dye Tomorrow'? It'll look like a morgue."

"Yet another reason to rethink that name."

"You've hated it since you were little. Why would I change it now?" Karina blew a kiss at Richard. "Honey, I think it looks perfect. It's bright and eye-catching."

Leo crossed her arms. "It's certainly eye-catching."

Richard had climbed down from the ladder while they talked, a wet paint roller still in his hand. He planted a kiss on each of their foreheads. "Leo, it's your mom's store, and it will certainly catch some eyes—though not as many as the good-looking store owner."

"Gross." Leo rolled her eyes at the smirk on her parents' faces. They were always like this together; they'd met as flower-child humanitarian workers in El Salvador, changing the world one fair-trade farm and small business at a time. They got married and then had Leo, eventually moving back to Karina's hometown so she could open up her dream salon and so Leo could start school. Richard had gotten a teaching certificate so he could have the same hours as his daughter; her mom had transformed from hippie traveler to kooky hairstylist. Her parents had been sickeningly, adorably in love their entire marriage.

Looking at the sign now, Leo realizes her mother probably has not painted it since that day. She adds "repainting the salon sign" to her mental list of things to do while she's home this summer. And it *is* only for this summer.

She cannot face the idea that this is her life now, that at

thirty-three—with a master's degree in rhetoric and a doctorate in English literature, an award-winning dissertation on E. M. Forster's subversive postcolonial representational tactics, three peer-reviewed articles, two grant-funded research fellowships, and twelve conference presentations to her name—she has no better option than to move into Kay's pool house and become a pity-job real estate photographer.

Two loud voices interrupt her train of thought, which, considering the path it was taking, is probably a good thing. "Gah, babe, she's the *worst.* Did you see her face on that float?" Leo can best describe the woman's speech as a piercing whine.

"Oh, I saw it, babe," a man responds in a rumbling voice.

Derrida snaps his head up. Leo half turns, the worries about her mother scattering in instant delight.

There in the flesh are Chaz Nickolson and Kymber Owens. Chaz is wearing a navy tank top to show off his ripped arms, and red workout shorts that skim his well-built thighs. His dark hair is slicked into a man bun, and as he walks from the shadow into the light, he pulls aviator sunglasses off his head and slips them on in one smooth movement. Beside him, Kymber—dressed in a navy sports bra and red-white-and-blue Lycra shorts—gazes adoringly at him, shades already on. She takes three steps to his one, glancing around to see who is watching. Leo can almost hear the soundtrack in their minds as they strut down the street.

She whips out her phone and dials without looking. Emily answers: "Where are you?"

"At Mom's salon. Five minutes here, and I already spotted Chaz and Kymber."

"Oh, babe, are they babeing each other?"

"Babe, so much babeing."

Emily snorts. "Welcome home, babe. Welcome home."

2

Leo tugs Derrida's leash gently and follows Chaz and Kymber as they walk south. She knows that Chaz's business, DreamBawd Gym, is down the street from Hair Today, Dye Tomorrow—on the other side of the downtown square surrounding the courthouse. But Chaz is walking in a different direction, and she realizes he's headed to the float-preparation area. She's instantly, punch-drunkenly giddy. The highlight of returning to Blue Oak will definitely be watching Chaz's ridiculous behavior in real time in the town's over-the-top Fourth of July parade.

She's known Charles Nickolson through almost all the phases of his life, the way you know everyone in a small town, though he wasn't someone she paid attention to until a few years ago. When he was young, everyone called him Chuck. But he'd had what Leo's undergrads called a "glow up" before starting high school. Chuck told everyone to call him Charlie when he showed up cute, muscular, and tall the first day of freshman year. As Charlie, he led first the junior varsity, then the varsity football teams to victory after victory, making him a local celebrity in Texas. He was a senior Leo's first year in high school; he was in the same class as Emily's older sister, Beth.

Like the whole starting line of the football team, Charlie had been a pallbearer for Dominic Garner, the cousin of Mack

Garner—one of Leo's childhood best friends. Dominic, an exalted senior, was so much cuter and more adult seeming than Mack, her overgrown puppy of a friend. She'd been devastated when Dominic died suddenly at the very end of his senior year in a freak accident. Leo's last memory of seeing Charlie Nickolson in person was at Dom's funeral, dressed in an ill-fitting suit.

For the rest of high school, college, and most of her twenties, Leo forgot that Charlie Nickolson existed. And then one day in 2015, not long after starting her doctoral program at Columbia, she got a text from Emily. *Is this Charlie Nickolson with Bodhi? Do you remember him? Beth says it must be.*

It was a screenshot from the account of a yoga influencer named Bodhi Bruce whom Emily and Leo loved to hate-follow on Instagram. Several months before, when Leo was complaining about a particularly rough researching day, Emily had sent a misspelled inspirational quote (*Your the center of your dreams*) from Bodhi's Instagram account to give Leo a laugh. After that, they often sent each other Bodhi's pearls of "wisdom." Mostly, Bodhi shared quotes that were notoriously misspelled or that plagiarized famous authors. She was also fond of sharing workout videos with genuinely terrible form but intentional crotch shots.

It turned out that Emily and Leo were not the only ones hate-following her; Emily found an entire snark subreddit devoted to categorizing all the ways that Bodhi Bruce—whose real name was Brittni—had a concerning social media presence. Soon Emily's and Leo's favorite shared hobby was reading the hilarious chats by smart (mostly) women who were waking up to the problematic ways influencers like Bodhi made them feel bad about their bodies and themselves.

They'd been following Bodhi for a while, and were well-versed in what the subredditors called the "Bodhi-verse," by the time Emily texted Leo the possible picture of Charlie Nickolson. Leo zoomed in on the photo. Bodhi stood in a black sports bra and black leggings on a gym floor taking a mirror selfie in her customary pose: left arm flexed, left leg cocked slightly, hips tilted so that her waist looked even smaller. Behind her, a tall white man with a brown man bun wearing a tank top that showed his armpit hair also flexed his muscles and made a duck face for the camera. A face that looked just like an older, fuller version of the Charlie Nickolson she remembered.

She texted Emily back. *OMG, is our high school quarterback Bodhi's new boyfriend? And does his tank top really say "Chaz Your Dreams"?*

Stop it. Hold on, I missed the shirt. Leo waited while the three dots appeared on the screen. *Confirmed. It does, in fact, tell us to chaz our dreams. Have you been chazzing yours, Lee?*

I don't even want to know what that means, but I immediately need to take a shower. Is that today's post? What do the snarkers say?

I haven't gotten that far yet. This post is twelve minutes old.

Within minutes, Leo and Emily were talking over each other on speakerphone. They quickly confirmed several things: Bodhi's new boyfriend was, in fact, Charlie Nickolson from Blue Oak, Texas, who had apparently changed his name again to Chaz. At some point, he'd broken up with the last girlfriend they knew about, his high school sweetheart, Tiffani, who they were pretty sure he'd married. He'd become a low-level fitness influencer whose signature line was, in fact, "Chaz Your Dreams!" Emily later told her wife, Tess, that if the mantra hadn't been quite so obnoxious, she and Leo might have left well enough alone, and Chaz's chaos wouldn't have become so central to both of their lives. But the mantra, and Chaz's entire social media personality, were so deeply irritating, so wildly problematic, that the choice had essentially been made for them.

Anyway, it wasn't like they could avoid him; Chaz was everywhere. The meme of Chaz reacting to Bodhi's product placement from Goop in 2017 (jumping back while yelling "Did you say *vagina egg*?") felt like it was on every Millennial's algorithm for at least a year. The think-pieces about "Yoni-Gate" in *The Cut* and *Jezebel* were written by reporters who were obviously in the snark group. It was a heady gathering place for pop-culture-loving nerds. For Emily and Leo, it became their internet home.

And then, at the end of 2018, suddenly and inexplicably, Chaz and Bodhi broke up. The subreddit immediately divided—on one side, those who thought Chaz should remain a subject for the sub, and on the other, those who thought the group should focus solely on Bodhi. Until one user, u/SmallTown-Snarker, made a comment that got 1.5k likes and twelve awards: she would start a separate subreddit just for Chaz.

And that was how the r/ChazNickolsonSnark subreddit was born.

• • • • •

Welcome, you gorgeous snarkers, to the snarkiest place on earth! We launched our own little snark show in late 2018 to talk about our favorite wannabe (but never will be) almost-celeb, Charles "Chaz" Nickolson.

CHAZ: Obviously a snark group called "Chaz Nickolson Snark" is about the big man himself. Chaz grew up in Blue Oak, Texas, a small suburb of Austin where he led the high school football team, the Blue Oak Bandits, to multiple victories—can't fight the BO! He went to Texas Tech for college, and then moved back to Austin. The early years of Chaz's marriage to our Gal Pal Tiff and what he did in those years is not really known and seems, honestly, kind of boring. This was before he became the quadfecta* of influence that he is now.

QUADFECTA: As he will proudly tell anyone who will listen, Chaz Nickolson is:

1. A real estate agent.

2. A CrossFit gym owner (it's called DreamBawd in what we think is supposed to be a pun, but . . . how? Is the gym itself bawdy? The bodies bawdy? The mystery remains), which he runs with his best friend / partner in crime, Grant Ford (more about Grant, the LeFou to Chaz's Gaston).

3. An internet pastor (his "chapel" is a conference room he calls "DreamSoul" in the gym).

4. And, of course, a social media influencer.

CHAZZERCISERS: That's you and the intrepid group of 17k (and growing!) snarkers who have joined in to witness and comment on Chaz's . . . exploration of himself and his place in the world. We're not really going to Chaz our *own* dreams, but as Chaz, well, chazzes *his* dreams, we show up with the popcorn. And receipts. And hand sanitizer for all that chazzing.

KYMBER OWENS: Kymber is Chaz's current girlfriend, after he broke up with Bodhi and went through a string of girlfriends we call Bodhi-Lites. Kymber exploded into our lives in 2021, at the height of the pandemic when so many of us were at home bored or scared. Where would we be without her unhinged rants, always spoken over Chaz's shoulder into the camera? Without her poor-form fitness videos that mostly just feature her booty? (Literally: do not ever copy her unless you want a back injury.) Her vague-posting whenever she and Chaz are experiencing trouble in paradise? Her constant gum-smacking? Her collagen-plumped duck lips?

And always, babe, *always*, is the babeing. There's so much babeing. Did you know, babe, that even when things are, like, hard, that I'll always be here for you, babe? Babe, you're so right. Even when they fight, babe, they're, like, still going strong, because, like, babe, their love is *real*.

The sub is grateful for that, at least, because, babe, if they broke up, what else would we snark on with our tens of thousands of online besties?

•••••

For five years and counting, Leo (as u/SnarkySnarkFunkyBnch) was the administrative brawn behind the brains of u/SmallTownSnarker (Emily). Leo wrote the FAQ page (a nice break from literary analysis), and they both kept a light hand on discussions in the group. They made sure that there were no references in any of their posts that would lead the rest of the group to find out their identities.

This task got harder when Chaz moved back to Blue Oak, where Emily and Tess had been living since getting married after college. Leo quietly worried at times that the ethical boundaries in online spaces were not clear-cut. As moderators for the subreddit, Emily and Leo are de facto experts on all things Chaz Nickolson. When Chaz decided to become a real estate agent and start a rival Facebook page to get business away from Schneider Realty, Emily learned about it first through snarkers making fun of his YouTube channel. Emily and Kay—who did not know about her daughter's snark group, but knew Chaz was gunning for their business—decided that, in response, they needed to amp up their own presence on Facebook.

When Emily asked her to do some extra contract work as a Facebook admin, Leo made a burner Facebook account (Bertha Rosenhaus; in her sixties; a divorcée who used the term *divorcée* and who was living in her daughter's house in Blue Oak to care for her grandchildren after school). Leo had deactivated her own social media accounts after hearing too many stories from academics on the job market. But as Bertha Rosenhaus, she immediately found herself enmeshed in the petty grievances of the Schneider Realty Blue Oak Neighborhood Facebook group, where the administrative work was significantly more demanding than on the snark subreddit.

"Bertha Rosenhaus" also joined the Chaz Your Dreams Realty Blue Oak and Area group as a spy.

In the years when Leo was completing and defending her dissertation—then beginning the first of a string of one-year, nonrenewable teaching positions—the rival Facebook groups felt like a novel where she got to read all about people in her hometown. She saw their lives playing out in discussions about coyotes in the greenbelt, trash pickup changes, weekend disturbances three doors down, incorrect Amazon deliveries, drivers going too fast through stop signs, recommendations for doctors and roofers and painters and dog-sitters, winners of the local pie-eating contest, curbside furniture giveaways, and pleas to find missing cats (which probably had much to do with the apparent influx of coyotes in Blue Oak). She helped Kay Schneider Realty keep its Facebook page—a key component for the Boomer and Gen X clientele—sharp and marketable in comparison to Chaz's group. It was exactly the level of interaction she wanted with her hometown: as if she was peering through a window into its secrets but not having to actually interact with anyone as herself.

And Leo also stayed with Emily as fellow mods and chief snarkers of the Chaz Nickolson Snark subreddit. As their mothers used to say, if Emily killed someone, Leo would bury the body: Emily was the force, Leo the support. That dynamic never changed.

And now, for the first time since Emily had launched the snark subreddit, Leo was following Chaz and Kymber in real life.

• • • • •

Leo turns left at the corner that Chaz and Kymber took a minute before, onto the street where the parade is lining up. It's packed. Blue Oak High cheerleaders stretch in blue-and-gold uniforms; a group of girls in black dresses with a green Celtic letter *S* emblazoned on them are tap-dancing in the street.

Kymber and Chaz amble a few floats ahead of her. And then Leo stops in wonder.

Four floats down, there it is: Kay Schneider's face, as tall as a house. Cutout Kay is smiling, her hair bouffant-big, her smile eerily white. A giant tiara of wires frames the face; an enormous baby-pink scepter rises from the float, topped with a sparkling gold knob. Leo attempts to swallow her laugh; Derrida glances up at her. She pulls out her phone and takes a quick snap to send to Emily with the text: *Your description did not do this justice; this thing is massive and that scepter is the most obscene thing I've ever seen.*

There's an immediate response ding: *Is that Kymber?*

Leo looks carefully at the photo, then at the float in real life. Sure enough, Kymber rounds the corner from the back of the cutout head, walking on the Schneider Realty float, fiddling with the wires around Kay's head.

Leo's phone rings and she answers without looking. Emily is irate. "Is Kymber on our float, Lee?"

Leo pulls Derrida behind a pickup truck a few hundred feet away, out of sight of Chaz and Kymber, her voice low. "She is. Want me to stop them?"

"Not this time. We're going to get the evidence we need to stop them. They're not getting away with this—not anymore!"

3

"We need photos of them in the act. Are they destroying anything?" Emily whips the minivan around the pre-parade crowd.

"I can't tell." Leo's whisper is loud over the car speakers. "She's behind your mom's ginormous head."

"What's Chaz saying?"

"I can't hear him. You're talking to me."

"I'm parking the car right now. Go."

"Okay. See you in a sec."

Two and a half blocks from the float-staging area, Emily parallel parks between two pickup trucks, then half runs in the heat, waving vaguely at neighbors who call out to her. She glances up at the street signs to be able to tell Leo where she is and grins, like she does several times a day.

Leo shot out of town as fast as she could, leaving for NYU as an undergrad, then the University of Chicago for a master's degree, then back to New York for a PhD at Columbia. In those years, she barely came back to Blue Oak. And yet her fingerprints are still all over the town.

When Leo and Emily were growing up, the streets all had basic names; Emily had just parked near the corner of what had been Main Street and North Thirteenth Street. A decade ago, unbeknownst to Emily, her mother had texted Leo asking for a list of thirty well-known but underrepresented writers. Thinking she was contributing to an exceptional TBR pile, Leo took a week to send a carefully compiled list; Kay simply texted *Thank you!* with a thumbs-up emoji.

Leo never even thought to mention it to her best friend.

Six months later, Emily noticed they were putting up street signs around town. Five streets in, she stopped and pulled her phone out. She sent picture after picture to Leo with the caption: *Did you do this?*

Leo called her, laughing so hard she could barely breathe. Of course Kay had not been asking for books to read. She was a longtime member of the Blue Oak City Council, and now each of those authors was a street name.

Blue Oak takes its motto—"Keep Blue Oak Weirder"—very seriously. Everyone who grew up here knows the story: the town voted in some city ordinances in the 1970s to make the city intentionally diverse; they dismantled the racial covenant clauses on the city's books, created mixed-income neighborhoods, and actively recruited former refugees and immigrants not always welcome in other parts of Texas. Leo had not fully registered until she was an adult how different her childhood had been, with its small-town community made up of people from all walks of life. It was beautiful, but it could also be a bit cloying; Leo once described her home's vibe to a friend in New York as "a smug DEI committee but make it a town."

Which is why Emily is now squinting against the sun on the corner of Lorraine Hansberry Boulevard and Kazuo Ishiguro Street.

The aging hippies on the council view Blue Oak as the last bastion of weirdness near Austin. Emily's heard them gripe for years: Hippie Hollow is all touristy now and you can't even sunbathe nude without somebody surreptitiously snapping a picture. Downtown Austin is no longer the hangout of tattooed buskers; it is chock-full of tech bros on scooters and Botox-filled lifestyle gurus in wide-brimmed hats. Even Matthew McConaughey has gone from smoking doobies while saying, "All right all right all right!" to hawking Lincolns.

Emily would never tell her, but she secretly relishes the fact that Leo's love of reading is represented in the very street names of their hometown. Even though Leo's been long gone, some core part of her is still here, rooted in this place.

Several houses away from her best friend, Emily stops and hides behind a tree, her mood immediately souring. From this angle, Emily clearly sees Kymber examining the wires around Cutout Kay's left ear. Chaz is pointing at the float, obviously directing Kymber. Emily snaps photos with her phone.

Leo calls and Emily answers with the AirPod dangling in her right ear, still snapping pictures. "Where are you?"

"Behind the Nacho Daddy's float. Is this a . . . taco?"

"Oh, the vagina taco?"

Emily spots the top of Leo's bun on the other side of a float three to her left from where Kymber and Chaz stand.

Leo whispers, "This is intentional, right?"

"Oh, they know what that taco looks like. That float alone brings half the tourists to this parade."

"Em, these big strands of lettuce are *fuzzy*. They *curl*."

"Yup. We all know. I see you. I'm across the street."

Leo pops her head up, topknot askew, and scours the street until she sees Emily waving from behind the tree. They grin at each other, and from across the street Emily can see Leo's mouth moving while her voice is low in Emily's ear. "Can you see Chaz?"

"Yes, and Kymber." Emily scoots to the other side of the tree for a better vantage point. "I want to know what Chaz is telling her to do."

"I'm going in."

Emily watches Leo huddle-walk between floats like a soldier avoiding sniper fire, Derrida behind her, ears at attention. In spite of her anger at Chaz and Kymber, Emily's smile tucks into her cheek. Leo's not tall, and she's wearing an outfit Emily knows she has owned since about 2012. Leo got bangs when *New Girl* was popular and the straight bangs—a dark contrast against Leo's pale skin—have lasted despite Emily's best efforts to convince Leo to move toward curtain bangs over the years. Emily thinks Leo likes them because they're a kind of protective layer she can pull over herself. With her oversize tortoiseshell glasses settled on the distinctive curve of her nose, Emily privately thinks Leo looks like an adorable owl, all beaky and soulful. Leo blinks her bottle-green eyes when she pulls into herself in crowds, observes and overthinks before she speaks, and cocks her head, bird-like, when something occurs to her. Unless Emily needs her—then Leo charges in without a second thought. It's just like Leo to arrive, reluctant and resentful, back to Blue Oak, but then drop everything and do exactly what is needed the minute a crisis arises.

Leo rises from her crouch abruptly, head slightly tilted.

Emily asks, "What is it?"

"Kymber and Chaz have no idea who I am. I doubt Chaz remembers me from high school because I'm so much younger, and Kymber's never met me."

"That's true."

"So this is an opportunity. I'm just a passerby checking out the floats. I'm going to go talk to them."

"I'm coming too."

"No, Em." Leo starts walking nonchalantly past the next float, a tasteful open book with a large beer stein, and black-and-white font that reads *Top Shelf*, the downtown bookstore/bar. "You keep taking pictures. We need a better strategy than just yelling at them."

"But they deserve to be yelled at." Emily pouts.

"They do. But this is better. Record the audio on the phone."

"I don't know how to do that."

"Google it, Em. 'How to record a phone call on an iPhone.' Gah, *why* is this town so into the Fourth of July parade? Is there just nothing else to do in Blue Oak?" Emily glances up as Derrida sniffs the last float before Schneider Realty's—a giant ship's prow with the words *Thai Tanic* in a sea of roiling papier-mâché pad Thai noodles.

"You're allowed one small-town dig, and that was it; this town makes bank on holidays. The better the show, the more money we make."

"Okay, that's respectable."

Emily fiddles with her phone, hoping that she's clicked the right button after her quick Google session. "Go get 'em, I think I got the phone figured out."

Emily watches Leo straighten her shoulders and tug on Derrida's leash. "I'm going in."

"This one, babe?" Kymber's voice is clear over Emily's phone. Chaz's response is muffled. Emily watches in indignation as Kymber plucks at the wires Tess rigged to light the tiara and scepter. Kymber continues. "I don't think that's how it's supposed to . . . What if I . . . ?"

"Hi!" Leo shades her eyes, holding Derrida's leash firmly.

Kymber glances down. "Hi."

Chaz scoots around the float. "Well, hello!" Emily grits her teeth. Why does everything out of his mouth sound so smarmy?

Leo's voice again. "Would you mind telling me where the parade starts?"

"Over that way." Chaz points, flexing his biceps while he does, and Emily rolls her eyes. You can almost hear him saying, *Welcome to the gun show.*

"Perfect, thank you. Is this your float?"

"No." Chaz laughs derogatorily. "This giant-head float is definitely not ours. I'm Chaz." He holds his hand out and Leo shakes it. He pumps twice, then places his hand on her shoulder. Derrida's ears go back. Good, Emily thinks; the dog doesn't like Chaz any more than she does. And he clearly doesn't remember Leo, as she suspected he wouldn't. "Full name Chaz Nickolson, a local entrepreneur with multiple businesses you should know about: I own a real estate company, and a gym. Are you thinking of moving here?"

"I mean, not really. So this is . . . not your float?" Leo infuses her voice with confusion.

"It's our friend's." Chaz's voice is even and controlled. Emily almost spits in anger. She checks to make sure the iPhone is still recording.

"Was there something wrong with it?"

"Oh, we noticed a couple of wires were sticking out."

"What kind of wires?" Leo's voice drips with innocence.

Kymber hops down from the float. "It's fine, I fixed it."

"Are you an electrician?"

"No, but I'm handy." Kymber smirks, dusting her hands on her shorts like a mechanic.

Emily snorts and mutters, "More like *handsy*."

Leo ignores her friend's voice in her AirPod. "I have some experience with wiring. Do you want me to look at it?" Emily flat out laughs, muffling her voice in her closed fist. Leo can barely handle a screwdriver, much less fixing anything electrical.

"I got it." Kymber's voice drips honey. "Chaz, we probably better head over to our float."

Chaz's tone is condescending. "I'll just check your work first."

"Chaz, babe, we really should get to our float."

"Just a sec . . ."

"Babe. *Now*."

Emily follows Kymber's line of sight: Detective Jake Nguyen is walking down the street.

Chaz glances up and clocks the detective. "Everything seems good to me, great job, babe!" He backs away from the float, shoulders back, cracking his knuckles as they walk. Kymber is a sleek cat, poised and pleased.

Emily hurries over and is crossing the busy street as Jake notices Leo; he frowns, and then smiles broadly, tugging off his reflective sunglasses. "Leo Holloway, I never thought I'd see the day!"

Leo glances down behind her, and then turns. She tilts her head slightly, checking out Jake's tan uniform, before smiling. "Jake? Jake Nguyen?"

"That's me! What are you doing . . . ?" His next words are drowned in a blast of sound as the Blue Oak High School band starts up. Derrida ducks and growls, ears flattened, and Leo reaches down to pet him as he shoves his head against her leg.

Emily catches snatches of Leo's words over the slightly off-key band as she walks toward the float. ". . . just for the summer. I'm going to help out Kay . . . for a few weeks, really . . ."

Jake's voice is louder. "Yeah, I knew you'd be back. Emily told Becky, who told me." Jake's older sister, Becky, had been in Leo's year in school and is a nurse at Blue Oak Hospital now. Leo and Emily had had many sleepovers at Becky's house when Jake was a squirt of a kid three years younger; he's definitely not a squirt now. "Are you helping out with the float?"

Emily answers. "Of course not, I would never trust her to actually do any work on our float. Hi, Lee." Emily hugs her friend quickly, then puts her hand on Jake's arm and shouts to be heard as the tuba section launches full throttle into the song. "Jake, Chaz and Kymber were just here. We finally have proof! You *have* to arrest them."

4

Want to file an official report?" Leo notices how Jake's voice immediately switches into a calm register.

"Probably, but let me check with Mom first. The rest of the fam and Leo's mom are right behind me. I got pictures." Emily's ears are pink and Leo knows it's not just the heat; they always turn pink when she's angry. They stand out in sharp relief against her short blond hair. Emily fumbles for her phone, opening it and holding it out to Jake. "And Leo talked to them while I recorded their conversation on my phone."

"Wow, the two of you are trying to put me out of a job." Jake takes it and squints, thumbing through the photos.

While he looks, Emily squats and rubs the dog's ears. "How's my best boy? Did you miss me, Derri-dog?"

Jake holds his fist out for Derrida to sniff. Just then, the band strikes up again. Derrida's ears go down and Leo can feel his growl up the leash. She tugs the dog closer to her, and Jake steps back as she leans down to put a comforting arm around Derrida.

Emily raises her voice. "We finally caught Chaz and Kymber red-handed."

Jake zooms in on a photo. "They were on the float?"

"Messing with the wires," Leo supplies.

"Why would they do that?" Jake asks.

"You know about the tension between Schneider Realty and Chaz Your Dreams?" Emily says.

"Pretend like I don't."

Emily sighs but continues loudly, struggling to be heard over the band. "For the last few years, Chaz has started an all-out campaign against Mom's business. It started with brochures in every mailbox in Blue Oak about why he was the only Realtor to be trusted."

Leo adds, "He implied that Kay was old and senile and didn't know what she was doing."

Emily continues, "And then he started that rival Facebook page, cutting into one of Mom's early online tactics to build business."

Jake has had his ear turned toward them to be able to hear them, but faces them now. "But surely there are lots of growing real estate competitors in the Austin area."

Emily nods. "Sure, and Mom's handled all of it. In fact, she often mentors other agents. And yet he still implemented a campaign of targeted harassment trying to undercut our business."

"Did it work?" Jake's eyebrows are raised.

Emily shrugs. "More than we wish it had. Things have been . . . harder since he started. And lately there have been several acts of intentional vandalism in our houses. Nothing massive, but enough that the houses seem shoddier or less cared for. If a house isn't pristine when it shows, we can lose thousands. We clean and stage a home so it feels aspirational. We definitely don't want wires sticking out of a wall or cabinet doors hanging off or a puddle of pee in a corner."

"All of those things happened in Schneider Realty houses?"

"Yes. In the last few months."

"Why didn't you call the cops?"

"Mom talked to Quackenbush, but we couldn't prove anything. Except for the pee, it's all been pretty innocuous, just enough to look like we don't take care of our properties. Even that was childish and gross but easily cleaned up. We've been trying to figure this out, and we all suspect it's Chaz and probably Kymber or even his business partner, Grant, helping him. And now we have proof." Emily takes back her phone, thumbs to a picture, then holds it out to Jake. "See? Right there. Kymber did something to the wires, I'm sure of it."

Leo speaks up. "They weren't trying to hide the fact that they were messing with them; they acted like they were friends with Kay because they didn't know who I was."

Jake nods. "I'll go talk to Kymber and Chaz right now. Do we need to find an electrician or something?"

"No, Tess is an engineer. She did all of the wiring, so she'll be able to check it out."

He slips his sunglasses back on. "Text me if Tess finds anything, and send me the pictures and recording. I'll follow up with you after the parade to see if you want to file a report. Leo"—he holds up his hand in a wave—"glad you're back. Looking forward to catching up later."

He takes off at a light jog; Leo watches him until he turns the corner behind a float, then turns back to Emily, who has her eyebrow raised.

Leo rolls her eyes. "What?"

Emily shrugs. "Sorry I didn't let you know sooner about Detective Hottie over there. I might have gotten you to move back a while ago, but he wasn't on my radar."

"You probably didn't even notice."

"Please, Lee, I may be queer, but I have eyes. Still, I was betting on another tall, dark, and handsome blast from the past to convince you to stay."

"I told you already, Mack and I are old news. That was my senior year in high school."

"Which makes him the one who got away."

"Which makes *me* the one who got away."

"Fine, while *you* got away, he got a great degree, moved back home, became a successful business owner, and an extremely respected member of a community who really appreciates him. I, at least, appreciate his *thighs*, Lee."

"You are *married*, Emily."

"To a woman who *also* appreciates Mack's thighs, Lee." She smiles. "Now, I might need to add Detective Hottie to my schemes. Did you see those biceps in that tight shirt?"

"Seriously, Em, we have enough going on without you trying to pick out a hometown hero for me to bang." At 'hometown,' the band abruptly stops, and Leo's voice rings out in the sudden silence. Leo cringes and hunches her shoulders.

"Auntie Weo?"

Emily guffaws, then reaches down to pick up her youngest. "Hyacinth! Auntie Leo was just talking about banging the drums. Did you hear the drums?" Hyacinth's cherubic face lights up.

"They were *big*! And *woud*!" Hyacinth puts her hands on her ears.

"That was too loud for me!" Emily kisses her daughter with a loud smack.

Leo snuggles up behind Hyacinth and grabs her under the arms. "Loud, huh? What about this?" She gives a big raspberry kiss to Hyacinth's neck, and the girl peals into laughter. "I missed you, Hy-Hy." And it's true. Perhaps the *only* thing Leo has missed since she moved away is spending time with Emily and her kids. They'd traveled to see her a few months before, for spring break, but she realizes with a pang that they've already changed in that time.

"I miss you, Weo. Today's a *parade*! And it's going to go *boom*!"

"The parade is not going to go boom, Hyacinth, it's the fireworks afterwards." Hudson, her sturdy six-year-old brother, rolls his eyes as he comes up. Leo opens her arm and he gives her a side-arm hug. Just then, she feels an additional two arms below her waist.

"Leo!"

"Hattie! Hudson! I've missed you both!"

All three of the kids—Hudson, who is six, Hattie, who is four, and Hyacinth, who is two—wear matching red-white-and-blue outfits that Leo is confident Kay didn't tell Emily about until she'd already given them to the kids as presents.

Then suddenly the rest of the family swarms in. Kay has on a red-fringed tunic and envelops Leo in a small cloud of lavender spray. Her husband, Phil Schneider, accountant-pale in a blue button-up Dri-FIT shirt and cargo shorts, asks how Leo's car held up on the drive in. Tess, in a navy sundress that sets off her long brunette hair and cornflower-blue eyes, gives Leo a quick kiss on the cheek, then joins Emily to examine the wiring on the float.

Leo feels a hand tugging at Derrida's leash. "Does 'ittle Derrida wanna come with Granna?"

Leo turns to Karina. "Hi, Mom. Who's Granna?"

"Well, since this is the closest thing I'm probably ever going to have to a grandchild, I might as well embrace it, don't you think?" Karina tugs the leash away from Leo. She gives Leo a side hug almost as awkward as Hudson's; her bronzer is two shades too dark for her light skin and her bright-auburn hair sticks up a full inch from her scalp in a gloriously crisp Aqua Net helmet. Leo gets a little hair spray on her lips and tries not to overtly wipe her mouth. "Glad you're home, Leonora."

"Good to see you, Mom. You're really ready for the parade." Karina has on a red sparkling dress that flares at the waist 1950s-style, with a crinoline underskirt, and four-inch blue velvet platform heels.

"You have to give the people what they want. I'm doing a live haircut on the float."

"Are you really?"

"I am! But right now, Granna's taking her precious granddog on a walk! And to find a treat!" Derrida's tail thumps at the word he knows well.

"No people food, Mom! And we're not doing 'Granna'!"

Karina waves her hand dismissively over her shoulder and Derrida follows her, tail high.

Emily, who had been catching Tess, Kay, and Phil up about Chaz and Kymber on the float, squeezes Leo's shoulder and speaks softly into her ear. "Honestly, you have to give her credit. She worked in a passive-aggressive grandmother comment within five seconds of your arrival."

Leo barely stops herself from rolling her eyes. The feeling of reverting back to being a moody teenager threatens to strangle her. She'd spent the drive down to Texas planning on having mature interactions with her mom, who had clearly not gotten the memo.

Leo watches her mom leave, then turns back to Emily, who is leaning down listening attentively to one of Hattie's interminable stories. Leo adores Emily, and doesn't begrudge her a moment of happiness with her wife and kids, but whenever she's with all of them, Leo is acutely aware of the differences in their lives: Emily has a lovely home, a good job, a healthy long-term relationship, a thriving career that benefits an entire community, three well-loved kids. Emily's navy tee with a star in the middle works perfectly with the whole family ensemble; they could pose for a catalog picture right now. Leo has a dog she's temporarily lost to a passive-aggressive mother, and an outfit she's had for at least ten years. She sighs. Coming back to Blue Oak like this just makes her feel like she's going backward in life.

Emily kisses Hattie's head and turns back to Leo. "I love that kid, but she can talk a blue streak." She registers Leo's expression. "We'll find some alcohol and work on our mommy issues soon. But the parade starts in"—she glances at her watch—"t-minus twenty minutes. Gah, I'm becoming Kay." She shades her eyes and yells up to her wife, "Does everything look okay?"

Tess answers, "I can't tell if they messed with it. I'm checking the wires now."

Kay claps briskly twice and yells, "People, we're t-minus twenty minutes!" Emily grimaces and Leo chuckles.

The crowd has really filled in. Emily has to shout: "Wanna join us on the float?"

"No, I'll grab Derrida and find a place to watch this whole . . ."—Leo gestures vaguely—"situation." Someplace out of the way, she thinks, where she can see everything but not have to talk to anyone. She only has a certain amount of energy in the day. The idea of spending the next several hours in pressing heat, running into people who want to hear all about her while she tries to explain why she's moving home in disgrace, sounds like a level of her own personal hell—especially after driving for two whole days.

"Okay, if you're sure."

Tess jumps down, wiping her hands on her sundress. "Everything connects and it doesn't blatantly seem off. I don't know, maybe Chaz and Kymber were just admiring our handiwork?"

Emily snorts. "I'm *sure* that's why they were on our float."

"Well," her wife continues, "I don't see anything for now. Still, maybe we should pull the kids in the wagon rather than putting them on the float?"

The kids immediately clamor at their moms, and Hyacinth's wail goes nuclear. Emily yells over her daughter and the marching band—are they getting louder? "Better get out while you're ahead. We'll meet you at the park for fireworks afterwards?"

"See you then!"

As Leo walks away, Hyacinth wails, "I want the fwoat, I want to hear the *boom*!"

5

Downtown is cacophonous. Lieutenant Laura Esquivel walks along the parade route beside her boss, Detective Jake Nguyen, hating the heat and the crowd and this holiday with all her heart. But her face shows none of it. Black hair slicked back into a bun, uniform pressed and fitted; Esquivel's expression is as stoic as ever, except her vigilant brown eyes, which roam the crowd behind mirrored sunglasses.

Batons with streamers whirl in the air as the high school band leads, the tuba players red-faced in the heat, the drums heart-thudding. Cheerleaders tumble after them, flying in sparkling, dizzying formations. Sheriff Quackenbush sits enthroned on a float of teenage girls wearing tight-fitting formals, the finalists in the annual Miss Blue Oak contest on their way to the coronation at the fireworks show. He lives for this day; it's part of why Esquivel hates the parade so much. Anything that makes Quackenbush this happy cannot be good.

The floats are interspersed with vintage trucks covered in balloons and streamers and signs. A 4-H club tries to herd unruly goats. The fire truck passes with a deafening wail of its siren. The buttery-sweet aroma of kettle corn mingles with the earthy scent of sweaty bodies packed closely together.

She and Nguyen pause on one of the corners of the town square where they can observe the crowd and the parade from every direction. Behind the fire truck is a dusky-blue 1973 Ford Bronco; in the driver's seat of the vintage car is the young Black man Esquivel knows runs the sprawling ranch and bed-and-breakfast on the edge of the park, his cowboy hat resting low on his brow. She has met Mack Garner a few times. She doesn't particularly like him, but that doesn't mean much; it's rare for Esquivel to like anyone. She finds Mack Garner unobjectionable—high praise.

The music of the band fades slightly as it leads the parade north to Deep Hollows Park, where it will pass the delighted tourists drinking cocktails with cutesy patriotic names on the porch at the Garner Ranch restaurant. The parade will end in the parking lot near where the Hollows Creek flows, not far from the pool formed by a natural pit that is virtually bottomless. Nicknamed "the Deep," the two bodies of water give the park its name, though the Deep has been fenced for a generation. Esquivel makes a mental note to stop at the Deep later to make sure no one has jimmied the locks. She's heard the stories.

A wave of laughter and exclamations begins to Esquivel's left, and she glances up to see the next float. On a pink-and-teal float that looks like it was designed by Miss Piggy, Karina Holloway stands on a raised platform behind a real mirror-and-chair station. The other stylists sit on the sides of the float in red-and-blue sparkling outfits that clash horribly with the pink. Esquivel notices that Karina's bouffant hair, not to mention her outrageously tall platform shoes, gives her an extra two inches of height. Her sparkling dress is blinding.

Karina holds scissors to the cascading hair of the client in the chair. There's a bump in the road, and the crowd gasps as a thick lock of golden hair comes off in Karina's hand. She holds the hair up with an exaggerated *oops* expression, and Esquivel's smirk almost makes it to her face. Almost.

The kaleidoscopic floats continue: a slowly rotating pie on the I Spie float, the beer stein and book of Top Shelf, the Nacho Daddy's suggestive taco. As the Thai Tanic monstrosity turns the corner, a pair of young waiters strike the Jack-and-Rose pose from the bow of the ship, and the crowd goes wild.

And then, right behind it, is the enormous face of Kay Schneider, the Queen of Blue Oak. Nguyen and Esquivel stride with intention through the crowd. Nguyen had filled Esquivel in—Kymber and Chaz had been all affable laughter and "No, Officer, of course not" when he talked to them—but Nguyen was not convinced. They plan to walk with the float for the rest of the parade, just to be sure.

The tiara flashes brightly around Cutout Kay's head, and the scepter, which is absolutely phallic, lights up from top to bottom, pink and then gold and then flashing before starting over. Esquivel squints behind her sunglasses, warding off a sensory overload. Kay's voice booms from a microphone (very *ignore the man behind the curtain*, Esquivel thinks): "You're okay with Queen Kay! Come to the Queen of Blue Oak for all your real estate needs!"

Phones whipped out, the people around them guffaw—a reaction Esquivel doesn't think Kay intended—when suddenly, Kay changes the script: "You're okay with . . . *what*? Are you . . . ?" Then a piercing scream into the microphone.

Esquivel bursts into a run as the left side of Cutout Kay's face explodes in flames.

6

Leo grabs Derrida's leash and shoves her way through the scrambling crowd toward the fiery float. Racing into the street, she snatches up a wailing Hattie and frantically looks for the rest of the family. The smoke is billowing around the vehicle as flames quickly engulf Cutout Kay's face.

"Hattie? Hattie!" Emily's cries are frantic.

"Here! I've got her, Em!" Leo runs toward her best friend, who is clutching Hyacinth in her arms with a hand on Hudson's shoulder. Hattie holds her arms out, sobbing, and Leo hands the girl off to her mom.

Emily's voice is throaty. "I've got them all. We're getting away from the smoke. Go tell Tess. And find Mom."

Leo nods once. Derrida lopes beside her, herding instincts activated. She navigates through the smoke to the other side of the street and finds Phil supporting Kay, bent over with her tunic up to her eyes, on the courthouse lawn. "Kay, are you okay?" Leo grimaces at the unintended repetition of the real estate slogan.

Kay nods slowly. Phil gazes at her, then back at Leo. "The kids?"

"With Em on the other side of the street. I haven't seen Tess, have you?"

"She was just here," Phil says.

"I'll go find her." Leo rushes off and sees—is that her mother? Double-fisting her hair scissors like a Charlie's Angel, dashing by in four-inch heels? The smoke is thicker here. Head down, Leo runs right into a wall.

Or not a wall. A person, with strong hands that grasp her elbows immediately and pull her away from the fire toward the courthouse. Coughing, she closes her eyes and allows the hands to move her out of the way. Derrida whines plaintively. She should not have run with her dog through the smoke. She tries to open her eyes, but they're smarting so much she can't see.

"Leo! Here, take a drink." She squints and sees that the voice belongs to Mack. His hair, which had been longer in high school, is cut close on the sides, and he has stubble that makes him look older. But his infectious grin, despite the circumstances, is exactly the same: he's a basketful of golden retriever puppies in the body of a working cowboy. He holds out a YETI tumbler, and she gulps down a few swallows, then closes her stinging eyes again. He gently takes the cup back and she hears a glugging sound before feeling a cool wet cloth on her face. "It's my clean bandanna, don't worry. Can I give the dog some water?"

Leo wipes her eyes. "If he'll let you." She pulls the bandanna away, but her eyes still burn, so she returns it to her face.

"What do you mean, if he'll let me?"

Leo laughs when she can finally open her eyes fully. Derrida is lapping water out of Mack's cupped hand, and the dog's face is wet from where Mack already poured water over his eyes and nose, tail thumping hard. Mack hands the half-full YETI back to Leo. "Finish this off. It didn't touch the dog. You'll need it."

"Thanks." She gulps the water, blinking up at him rapidly.

He hesitantly cups her face, his brown eyes peering into hers. "How are you feeling? Any better?"

"Yes, thank you." She wipes her eyes gently again with his bandanna. He mutters something under his breath that she can't quite hear; she only catches "forgot how green your eyes are." Her heart beats a little faster. She changes the subject. "Did you see Tess?"

"She was crossing the street on my way over."

"And my mom? Is everyone—?"

"Stand back!" A firm voice rings out. The crowd has already thinned considerably. Mack gently takes the dog's leash from her hand and tugs them back several yards to a sprawling oak tree, one of the dozens planted all over the historic courthouse grounds that give the town its name. "I'm sure everyone is fine. I don't think there were any injuries." They stop in the shade and the dog settles at Mack's feet.

By the road, Jake is directing civilians away from the burning float, voice authoritative, jaw clenched. The fire truck had just turned the corner on the parade run, and now four firefighters run back with extinguishers for the electrical equipment. A few minutes later, the rest of the crew douse what's left of the float with the hose from the truck they've angled back on another corner of the courthouse square. Within minutes, the Schneider Realty float is a heaping, smoking, soggy mess. One small piece of Cutout Kay's face sags into a lopsided half grin.

With the smoke clearing, Leo sees that the plaza has emptied; only a few stragglers remain, recording the hubbub. Across the street, Emily and Tess, arms around each other and the children, stand beside Phil and Kay and a loose group she recognizes as the other Schneider Realty agents and staff. Beside them, Karina holds a pair of scissors, and next to her is a woman with a pixie cut clutching a long platinum wig whom Leo now recognizes as one of the hairstylists—that explains the haircut client. Karina spots her across the street and lifts a hand; Leo waves back.

"Thanks, Mack." She reaches her hand out. He grabs it, intertwining his fingers with hers. Startled, she pauses—she was reaching for Derrida's leash.

"Of course. What a welcome home for you!"

"It was adventurous, that's for sure."

"Leo, I'm glad you're—"

A piercing voice comes from around the corner of the courthouse. "Babe, you tell 'em!"

"That's right, babe, I will." Leo stiffens as Chaz and Kymber stroll into view, selfie stick held high. Chaz's best friend and business partner, Grant Ford, follows a few feet behind, out of the camera shot. He keeps his hands in his gym shorts pockets and glowers at Chaz and Kymber, who ignore him completely. Chaz continues into the camera. "So many people want to DIY electrical work in their homes, but that is always a terrible idea. I'm a big fan of DIY, I really am."

"I loved your DIY headboard, babe!"

"I know, babe, it turned out great, didn't it? So *solid*." Chaz leans down to kiss Kymber, careful to frame the kiss with his selfie stick. She smacks his lips, then turns to the camera and gives a cheeky wink.

Mack grumbles quietly. "Of course that bastard is here." He squeezes Leo's hand, which he's still holding.

Leo gently pulls her hand away from Mack's and steps out from under the trees. Mack follows, still holding Derrida's leash. As Leo follows Chaz down the street, the dog pulls toward her, so Leo takes his leash with a small smile at Mack and says, "Come on, I want to hear what he's saying."

Several feet away, moving swiftly toward the wreck of the float, Chaz continues. "When it comes to electrical work, you need to be especially careful. I hate to take advantage of a situation like this, but I feel like I have to. It feels irresponsible *not* to."

"It would be *irresponsible*, babe, and you've never lied in a Chaz Chat."

So Chaz is broadcasting this video in a Live feed to his almost half a million Instagram followers. He calls these candid videos "Chaz Chats," and hosts at least one a day, often multiple. The snark subreddit lives to skewer the Chaz Chats.

"Correct. I am a man of integrity, and I feel compelled to show you the result of what DIY electric work can do. Today is the Fourth of July, and my real estate competitor, Kay Schneider, had a float in our town's big parade. We had a float too, and it was going great, wasn't it, babe?"

"Oh, *babe*, it was so cute, with all our little patriotic workout clothes?"

Leo glances at Grant. The subreddit group has always wondered about Grant's role when Kymber and Chaz are on camera; it's clear from many of the videos that he's nearby, but he's rarely featured in any of them. The sub is divided: Many feel that Grant finds his best friend's online persona secretly repugnant. Others think he's a willing participant in the shenanigans; Grant is the full-time manager/co-owner of the DreamBawd Gym. Watching him now—stocky shoulders tense, DreamBawd Gym baseball cap pulled low—Leo wonders if the section of the sub that thinks Grant is turning against Chaz might be right.

Chaz glances down at Kymber, chin tilted toward the camera. "I don't know about cute, but the DreamBawd Gym slash Chaz Your Dreams Realty slash DreamSoul Chapel float was pretty great. We all did workouts to the best playlist ever."

"Chaz Jams will *pump you up*!" Kymber open-mouthed laughs, gum dangling from the corner of her lip.

Chaz chuckles too, and then his face instantly turns faux-somber. "But you know what we *didn't* do? We didn't have any electricity on our float. Or wiring that we don't understand. You know why? Because I'm smart enough to know my limits." Chaz tucks his chin down conspiratorially for the camera. "There may not be much, but I know what I'm *not* good at. And that's electrical work. Because look." He presses a button on the screen and flips the camera. "This is what's left of Kay's float. Now, I don't know what happened exactly, but I know her daughter and grandkids were on that float. And that they did some kind of electrical work because they had that mess of lights. What was that thing around her giant face?"

"Maybe a crown?" Kymber smacks her gum loudly and shrugs. "There was one of those big stick thingies too."

"A scepter, you dolt," Emily shouts, and Leo turns to see Emily, Kay, Phil, and Karina walking up behind her. Chaz glances over and angles his camera again to capture the conversation as Emily continues. "That *stick thingy* was a scepter, which you'd know if you'd ever read one single book all the way through, instead of just standing smacking your gum like a . . ." Kay snaps her fingers once and Emily stops immediately. Kay rarely got angry when the girls were young, but they knew the second she snapped her fingers that she was done.

When she speaks, Kay's voice is quiet, which Leo recognizes as her dangerously angry tone—when they were little, she and Emily called it Kay's "NPR voice." "Son, you had better turn that video off. Now."

"Why, worried he's going to tell everyone how terrible you are?" Kymber sneers.

Kay looks Kymber up and down as if she's a bug under her shoe.

"Young lady, I am not speaking to you. Bless your heart." Leo breathes in sharply; that phrase in that tone from Kay's mouth is pure venom. "Kindly refrain from speaking to me again." She turns back. "Charlie."

"Chaz," he mumbles, running his hand through his hair.

"Fine, *Chaz*. I have put up with a lot from you." She points a finger at him. "I offered to mentor and help you start your business, but instead, you have insulted and undercut me from the beginning. And now you're standing here hiding behind your little camera . . ."

"It's a Chaz Chat."

Kay raises an eyebrow and Leo holds her breath. Kay's words are clipped. "Hiding behind your little camera, having a *chat* with your followers on the internet, and I am *done*, do you understand me?"

"No, I don't understand you . . . Hey!"

Kay glides over and puts her arm on Chaz's forearm, lowering the camera until her face is framed. "Well, hello, y'all." Her voice is honey. “I’m Kay Schneider, better known as the Queen of Real Estate here in our little ol’ town of Blue Oak.”

“This is not . . .” Chaz attempts to pull his arm back, but Kay digs her nails in slightly.

“Young man, so help me, I will *call your mama.*” Chaz immediately stills. “Much better. I’m going to tell all your little followers what really happened. These two came before the parade started and tampered with our float, which was constructed by the very best electrical engineer on the planet—my precious daughter-in-love, Tess.”

She turns to Chaz, arm still on his. “But now you’re telling all these people on the internet that, what, Tess or I did a slipshod job? I’m so mad at you, I could spit nails. How *dare* you act like we would do anything to put the lives of *my* babies in danger? What is wrong with you, son?” Her voice cracks. “You’ve been sabotaging our listings for months, and the only reason we haven’t gone to the sheriff is because we couldn’t prove it yet. You messed with our wires so you could record this whole little drama on your camera and say, what, you’ve beat me? You’re better than me? Fine, you win! You can have the whole gosh-dang real estate market in Blue Oak, Texas, if you need it. I would quit real estate in a heartbeat if it meant protecting my loved ones.” She steps back, withdrawing her hand, mouth pursed. “Do not come for me again, Charles Nickolson, or I will call more than just your mama. And do some soul-searching about what actually matters to you. Because, right now?” She waves her finger up and down at him. “You’re all *hat* and no *cattle.*” There’s a moment of stunned silence. And then—

Kymber takes a step forward. “You old *bitch.*”

Leo runs and intercepts Emily, holding her with both arms as she rushes at Kymber. Derrida growls in front of them. Emily shrieks, “Did you just call my mother a *bitch*, you soulless, vapid, piece of—”

“Emily Katherine Schneider-Embry!” Kay raises her voice.

“Mom, seriously! Do not full-name me right now!”

Mack comes around and puts an arm in front of Emily, helping Leo hold her as Emily squirms to get at Kymber. Emily says, "I swear, if I see you around town, I'm going to . . ."

Chaz, still filming, grins maliciously. "I think you might want to rethink your anger over here. If it were me, I'd wonder why your mom wanted to hurt you and your kids. She talks a big game, but I think she planned to do some damage today."

"This is an outrage!" Kay's voice is sharp and loud; hands on her hips, she's shouting in Chaz's face. "I've had enough!"

"Whoa, *Queen Kay*, back up!" Grant is standing beside Chaz now, arms folded, pecs flexed.

"Say it again." Kay's face is red, and she is facing Chaz, not Grant.

"Back. Up," Grant responds, voice deeper.

"Not you. Charlie, say the part where you accused me of wanting to hurt my babies."

Chaz's smile is malevolent. "Your *babies*, huh? You mean, your daughter and her *wife* and her *wife's* kids . . . ?"

Kay pulls her right arm back and punches Chaz Nickolson so hard in the face that he stumbles back, dropping his camera and falling flat on his ass.

Chaz scrambles up. "Oh, that's it, I'm done." Grant tugs him up and they both turn on Kay.

But Mack is already there. He shoves Grant backward, and then whirls to punch Chaz hard, once in the stomach and once in the face. Chaz falls again—this time out cold.

7

Because the altercation became physical, Jake Nguyen herds the whole group to the sheriff's station to file a report. Karina and Leo walk together several feet behind the others. The female sheriff's deputy introduces herself as Lieutenant Esquivel and says that the two of them can go, but they both refuse. As the deputies lead the angry group around the courthouse square to the nondescript office building that is the sheriff's station, Karina speaks in a low voice to Leo. "This whole thing is a mess that's been building for a long time. I'm sure Emily has talked to you about Chaz Nickolson and the way he's gunning for Kay's business?"

Leo gives Karina a quick side-eye. "Yeah, Mom, of course; he set up that rival Facebook page I've had to deal with as their social media manager. And Emily tells me all the time about how they suspect he's been messing with Schneider listings."

Karina is silent while they tromp down the sidewalk, unsure what to say next. "Well, he's been rude as all get-out since he came home. He's just always saying things to Kay and Emily. One time, someone peed in one of their houses."

"But there's technically no proof it was Chaz."

"Kay thinks it was. It made her madder'n a wet hen."

"Yeah, Em told me. I got to say, Chaz had it coming. I saw Kymber and Chaz messing with the float beforehand."

"You saw it?" Karina's head snaps up.

"Yes, I took video and photos."

"Can I see?"

"Sure, but I'm going to hand it to the deputies."

"Let me look first." Karina watches the videos for the rest of the short walk to the sheriff's station, then texts the videos and photos to herself before deleting the text from Leo's phone.

"Why'd you delete that?"

"Plausible deniability." Karina follows the group without another word. Her shoulders are stiff, but her heart aches. She wants, more than anything, to gather her daughter into a long, lingering hug.

Nguyen and Esquivel divide the groups and take everyone past the wooden counter and upstairs, leaving Karina alone in the waiting area with Leo.

She steels herself. It's better this way. Leo looks so much like Richard; even her glasses look like Richard's, though his were always falling and he had to push them up his distinctive nose, which his daughter inherited in a more delicate form. When Karina grabbed Leo's dog earlier, she moved just out of eyesight so she could drink in her fill of her daughter. Leo has Richard's presence too, the way his mind was always clicking and whirring like a mechanical clock. The way he could be unobtrusive but still somehow deescalate the tension in the room by asking questions of others, by listening well, by noticing things few others did. The way he would pull into himself when he was tired or upset or hurt, a shelled creature withdrawing into a private world. Karina could see the exact moment when Leo tugged all parts of herself away from her mother, protecting herself.

It breaks Karina's heart every time. And still, what can she do? Karina sits two chairs away from her only daughter, whom she hasn't seen in months, and plays *Candy Crush* on her phone for the next two hours.

• • • • •

When it becomes clear her mother has nothing to say to her, Leo gazes around the room, shaking the wooden chair she's sitting on with her bouncing right leg. The sheriff's station used to be part of the courthouse, but as the town expanded, they moved much of the day-to-day business to an old storefront. Like many of the other stores in downtown Blue Oak, the front wall is all glass, with an empty space where a department store might have put mannequins years before. The sheriff's station has nothing in that space, just faded tan carpet and a few dead bugs. Next to the display-window area is the waiting room where Karina and Leo sit, in two of the four chairs huddled against one wall.

Derrida puts his head on Leo's shaking leg and she stills. She finally pulls her phone out, checks on the neighborhood Facebook page and, with her phone tilted away, the snark subreddit. A user shared a video of the Chaz Chat, and it's blowing up in the group. Leo can't wait for Emily to read what the community is saying about Kay being a badass.

Lieutenant Esquivel comes downstairs to speak to Leo and get her pictures of Chaz and Kymber on the float. After she is gone, Karina and Leo return to their silent, shared vigil—in the same room but miles apart.

One by one, after making a statement to the deputies, their friends trickle out of the upstairs offices; Emily is first, and she leaves to join Tess and the kids at the Deep Hollows fireworks show. She invites Leo, but by that point, Leo is so exhausted that more people time in the heat sounds awful. Leo almost leaves for the pool house, but then Mack walks down the stairs.

Leo stands when Mack pushes the half door in the middle of the wooden counter open. "How'd it go?" she asks.

"Fine. I talked to Jake. That guy's kind of rude, don't you think?"

Leo shrugs. "I mean, I don't know him that well as an adult, but he didn't strike me as rude. What did he say?"

"Just a lot of questions about why I hit Grant and Chaz, and about my history with Chaz. He wanted to dig into Dom's death, and I just kept saying, 'Listen, man, they were coming for Kay and I defended her. It's as simple as that.'"

"Why would he ask you about Dom?"

"Because Chaz and Dom were friends, and he knows Mel and I have always thought Chaz was a jerk." Mack's sister, Melody, was less than a year older than him, and the two had always been close, especially after losing the cousin who was like a big brother to both of them.

"Do you think Chaz had something to do with Dom's death?"

Mack ran his hand down his face. "I don't know, he's just . . ." He pauses, considering for a minute. "It's the same stuff as before, with Dom and the whole football team, just fifteen years later. Chaz hasn't really changed, except to get worse, and over the last couple of years, he's been everywhere in this town. Melody and I have made no secret of the fact that we don't love his whole 'celebrity speaking to the peons' shtick. But I really did hit him because he was coming after Kay."

"What a ridiculous situation."

"Jake told me that I need to leave before Grant or Chaz come down. I'm glad you're here. Emily said you have boxes to unload?"

"I do, actually."

"Can I help?"

"Honestly? That would be—"

Karina interrupts her. "You could help her by throwing away that terrible futon she's drug all over kingdom come."

"Thanks, Mom. I've slept on it every time you've come to visit, so it's not like you've ever had to deal with it." Leo is too tired to keep the acerbic tone from her voice.

Mack breaks into a charming grin. "I'm a futon-moving expert."

"Thanks, Mack. Can I . . . That is, I hate to ask you . . ."

"Leo, stop worrying." His grin crinkles his eyes. "What do you need?"

"Is there any chance you could help me tomorrow night? I'm too tired to face anything but a shower and bed tonight."

"Of course. I'll walk you to your car and we'll set a time." Mack turns and touches the bill of his cap at Karina. "Night, ma'am. Please give my love to Miss Kay and tell her I'll call her tomorrow. Need anything?"

"No, thank you. I'm fixin' to leave too, as soon as they're done."

"Well, don't stay too long."

Leo pauses, and almost waves, but decides it's time to get her money out of years' worth of therapy: she kisses her mom on the cheek, and walks out.

Mack is beside her, and the air is thick with humidity. His charming grin has softened into a gentle smile that Leo prefers. She expects him to start speaking immediately, but he just walks with her companionably. The streetlamps have kicked on in the dusk, and Derrida sniffs the sidewalk and grass eagerly as they walk across the street from the Blue Oak Courthouse square toward the salon.

"How's your hand?" Leo asks, breaking the silence.

He grimaces ruefully. "My hand is sore, but now that we're away from the sheriff's station, I'll admit: It felt really good to punch Chaz. He's been asking for it for years, and now at least I have a good excuse for choosing violence."

"Do you think you're going to get in trouble?"

"Nah, I know a good lawyer." His smile turns boyish and Leo feels her heart skip a beat. She looks down at Derrida quickly, tugging his leash. She does not have time for heartbeat skipping. She's only here for the summer.

The conversation after that is light. Mack tells Leo about Melody's young son, Nico—short for Dominic. Melody married her high school sweetheart after law school and had the family's only grandbaby, whom Mack says is "spoiled rotten in the best possible way. I assume you want to see pictures?" And he pulls out his phone to show her several from a recent family photo shoot. Leo dutifully takes it and thumbs through shots of a curly-haired toddler with his uncle's dimples surrounded by five adoring adults. She recognizes the fence in the background from Garner Ranch—Mack's grandparents had been among the first Black families to buy land when Blue Oak changed its policies in the civil rights era, and Leo knows how much it means to Mack's father especially to be holding his grandson on land his parents owned. Family is everything to the Garners.

"How *is* your dad doing?" Leo asks, handing the phone back. Mack says that his dad has been really responsive to the latest Parkinson's treatment and then changes the subject. They spend the rest of the walk catching up on mutual friends who have stayed in town.

Finally they arrive at Leo's Subaru.

"What time tomorrow works for you?" Mack asks.

"I'm pretty open."

"I'm off after dinner service starts. Seven forty-five or so? It'll be cooler then."

"Sounds great. I'll have this monstrosity"—she gestures to the U-Haul—"ready to unload, and I can only lift so many boxes of books."

This time when Mack grins, wrinkles creasing at either side of his warm brown eyes, she sees the exact instant his dimples appear. "I'm happy to be your muscle anytime, Leo." He opens his arms for a hug, and she hesitates only for a second before stepping in. He holds her for several seconds before whispering, breath tickling her ear, "Glad you were okay today."

From the direction of the park a few blocks away, fireworks burst in the night sky.

8

Voicemail on the phone of Mack Garner, 8:32 p.m., July 4: "Hey, it's me, hope you're okay. I heard you punched Chaz Nickolson? And that you went to jail? And also that Leo's back in town? You better call me ASAP. I'm more worried about Leo than jail; I hope it wasn't too hard to see her after all this time. I know you always want to play it cool, but I also know you are absolutely *not* cool, and well, that there's still . . . you know . . . some stuff there. Call me if you get this in the next thirty minutes or so. I have something to tell you."

Voicemail on the phone of Mack Garner, 8:56 p.m., July 4: "Me again. I hope everything's okay tonight. Sorry for the double call, but I wanted to let you know that we just had a major step forward in our little investigation. I hope you didn't say anything about it to Chaz tonight when you punched his face—seriously, *call me back*. Anyway, my coworker's client invited her to an exclusive party tonight, and guess who is going as her plus-one? I'm five minutes away right now! And you're never going to believe where it is: Bodhi Bruce's house! I'm going to have to figure out how to slip away from the party to, I don't know, rummage through her filing cabinets? Does Bodhi have filing cabinets? Probably dig through her computer? This is all last minute, so I haven't worked out my strategy yet, but before I leave, I'm getting answers. We're bringing him *down*. Love you, bud. Call me as soon as you can."

9

That night in Blue Oak, everyone agreed that the fireworks show at the park was the best ever. When the fireflies and streetlights are all that remain to puncture the inky blackness of midsummer, two very different conversations happen between two sets of best friends, communicated over two separate channels.

The first conversation takes place over private DMs between the moderators of the r/ChazNickolsonSnark subreddit.

U/SNARKYSNARKFUNKYBNCH: So, your mom punched Chaz. That happened.

U/SMALLTOWNSNARKER: OMG, my mom punched Chaz. And Mack punched Chaz. And I heard you left with Mack.

U/SNARKYSNARKFUNKYBNCH: I did.

U/SMALLTOWNSNARKER: And?

U/SNARKYSNARKFUNKYBNCH: And what? He's going to help me move some things.

U/SMALLTOWNSNARKER: Mmmm, Mack in Wranglers moving boxes. Or better yet, shorts. With those thighs.

U/SNARKYSNARKFUNKYBNCH: You're obsessed with his thighs.

U/SMALLTOWNSNARKER: Again, I have eyes. You have to admit, he grew up to be very good-looking.

U/SMALLTOWNSNARKER: As did Jake.

U/SNARKYSNARKFUNKYBNCH: Ok, I'll admit it. I'm not interested in anyone right now, but as you keep saying, I have eyes. What's in the water here in Blue Oak?

U/SMALLTOWNSNARKER: I shouldn't have made my pitch "move here because we'll pay you a living wage" but "move here because two of our high school friends are hot."

U/SNARKYSNARKFUNKYBNCH: CHANGING THE SUBJECT. How is your mom?

U/SMALLTOWNSNARKER: Honestly, she's really sad. Her hand hurts, and she feels bad that she punched him. But she doesn't mess around.

U/SNARKYSNARKFUNKYBNCH: I, for one, was hella proud of her.

U/SMALLTOWNSNARKER: Charlie was already bad, but as Chaz, he keeps surpassing my basement-level expectations of how low he will sink. Almost burning down our float to stage some kind of Insta Live drama—it's unreal.

U/SNARKYSNARKFUNKYBNCH: How are you?

U/SMALLTOWNSNARKER: Pissed as hell.

U/SNARKYSNARKFUNKYBNCH: Are you going to be OK?

U/SMALLTOWNSNARKER: I mean, I might murder Chaz—or Kymber—next time I see them. Other than that, ok. Grateful to be able to vent my feelings in snark.

U/SNARKYSNARKFUNKYBNCH: Did you notice Grant in all of it?

U/SMALLTOWNSNARKER: No, just when he came after my mom. Did you?

U/SNARKYSNARKFUNKYBNCH: Yes, in person but also in the video. He looked pissed the whole time.

U/SMALLTOWNSNARKER: At Chaz? At Kymber?

U/SNARKYSNARKFUNKYBNCH: I don't know, maybe both.

U/SMALLTOWNSNARKER: He was obviously still enough on Chaz's side to try to attack my mom.

U/SNARKYSNARKFUNKYBNCH: Totally. I just . . . what in the world just happened today?

U/SMALLTOWNSNARKER: Chaz Nickolson decided to welcome you home with a bang.

U/SNARKYSNARKFUNKYBNCH: Did you just make a joke about your mom's float exploding?

U/SMALLTOWNSNARKER: Too soon?

U/SNARKYSNARKFUNKYBNCH: You tell me.

U/SMALLTOWNSNARKER: You know dark humor is my love language.

U/SNARKYSNARKFUNKYBNCH: I do. Are you really OK?

U/SMALLTOWNSNARKER: I think so. I'll chat with my therapist this week. It scared me to have the kids in danger and not be able to find Tess. I think I'll have nightmares for the next few weeks.

U/SNARKYSNARKFUNKYBNCH: I would too. I'm here to talk whenever you need to. Love you, Em. Let's chat tomorrow.

U/SMALLTOWNSNARKER: Yes, but not till after lunch. The office is closed and there's nothing to discuss that can't wait.

U/SNARKYSNARKFUNKYBNCH: Are you forgetting about the high-needs Facebook group? It's July 4th, Em, and the dogs are SUFFERING because of the FIREWORKS. The people are ANGRY.

U/SMALLTOWNSNARKER: I hate the fireworks debates.

U/SNARKYSNARKFUNKYBNCH: If we don't debate on FB, how will we judge our neighbors and prove we love cats more than people?

U/SMALLTOWNSNARKER: Uggggh, please ignore those people until at least tomorrow.

U/SNARKYSNARKFUNKYBNCH: Already planned to.

U/SMALLTOWNSNARKER: Call you tomorrow.

U/SNARKYSNARKFUNKYBNCH: Good night!

U/SMALLTOWNSNARKER: Night, Lee.

U/SMALLTOWNSNARKER: I'm so glad you're home.

• • • • •

The other conversation begins with a series of clicks from Kay's closet, inside a pink frilled box Beth made for her in middle school art class and where Kay has piled a few silk scarves to disguise the equipment; a hole in the bottom of the box hides the cables that extend into Kay's elaborate, gold-trimmed chest of drawers where she keeps what she calls her "unmentionables." Saying "unmentionables" repeatedly has successfully kept her children and grandchildren from digging through the drawers over the years.

Phil hears the repetitive clicks from their bed, where a presidential biography is propped on his belly against the flowery comforter, but he waits a couple of minutes before taking his reading glasses off. "Kay? Kay!"

There is no response. He heard her turn the tap on in the bathroom a few minutes ago, followed by several splashes. The clicks continue, but neither of them have the hearing they used to. It isn't worth yelling about. Might as well let her get ready for bed first. The person on the other side will wait.

When Kay walks in a couple of minutes later, still rubbing moisturizer on her neck with her lavender silk robe blowing out slightly behind her, he glances up at her over his glasses.

"Incoming, honey."

"Oh, okay. Thank you. Have you seen my glasses?"

"On your head." He smiles at her affectionately.

"Of course. There they are. Thank you." Kay pulls jewel-encrusted glasses down over her nose. "Now where is . . . ?"

"Here you go." Phil holds out a pencil without looking up.

Kay grabs it and leans in to kiss his forehead. "I'd be lost without you."

He smiles vaguely, already back in the book.

Kay heads into the walk-in closet, pulling the door tight behind her out of habit; there aren't any kids or guests to hear, but it's always better to keep the protective rituals in place.

The clicks come through again, as they have every minute on the dot since the transmission began. It is the usual code, so Kay doesn't write the letters down in the notebook she keeps beneath silky underwear in her top drawer.

KKRUTCIS

She knows it means *Karen K., are you there? Come in. Stop.*

She pulls her own telegraph key out of the pink-edged box, removes the sounder so she can hear it clearly, sets it beside the notebook with the pencil at the ready, then pulls out the straight key. She opens and closes her right fist a few times—it is very sore, and will probably be pretty bruised tomorrow. She's iced it since they got home, but there's only so much she can do.

Her left fingers curl slightly around the small lever—thumb and middle finger around the end, pointer finger at the top, wrist limber in case the conversation takes a while. She types:

HKJS

It means *Here, Karen J. Stop.*

The clicks continue for the next several minutes, the scratching of Kay's pencil on the yellow pad the only other sound in the muffled closet as she painstakingly turns their personal code into letters. Kay finds comfort in the rhythm of transforming dots and dashes into sentences after each *stop.*

Perhaps it's silly, their commitment to an antiquated form of communication, but Kay has learned to trust her friend. Karina has found more than one bug in her home over the years.

And there was that one awful time when all Karina's fears turned out to be painfully, desperately well-founded.

Even if it is has shifted mostly into paranoia now, Kay still loves the feeling of being a clandestine accomplice in some secret operation.

Kay gives Karina stability and connectedness; Karina brings Kay a sense of adventure a girl who has lived almost her entire life in Blue Oak sometimes missed—though the idea of Karina as an adventurer would have shocked Leo.

Kay reads back over her notes from their conversation, translating their code into legible English in her mind.

KARINA: Doing okay?

KAY: Surprisingly, yes. It felt really good to hit that young man. I should feel terrible saying that, but I don't.

KARINA: He had it coming and I'm proud of you for standing up for yourself.

KAY: Thank you. I shouldn't have done it through violence. But no one insults my family.

KARINA: Damn straight. Do you think the sheriff's department will prosecute you?

KAY: Jake said no, and it sounds like Chaz isn't pressing charges. But there's also a very good chance Chaz will sue.

KARINA: Are you worried about it?

KAY: I don't know. Not much I can do tonight. But even if he doesn't sue, he just makes our lives so unpleasant. I hate the feeling that he's always lurking, ready to sabotage us somehow.

KARINA: Especially after what he pulled today.

KAY: That was so scary, Rina.

KARINA: I know, honey, I'm so sorry. I'm glad everyone is okay. It could have been so much worse.

KAY: We talked to Beth tonight and she thinks we should press charges or file a restraining order first. We have the evidence that Leo took on her phone. The sheriff's department has it too.

KARINA: I saw it. I don't know if it'll implicate Chaz, but it probably would Kymber. He was smart and had her doing his dirty work.

KAY: Smarmy bastard.

KARINA: There will be time to worry about it tomorrow. For now, I'm just glad you're all okay.

KAY: Me too. And don't think I didn't see you hoofing it back over to us, running like you'd been trained by special ops and not like a hairdresser.

KARINA: How do hairdressers run?

KAY: Not like that.

KARINA: Do you think anyone else noticed?

KAY: Leo didn't. I saw her with Mack by the courthouse. She had smoke in her eyes.

KARINA: Was she okay?

KAY: Did you ask her?

KARINA: Don't do this, Kay. Not tonight.

KAY: There was an explosion that threatened my babies today, so I think I'll say whatever I want tonight.

KARINA: Fine, that's fair.

KAY: It's good to have your girl home.

KARINA: She looked good, didn't she?

KAY: She really did.

KARINA: I know I've been going back and forth about her coming home. I still think it's the wrong decision, but I was glad to be able to see her.

KAY: She was glad to see you too.

KARINA: It's alright. We don't have to lie to each other.

KAY: I would never. She was glad to see you. The only thing she seemed irritated about was the thing you planned: being the dog's grandmother.

KARINA: That was funny.

KAY: I'm going to say the same thing I've said all month: it is time to tell her.

KARINA: I'll say the same thing too: No.

KAY: Keeping this secret is going to destroy your relationship.

KARINA: Keeping this secret is the only thing
that has kept her alive all these years.
She might hate me but she's still here.

KAY: She doesn't hate you.

KARINA: We'll rehash this conversation
another time. Please don't press tonight, Kay.
My heart can't handle it.

KAY: OK. And even if I disagree with you,
I know you're doing what you think is best.
You are an incredible mom to Leo.

KARINA: Thank you.

KAY: I love you, honey.

KARINA: Love you too. Sleep well.

KAY: Good night.

KARINA: Over and out.

KAY: Over and out.

• • • • •

Kay puts the sounder and straight key back in the box. She carefully arranges slips and underwear and scarves over the false bottom before tearing out the pages from the yellow legal pad and taking them to the bathroom. As she always does, she opens the dusty matchbox on the shelf next to the stacked mauve towels. She lights the pages of yellow legal paper on fire, holding them above the toilet to catch the ashes. She grasps the paper between thumb and forefinger, moving her hand out of the way of the flames until all that is left is less than an inch. She drops the last bit into the water, where it hisses out. The smell of burnt paper is not unpleasant. She flushes the ashes.

She washes her hands and dries them carefully, applies a little more lotion, then turns off the light. She returns to her room, pulls back the covers, and slips into bed beside Phil, who is still reading with his lamp on.

"Anything new tonight?"

"No, she just wanted to chat about Leo."

"Leo looks so much like Richard." Phil sets his book down and tugs his glasses off.

"I know. She really does."

"Did Karina agree to tell her?"

Kay huffs out a laugh. "Of course not. She's the most stubborn woman that ever lived." Kay leans in for a kiss. Phil finds his bookmark, carefully marks his page, closes the book, and sets his glasses and book on the bedside table as she continues. "I missed Richard tonight in a way that I haven't in years. He should have been here."

"He should have been," Phil says. He reaches up and pulls Kay's glasses off her head, setting them on the nightstand beside his own. "We are very, very lucky, my love."

Then he turns the lamp off. A faint glow from the streetlight outside the blinds and the occasional stray firecracker provide the only light in the room. They do not say anything else for a long time.

10

In Blue Oak that night, two couples sleep cuddled together. A few minutes earlier, one of those couples narrowly avoided damaging their DIY headboard; laughing afterward, they spend the night tangled up, sleeping like the dead.

One man goes back to his place and tries to go to sleep, but he is distracted by the clean linen smell that lingers on the collar of his T-shirt. He showers and changes, but the aroma remains. Finally giving up, he leaves a little after 2 a.m. and goes for a long walk.

One person goes to bed having fully recognized for the first time that night that what they are feeling is a low hum of anger at their best friend.

One person drives home from a night checking on the cameras they installed in a nearby property a few days before, determined and focused and grimly glad for the first time in a long time.

One person enacts a plan that had been a long time coming.

And one person dies.

11

Leo sleeps until almost noon the day after July Fourth. She only gets up because Derrida whines. She lets him outside, then returns to her bed a few minutes later with a piping hot cup of coffee. She shoves her glasses on and ignores the grimy lenses, leaning back against the pillows and scrolling through the phone.

First she checks the Schneider Realty neighborhood Facebook page. It's mostly the usual July Fourth bickering. Bertha Rosenhaus is tagged in two posts for moderating. One of them came in around midnight last night.

Marcos Salinas

July 4

Once again: fireworks in the neighborhood are a bad idea. This happened to my friend's dog when he got scared, ripped through the screen door, injured himself and then died. Do you want deaths on your hands? Then stop with the fireworks!

The post has pictures of a mangled screen door with the frame dripping with blood, and a blood-splattered garage door. The blood is everywhere—it looks like a Jackson Pollock painting. Are these pictures actually from last night? Leo does not have the energy for this today.

There are forty-seven comments, the last few just repeating mod requests for the post to be taken down. Kay has a zero-gore policy in the Facebook group. Leo deletes the post and sends a stern warning as Bertha Rosenhaus to Marcos Salinas to abide by the group's community standards or be removed immediately.

She flips through other posts. Someone has left two boxes of men's shoes by their driveway for anyone who wants size eight men's shoes, *in case there are any other small men in the neighborhood.* Leo chuckles; there's clearly a Hemingwayesque story behind the boxes.

There are several more posts about fireworks. She used to watch the Facebook page with a sense of nostalgia. It's an odd feeling to be seeing this group now, tired from the same loud fireworks in the streets that the neighbors complained about. She might be on the side of the anti-fireworks crew now.

Two people want recommendations, one for a painter and one for a math tutor. Then one post makes her sit up slightly:

Jill Mendoza

July 5

I don't want to make anybody scared, but I love this neighborhood and I want y'all to be safe. Last night, I saw a silver Chevy truck driving through the neighborhood slowly. It was making a loop, and the driver was wearing a baseball cap and seemed to be looking into people's backyards. He went really slowly down Ralph Ellison St., turned right on Sandra Cisneros Ave. I saw him at least three times and he went slower each time. Just wanted to make y'all aware. Stay safe out there, neighbors! #neighborhoodwatch #wehavetowatchoutforeachother #nokidleftbehind #smalltowncommunity #lovewhereyoulive

Leo shakes her head slightly. She loves the hashtaggers who go nuts inside the group—where no one searches by hashtags.

And the odd-duck comment of the day that Leo lives for, this time from her favorite neighborhood crank:

Elvie O'Malley

July 5

I went outside this morning to water my garden, which I'm allowed to do because it's my watering day, and I realized that SOMEONE has been in my garden again. And no, it's not the deer. Could the deer do THIS? Someone stole the pristine white quarry stone border around my front garden, and replaced it with a dirty rock. Who would do such a thing? This used to be the best small town in the world. Now I'm not so sure.

The post has a blurry picture, obviously snapped with a flip phone, of a rock that looks almost identical to the rocks next to it, except perhaps a shade darker.

No mention of Kay slugging Chaz in the Facebook group, at least. She'll keep an eye on it for later.

Leo suddenly feels too tired to deal with anything else today. She sets her phone down on the bedside table, pulls the comforter up, and snuggles in with her coffee. She flips through the television apps on the Schneiders' large-screen TV for a few minutes, before settling on rewatching *Schitt's Creek* season 3.

• • • • •

Almost five hours later, Leo startles awake. She never naps; the feeling is disorienting. The TV continues, somewhere in the middle of season 4. She shuts it off, stumbling into the bathroom to shower and brush her teeth. Afterward, famished, she opens the refrigerator to find that it is fully stocked with healthy food. It's such a Phil move; there's nothing he loves more than filling his kids' refrigerators. She grins, snaps a picture, and sends it to Emily.

A few minutes later, Emily confirms it was Phil, and asks Leo if she wants to come join them at the kids' swimming lessons (*tempting but absolutely not,* Leo writes back, and Emily gives it a *haha*). Leo could go to her mother's, but doesn't feel inclined to make any more effort than necessary after the cold shoulder she got yesterday.

She has a little time before Mack comes to help her unload. She throws on her worn Tevas with her jean shorts and a Strand bookstore T-shirt and grabs her photography equipment. Worn-out from yesterday, Derrida barely lifts his head when she grabs her keys.

She feels a small shot of nerves as she locks her door, then checks the address in the Slack message Emily sent her—the first house for sale that she wants Leo to photograph. They're supposed to meet there tomorrow, but it will be golden hour soon. She'll spend an hour playing with angles before meeting Emily in the morning to actually do the walk-through.

She straightens her shoulders and breathes in deep. Tomorrow is her first day, but she tells herself she's up for this task. After all, her new job is just to take pictures: What could possibly go wrong?

12

Leo opens the lockbox without any trouble and enters the house on Zora Neale Hurston Street. She sets her camera and tote bag down on the floor when she gets inside; the sound of the door closing echoes through the almost-empty house. The flooring is rich stained oak, and Leo is glad she came—the light is already incredible.

She takes out her camera and puts on the wide lens to capture the room. It's a challenge she realizes she's interested in: to give a sense of the space and show small details but still make the picture feel like art. She takes some pictures of the living room and adjoining dining room; the stained glass accent at the top of the wide windows really gives the space warmth. On a whim, she focuses in on some of the staging furniture, like the curve of the vintage couch re-covered in emerald velvet, and the brass vase on the sleek farm table with a single faux palm leaf elegantly tilted to the right. She widens the shot, walking backward without checking where she is going, and almost falls over the low mid-century coffee table.

It wouldn't do to break the staging furniture on her first shoot.

The kitchen is much darker. Leo thinks the egg-white color on the walls and the Paddington-blue cabinets with brass handles look much better than the "before" photos Emily sent. But the windows are smaller in here and they're shaded by big trees outside. It's difficult to capture the depth of the room on her camera.

Through the viewfinder, in the corner of her shot, she sees some bundles in the doorway leading out to the laundry room: probably painters' cloths that they forgot to clean up. She positions her camera to avoid them.

She takes a few final shots, moving to the other end of the kitchen—and what is that smell? Once a rat died in her apartment wall and this slight odor has the same edge. With all the wildlife around Blue Oak, it could be a squirrel or armadillo or possum in the attic or beneath the house. She'll have to tell Emily before they officially list the place.

And they should clean up those painters' cloths too. Actually, she thinks, she'll just take a minute and gather them all up now. She can save Emily a little time in the morning.

She's moving to the laundry room door when Emily texts her: *Are you up for starting in the morning? 8:00 am at the newest listing?*

She glances at the time: 7:32 p.m. She hesitates, wanting to take pictures of the whole house. But it's a ten-minute walk back to the pool house, and Mack will arrive at 7:45. The laundry room will have to wait for tomorrow.

Leo calls Emily back and speaks the second she answers. "I was *just* thinking about you, are you psychic? I'm actually at the house right now. Came to get a feel for photos—I'll bring them to show you tomorrow."

"Of course you're working ahead of time, overachiever. I'll pick you up with Glazed and Confused and coffee."

"You're my dream woman."

"Please stop flirting with me, I'm already spoken for."

"Darn it, because I still have those photos from middle school when you had to sleep in headgear and you were *so sexy*." Leo smiles while she puts the last bit of camera gear in her bag.

"You told me you deleted those photos!"

"See you in the morning, Em! Bright and early! I like my coffee black; don't put any of your stupid creamers in it."

"You're getting peppermint mochas for life if you don't delete those photos!"

"They never existed, I was *kidding*, geez!" Leo turns off the kitchen light and starts moving through the house, shutting off the other lights. "And before I forget—there's a mess of painters' cloths in the laundry room. And a weird smell here. Do you think that's Chaz messing with the house?"

"Do you see anything else that's off?"

"No, just the cloths. Want me to move them?"

"No, they're fine. Sometimes the crew leave a few supplies if the walls are wet so they can touch them up later. I'll check it out tomorrow. See ya bright and early!"

Leo makes a loud kissing noise and hangs up. She didn't tell Emily that Mack is coming over; there's nothing to tell. He's just an old friend helping her unload a few boxes. No need to start Emily talking about his thighs again.

She turns on the ceiling fans to dissipate the smell. Maybe it'll go away before they get there in the morning.

As she's closing the door behind her, she hears a thud. She opens the door again and counts to thirty. Nothing. She must have imagined it, or it was out back.

Leo locks the front door behind her and carefully secures the key in the lockbox. Tomorrow she will deal with her mom and her new job and the rest of her life. Tomorrow, she tells herself as she walks back to the pool house under clouds tinged pink with the beginnings of a glorious Texas sunset. Everything will look easier in the morning.

13

When Leo arrives, Mack is waiting in the driver's seat of a navy truck. She regrets walking as she wipes her sweaty bangs out of her face and surreptitiously checks to make sure she doesn't have sweat stains on her tee. He opens the door, steps out, and grins.

"You been a Yankee so long you forgot it's too hot to walk places here?"

"I guess so. Thanks so much for coming." He walks toward her like he might hug her, and she smiles but holds a hand up. "I've been taking pictures and walking in the heat, so I promise you don't want to hug me."

"Nah, I don't care." He wraps her in a big hug and sticks her face in his armpit like when they were young. She laughs, and part of her warms at the familiar silliness of it. She hasn't been around anyone but Emily who knows her well enough to push past her reserve in a long time.

She backs away and says, "I smell terrible."

"You smell like clean laundry."

"Well, that's good. I was just at my first Schneider Realty house and there was some funky odor, so glad I don't smell like funk and sweat." She's been talking about smelling bad for too long, she realizes. She feels off-balance, unsure how to act. "You're okay to get started?"

He heads back to the driver's-side door. "I brought to-go tacos and margs from the restaurant. Let me put them in the fridge."

"Great. I'll throw on tennis shoes and grab the keys."

Fifteen minutes later, they are almost done unloading the truck. Leo is slightly embarrassed it doesn't take longer. She'd left most of her furniture on the curb with a FREE sign when she left because it didn't seem worth bringing. The pool house is like something out of a magazine—all creams and porcelains and ecrus with tasteful gold accents—making Leo's stuff seem especially shabby.

As Mack puts down a particularly heavy box of books, Leo is chagrined to notice that Emily was right—he does have very sturdy thighs that look pretty great in his workout shorts. Moving her boxes is not a terrible look for his muscles in that black tee either.

"Last load?" Her voice cracks slightly and she thumbs over her shoulder like a cartoon character. She turns and trips on nothing as she makes her way out to the U-Haul. Mack graciously doesn't say anything.

Once they finish, Mack takes off his baseball cap and wipes his forehead with his forearm, then pulls out his phone. "Ready for tacos and margaritas?"

"Absolutely."

"I'll heat up the tacos and meet you outside. We can dip our feet in the pool while we eat."

A few minutes later, Mack and Leo sit beside the pool with a veritable feast. "This smells incredible. Did you make all of these?" Leo asks.

"Not tonight, but a lot of these are my recipes." He points to four of the tacos. "Those are al pastor on corn, obviously."

"My favorite."

"I remembered." He grins, pleased, and holds up his glass. "First, a toast. To the hometown girl, home at last."

Leo feels herself blush. "I don't know if I'm 'home at last.' "

"Home for now, then." He takes a sip of his margarita, and Leo has to keep herself from watching his Adam's apple.

She takes a bite of taco, a savory bite of well-spiced al pastor meat brightened by pineapple and tempered by the handmade corn tortilla. "Okay, I take it back, I'm moving home for the tacos."

"Why do you think we all stay in Texas?"

"Oh, I know why. Tacos and H-E-B."

Mack grins at her, biting off half the taco. "Exactly. Best grocery store in the world." As he sets it down on the take-out container, he flexes his hand slightly.

Leo gestures with her chin. "How's your hand?"

Mack opens it again. "It'll be fine. It was worth it. Chaz was due a good punch in the face."

"Did he press charges?"

"Not yet. If he does, I doubt they'll stick. Not against me, at least. Melody says mine was clearly defense of an elderly woman. I'm pretty sure Kay will have better grounds for pressing charges than Chaz; it seems clear they messed with her float."

"Don't let Kay hear you call her elderly."

"Yeah, I would never. More like, that's what I think a good lawyer would say in court. I don't think Chaz will get very far in town if he presses charges, especially not after this. Can you imagine making *Kay Schneider* so mad she punches you in the face?"

Leo snort-laughs and then blushes; she hates how she always snorts when she's laughing her real laugh. For an instant, she thinks about comparing the fight to one of her favorite literary brawls, in the 1970s when Frank Chin and the Chinatown Cowboys confronted Maxine Hong Kingston at a speech. She opens her mouth to make the comparison—who could yell at Maxine Hong Kingston? The same people who could yell at Kay Schneider!—and realizes it would be impossible to explain. She has spent her entire adulthood building up expertise in an area no one else cares about. With a twist of her mouth, she turns back to the pool, and says, "Yeah, it was quite the kerfuffle."

"It was, indeed, a *kerfuffle*." She glances up at him and he's grinning.

"You're making fun of me!"

"Not at all." The look on his face is fond amusement. "Leo, I have never met anyone with a mind like yours."

She glances down at the pool and trails her fingers over the water. She isn't ready for anything that gets close to a talk about their romantic past. They'd been friends who started dating exclusively in the fall of their senior year, and were inseparable until Leo's father died the following May. Mack, nursing grief of his own, understood completely. They broke up amicably, and drifted apart when they went off to different colleges.

After a beat, she returns to the subject. "So you think Kay should press charges against Chaz?"

"Yeah, definitely, before he's able to charge her. Chaz might have an in with the sheriff's department."

"You think Chaz has an in with Jake?"

"Nah, with Quackers, who will always football-worship Chaz and any other Bandit first-stringers. Other than Quackers, everyone who has been here longer than five minutes hates Chaz."

"Including you?"

"Of course including me." He looks up at Leo, the low pool lights dancing on his face. His lashes have always been so long. "You know that better than anyone."

"I used to know that, but it's been a long time."

"Why has it been so long, Leo?" His voice is soft.

Leo takes a long swig of her drink and kicks her feet in the pool for a minute. "It's hard to come back. Hard to miss my dad. My mom is . . ." She waves her hand vaguely.

"Cold?" Mack supplies.

"Right?" Leo turns to face him.

"Yeah, it was weird. She's not like that normally, but it's as if the minute you got here, a wall went up. I could see it last night."

"Emily thinks that too. Mom goes on cruises all the time, but can barely come see me, and she always has excuses why it's not a good idea for me to visit here. Eventually, I got used to not coming back. I feel like . . . I don't know. This town hurt me." Leo lies back against the quarry stone surrounding the pool, her feet still in the water. After a minute, Mack lies back too.

Leo listens to the gentle whir of the pool filter and the thrumming cicadas for a while before starting again. "It hurt you too, but you came back anyway."

"I did. And I think it hurt me in a different way—it's more like, I felt some really sad things here in Blue Oak, but also . . ." Mack pauses, looking at the sky, putting his thoughts into words. Finally he continues. "This town can be ridiculous and frustrating and it drives me nuts, and yet there's something in Blue Oak I've never found anywhere else. A real community with real people from all walks of life. To me, it's worth protecting and saving."

"That's very white knight of you." She turns her head to look at him.

He gazes back, his brown eyes shining in the soft lights around the pool. "That's very Black cowboy of me."

Leo's chuckle is soft. "Fair enough. And I'm glad you've found a sense of purpose. But that's not my dream."

"Careful." Mack's voice holds a hint of laughter. "Blue Oak has a way of getting under your skin."

"Yeah, no thanks. This town is a great place, for some people. For you, and for Emily and Tess. For my mom and Kay. But not for me." She sighs. "And anyway, it doesn't matter. I'm back for a few weeks with a wasted career and nothing to show for it but some boxes of books, a sad futon, and my dog . . . I sound like a country song. These margaritas must be strong."

Mack smiles. "They are strong, which is why I'm about to say something I should probably wait to say."

When he smiles, his eyes crinkle around the corners and the dimples that have always been her downfall pop. "Leo, will you go to dinner with me on Saturday?"

14

At 7:57 the next morning, Emily drives up to her parents' pool house after picking up doughnuts, ready to go inside and bang on the door until her chronically late best friend rolls out of bed. Her mouth actually opens in shock when the gate opens and Leo steps out, wearing a yellow sundress with her favorite Birkenstocks.

Leo rolls her eyes. "Fix your face, I'm ready to go."

"I have never, in the history of our friendship . . ."

Leo doesn't even smile. "I couldn't sleep last night. I woke up around four a.m. because something was bothering me about the house."

Emily takes the first left. "The pool house?"

"No." Leo's voice is impatient. "The Zora Neale Hurston house. It was . . . something about the smell. And . . . I don't know, I can't stop thinking about it."

"Well, we're going there now."

Leo's right leg shakes impatiently as Emily turns. Leo pulls her phone out and opens the snark subreddit while saying absently, "Also Mack thinks that your mom should press charges against Chaz before he presses charges against her."

"Oh, Mack thinks that, does he? Mom's talking to our lawyer this morning. But when did you see Mack?"

As Emily parks, Leo sits straight up, still staring at her phone. "Wait a minute. Is that . . ." She enlarges a photo in the latest subreddit post with her thumb and forefinger.

Emily smiles in amusement; Leo's so single-minded when she's into something. "Lee, did Mack come over . . . ?"

Leo shushes her impatiently, thrusting the phone in her face. "Em, *look*."

15

Of the 17,652 members of the r/ChazNickolsonSnark page, 27 were active at 7:51 a.m. on July 6 when u/Oodlesof-Schnoodles shared three photos on the main thread with the caption: *Has Chaz finally lost the plot? What the hell is happening? Go watch his IG Live. This is wild!*

The first three photos are blurred screenshots u/Oodlesof-Schnoodles took of Chaz's Instagram Live, where he is streaming his latest "Chaz Challenge." This is different from a Chaz Chat—Chaz Chats happen any time Chaz is in the mood to talk live to his followers, which is almost all the time. A Chaz Challenge is when Chaz joins a Zoom meeting with special clients who have paid a premium to have small group check-ins on their fitness journey, one of the "premier" services that Chaz Nickolson offers on his website as his clients Chaz Their Dreams.

While the clients are in their Zoom meeting, Chaz often streams on Instagram Live. He points his phone camera at his laptop screen, each recording the other in a twenty-first-century infinite reflection: he is filming himself filming himself. As one user put it once:

U/SNARKASAURUS • 3MO: It's an endless loop of Chaz—heaven for him, hell for everyone else.

In today's version, Chaz's laptop is sitting on a kitchen counter, and the Zoom meeting shows ten clients waving at the camera. Normally, Chaz's camera is on, but today it's off. His box in the meeting is a static headshot of himself praying.

U/OodlesofSchnoodles's next comment under her post says it all: *Can't even be bothered to turn his own camera on. What a douche.*

• • • • •

The "über-secret" Chaz Challenges are a core moneymaking part of Chaz's fitness-influencer business—one the subreddit is always, always interested in. The price of this service is not listed on the website, but the subredditors—who call themselves "Chazzercisers"—live to uncover these types of mysteries. One woman joined on Chaz's website right up to the point where she had to put in credit card details; that's how the subreddit found out that the twelve-week Chaz Challenge Course costs an up-front fee of five thousand dollars.

One subredditor uploaded a video showing Chaz at a small desk in what looked like his gym office, yelling into the screen of his laptop, "You just *sit there*! And eat *cake*! All day, stuffing *cake* into your *cake hole*!" The subreddit went wild for this proof that Chaz not only shamed the people who paid him money to be "trained," but he wasn't even original about it; the video went on for fifteen minutes and he said *cake hole* nine more times.

More information was relatively sparse until a few weeks ago, when a disillusioned former Chaz Challenger joined the group as u/GoldenDoodles1968 and made a comment that she was *sick of Chaz's BS* and was ready to dish. As the group mods, Emily and Leo set up an Ask Me Anything conversation—an AMA—with u/GoldenDoodles1968. It went on for five hours until u/GoldenDoodles1968 finally said her carpal tunnel was too bad to keep going. By then, the Chazzercisers of the subreddit were thrilled. The secrets had been spilled.

U/GoldenDoodles1968 told them that the Chaz Challenges

started at five thousand dollars, but there were all kinds of product pitches from the "DreamBawd Team," and the Challengers readily bought all the "life-transformative" products that were sold to them—fitness gear, shakes, supplements, and protein bars. The meetings often started with thirty minutes of Chaz ranting (she confirmed he loved to say *cake hole*, as well as *activate*, *synergize*, *leverage*, and *low-hanging fruit*). That was followed by a good fifteen minutes of "tips" like, "Why would we glorify people who can't control their weight? Laziness isn't hot." Or "Get on your treadmill and run like all the carbs in the world are chasing you."

To the delight of the snark group, u/GoldenDoodles1968 gave them insight into the mysterious "team" that Chaz refers to at least five times a day. The illustrious DreamBawd Team was actually just a few part-time trainers who came and went (including some girls he dated after he broke up with Bodhi and before Kymber), but it was mainly Chaz's business partner, Grant Ford, and an overworked intern named Lily Ferrero that the sub suspected did most of the work.

Lily—a junior kinesiology major at nearby Texas State University—led the meetings most often when Chaz wasn't there, reading from Post-its that Chaz gave her with cryptic notes like *Tell them it's not working* (though none of them knew what "it" was), or repeating *Nothing tastes as good as skinny feels* five times.

After that AMA, every time Chaz posted on Instagram with his signature shot of himself filming himself filming himself, usually with the hashtags #ChangingLives #DreamBawd #ChazYourDreams, the subreddit went bonkers.

That's why when u/OodlesofSchnoodles posts those screenshots, it takes a minute for the group to register that something is different about today's Chaz Challenge.

• • • • •

The discussion begins along the usual lines.

Nine posts call out Chaz for his unwillingness to show his own picture while not protecting his clients at all, including:

U/EDUCATOR4LIFE • 18 MIN. AGO: I thought we agreed to cover the participants' names?

U/MONICALEWINSKYLOVE • 18 MIN. AGO: They're grown-ups, if they pay for this, they know Chaz is going to share it. For the millionth time, Challengers are fair game, children should be shielded.

U/Educator4Life and u/MonicaLewinskyLove continue their discussion for seventeen posts that most longtime users scroll past; these two have this discussion almost every day. Another string of posts calls out the subredditors for watching the Live (*We shouldn't give him the views!*). This, too, is a familiar discussion.

Eight posts below that, things start to shift. As they often do, the people who have been watching Chaz's Instagram Live from the beginning narrate the play-by-play for others who have jobs or responsibilities that do not allow them to drop everything to snark on their favorite influencer. The commenters start noticing that today's Live seems odd: Chaz normally yells or jumps in to announce himself, but today he just silently films the meeting.

As the Chaz Challenge streams on, the participants in their Zoom boxes look at their cameras uncomfortably. Eventually, one of the women in the top left asks, "Hey, Chaz, are you there?"

This is the first screenshot that u/OodlesofSchnoodles posts.

He finally speaks, the canned opening he says in every Chaz Challenge, "Welcome, Challengers! Be ready to *Chaz Your Dreams*!" They're supposed to say his signature phrase with him; the women in the Zoom dutifully repeat the phrase a beat after him, with varying levels of enthusiasm.

Then Chaz takes a step back to get a wider shot of the laptop. It's set on a beige counter in a kitchen with blue cabinets and a stained glass window, not his usual starkly white kitchen. U/OodlesofSchnoodles screenshots that view too.

His voice rings out again off camera. "Look at all your beautiful faces! But soon these faces will be even skinnier and more beautiful! We're in the middle of the hard, but we can do hard things together!"

Then, inexplicably, he sets the phone down with the camera still running. The video captures the white ceiling, with a dash of sunlight across its white surface. Chaz says, "Lol, looks like we're having technical difficulties!"

U/OodlesofSchnoodles's third screenshot is the view of the ceiling.

A minute later, they can hear one of the women in the Zoom meeting say, "Chaz . . . are you still there? Chaz?" There's no response; no clacking of the keyboard to show he's trying to fix the meeting, just the camera still recording the white ceiling.

U/TEAMDWIGHTNOTJIM • 17 MIN. AGO: What is going on? He can't be bothered to even speak to the women literally paying him thousands of dollars to have their privacy violated on his IG? Is he so used to filming he doesn't even realize the camera is still going?

U/ALOHAALOHA765 • 16 MIN. AGO: Just starting this video. What is happening? Where is he?

U/EDUCATOR4LIFE • 15 MIN. AGO: He doesn't even bother to turn his Insta Live off when he's not talking. Is he peeing while the camera is pointed at the ceiling in this video? IS HE PEEING?

U/SNARKALICIOUS • 15 MIN. AGO: He's probably running to get Lily to help with his "technical difficulties" since he can't do anything himself.

After several minutes of dead airtime on the Live, in which it sounds like most or all of the Chaz Challenge participants log off, the hundreds of subredditors watching the recording in almost real time on Instagram hear a knock at the door. It is followed by Chaz's voice several feet away, off camera.

"Hey, how's it going?" The end of Chaz's last word is clipped, as if he swallows his sentence.

"This is an outrage. I've had enough!" The woman's voice sounds slightly tinny, but her anger rings through. The door slams shut. There are no other words spoken.

After twenty-eight seconds, there is a loud thud. Two minutes and thirty-seven seconds after that, there is another thud. Twelve seconds later, they can hear the door open and close again. This time, there is also the metallic jingling of a key. And then the snick of a latch being bolted in place.

U/TEAMDWIGHTNOTJIM • 13 MIN. AGO: What the hell was that?

U/ALOHAALOHA765 • 13 MIN. AGO: Are those noises? Is he doing the dirty?

U/EDUCATOR4LIFE • 13 MIN. AGO: What was that? That doesn't sound good.

U/OODLESOFSCHNOODLES • 13 MIN. AGO: That silence is ominous.

For more than twelve minutes, the video is silent, the camera still on, pointed toward the ceiling. The discussion in the subreddit grows increasingly heated as group members debate what to do. But then, at almost fourteen minutes into the video, they hear the sound of the door being unlocked again.

Real-time comments explode. For forty-seven seconds, the Chazzercisers listen together as they hear two new women's voices in the same room.

Voice 1: "Why is his laptop in here? Is that his phone? Chaz? Chaz!"

Voice 2: "Em, that's the same smell I noticed earlier, I wanted to tell you—"

Voice 1: "Gah, it stinks! What *is* that? Chaz!"

And then, at fifteen minutes and seven seconds, there is a single piercing scream.

After six seconds, another.

As if they had held their collective breath and then let it out all at once, five subredditors comment at almost the exact same time.

U/TEAMDWIGHTNOTJIM • JUST NOW: I'm calling the police.

U/SNARKALICIOUS • JUST NOW: Do we know where he is?

U/ALOHAALOHA765 • JUST NOW: Someone call the police!

U/EDUCATOR4LIFE • JUST NOW: I don't care how much we hate him, I'm praying for him and Kymber right now.

U/MONICALEWINSKYLOVE • JUST NOW: OMG OMG OMG OMG OMG.

Eleven seconds later, one of the women who has been screaming stops. "Em, take a breath. Em!" The other woman pauses as the other voice continues. "I'm going to call the cops. Is this your phone? No, you have your phone. Sorry, I . . . Walk back ten steps and then put your head between your legs. This is Chaz's phone. It's still recording."

A hand appears over the camera, then hesitates. "I don't know what to do. I don't know . . . Yes, just like that, head between your legs. Here, quick, hand me your phone. Mine's in the car. Perfect. Deep breath in, hold. Deep breath out, hold. Good."

The hand disappears. There are three high-pitched beeps

outside the phone frame. “Hello, I’m at 1405 East Twelfth Street, sorry, Zora Neale Hurston Street in Blue Oak. I want to report a . . .” The woman sucks in a shaking breath. “I’m turning this off. They can’t find out this way.”

Then a single finger comes back into the frame.

Abruptly, at sixteen minutes and thirteen seconds, Chaz’s Chaz Challenge on Instagram Live stops.

16

Jake hands Leo an ice-cold can of Coke, then sits down beside her on the curb. She has no idea how long she's been here. It is over a hundred degrees in the shade, yet she is shivering.

She can't stop her mind from replaying what just happened. When Leo saw the most recent post in the subreddit about today's Chaz Challenge on the drive over, she noticed that one of the three photos showed Chaz in the kitchen she had just photographed the day before. Then—

Rushing into the house behind Emily, intent on finally catching Chaz in the act of sabotaging Schneider Realty.

The stench as Leo wrestled the key from the door.

Signs that Chaz had been there. His laptop open on the kitchen counter.

His phone beside it, Instagram Live on, camera still recording. Leo had been looking at the phone when Emily screamed.

And screamed.

And screamed.

Leo behind her, putting a hand on Emily's shoulder to calm her down.

And realizing that Emily had screamed because Chaz was lying dead in the laundry room.

Bile rose in her mouth: The painters' cloths she'd almost cleaned up the day before were not the workers' leftover mess.

They were wrapped halfway around Chaz, with one part under him and the other part swooping over his back, hiding his legs and feet from the door. She had to squat down to confirm what she was seeing, as if Chaz were playing hide-and-seek.

The images jittered and fled from her mind. She couldn't piece them together.

Chaz's charcoal tennis shoes under bare, hairy legs.

Chaz's red workout shorts.

A navy tank top, bunched slightly at the side.

Chaz's face, with evening stubble, hair undone from his usual bun.

Chaz's unseeing eyes, open and staring past them.

Those eyes shadowed by the cloth that partially covered his face. Cloth that had been there yesterday. *Chaz* had been there yesterday. Chaz's dead body had been there yesterday. While she was alone in the house. Taking pictures.

Blood was soaked into the cloth, so dark beneath his face it was almost black.

No blood on his cheeks or his nose or his mouth. One thin trickle of blood smeared across his forehead.

The phone call she made with shaky fingers. Had she used Chaz's phone? No, she thought, she'd watched enough *Law & Order* to know she shouldn't move his phone. On her phone? No, it had been in the car. She flashed to Emily's face—tear streaked, horrified—when she finally looked at Leo. Emily, who looked as if she'd aged ten years in two minutes.

Leo remembers now: she called 911 on Emily's phone.

Sitting here on the curb, Leo feels herself slipping in and out of coherence. How long after she called did the cops come? How did she end up out here on this curb? She remembers pressing stop on Chaz's video. Did the subredditors see her face? Leo tries to corral her mind, but her rational thoughts scrabble away like feral cats. Where is Emily? Leo licks her lips, shakes her head slightly from side to side.

"I don't know if it's true." Jake's voice brings her back. He's beside her, finger gently tapping her unopened Coke can. The metallic cold is bracing on her fingertips. "But my mom always insists sugar helps with shock."

"Thank you." Leo glances down numbly at the can in her hand.

"I'm going to wait for you to open it and drink it first." Jake bumps her gently with his shoulder. Leo obediently pops the top open and takes a few sips. Her stomach roils but she drinks anyway. After a minute, she can feel a jolt from the sugar. Whether it's real or psychosomatic, she doesn't care. It does help.

"Where's Emily?" Her voice is hoarse.

"Deputy Williams took her home. She wasn't able to talk very much. She'd already called Tess, and it became clear I either needed to get Emily home, or have Tess here with the kids at the crime scene, and they don't need to see that. Williams will stay with her for now and bring her into the station in a little bit to answer some questions."

"Questions? Are we suspects?" Leo glances at Jake for the first time but he doesn't look back. He watches the deputies and the DPS officers coming in and out of the house next door, the house Leo took photos of only yesterday. It feels like a week ago that she captured the play of light through those windows.

"Since you're the ones who found the body, we're going to have to talk through the details of what happened, why you were here, why Chaz was here, what you know. Especially after what happened at the parade, and the tension between the Schneiders and Chaz." Leo notices Jake doesn't answer her question.

She takes another sip of Coke. For a long moment, they sit in silence. Jake turns to Leo. "While we're sitting here, is anything out here different than it was before, when you arrived at the house?"

"Besides the ambulance and cop cars?"

"Yes, besides those. Were there any other cars outside the house?"

Leo looks around. "I don't think so."

"Not in the driveway? Or parked nearby?"

"There was that blue truck in front of the house." Leo points.

"That belongs to that neighbor. I checked. Nothing else? Did you see anyone come out of the house? Or anyone pull away from the curb?"

"No, we didn't see anyone's car or anyone leaving. I didn't think to check, though. I might be wrong."

"That's okay. It's helpful sometimes to take a minute to go over details." He dusts his hands on his knees and stands up. "Are you okay to stay here for a bit longer? The neighbors offered to let you go into their house, but they're chatty."

"I'd rather be alone."

He nods. "I figured. If you get too hot, you can sit in my truck. It's over there." He points to a black Ford truck three houses down, then pats his pockets. "Here are the keys. They're going to bring the body . . . they're going to bring Chaz out in a few minutes. You don't have to watch, but I need to stay until they do that, then I can take you back to my office so we can talk in the air-conditioning. Does that sound okay?"

Leo nods vaguely. Jake leans forward and then frowns, pulling his sunglasses off till he catches her eye. She focuses on him.

"Actually, why don't you go get in my truck and crank the AC up right now?"

She nods again, and he helps her up.

"AC on, okay? I'll bring you some water once you've finished that Coke. Are you hungry?"

"No . . ." She pauses to clear her throat. "I had a granola bar after my run this morning. Emily brought doughnuts, but we didn't have time to . . ." Her voice fades.

"All right. As long as you've had something this morning. For now, go sit in the car. There are plastic bags in the glove box if you start feeling queasy. It's common. I'll see you in a minute."

Leo walks shakily toward his truck. She turns the vehicle on, shifting the AC vents so they blow on her. The only sound is the whir of the air in the car. It smells like Jake, citrusy laundry soap and a slight scent of cedar.

She hears voices and the front door to the house opens. The door is canary yellow, probably a Schneider Realty upgrade. A paramedic walks backward out of the house, her hair pulled into a low blond ponytail. Leo's eyes suddenly sting. She cannot watch.

She looks down at her fingers. She picks at a hangnail. She takes another sip of Coke. She glances up. They are at the ambulance now, opening the doors. Her stomach lurches. She looks down again, at her feet this time, and then at her phone. She has several missed calls, mostly from Karina but a few from Kay.

Suddenly she wants her mother desperately. She cradles the phone in her hand while she texts:

Hey, Mom. I can't talk right now. I'm with Jake. We found a dead body. It was Chaz. I don't know what happened. They took Em home. I'm going to answer some questions in a few minutes at the sheriff's station. I'll let you know as soon as I know something or if I need anything. I love you.

Three dots appear immediately followed by her mother's simple text: *I love you too.*

She tenses. It is incredibly out of character that her mother is not insisting on coming to the station, that she has not appeared already at the crime scene. Maybe, for once, her mother is going to wait until Leo tells her what she needs before acting, but Leo doubts it. Her mother will show up soon, just one more thing for Leo to worry about. She lets her breath out in a whoosh. Only then does she realize that she's crying.

The driver's-side door opens. Jake makes a concerned face as he gets in. Without saying a word, he pulls a small packet of tissues out of a pocket in the door and hands it to her. She clutches the tissues in her fist for the three-minute drive.

• • • • •

Jake takes Leo back to the sheriff's station where Karina and Leo waited on July Fourth after Kay and Mack punched Chaz. He parks in the back, and leads her through the back door behind the wooden counter, past several empty desks, and gestures up the stairs. "Why don't you head upstairs to my office? It's the first one on the left. I need to make a quick call and then I'll be there."

Jake's office is cramped with barely room for the oversize desk and two slightly worn pleather chairs, with a painted-shut window overlooking the main street in town. The bookshelves behind his desk feature family photos: Leo sees one from Becky's wedding, featuring a large Vietnamese family whom Leo recognizes as the entire Nguyen clan, most of whom have lived in Blue Oak for decades. And another that's older—Becky and Mrs. Nguyen are sitting on a beach blanket, and in the middle behind them, a young Jake has one arm slung over each of their shoulders as they all grin widely at the camera. The photos are a welcome distraction.

When he walks in, Jake holds out a bottle of water for her and Leo thanks him, putting it down on the desk. She watches a drip of condensation on its side.

Jake places a mug of coffee on a coaster on his side of the desk and sits down, leaning in slightly. "Look, Leo, I highly doubt that you finally came back to town just in time to brutally murder an old high school acquaintance in a house your best friend's mom is about to list. But I need to be up-front: It's a weird thing to be a detective in your hometown. Sometimes I have the home-field advantage. But I try very, very hard to always be aboveboard. I record all of my interviews and take careful notes. It's not an easy time to be a cop, nor should it be—there are a lot of bad cops out there. I never want to choose sides or cut corners." He pauses to take a sip of coffee. "I'm especially not going to cut corners for someone whose face I've seen covered in zit cream with those weird things between your toes while you and my sister gave each other pedicures."

His slight smile fades as Leo looks at him. She feels too exhausted to pick up on the joke.

"I hadn't thought about how hard it must be to be a detective in Blue Oak," she responds.

"Let's just say you're not the only one with a complicated relationship with this town." He straightens in his chair. "I want to ask you some questions and record our conversation. Is that okay with you?"

Leo nods as he pulls a small black voice recorder out of his pocket.

"Would you mind saying that on the record?"

"Sure. It's okay for you to record our conversation."

"You understand that you're not under arrest and do not have to answer any questions and that, if at any time you feel like you want a lawyer, you can say so."

Leo glances down at the voice recorder. "I understand. I don't need a lawyer."

"Thank you. Let's begin with your name and what you do."

"Leo Holloway. Leonora. Leonora Jane Holloway."

He nods. "Leo is fine. Leo, why were you at the house on Zora Neale Hurston today?"

"I just started working for Schneider Agency as a photographer. Today. Today's my first day."

"What time did you get to the house?"

"Which time?"

He raises his eyebrows slightly and makes a note on his yellow legal pad. "How many times have you been there?"

"I went yesterday evening and then first thing this morning with Emily."

"Why did you go yesterday?"

"I wanted to get started taking some shots by myself. I don't really know what I'm doing. Em and I were going to use this first house as a training exercise to get a sense for the kinds of shots she wants and how to list them on the website."

"How long were you there the first time?"

"Thirty or forty minutes, maybe? The photos will have time stamps."

"Can I see them?"

She unzips her backpack and pulls her camera bag out, then tugs out her camera. She turns it on and flips back to the first pictures. "Here, you can look through these."

Jake takes the camera and looks through the images. "Who has a copy of these?"

"No one. I haven't even downloaded them yet."

"I'm going to need to keep this camera, I'm afraid."

Leo nods. "For how long, do you know? I hate to leave Kay and Emily waiting."

Jake turns the camera off. "I don't know yet, but I'll try to make it reasonably fast. I'm sure it'll be okay with everyone if you're not taking pictures for a few days after such a traumatic event." He sets the camera down and seems to be weighing his next words carefully. "I get that you just started in a new job, but this definitely changes things. You're not going to be able to use these photos or list the house until this murder is solved."

Leo swallows around a sudden lump in her throat. Of course the house can't be listed anytime soon. She shakes her head slightly. Her head feels like it's full of cotton. She wonders if she is still in shock.

"Let's take a minute," Jake says, watching her face. A text lights up his phone and he glances at it, then stands. "Esquivel is here. I'm going to take these down to her to log in. Need anything?"

"Can I go to the bathroom?"

"Of course." He stops the recorder and gestures for her to walk out the door first. "Second door on the right. See you in a few minutes."

In the harshly lit bathroom mirror, Leo examines her reflection while washing her hands. Her eyes are red-rimmed and puffy; the yellow sundress she put on this morning—was it only a few hours ago?—makes her look washed-out. Her hair is in her usual messy bun, bangs plastered to her forehead. She brushes them with her fingers. She wishes distantly that she looked better, then immediately feels awful. How could she be thinking about looking good in front of Jake when Chaz is dead? She swallows, drying her hands with a paper towel. More than anything in the world, she hates this feeling of being out of control.

It hits her like a wave: Chaz is dead. Chaz, who she spent so much time over the last few years snarking on. She watches as the blotches work themselves up her chest and neck. What has always seemed harmless and funny when the subreddit was a secret now seems childish, even mean.

Leo grabs the sink to steady herself as the realization sets in of where Jake's questions could lead. The scenarios play out in her mind like chess moves—if she doesn't say anything, if she waits to say something, if Jake finds out, if Emily reveals it all. Her grip tightens, but she swallows more easily.

The realization has cleared her woolly mind. This, at least, she can control. Because there is only one scenario that works, that doesn't lead to more trouble in the future. She thinks it through one more time—a chess player tapping her finger on a piece before withdrawing her hand. She nods at herself in the mirror. She is certain.

With a measure of calm she did not feel earlier, she walks back to Jake's office. He's already there waiting.

"Jake, I have something I should tell you first."

He holds up the recorder. "Okay if I keep recording?"

Leo pauses, looks at the voice recorder, takes a deep breath, and begins.

17

Sheriff Stan Quackenbush is irate. This is not new. Quackenbush spends most of his time driving around Blue Oak in a huff.

Quackenbush grew up in Blue Oak, Texas. He met his wife, Susan, at Blue Oak Elementary; they started dating their sophomore year at Blue Oak High School, and he married her after their junior year at Rollingwood Baptist College thirty minutes away. He's proud to say he has never lived anywhere but Blue Oak. He knows every inch of this town—or he used to.

Quackenbush hates change. And living in Blue Oak for more than five decades, he has seen nothing but change. It used to be a small town, Austin's *Leave It to Beaver*-esque southern neighbor, but the city crept to the edges of the municipality and brought a culture that changed the heart of what he loves about this place. He ran as sheriff decades ago to protect this town. In his heart of hearts, he hoped to be a Texas Ranger. But Quackenbush was small as a kid and remained short as an adult; he blames his diminished height for his four failed applications to be a Texas Ranger. Though they got rid of the height restriction in the early 1970s, at five foot five, Quackenbush knew it was a losing battle; the iconic white hat would've just slipped down around his ears, he told himself disparagingly in the mirror after he got that first rejection.

He found his place as a sheriff. He has run unopposed for the last twenty years. Quackenbush knows now—because his preacher pulled him aside last year and told him God had delivered this word especially for him—that God put Quackenbush on this earth to protect the bit of land that makes up Blue Oak, Texas.

Which is why Quackenbush is so angry today. It's not his normal irritation at new buildings or new signs or new city codes. This is a holy, focused rage. Charlie "The Bear" Nickolson moved back to Blue Oak a few years ago, and now he is dead. The Bear coming home was the only kind of change Quackenbush liked—a change that made things closer to what they'd been. Quackenbush never missed a Blue Oak High football game, especially in the years when Nickolson had been the best quarterback for five hundred miles. Charlie and his best friend, Dominic Garner, had dominated the field in every game—The Bear and The Boss led Quackenbush's home team to State not once but a record three times. It didn't matter that when Quackenbush was in high school, he'd been a third-string safety who only played in four varsity games; he had the letter jacket still hanging in his closet and he would always be a proud fighting Blue Oak Bandit—BO for life.

Quackenbush had just started in his role as sheriff when Dominic Garner died. That death had been formative for him. He'd seen how cut up Charlie Nickolson had been. Charlie was always a good egg; just look at how he'd come back and opened up that gym and helped the people of Blue Oak get healthy. Charlie offered his workout facilities and expertise to the high school coaches to get this generation of Bandits up to speed for the upcoming football season, taking 10 percent off his usual fees for the off-season workouts. Even when Kay Schneider and the rest of the city council made Charlie give his gym that cutesy-ass name, Charlie went along with it, proving he was still the same golden-hearted boy of all those years ago.

And now he is dead.

Quackenbush's anger at the death of Charlie "The Bear"

Nickolson has given him clarity and toughness. He knows now that his preacher was right last year to say that only Quackenbush could keep evil at bay in Blue Oak.

Quackenbush is here to do the Lord's work. He lifts his right hand in a tight fist and knocks, two staccato raps on a fiberglass front door. He stands tall, or as tall as he can. In the second before the door opens, he feels a surge of gratitude that he was called to this place and this time to do what few have the courage to actually do.

The door opens. He holds out his badge, though it's unnecessary—they know each other well. He gazes up and speaks first.

"I think you and I both know why I'm here. We can talk here, or down at the courthouse. But I know what you did. And you're not getting away with it."

18

After an hour of talking with Leo in his office, Jake pauses his recorder and sits back, stretching, in his chair.

"That is . . . I mean . . ." He gazes up at the ceiling. "I'll just say, this is not where I thought this conversation was going when you started."

Leo sips at her water, chagrined. She'd told Jake everything—about her and Emily modding the subreddit, about the weird feeling that something was off with the cloths and the funky smell in the house the night before, about seeing the screenshots on Reddit and recognizing the kitchen, about rushing into the house and finding Chaz's body.

Jake clicked through the subreddit on his computer; the group had exploded since Leo cut off the Instagram Live on Chaz's phone. One of the more recent posts had a full-screen recording of the Instagram Live, from the moment when it started until its end. Hundreds of subredditors had commented, speculating on what exactly had happened.

Jake and Leo had just finished watching the video before he turned the recorder off. When it's over, her body feels buzzy, too warm and agitated. She does not want Jake to know these things about her, things she never had any intention of revealing to anyone. She still thinks it was the right decision to tell Jake about the subreddit; there was no way to reveal why they ran into the house without talking about it. But she likes to be in charge of how people perceive her. His neutral expressions and careful questions do not give her any insight into his thoughts. As she finishes going over it, she feels vulnerable and exposed.

"Can I . . . Do you mind if I try to talk this through with you?" Leo recognizes even as she asks the question that she is trying to wrangle back control of the situation, to approach the situation as a researcher might.

Jake reaches for the recorder again. "Should I turn this on?"

"You can, but this isn't a witness statement. I just—I need to process this."

"Go ahead." He leans back, crossing his arms.

"I smelled Chaz's dead body yesterday, and the pile of cloths was obviously there already."

"That seems likely."

"Was he killed yesterday?"

His eyes don't give anything away. "I can't discuss those details with you, but the body is undergoing an autopsy while we speak."

"Already?" Leo scrunches her face with disbelief.

"What are you implying?"

"I'm not implying anything. Blue Oak is a small town. Don't you have to, I don't know, send . . . the body to Austin?"

Jake sighs. "Blue Oak County Hospital houses the medical examiner's office used for five counties. Our ME is very good, and before you ask, she lives here because she likes ranching and got tired of the big city. She's a friend of your mom's. And she happens to like my mom's cooking, and I'm not above pulling in favors when I need it. So yes, the body is already undergoing an autopsy."

"Okay, of course." Leo has clearly hit a nerve with Jake. She moves on. "The blood around Chaz's head was dried. And there wasn't much of it, or it wasn't, I don't know, splattered against the walls or something." She swallows bile, and sips more water. "It seems likely that he was killed someplace else, and that his body was placed there earlier, like maybe earlier in the day or the night before, by someone who had no idea I'd be in the house."

He dips his head, conceding her point without giving her an answer to her implied question about the murder timeline.

"No one knew I was going over there last night; Emily didn't even know. The agents at Schneider Realty have a pretty strict communication system over Slack since they work so collegially, so they're supposed to log when they go to and leave a property. I had the lockbox code but didn't log it into their system because I wasn't technically employed."

Jake waits patiently while she puts her next thoughts together.

Leo continues. "So maybe I almost stumbled over someone murdering Chaz. Or dragging his body in. Except . . . the smell was already there, faint but present. He had to have been there for some time, at least. So maybe the body wasn't . . . fresh."

"Was it hot in the house?"

"Yesterday?"

Jake nods.

"No, not particularly. The AC was on."

Jake makes a note. "What do you think of this video, then?"

Leo starts to feel a bit better. Providing an analysis of media is comfortable—far more comfortable than everything else that's happened this morning. "Someone went to a lot of trouble to make it seem like Chaz was at that house this morning. We all thought it was Chaz taking that video, and you can tell the subreddit immediately turned on him for not turning his camera on and all that. But there was something . . ." She pulls Jake's laptop over, with the subreddit open, and clicks through it for a minute, then nods. He watches her, waiting. "You can tell this felt different to people even early on. Chaz never misses . . . missed an opportunity to make something about himself. His silence, his short words, the turned-off camera, the conversation several feet away . . ." She sits back in her chair and continues. "I have no idea why, but someone obviously killed Chaz earlier, and then went to a lot of trouble to make it sound like it actually happened this morning. Though, was it about timing?" She almost stands up to pace, but stops herself.

"Say more." Jake leans forward. Any other time, she might have been distracted by his piercing dark-brown eyes. But now she's in full-on researcher mode.

"Did they go to a lot of trouble to make it seem like Chaz died today? Or was this more about framing someone than, I don't know, confusing you about the cause and time of death?"

Jake snatches his pen and starts jotting in his notebook. "Do you recognize the woman's voice in the video? The woman at the door?"

"Something about it is bothering me, but I can't . . ." She shakes her head again. "I can't figure out what it is. It'll come to me." This, at least, she knows.

"For now, we'll need to log all of this into evidence. Lieutenant Esquivel has a colleague we often work with on a consulting basis for digital cases. I want to explain all of this to Esquivel, then I'd like you to tell her your password, and let her change that password so that she can access everything internally in the Reddit group. She'll also make it so that you and Emily do not have administrative access for however long it takes us to document what we need."

Leo sits back, a little stunned. "I mean, if you think that's necessary."

Jake nods tersely. "I do."

"Can I tell Emily?"

"I'd rather you didn't. I'm going to interview her soon and I'd rather you not speak with her beforehand. I don't want it to affect our evidence in this case."

"You think I'm going to get my best friend to lie to you, after everything I just told you?"

A small furrow appears in Jake's forehead and he takes a deep breath. "Remember what I said about being absolutely by the book, Leo? This is one of those times."

"Fine." Leo's too tired to hide that she's upset. "On one condition: let me leave a mod message on the subreddit telling them not to speculate and that we're cutting off all communication for now. They're used to being able to DM us if something goes wrong, and if we suddenly leave right after that video was posted, it'll be anarchy. You'll have a group of voracious snarkers landing in Blue Oak with fake journalist passes trying to solve this thing. Wait." Her stomach drops. "Has anyone told Chaz's family? And Tiffani? And Grant?"

Jake leans forward. "Leo, we're very good at our jobs. That's most of what Esquivel has been doing today. She texted an hour ago to tell me all of the next of kin and close friends have been notified." He taps with his pen on his notepad and gazes at her for a second. "I'm okay with you doing whatever you need to in the group, as long as you do it in front of Esquivel. Is that okay with you?"

Leo nods, then looks at the recorder. "Yes."

She follows Jake down the stairs, shoulders slumped. His phrase—"evidence in this case"—makes what had felt like a lighthearted hobby seem so sordid.

A wave of heat passes over her. She knows she had nothing to do with Chaz ending up dead in some painters' cloths in an empty house this morning.

So why does she suddenly feel so guilty?

19

Esquivel looks up as Detective Nguyen leads a woman in a rumpled yellow sundress down the stairs into the desk area of the cramped sheriff's station. The historic redbrick building on the corner of Phillis Wheatley Street and Lorraine Hansberry Boulevard is not as pretty as the county courthouse. As sheriff, Quackenbush has an office in both, but he prefers the courthouse office, near the holding cells—which in Blue Oak are only occasionally occupied, usually by drunks sleeping it off. That means Jake and Esquivel can often go days without seeing their boss. A little separation of church and state, if you will. The youngest full-time deputy, Dusty Williams—a white man who has never said *aw shucks* in Esquivel's hearing but might at any moment—stays mostly with Quackenbush. Jake and Esquivel almost exclusively have the run of the sheriff's station. When they need more officers, like they do right now, they work with the Texas Department of Public Safety to bring in extra person power, but usually, it's just the four of them in Blue Oak.

From Esquivel's desk at the back of the room, she can see every entrance clearly: the front door and the public counter, the back door to the parking lot, the two conference rooms, and the stairs.

Esquivel does not like to be surprised. Ever.

"Hey, boss." She straightens a pile of papers that does not need to be straightened.

"Esquivel, this is Leo Holloway. Leo, Lieutenant Laura Esquivel." Esquivel stands and shakes the hand of the woman behind Nguyen. She registers every detail of Leo's appearance and instantly files them away.

She gives herself a mental gold star for both cataloging the details and doing it quickly, hopefully without Leo noticing. That is always the hard part—observing is easy, but it makes people uncomfortable. She gazes squarely into Leo's eyes and gives herself another gold star for the solid amount of eye contact.

Leo looks back at her for a moment as they finish their handshake and Esquivel feels a flash of recognition—Leo is observing her as closely as she is observing Leo. She swallows a smile. She finds herself feeling warm toward Leo—a very rare thing for her.

Leo drops her hand and steps back. Esquivel notices Nguyen keeps his hand lightly on Leo's elbow, almost as if he doesn't register the contact.

"We're going to have to pull Macy Johnson in on this one, Esquivel. Get her on the phone and I can explain to both of you what we're going to need her to do." He gestures for Leo to sit and pulls another chair over to sit with them.

Esquivel picks up the receiver on her desk telephone and makes a show of opening a drawer and looking up a number she knows by heart. And she doesn't put the phone on speaker yet because . . .

"Hey, baby." Esquivel has talked to Macy about this, that any call not from her personal cell phone would always have to be professional since Esquivel has no plans to reveal their relationship to anyone at work, but does Macy listen? Again, Esquivel has to swallow a smile.

"Is this Macy Johnson?"

"Oooh, are we doing professional talk now?" Esquivel pushes the phone even closer to her ear, hoping that the other two can't hear Macy's voice.

"Hi, this is Lieutenant Laura Esquivel. We worked together a few months ago on the Anthony Crabb case?"

"Right, of course, that rings a bell. I think I might remember you." Macy's laughing.

"I'm here with my boss"—the tiniest emphasis on that word—"Detective Jake Nguyen and a witness. We'd like to pull you into a murder case. Are you available this week to take it on?"

She hears cloth rumpling and the electric hum of Macy's wheelchair moving; Macy was either in her bed or on the couch in the nest of blankets she makes while gaming, but she's heading now to her office.

"I am available. A *murder* case?" Esquivel hears the mix of concern (for Esquivel) and excitement (for herself) in Macy's voice.

"I have Nguyen here now to explain. Can I put you on speaker?"

"Of course." Macy's tone is clipped and professional. Esquivel is relieved by the change. Secretly dating a world-renowned hacker who moonlights as a sheriff's department consultant and has a subversive sense of humor keeps her life interesting. She presses a button on the phone, places the receiver down, and moves it closer to Nguyen and Leo.

"Macy, how are you? Nguyen here. Thanks for agreeing to help out."

"Absolutely, Detective. Happy to do whatever you need."

"I'm assuming the usual rate works?"

"Sounds good."

"Esquivel will send over the contract after this call. And the NDA you signed for the earlier cases still applies."

"Of course." Esquivel pictures Macy, wearing the *She-Ra* T-shirt and gray pajama pants she'd had on this morning, her pink-orange-green-teal hair in Princess Leia buns, hands on her ergonomic keyboard, ready to start typing notes. Macy loves murder cases, and Esquivel loves Macy. Inside, she's delighted to be able to bring this case to Macy; outside, her face is stony.

For the next ten minutes, Nguyen and then Leo catch Esquivel and Macy up about Chaz's death and the subreddit. The whole time they're talking, Macy clacks away on her keyboard.

"Do you have reason to think anyone in the group is a suspect?" Esquivel asks.

Leo considers the question. Esquivel appreciates that she takes time to think before speaking. "I don't know how to answer that. I don't really know who's in the group, since most people rely on usernames. It's possible that there are lots of people in Chaz's real life who know about or have joined the group. A suspect could be part of it."

"How many people are in the sub?" Esquivel asks.

"Almost 18,000," Leo says.

"Actually, you're at 24,124," Macy corrects her.

"Wow. That's jumped up a lot." Leo opens her laptop. "They must be going nuts over the video."

Nguyen's phone buzzes. "I'm going upstairs to take this call. Leo, I'm leaving you in good hands." He touches her shoulder as he walks swiftly toward the stairs, phone already by his ear.

"I guess I'll just make my mod statement and then tell you my password and you will take it from there?" Esquivel knows this business of Leo handing over her passwords is legally necessary, of course, but she also knows Macy has already hacked into the group and could lock them all out right now if she wanted.

"Yes, that'd be great," Esquivel says.

For the next few minutes, Esquivel listens as her secret girlfriend and the person that she suspects Nguyen might be interested in have an engaging conversation about the subreddit.

While they talk, Esquivel creates an evidence folder for Macy to upload the documents using Quackenbush's preferred, if outdated, method—one that is easiest to print since he still largely refuses to even log onto a computer. She makes the first document: a screenshot of some entries in the group's wiki. She'll let Macy document the rest of the page, but having this as a template will make it easier. She can already tell the

"Cast of Characters" section—detailing the people in Chaz's life and circle—will be especially important.

In no other case she's ever investigated has someone basically just handed her a list of suspects to look into. For the third time in the last hour, she has to swallow a smile.

Esquivel shares the folder with Macy, who she knows will begin while they're still talking; Esquivel has watched Macy work, and her ability to do seven hundred things at once is truly remarkable.

Macy will get the evidence that the sheriff's department needs. And Esquivel is confident that Macy hears what she does—the worry and care in Leo's voice, the desire to protect Emily, the fear that the tens of thousands of people in the subreddit will overreact as the news about Chaz's death gets out.

"Hey, Leo?" Macy interrupts a long sentence as Leo tries to explain the dynamics of the group to her. "Can I just offer something to you? I'd like for you to give us your cell phone number. I am definitely going to do the archiving work the sheriff's department needs me to do, but it's in the best interest of this case if I also do a little babysitting of this sub, it sounds like. Does that seem right to you?"

"Yes." Leo's voice is low. Esquivel watches her, noticing that she seems weighed down by fatigue. Leo's eyes are red-rimmed, making them look even greener.

Macy goes on. "Okay, let's make a deal. I think that mod statement you wrote is good. It's live now; I'll keep an eye on the comment section today. If anything gets wild, I'll text and let you know. I'm going to be spending a lot of time on this sub. I'm not going to delete comments because we want to see where the points of tension are. That actually might give us real-life information that could be crucial. But if I need anything, or if I feel like, I don't know, someone is about to get on a plane to come to Texas or something, I'll check in with you. How does that sound?"

Leo sighs. "That sounds good, actually. I just . . . I don't want to leave the group alone right now."

Esquivel clears her throat. “Ms. Johnson, do you have what you need for now?”

“Actually, Lieutenant, I have some questions I’d like to ask Leo while we’re here. I think you might be interested in hearing these answers too.”

“Proceed.”

Macy pauses briefly. She’s going to tease Esquivel mercilessly about that one-word response later.

“It was just the two of you as mods?” Macy asks.

“Yes, we thought about adding others but never did. It’s a pretty easy mod role; we occasionally delete wackadoos. Definitely anyone who shares pictures of kids’ faces without permission. Anyone who touches the poop. That kind of stuff.”

“Touches the poop?” Esquivel speaks up.

“Engaging with the subject of the snark group.” Macy’s voice is quick, and her fingers never stop typing. “Reddit shuts down subs if they harass people. They’re pretty strict about that, so it’s a common rule.”

“Was Emily touching the poop by interacting with Chaz in person?” Esquivel clicks her pen to take notes on her legal pad.

Leo answers. “No. Touching the poop is like leaving a comment on an Instagram post that says ‘I read about you in this snark group and we all hate you!’ Maybe if Emily weren’t moderating under a hidden identity or something, it might be considered touching the poop. But when Em engaged with him, she was careful to make sure that she didn’t let it slip into the sub. Most of the posts weren’t from us, anyway. We were mainly moderating other people’s posts.” She stops and bites her lip. “I doubt anyone in Blue Oak even knows about the subreddit; it’s a pretty obscure corner of the internet.”

Macy speaks up. “I want to watch this Insta Live video with you here, Leo, if that’s okay with you, Lieutenant.”

“Okay.” Esquivel watches Leo steel herself and decides she’d like more information too. “Actually, Ms. Johnson, let’s do it at the same time and you mute yours.” It takes them a minute to get the video up and loaded on Esquivel’s laptop.

"Wait." When Macy speaks, Esquivel stops her fingers from touching the play button. "This video is what the sub refers to as a 'meta-recording'?"

Leo answers. "Yes, a Chazzerciser uploaded screenshots of the meta-recording of the Chaz Challenge where he Lives himself while Zooming with the Challengers."

Esquivel allows herself a small laugh. "That sentence just gave me a headache. Say that again in English."

Leo smiles wanly. "Today's post was pretty common in the sub: A subredditor, which we call a 'Chazzerciser,' just to be . . . anyway, she screenshotted Chaz's Instagram Live. Then a bunch of subredditors watched it on Insta while it was streaming and talked about it in the sub. Chaz usually filmed himself with his phone while also on his laptop in a Zoom meeting with the members of his paid-for Chaz Challenge. Today, he moved his phone around . . . or, I guess, someone made it look like he moved his phone. Emily and I could see the recording taking place in the house we were outside of. We thought it was proof that we'd caught him on their property. We'd suspected him of sabotaging Schneider listings before."

"And you thought Chaz was there in that kitchen when you ran in?" Esquivel's voice is firm.

"I mean . . . the video of him in the kitchen was on his Instagram Live, so we thought he was in there. Obviously it wasn't him, though; he was already dead."

"Did you see anyone else in the house or outside of it?"

Leo pauses. "We didn't. Jake already asked me. The Zoom camera was off. And we didn't see anyone coming or going from the house while we were there."

Esquivel nods. She asks Macy if she's ready to start, and then presses play. Macy listens over the speakerphone, the sound of her tapping keyboard the only thing that breaks their silence for all sixteen minutes and thirteen seconds of the video. Esquivel pauses only four times: First, when the laptop open with the Zoom meeting comes onto the screen; Leo points out that Chaz's user square is a static profile picture because his Zoom camera is off. Second, she shows them the cabinets and distinctive window in the frame and pulls up u/OodlesofSchnoodles's screenshots that prompted her to run inside with Emily. Third, when they hear someone speaking; Leo asks them to stop and beats her fingers agitatedly on the desk, thinking, but she can't place what is familiar about the voice. And finally, Esquivel pauses when they hear a distinct thud; Leo answers Esquivel's question about whether she knows what those noises are by saying she doesn't. "Unless it's someone trying to make it sound like Chaz was being murdered right then."

The video plays on, the phone focused on the ceiling, for several more minutes. Leo visibly pales when they hear Emily screaming and then herself screaming. They finish the video out, on that cliff-hanger of Leo dialing 911.

Macy is silent for a minute. "The sound quality between your voices and the voice at the beginning is really different. I'm going to run some analysis on the sound first thing."

Leo suddenly sits forward eagerly. "Can we watch that part again? This sounds absolutely nuts, but that voice sounds like . . ."

A clanging metallic noise startles Esquivel and Leo—the cannonball that is Leo's mother, shoving open the glass front door. She spots Esquivel first.

"Where is my daughter? What the hell have you done with her?"

Leo stands up. "Mom. I'm right here."

"Leo, it's time to go! They've just arrested Kay!"

20

Quackenbush tries to suppress his joy as he perp-walks Kay Schneider out of her house with her hands cuffed behind her. "You just never know about people," he always tells his wife; she used to nod along to these little pearls of wisdom from him, but now she tends to offer a dismissive "yes, dear" midway through his thoughts. As he tucks Kay Schneider's head into the back of his vehicle, he murmurs to himself. He was right; of course he was right. *You never really know about people.*

Kay Schneider looks like a Stepford wife, albeit an older one: a successful real estate agent, pillar of the community, doting wife to Phil, mother to those two girls, grandmother to three. But lurking beneath the surface of that exterior is a dark core. Kay Schneider is a stone-cold killer.

And—this time he doesn't stop himself from smiling; it doesn't matter, because he's in the front of the car now and Kay can't see him—Quackenbush knew it all along. Hadn't he always suspected that there was something hiding beneath the surface of the person whose entire life's goal seemed to be causing chaos in the town that Quackenbush loves so much? Hadn't he known, in some secret part of himself, she was up to no good? He really should have been a Ranger. His instincts are always spot-on.

Of course—now the smile dims slightly—Quackenbush hasn't been able to *prove* it yet. He has good circumstantial evidence, though. He heard the recording himself. He recognized, when no one else did, whose voice was speaking to Chaz at the beginning. He jumped to arrest Kay before she could destroy evidence—every second counts in a murder investigation. Real detective work is five parts intuition and one part hard work, and this time his gut is telling him that Kay did it.

That nugget about intuition and hard work is one of his favorites, shared almost daily with his protégé, little Jake Nguyen. It's true that Nguyen came to the department with more training and education than Quackenbush had, but Quackenbush clearly knows more; Nguyen might have learned how to be a detective in school, but Quackenbush went to the school called *life*. He smiles again. Young Nguyen will learn someday. This case will be a great chance to train him. Quackenbush is downright glowing by the time he pulls up to the county courthouse at the center of town. He will book Kay Schneider—a pleasure he never anticipated having—then spend the next few hours closing the case up. When he is done, he will walk Nguyen and Esquivel and maybe even Williams—he's feeling particularly generous today—through what he did, step-by-step and slowly, so they can learn.

The entire time she's been in the back of the car, all four minutes, Kay Schneider has been silent. As they park, Quackenbush glances back. She smiles at him politely, absolutely unruffled. "Thank you, Sheriff Quackenbush, for bringing me here safely. If you don't mind opening the door for me, I'll walk with you into the station."

Quackenbush is immediately incensed. Of course he's going to open the door for her. It's locked from the outside. She doesn't have a choice!

The euphoria of bringing Kay to jail in handcuffs fades. It's less fun if she's not flustered. Then Quackenbush remembers: by law, he has forty-eight hours before he has to charge her or let her go.

That's plenty of time. Anything can happen in forty-eight hours. Even proving that she is a murderer. He smiles broadly.

He finally has Kay Schneider exactly where he wants her.

21

Karina is quivering, her shellacked helmet of crimson hair practically vibrating. Normally Karina's paranoia drives Leo absolutely batty, but this time her mom's response is justified. "What happened with Kay?"

"Sheriff Quackenbush arrested her."

"You're sure she wasn't just being brought in for questioning?"

Karina's voice is clipped and she walks briskly toward her Nissan Altima. "Please. I know the difference between being taken in for questioning and an arrest."

Leo pauses, cocking her head at Karina. Has her mother started watching crime shows in her free time?

"Leo, let's go!" Karina says, starting the car. "We gotta find out what's goin' on!" Leo shakes her head. She's had a very long day and it's only late morning.

Her mom drives around the corner and parks the car haphazardly.

"Mom, we could have walked—" But Karina is already blazing into the historic courthouse. Leo walks behind her.

"Hey! *Hey!*" Karina shouts at a young DPS officer who is just closing a door behind him. "We demand to know what's goin' on!"

The officer stands with his hand on the doorknob, obviously torn about what to do. Leo puts a hand soothingly on her mom's arm. "Mom, let's just take a seat and wait for him to get us more information when he can, all right?"

Karina shakes Leo's hand off. "Stop talking to me like I'm an old woman! I'm not gonna just wait here!"

"Mom, you need to calm down."

"Do *not* tell me to calm down!" Karina turns to Leo and looks at her for a long moment. Leo sees something strange in her eyes, something that is both calculating and anguished. Karina takes a deep breath and her entire body language changes; she had seemed poised to charge down the hallway, past the metal detector and security entrance. But now it's like she pulls her energy back. She grasps Leo's hand and lowers her volume. Again, the tone of her voice changes. "I'm not . . . I can't do this right now. They've arrested Kay. We have to do something."

"Why in the world would they arrest Kay?"

"I don't know, Leo. I need to make some calls." She storms outside.

Leo sits down and pulls her phone out to distract herself. She notices in a detached way her hands are shaking. She thumbs to her Facebook app and opens it.

There's a new post that accompanies a picture of a large German shepherd with a red bandanna:

Liz Frenetti

July 5

Today, Duke and I are praying for all those who have PTSD, who served our country so bravely and now must face a return of those fears when selfish youths and others refuse to adhere to community guidelines, and instead, inflict the fear of WAR and TRUAMA on these brave soldiers. Duke salutes you and your fur-babies.

For a brief minute, Leo thinks about screenshotting the post to send to Emily, who would love both the salute to fur-babies and the worries about "truama." But then Leo remembers where she is.

She looks up sharply. That post she deleted earlier, the one with the blood-soaked garage door that looked like a crime scene: Could that have been an actual crime scene? She's not a forensic investigator, of course, but there was hardly any blood around Chaz. Could he have been killed in another location?

She opens the app on her phone and goes to the deleted posts. Who is Marcos Salinas, and what is his connection to Chaz?

Maybe Leo was too focused on the subreddit. Chaz had a whole other life she never really knew about offline. She has to call Lieutenant Esquivel and tell her about that post. There was another one, too, that might be important, about a truck driving around the neighborhood. She wishes Esquivel and Macy had given her their numbers or emails instead of just taking hers.

She has her phone out, trying to find the number for the sheriff's station, when her mom walks in briskly, still on the phone.

"Well, tell the Member when she can find five minutes, she owes me a huge favor and I'm calling it in. I have to go. I'll call you back." Karina hangs up. "Are they out?"

"No, not yet. Who is 'the Member'?"

Karina's face looks stricken for one second, and then returns to a scowl. "What are you talking about, Leonora?"

"You just said 'tell the Member.' "

"Why would I say that?"

Leo throws up her hands. "I'm literally asking you that!"

"I think I said 'remember.' I was calling an old client who might be able to help us with the legal end of things if Quackenbush doesn't let Kay go soon. She owes me a favor."

"That's not what you . . ." Leo takes in a deep breath and releases it slowly. "You know what? Never mind. Are you doing okay?"

"They arrested and Mirandized Kay, Leonora. No, I'm not doing okay. And they're still questioning Emily. I bet you're not okay either." Then she stops and begins again, her voice softer. "Leo, Kay's in big trouble. Quackenbush has been in charge for a long time and he's old-school. If he thinks he has a good case against Kay, he won't hesitate to move against her—and quickly. I'm not worried that he *has* a case against Kay, I'm worried he *thinks* he has a case against Kay, and that he'll steamroll the evidence to make it fit the narrative in his mind. I'm assuming it's that video."

"That's it, that's what was bothering me. That's Kay's voice on that video." Leo's voice is low, to herself, but her mother hears her.

"Of course it was. I recognized it immediately. You didn't?"

"Wait, when did you see it? Are you on Instagram?"

"Almost as soon as it came out. One of the other stylists' daughters runs our salon account, and she was at the salon this morning. We all watched it."

"You have a salon account?"

"Of course we do. We live in this century. And it was also in that snark group about Chaz."

"You know about the subreddit?"

Karina snorts. "I think everyone in Blue Oak knows about it. Those people are *funny*."

"Are you in the snark group?"

"No, but I read it sometimes. Kay sends me screenshots."

"Kay knows about the snark group?"

Karina revolves her hand a few times, like *catch up*. "Everyone in Blue Oak, Leonora."

"Okay, well, that's a lot to process."

"Also, the Baptists sent it out on their prayer chain."

"I'm sorry, what?"

"The video that looks like Chaz filming himself on a Zoom meeting, and then you screaming at the end, it's on the Baptists' prayer chain. Everyone in town has seen it by now. The minute I heard her say, 'This is an outrage!,' I knew it was Kay."

Leo gets up and starts pacing by her mother's chair, trying to rein in her thoughts. "But Kay wasn't there. Em and I were parked out front. We would have seen her."

"Of course she wasn't there. Kay didn't kill anyone."

"That video was obviously a setup. Chaz had to have been dead for a while by then."

"How do you know that?" Karina's voice is sharp.

"I went to the house the day before to take pictures and could smell the body faintly; I saw the painters' cloths he was wrapped in, but didn't get close enough to look. But he was definitely there, already dead."

"You were in the house *last night*?" Karina's entire body quivers, like a tiny mouse who has spent too much time rooting around in a Sephora.

"I mean, yes, but I also found the body this morning."

Karina stands immediately. "I want you to go home right now. I'll drive you. Let's go."

"Mom, you're being ridiculous. It's fine. Kay is being framed, and I want to help."

"You will do *no such thing.*" Karina's voice is steel. "You will go home and lock your door. You were already in the house the day before, and your voice is on the video too. I don't want the killer anywhere near you. I'll take care of this." She narrows her eyes, her smoky makeup increasing the drama of her glare at her daughter.

Leo holds her hand up. "Mom, this is *enough.* This is way above both of our pay grades. But you are *not* going to start with this paranoid stuff again. I'm not going home and locking the door. No one knows it was me. I know the snark . . . I mean . . . Listen . . ." Leo sucks in a deep breath.

"Leo?" Jake's voice echoes off the marble floors as he walks swiftly out of the hall and past security.

She turns. "Yes?"

"Hi, Mrs. Holloway."

"Jake." Karina nods.

Jake's hair is sticking up slightly as if he's run his hand

through it in frustration. "The sheriff just had a search warrant approved for the Schneiders' home, and it includes the pool house where you're staying, Leo. So I need you to come with me."

Karina puts her hand on Leo's arm as if to stop her. "Leo, no." Her tone is not angry but anguished.

"Mom, it's going to be fine." Leo puts her hand on her mother's, squeezes it briefly, and then gently takes it off.

Jake is already walking out the door. "Let's go. We have no time to waste."

22

As they walk to Jake's truck, Leo tells him about the Facebook posts, and he fires off a text before putting his truck into reverse.

"Sounds good. I'll have Macy look into it."

"Does she want me to give her my password?"

Jake puts his hand on the back of her headrest as he looks behind him to back up, ignoring the rearview camera that shows the exact same thing. "Sorry, Leo, but I'm not worried about that for now. Macy's very good. And I have exactly three minutes to tell you something that is so unprofessional, it could end my career, and I don't have any time to waste."

"I'm sorry, *what*?"

His jaw tenses. "Quackenbush should not be running lead on this case. He's well-intentioned, and he has an unwavering sense of right and wrong. But in this case, it's the worst possible scenario for Kay. By the time I'd interviewed you, Quackenbush had wrapped the case up in his mind. He's on his way right now to dinner, and then he'll head to the Schneiders' to gather whatever evidence he thinks he needs to tie it up with a bow. I'm trying to beat him so that I can stay on top of it; he views this as a mentoring opportunity for me, and I view it as a way to prevent him from miscarrying justice in an egregious way."

"Good grief, Jake."

On the left, they pass Garner Ranch and then the Episcopal church that Leo's and Emily's families have attended since she was little. "I know Kay didn't do it. It's too neat. And honestly, she's too smart for that. If she'd killed someone, I doubt we'd know about it."

"Are you saying Kay didn't commit this murder because she would have committed a smarter murder?"

Jake smiles without humor. "I'm saying this is not adding up to me the way it does for Quackenbush." He flips his blinker on and turns right onto Kate Chopin Drive.

"Obviously I think you're right. But why are you telling me this?" Leo instinctively looks out the window on the right when they pass her childhood home. She hasn't even stepped inside it yet.

Jake pulls his truck by the curb a few houses down. He sits in silence for a moment. Leo waits.

"I . . . Leo, I need to be really careful here."

"Can I guess?"

For the first time, he meets her eyes, and Leo sees distress. There is also—for one second—a spark of heat.

Leo's voice is low. "You're afraid Quackenbush will ignore important evidence in favor of finishing this case up quickly."

Jake raises his eyebrows and bites his lips—confirming without actually saying a word.

"So Quackers is quackers."

Jake smiles slightly. "You could say that."

"Can I offer a suggestion?"

Jake shrugs. "Leo, if you have ideas, of course you should come to me with those."

Leo continues. "I know you have Macy working on the sub-reddit, but I know things it might take her weeks to find out. Like, Chaz's ex-girlfriend Bodhi is a mastermind at digital editing. In the last several months, Chaz and Bodhi have been seen at some of the same parties. There was chatter in the Chaz-verse that he was moving back into their shared spaces;

he did some collabs with internet-famous people in her circle that really pissed her off."

Jake pulls his notebook out and scribbles rapidly.

"And they had a big fight a few weeks ago at a VIP party at Stubb's."

"What about?"

"No one knows. Kymber was filming a Live of them at the concert when Bodhi appeared in the background and yelled, 'You bitch!' Even the YouTubers covered it."

"The YouTubers?" Jake frowns.

"Yeah, there are three or four who always cover Bodhi especially, but sometimes Chaz and Kymber too."

Jake looks up. "My cousin's kid is into YouTubers who just play *Minecraft* all day."

"Same idea. These people replay videos the influencers upload and make commentary on them. The video about Bodhi was with Tanya Tells All. She's one of several people in the sub who makes a living creating YouTube videos about online celebrities."

"There really is something for everyone on the internet." He pauses and looks out the window, then back. "Okay, so you're making an official suggestion that I should talk to Bodhi?"

"Yes, officially."

Jake taps on his phone, and Leo's buzzes in her backpack. "I just texted you, Esquivel, and Macy. As soon as you're done here, leave all of us a voice memo—not a text—with all of that information."

He opens his door and she follows.

"Are you going to interview Emily?"

"I can't right now. And you can't talk to her either, not until I've had the chance to." As they walk toward the back gate leading to the pool house, he continues: "Go inside and I'll stand at the door while you pack a small bag for tonight. And then you'll need to head to your mom's house. I want you to keep your phone on and available; I'm hoping we can go tonight to interview Bodhi."

"We?"

"Yeah, I'd like you to come with me. Probably as an outside consultant like Macy. I might even pay you." She looks at him for a minute as they stand by the pool house door. His eyes are opaque, and Leo recognizes that distant expression—his brain is going a mile a minute. It's exactly how she feels when she's in the depths of researching.

Without a word, Leo goes inside; a few minutes later, she returns with a couple of tote bags, her pillow, her backpack, and a leashed Derrida, who sniffs Jake's pant leg. Jake steps back.

"He's super friendly, I promise."

Jake holds his fist down low for Derrida to sniff, and Derrida growls deep in his throat.

"Derrida!" Leo tugs on his leash. "I swear, he's never like this."

"He probably smells my cat. Do you have everything you need?"

She opens up her tote bags for his inspection. "Do you need to look through this?"

"Did you hide any murder weapons?"

"Just a candlestick, a rope, and a lead pipe. The rest are with Colonel Mustard."

Jake raises his eyebrows. Leo speaks quickly. "Sorry, I make bad jokes when I'm stressed."

"We all handle it our own way. Go on to your mom's. I'll text you soon."

Leo walks toward the back gate and Jake turns toward the house, where Esquivel has already unlocked the patio door and turned on all the lights.

"Oh, and Leo?"

She looks over her shoulder. He's standing near the pool. The wind stirs the branches of the live oak tree, and the sun dapples the ground around him, ruffling his thick black hair. His mouth is a thin line, and in the changing light, his cheekbones could cut glass.

"We don't know who we're dealing with here, and we don't know what they know about you. Don't answer the door unless it's Esquivel, one of the Schneiders, your mom, or me."

"I'll be careful, Jake." He gazes at her for one more second, likely noticing that she did not agree exactly. She doesn't like being told what to do. Finally he dips his head, and then walks across the yard to the deck and in the Schneiders' back door.

• • • • •

Several minutes earlier, in two other vehicles riding away from the courthouse, the conversations are very different.

In a Blue Oak PD squad car, Esquivel places a call.

"Hi, love." The voice is muffled.

"Are you eating chips?" Esquivel's face is unchanged, but her tone is slightly amused.

"Maybe. You're calling me. I can be doing whatever I want to be doing," Macy replies.

"True. Found anything yet?"

"I did. But I want to wait for a bit. You know how I love a big reveal."

"You really do." Esquivel shakes her head, though Macy can't see her.

"Later tonight, can we replay our conversation from earlier?" Macy can barely keep the grin out of her voice.

"What do you mean?"

"You know, where you say 'Proceed' in that bossy voice."

"Stop." Esquivel rolls her eyes.

"You love me."

"I do. But you really are going to have to be professional, or we'll lose the chance to work together like this. Everything has to be usable in a court of law—expert-witness-with-a-PhD-from-MIT-level usable. No hacking." Esquivel's voice is firm.

"*No* hacking?"

"Well, no detectable hacking."

"I'm so offended right now. As if anyone could ever detect my hacking."

"I'm sorry, you are a genius," Esquivel says, conciliatorily.

"*Proceed*," Macy purrs.

Esquivel allows herself one grin, then her voice gets quieter. "We're going to have to work fast."

"Because usually I like to take things slow."

"I'm serious, Mace. Quackenbush is being Quackenbush."

"What does that mean this time?" Macy stops joking immediately.

"He's decided the killer is an innocent woman because he's gullible as hell."

"This is about justice for women?"

"Justice for women."

"I'll be back with more in an hour."

"Thank you." Esquivel is out of the car and walking toward the Schneiders' before Macy hangs up the phone.

• • • • •

After putting their minivan into drive, Tess reaches across the console and grasps her wife's hand. The console holds the usual chaotic evidence of their family: Hyacinth's latest dried paint scrawlings on construction paper sent home from preschool, a half-empty juice box and a sippy cup in the back cup holders, and two travel mugs of day-old coffee in the front set. There are Band-Aids, two pairs of sunglasses, a bright-yellow bandanna, and a crayon half melted onto a napkin. Emily nestles her hand into the mess, holding on to Tess till their knuckles are white.

Emily doesn't pretend she's not crying. Tess drives with her left hand for two blocks and then looks at Emily. "I called Dr. Dansby. She cleared her schedule for a virtual appointment tonight at seven and said to tell you she'll take as long as you need, and she can come to the house if you'd rather."

Emily's voice is tight. "Virtual is fine. Do the"—she clears her throat—"the kids know?"

"The girls saw your mom get arrested." Emily's face is white. "We told them Quackenbush was playing hide-and-seek; they don't really get it. My mom came as soon as I called, and picked the girls up for what they're calling 'Surprise Grandparent Camp,' and my dad already got Hudson from baseball."

Emily nods absently. "I want to see them."

"I know, sweetheart. I know." Tess kisses Emily's hand. "Mom and Dad told them I'm taking you on a surprise date. There's just no reason for them to see you this upset. We'll call tomorrow."

Emily's face streams with tears. "Yeah. Okay. Thank you."

Tess pulls into their driveway, to the left of the bicycles and sparkle Hula-Hoops and a jump rope still on the pavement, right over the sidewalk chalk drawings of flowers and a rainbow and a wonky stick-figure version of their family of five.

Tess leans across the minivan. "Honey. Let it out." Emily's sobs are open-mouthed as she hugs her wife across the glorious, lovely mess of their good life together.

23

Leo walks into her mother's house. The aroma in the entryway—aging boards warmed by the sun—immediately signals "home" to Leo's tired body. She feels her shoulders relax even as her heart aches.

In the years since Richard died, her mom redecorated the house in what Leo calls (only to Emily) "Skittles Country Chic." A painting of a cow in Andy Warhol's Technicolor palette with none of Warhol's artistic ability hangs over the magenta couch. The kitchen has a collection of psychedelic-colored chickens. The whole thing gives Leo a headache.

As she goes to her old bedroom, each place she passes holds memories of her father. The kitchen counter, where Richard made her pancakes in middle school when she struggled to make friends because Emily was a year younger in school and Leo's bookish reserve came across to everyone else as unfriendliness—Karina often advised Leo to "get out of her bubble," but Richard just piled her plate with pancakes on Saturday mornings until she felt able to talk it through.

Before, the hallway to her bedroom had been filled with Richard's photographs taken over decades: first in El Salvador and on their many trips around Central and South America, featuring her young parents with smooth skin and earnest faces and 1980s short shorts. And later, when Leo was growing up, so many pictures of her: holding a flower in a chubby toddler hand in El Salvador, running away from the camera with Emily at Easter when she was eight and Emily seven, laughing at Christmas when she was thirteen with braces (a picture she hated but her father adored). Those pictures are now stored away somewhere, Leo assumes. The flamboyant farm animals continue into the hall.

In her childhood bedroom, the pale-blue walls and navy bedspread, untouched by Karina's redecorating scheme, make her feel as if she could just slip back in time. If she goes to sleep now, maybe her father will wake her up early for a run or to capture the light with their cameras as the sun tips over the edge of the horizon to begin a new day.

As she places her things down on her white childhood desk, Leo remembers a moment she had forgotten—when she was a teen and her mother hosted a birthday party for Kay, and the living room was crammed with old friends. Leo enjoyed it for a while, but eventually had gotten tired and ducked into her room. After a while, Richard came to find her, and they sat on the floor together leaning back against her bed, laughing affectionately at Karina's voice rising above the others, her Texas accent clear, her joy infectious. Richard had shaken his head, but his smile was genuine when he told Leo, "If it were just you and me, amor, we'd never talk to anyone, just live alone with books and cameras."

"Sounds pretty great to me," Leo responded.

"For a while, sure, but being an island is pretty lonely. I learned a long time ago that if I'm an island, your mom is my bridge, and I'm much happier this way." He kissed Leo on the forehead and got up to rejoin the party. A few minutes later, when Leo went back to the living room, her dad was sitting in an armchair in the corner, arm slung around Karina's waist as she perched on the armrest. Leo had rolled her eyes; her parents always had their hands all over each other.

Now, in the silent house, with dust motes dancing in the light from the slatted blinds, she is struck with clarity: her mother's joy has been gone for a long time. And Leo has become the island her father warned her she might one day be.

She toes off her shoes and drops onto her bed; her body is crashing and she closes her eyes. In the seconds before she drifts off to sleep, she sees Chaz's open-eyed stare under the tarp and shudders. Then she catches a whiff of her father's piney aftershave as he leans down to kiss her forehead.

Impossible, she thinks, and falls asleep.

• • • • •

Hours later, the light through her bedroom blinds is dim and her mouth is dry. Leo pads out to the kitchen and pours herself a glass of water. Her mom is home, but she's on the phone. When Karina sees Leo, she closes the door to her bedroom to continue the conversation. Leo checks her own phone, but the only text is from Emily to say Kay is still with the sheriff. A few minutes later, Karina comes out and catches Leo up briefly: the sheriff was undeterred and Kay will spend the night in sheriff's custody.

Leo makes the two of them sandwiches while Karina takes a shower; her mom takes hers back to her room to eat after drying her hair and leaves the door closed. Emily gives her text a thumbs-up when Leo tells her to keep her posted. Eventually, Leo turns the TV on and numbly watches *The Office*.

• • • • •

Around 8:45 p.m., there's a quiet knock at the front door. Derrida jumps up when he realizes there's a man outside. Leo grabs his collar and holds him back as she lets Jake into the room lit only by the TV.

"Hey, Leo." Jake takes a step back as Derrida growls deep in his throat, hackles rising. Jake swallows.

"Derr, to your mat!" Derrida goes to a towel on the floor by the wall, but whines at Leo expressively. "Enough!" Her voice is firm. "Jake is a friend. *Friend*."

Derrida puts his ears back and whines once more for good measure, sounding like a grumbling teenager being grounded.

"Wow, that is an expressive devil dog."

"Are you afraid of dogs?"

Jake shakes his head. "No, just more of a cat person."

She calls Derrida over, has Jake hold his hand out, and allows Derrida to smell it while Leo pets him and praises him in a crooning voice. Soon, Derrida is sitting belly up, thumping his tail while Jake rubs his stomach.

"Honestly, this isn't bad. Not a purring cat, but I appreciate belly rubs at the end of a long day," Jake says, kneeling on the floor.

"How'd it go at the Schneiders'?"

"There were . . . some unexpected developments."

"If you found sex toys, I don't want to know."

Jake smiles slightly. "I think . . . honestly, I don't think this hurts to tell you, and it might help me. Why does Kay have a telegraph-operating setup in her closet?"

"A what?"

"An old-fashioned telegraph machine."

"Like, Morse code? Dots and dashes?"

"Apparently."

"I have no idea. Are you sure it's Kay's? That sounds like something Phil might be into; he had a few years where he was really into model trains, and now he's an avid birder and master naturalist."

"It was set up in Kay's underwear drawer."

"Then it's definitely Phil's. That's probably his favorite drawer in the house." Leo rolls her eyes.

Jake pauses for a second, considering his words. "There was . . . well, I'm not sure how much I can tell you right now, so let's just say that there's no direct evidence pointing toward Kay being a murderer, but that's not enough to deter Quackenbush. The best option is to get some definitive proof that someone was framing Kay."

"Then let's do that."

"Can you come with me? I appreciated your insight into Bodhi Bruce. We got ahold of her assistant, and if we want to interview Bodhi, it has to be tonight. I'd normally never ask this, but, well . . ." He rubs his hand on the back of his neck. "You're clearly an expert on the, what did you call it? Chaz's universe?"

"The Chaz-verse. And the Bodhi-verse."

"Yes, exactly. I agree it would take me months to get the level of detail you know already. I'll have Esquivel set you up as a paid consultant tomorrow. Tonight, I want you there for anything I might miss."

Leo is already getting up and trying to smooth the wrinkles out of her yellow sundress. "Okay, I'll go. I want to do whatever I can to help."

Karina flutters into the living room in a brightly colored kimono, cosmetic face mask on. "Hi, Jake. Any news?"

Jake straightens up, and Derrida's tail slows forlornly, wanting more attention. "No, nothing to report. Do you know anything about Kay having a telegraph set?"

She waves dismissively. "That's Phil's. He's always into some hobby or another. You should see his birding T-shirts: 'I am not emu-sed' was his latest."

"That is . . . wow."

"Are you here to tell us there's no news?" Her hands are on her hips.

"Actually, I'm here to get Leo to help with an interview."

"Why would Leo be able to help?" Leo bristles at what feels like an implied criticism in her mother's voice.

"I thought I'd get her impressions of a conversation with an influencer."

"Oh, Brittni Bruce. But I'd rather Leo stay here."

Leo cocks her head. When did she tell her mother Bodhi's real name? "Mom, you have zero say on what choices I, an adult, get to make."

Karina puts her hands on her hips and then sighs dramatically, as if she's reluctantly acquiescing. "Fine, as long as you're with Jake."

"Literally, you cannot grant me permission."

Her mom ignores her and squints. "You should change before you go."

Leo's jaw drops. "Mom, this is hardly the time to argue about my clothes."

Karina holds up a hand to stop Leo. "Honestly, a little color does wonders for your features! But someone associated with the sheriff's department would not show up in a yellow sundress and old sandals."

Leo looks at Jake, who shrugs and says, "She might have a point."

After leaving Derrida with her mother (who coos she can't wait for "Granna time," to Leo's eye roll), Leo and Jake walk back to the pool house; he waits outside while she pulls on a slightly wrinkled pair of charcoal slacks, a light-blue button-down shirt, and black flats. At the last minute, she also tugs her hair down from a topknot and fixes it again, this time in the low bun she normally wears on the first day of classes to communicate that she is a no-nonsense teacher.

The cops are still searching the Schneiders' home, so Jake leads Leo out by the side gate. They aren't sneaking around exactly, but as Leo tugs on her backpack, she gets the feeling that Jake is also not advertising his plan to any other law enforcement officers.

She is not the only one keeping secrets, it seems.

24

Blue Oak County Sheriff's Department
1904 Phillis Wheatley St.
Blue Oak, TX 00130
(555) 512-6523

July 6

MEMO TO FILE

FORENSIC EXAMINER PROCESSING NOTES: Lt. Laura Esquivel (4132)

FORENSIC CASE NUMBER: 95613

EVIDENCE DESCRIPTION: Screenshot taken at 10:36 a.m., wiki page from the Chaz Nickolson Snark subreddit

BODHI: Everything you need to know about Bodhi can be summed up in the fact that a white girl from White Settlement (suburb near Fort Worth; true name; yep, the history is exactly what you think) legally changed her name to a Sanskrit word that means "awakening" or "enlightenment" but that has also become a shorthand for "yes, I am eating this açai bowl judgmentally at you."

Bodhi passed cultural appropriation in the rearview mirror years ago and has never looked back. She excels in her chosen career of ripping off other self-help gurus and plagiarizing their ideas in watered-down, more problematic renditions.

Whatever she was doing really worked for her until it wasn't: Bodhi passed a million Instagram followers back in the days when the Kardashians were still building their platform, fueled in part by being an early influencer for Goop (the famous vag egg video is here; yes, we know and you're welcome).

But for those of you who live under a rock, Bodhi fell from grace in April 2018 after what we now call Barista-gate (see below, or watch the full meltdown in all its glory on TMZ, read this write up on Newsweek, or the outstanding feature in The New York Times). Two weeks after Barista-gate, Bodhi and Chaz had their candlelit uncoupling ceremony that was widely and deservedly panned (watch this brilliant takedown by YouTuber and friend-of-the-sub Tanya Tells All). Now we chronicle Bodhi's increasingly desperate attempts to return to her glory days, and watch as things get worse and worse for Bodhilicious every year that passes.

Bodhi-Lites: Our own u/MonicaLewinskyLove coined this term for the interchangeably blond, fit, and young honeys Chaz hooked up with after Barista-gate. Some were bougie woo-woo, others were more hard-core fitness, but they all had one thing in common: growing social media followings. They hitched their star to Chaz, or he hitched his star to them, or they all . . . well, no one actually got hitched but there was a lot of hooking up and taking selfies, ostensibly to get more famous. Those were dark years in Chaz's life as he . . . found himself. Or found something, at least.

Chaz now employs a few of them in his CrossFit gym, and they pop up in videos every once in a while, but who can keep them straight? We cannot. We just call the blond ones Bodhi-Lites, and the brunette one . . . wait for it . . . Brunette Bodhi-Lite.

We're glad he dated one brunette. Diversity matters, y'all.

25

Jake breaks the silence several minutes after they get in the car. "Can you put together a timeline as I drive?"

"Sure."

"My notebook is in here." Jake pats his bag on the seat, and Leo pulls out the yellow legal pad he was writing in earlier.

She flips the page. "What do you want to know? I'm embarrassed at how well I'm about to do on this quiz."

"When did Chaz and Bodhi get together?"

"Chaz was married to Tiffani Miller either the year he graduated from Texas Tech or the year after; I don't know much about their marriage, only that Tiffani left him after a few years. In the subreddit—which, as far as I know, Tiffani has never engaged with—people refer to her as our Gal Pal Tiff, or GPT. It's a shorthand to say that she was smart enough to recognize Chaz for who he really is and that she would understand the snarkers too; I have no idea what she's really like, but we've created a whole character for her in the sub."

"I might get you to come with me when I interview her too, maybe tomorrow."

"Really?" Leo squeals. She immediately coughs to cover her mortification.

"Are you going to be all right doing this?"

"Yes, sorry. I'm going to play it cool, I promise. This whole thing is weird. I have an odd parasocial relationship with Bodhi and Tiffani, and I'm finding it difficult to . . . I don't know, regulate myself?" Leo runs through her mind for a comparable experience—maybe Elizabeth Gaskell meeting Charlotte Brontë, except, of course, she would never sanitize Bodhi's image for a myopic Victorian gaze. She shakes her head slightly and looks out the window; no one in her current life would understand that reference. She sinks down in the passenger seat.

Jake knits his eyebrows. "Is this too much for me to ask of you?"

"No, honestly, it helps to have something to do. Writing through a timeline feels cathartic. It's like research."

"Perfect. Think of yourself as my research assistant."

Leo perks up immediately; this is a role she understands. She scribbles for a few minutes while Jake drives. "Okay, Tiffani left him sometime in 2012. Chaz went through what the sub calls his Dark Ages: dating around and probably doing all kinds of substances, though that's mostly conjecture." She points to a few lines on the paper. "All my dates on this are approximate."

"Sounds good."

"He met Bodhi at a party in Austin after Austin City Limits, so probably . . . Let me just check the sub."

"Going through the subreddit this afternoon made me feel sorry for the guy."

"Yeah, as it grew, it got unwieldy. I'm with the people thinking critically about the self-help industry; I'm a little turned off by the people who seemed to be gleefully happy about Chaz's spiraling behavior."

"Was Emily?"

"What?"

"Gleeful?"

"I'm going to let you talk to Emily yourself about that."

"So yes."

Leo is silent for a minute. "Am I talking to Becky's brother, Jake, or Detective Jake?"

"They're one and the same."

"Not for me, they're not. I don't want to say anything that might incriminate Emily."

"I'll find it out anyway. Macy is very good."

Leo cringes again when she thinks of the DMs she and Emily never thought would see the light of day. "Let's say Emily was definitely angrier than I was at Chaz, and happier when things started falling apart for him. But that doesn't mean she killed him."

Jake nods. "If every person who was gleeful about snarking on Chaz were a suspect, I'd have more than twenty thousand suspects." He turns on his blinker to pull off into the Westlake area of Austin, and all the properties noticeably grow in size.

Leo looks around. "How much longer?"

"Five minutes or less."

"Okay, crash course, here we go."

• • • • •

THE BREAKUP: Popcorn out, fearless snarkers! If you're new to this little space, you might not have been there for the roller-coaster months in which Bodhi and Chaz's situationship was breaking apart faster than icebergs on a warming planet (too depressing?). But we're tired of answering these questions in the comments, so we decided to write out the timeline here.

OCTOBER 2015: When Chaz and Bodhi first hooked up, it was love at first sight: soulmates finding their twin, yin and yang, yada yada yada. Bodhi was Chaz's gateway drug into the big leagues of self-help and fame-seeking. Bodhi was the emotional and psychological savior and Chaz her adoring disciple. She constantly came down from the metaphorical mountains of enlightenment to bathe him and everyone else in the wisdom of her superior insight and chakra-opening love (yes, she said that; click here but don't say we didn't warn you; you can't scrub this video from your brain; we've tried).

Chaz was VERY good for Bodhi's business. Her numbers exploded when they got together, and Chaz built an almost instant platform overnight. They had great chemistry on camera. And they're both extremely pretty. Case in point: Bodhi convinced Chaz to play shirtless with puppies to fundraise for Austin Pets Alive and the viral post crashed the nonprofit's website. It got picked up by People magazine and Entertainment Weekly and all kinds of other places. They leveraged their "adorably fit, spiritually enlightened couple" shtick for extremely lucrative endorsements (no, we don't know how much, but if you do, we're all ears! DM the mods!)

AUGUST 2017, AKA CHAZ'S DARK AGES II: Bodhi kicked Chaz's ass to the curb via a released PR statement. Her "astrologer" (extremely sus woman who basically always tells Bodhi whatever she wants to hear) gave her a star chart (no, this is not how star charts work) telling her to "focus on your own journey of becoming and breathing" (Chaz kept her from breathing?). According to some posts by people who apparently encountered the pair in the wild, Chaz was belligerently drunk one too many times and Bodhi got sick of him. We don't know the full story, but we do know they were entangled financially and she worked hard over the next two years to untangle them. (We cannot recommend this series by the meticulous u/NanciDrew42 enough; come for the bullet points, stay for the extraordinary revelations about Chaz's finances.)

It seemed clear that Bodhi and Chaz were "charting their next steps together but alone," as she put it. Then . . . things got less clear. They were on again. Then off again. Then . . . on. Sort of. Then off. Then onnnnn, then whew, they were OFF again. There were so many quotes about "suffering" and "leaning in" and "the hard" we can't link to them all or we'd be here all day. But then, everything changed in . . .

JANUARY 2018: When Chaz disappeared. For weeks. There were no posts, no updates, no nothing. Then, in early March, almost exactly eight weeks later, Chaz shared this photo of a Gideon Bible in a shady hotel room and a very long word salad about finding the Lord. U/AxolotlLover figured out within five hours of the post where he was: a rehab outside of San Marcos, not far from Blue Oak.

That's where he met Grant Ford, by the way; more here on their relationship and the birth of DreamBawd Gym and DreamSoul.

You might think that's the end of Chaz and Bodhi, but think again. Their love could not be stopped that easily. They still had one more little nugget for us, which leads us to . . .

APRIL 2018, "BARISTA-GATE": For two weeks, Bodhi and Chaz got back together, all day, all the time; they posted truly a bonkers number of times about each other and love and all that schmaltz. And then, in late April, several separate videos from a Houndstooth coffee shop in downtown Austin—Bodhi tagged her location right before the videos occurred—made it to Twitter and then to us and then to TMZ.

Barista-gate was the beginning of the end for Bodhi Bruce's online reputation. Watch the full video here.

• • • • •

Jake pulls over on the side of a residential street. "We're right around the corner, but I want to see this Barista-gate video before we go in. Also, who are the people in this subreddit?"

"The Chazzercisers?"

"What?"

"That's just a funny . . . Never mind. They're from all over. We don't know who most of them are. Apparently there are people from Blue Oak, because my mom knew about it, which I still have not processed."

"Wow. I want to see the information about Chaz's finances. Will you send me the link to that post later?"

"Of course. Ready for Barista-gate?"

"Sure. This is Bodhi's video?"

"No, Bodhi took her own video, just a short one with the camera angled so it was mostly sunlight, two cups of coffee, and her silhouette kissing Chaz in the upper corner of the shot. But onlookers took their own videos and, well, you'll see—she looks awful, which isn't like her. She probably spends more money on extensions and filler and Botox than I've ever made in a year. Let's watch."

Leo presses play and hands her phone to Jake. An unholy screech fills the car. Bodhi is half leaning over a counter, where a young barista holds out a plate. The barista looks like she's in high school. She backs up as Bodhi leans in, spittle forming in her mouth.

"Where is your manager? I'm going to get you fired." Her hair is greasy, her nails chipped, and her makeup looks like she slept in it.

The barista holds out the plate. "I'm so sorry, ma'am, but you asked for avocado toast—"

"I asked for avocado gluten-*free* toast with no onions, and are there onions? Do those look like *onions* to you? Can you smell them even from there? *Those are onions!*"

The barista swallows. "I'm so sorry, ma'am . . ."

"*Ma'am*? What am I, fifty?" Bodhi shakes her head, her words slurring slightly.

"Let me just remake this . . ."

"You could have *poisoned me*. I could have *died*. Do you know what an *allergy is*?"

An older woman with a short haircut and a no-nonsense attitude flaps through the door from the kitchen. "Can I help you? Marissa, what's going on?"

"This little *bitch* is trying to *kill me*!" Bodhi's voice is shrill.

The manager holds up her hands like Bodhi is a skittish horse. "Whoa, now, let's just take a minute."

"I'm not going to take a minute! *Some of us* with refined taste can't allow *negativity* to interrupt our *chis*, but obviously *you people* . . ."

Chaz's body shields Bodhi from the camera, and her words

are garbled as the person filming moves to capture Bodhi's face again. It's clear Bodhi says something explosive because both the manager and barista suddenly step back as if she threw water in their faces.

The manager's voice is firm. "Absolutely not. You will not come into this business and use racist language against my coworkers and me. We've offered to remake your meal and you've chosen to verbally abuse Miss Gonzalez here. You are now banned from this establishment. I'll refund you whatever you paid this morning."

Bodhi continues to yell as Chaz tugs her out. "Do you know who *I am*? I will *destroy* your little business and make sure neither of you ever work again." The door slams behind them and the coffee shop erupts into applause as Chaz moves Bodhi down the sidewalk.

The video pans back to the barista, who is crying on her manager's shoulder while the manager holds a phone to her ear, and then cuts off.

Jake clicks the phone off and looks at Leo. "That was Barista-gate?"

"It was the beginning of the end of Bodhi's career as she knew it. Her sponsors dropped her like a hot potato. She's made like three different comeback videos, two of them apologies, but they don't take. Our subreddit numbers exploded as people came to rant about how Bodhi's 'silver lining' philosophy ruined their lives. Seeing how this 'enlightened guru' was actually an awful person yelling at a teenager revealed a lot about the self-help industry to some people who'd spent a lot of time and money investing in it."

"And she and Chaz?" Jake glances at his GPS and pulls back onto the road.

"The breakup was official after that. Chaz said he left her because he found Jesus—that's a whole other thing—but really, we all knew it was because the bad PR was here to stay."

"Ouch, that's cold."

Leo snorts. "It's the truth. Bodhi has family money, and she sold her line of yoga clothing for millions before Barista-gate, so she could easily turn off the cameras and live in privilege for the rest of her life."

"Is that what she's doing?"

"Are you kidding? For an attention junkie like that? No, she's desperate to get back in the public eye."

Jake pulls onto a winding road high on a hill above the city. "Did they get back together?"

"Nope. Chaz moved to Blue Oak, became a real estate agent, dated a bunch of Bodhi-Lites, and opened a gym. And then along came Kymber."

"Sounds like we have a lot more to talk about on the way back. We're here."

The truck eases into a circular driveway lit by tasteful lights protruding from the ground. A modern house made almost entirely of glass is ablaze with light. It sits on the edge of a steep drop, with the lights of Austin scattered below.

Jake and Leo step out of the truck. Just as they close the door, they hear a screech. Leo reaches for her phone, thinking she has accidentally played the Barista-gate video again, but it is off.

The screech becomes a scream. Jake takes off at a run toward the back of the house, Leo right behind him.

26

Karina watches Jake and Leo drive away, then counts to one hundred while she turns off lights around the house, leaving only a lamp on in the living room. She checks the security system; all the cameras—hidden in her garish chicken art—are recording. Hopefully, she'll only have uneventful videos of a sleeping dog to come home to.

By the time she's counted to seventy-nine, she's pulling off her kimono to reveal black cargo pants and a black tank top. By eighty-five, she's peeled off her face mask and is brushing her hair back into a ponytail at the base of her neck; it is always a relief to be rid of the big hairdo. And at ninety-nine, she is climbing out her bedroom window, black backpack strapped on tightly holding her tools. She glances back once—the pile of pillows looks like her sleeping body, not that Leo would check on her anyway. She secures and locks the window, and slips through the shadows into the night.

She has an investigation of her own to begin. She did not estrange her daughter to keep her out of Blue Oak for the last several years only to have Leo return and jump right back into a dangerous situation involving a murder. She should never have let Kay talk her into encouraging Leo to come home; Karina knew it was a mistake. Leo can go with Jake tonight, but tomorrow, Karina will put a stop to this.

First, she will focus on finding the killer before Stan Quackenbush ruins her best friend's life. After all, this is a job for the professionals.

And though her daughter has no idea, Karina Jones Holloway is a consummate professional.

27

Jake bursts through an unlocked gate, following a stone path around the house to the back porch. There is a pool and for a brief second, Leo flashes back to the night when Dominic died. She searches the well-lit turquoise water, but there is no body.

The screaming coheres into words. “Ellis, where is my *towel*?”

Jake stops short; Leo runs into his back.

Bodhi turns her naked body slowly, glaring at first. And then her narrowed eyes soften as she gazes up and down at Jake.

“Oooh, hello, are you my cop?”

A harried-looking assistant with a brunette pixie cut rushes through a back door. “Here it is. I swear I put some out . . . Oh. They’re right there.”

Bodhi turns back to her and almost coos. “I didn’t want *those* towels. I wanted *this* towel.”

Ellis looks up and startles when she sees Jake and Leo. “Hi, I’m so sorry, I didn’t hear—”

Jake raises his hand to take control of the situation. “No problem. My colleague and I heard a scream. We came back here instead of going to the front door. Glad you’re okay, ma’—miss.”

Leo almost snorts but does not.

Bodhi dries her face, then wraps the large beach towel around her, holding it loosely at her breasts.

Jake turns his head away. "Ellis, is it?"

The assistant nods in a daze.

"Excellent, would you mind?" Jake walks past Bodhi as if nothing has happened. Bodhi's mouth is pursed.

Ellis leads them into the house with granite floors, birchwood, and white and metal furniture. The calming effect of the monochrome decor is disrupted by an explosion of color in the form of scarves and clothes and yoga mats all over the floor and furniture. Three large suitcases are open on the living room rug.

Ellis scurries around the room, collecting lacy bras and leggings and three beach wraps from the couch. "Sorry, she's packing, and when she packs, it's a whole—"

She snaps her mouth closed as the back door slides open. Bodhi glides into the house, clutching the towel wrapped around her.

"I need to shower first. Chlorine is horrid for my hair. It'll only be an hour or so."

Jake says, "That's fine. We can return in a few days, but unfortunately, you'll be added to the no-fly list in the interim, so your trip is off. Unless you wanted to take a few minutes and talk to us now?" He smiles at her politely.

"Fine. Ellis, my robe." Ellis scuttles to a pile of clothes and holds up a white terry-cloth robe for Bodhi, who drops the towel seductively. Jake merely sits down, placing his voice recorder and notepad at the ready. Leo appreciates his contained restraint; his entire demeanor makes it clear this is not his first rodeo. He catches Leo's eye briefly and nods at her, indicating she should start.

Leo is caught off guard but recovers quickly. "Bodhi, thank you so much for seeing us on such short notice. We have some questions we'd like to ask you about your ex-boyfriend Chaz."

"Past lover. I don't say 'boyfriend,' it's so high school."

Jake speaks up. "Can we record our interview?"

"Of course." Bodhi sits back in a white overstuffed leather chair, head on one armrest, her feet hanging off the other. "I'm absolutely devastated about Chaz. I could feel it, you know? When he died? Like a rupture in the universe. I told Ellis, something awful was coming."

"Oh, when you thought it was a bad breakfast taco?"

"I did think, for just a little bit, that it might have been those terrible tacos you got me, but then I told you . . . didn't I tell you, around ten thirty or eleven . . . that I could feel something very wrong. It was like Mercury was in retrograde only bigger and more, like Venus was in retrograde or something."

"Venus doesn't go into retrograde for another—" Ellis says.

"It was like *Venus* was in *retrograde* because it was *more* than what I normally feel."

Ellis tightens her mouth like a sullen toddler.

Jake taps his notepad, his forearm flexing with the movement. "What time did you have this feeling?"

"Late morning. I've always been very cosmically in tune. One time . . ."

Jake continues. "And where were you on the Fourth of July?"

"Here. I had a going-away party."

"Are you moving?"

"No, but I am leaving for a chakra-cleansing retreat for five days, and I had to ensure I am at peace with all of my loved ones."

"Which loved ones were in attendance?"

"Ellis, where's the list?"

Ellis pulls out her phone. "I can text you the people we invited."

"Please." Jake takes a card out of his wallet and hands it to Ellis.

Leo sits forward eagerly, feeling a rush of confidence. Since moving back to Blue Oak and seeing Chaz's body, she has felt off-kilter, reacting to the chaos of the last several hours. But she knows the Bodhi-verse cold, and she always feels on solid ground when she's an expert on something. Leo loves to talk about research.

"While Ellis does that, Bodhi, can I name some people and you tell me if they came?"

"Sure. It's all online."

"Great. The Payal twins?"

"Yes, and Alisha had on the cutest . . ."

Leo talks over her. "Das Punk? Milo Sands? Abacus Abbott? Eddie Veneer?"

"Yes, all of them. Milo brought the whole band and Eddie brought this new Danish girl he's with."

"Cali Fuller?"

"No, she is no longer part of my circle of love and light."

"Oh?"

Bodhi sits up. "Did you know that she was passing off her salamba bhujangasana with a spinal twist as if it were some kind of signature move when everyone knows I've been doing that since my workout videos in 2016? That absolute faker."

"Who else?" Leo cocks her head to the right.

"Jannifyr Pyenson, Barley Adams, Glowe Gaines, Wicket Lewalski, Lulu Moura, I don't know . . . everyone. I don't want to list everyone. It's all online."

"How late did they stay?" Leo glances over at Jake to make sure he's okay with her line of questioning; she catches a brief look of pleased approval. She forges on while he pulls out his reading glasses and takes notes.

Bodhi looks at Ellis. "I went to bed around three a.m. Ellis is in charge of locking up. Ellis?"

"Barley and Wicket were the last to go, at four a.m. They were . . . indisposed before then." Ellis's voice holds an edge. Leo makes a mental note to fill Jake in later on the voyeuristic influencer couple who make Bodhi look like a Puritan.

Jake looks over the top of his glasses to focus on Bodhi. "Where were you between the hours of eleven p.m. and one a.m.?" The preliminary autopsy report must have come back, Leo realizes.

"Here. The whole time."

"Can anyone vouch for you?" Jake asks.

"Everyone can vouch for me. I'm sure it's all over their feeds too."

"Great, we'll look at that," Jake responds. "And what about security footage?"

Bodhi looks to Ellis, who sighs. "The video from the front of the house should be able to tell you who arrived when. We have cameras in the back to look like they're recording, but we don't actually get a feed from them."

"I like to have my secrets." Bodhi's grin at Jake is Cheshire-wide.

"Speaking of, I'd like to ask you a few questions about your past," Leo pipes up, hoping Jake is okay with her taking the interview in a different direction.

"Ask away. I live my truth with transparency."

"Your full name is Brittni Denae Bruce, correct? You were born on June 26, 1991?"

"Yes. All of that is right."

"You dated Chaz Nickolson from 2015 to 2017, right?"

"Correct."

"How long were you actually together as a couple?"

"What do you mean? We were together the whole time."

"So you made it appear, but was the relationship just a business deal? Because your financial records show the two of you entered into several real estate deals in 2016. Give me just a sec." Leo pulls out her computer and opens the financial thread in the subreddit from u/NanciDrew42, using her phone as a hot spot. "Here we go, sorry about that, government databases are not as fast as any of us would like." She resists the urge to look up at Jake so that she won't break character or see on his face that she's taking it way too far by pretending a snark subreddit page is a government database. "In 2016, you were listed on an LLC known to belong to Charles Nickolson, which is named . . . let me check." She toggles through the document. "Ah, yes, here it is. You Only Get One Shot LLC."

"You don't know that that is Chaz's."

"Actually, we do. We have a very astute financial team. At least three of Mr. Nickolson's LLCs have names from the lyrics of 'Lose Yourself' by Eminem." Leo slides into the confident tone she cultivated for academic presentations. "Two of those LLCs were established local businesses in Blue Oak: Dream-Bawd Gym, which he bought in early 2018 under Pied Piper LLC, and the Chaz Your Dreams real estate business he established later that year under Beat Goes On LLC. We know that you tend to use your middle name for real estate purchases. In February 2016, we have three houses bought by Denae Bruce and You Only Get One Shot LLC, and then five more between May and August 2016. The transactions stop for a while, but then between October 2016 and May 2017, there are"—she pauses to count—"more than twenty residential or commercial properties bought between those two entities. That includes this home, which Denae Bruce purchased from the LLC in August 2017. That is also, I believe, when you and Mr. Nickolson announced that you were no longer a couple. Is that right?"

"I don't remember when we made the announcement." Bodhi slumps in her chair.

Leo checks in with Jake, who looks at her with open admiration; Leo turns to Ellis. "You handle Ms. Bruce's social media as well?"

Ellis is trying to repress a smile at watching Bodhi be grilled. "Yes."

"Great, can we verify a few things?"

"Absolutely."

"Fantastic. Why don't you find that post and I'll ask about it again in a minute. While you do that, I want to dig into these purchases a bit. In July 2017, there were three properties bought by these two real estate partners that were poor investments. They were in locations that were not likely to grow, and the asking price was significantly over the going rate—not by a little bit but by millions. Does any of this ring a bell, Ms. Bruce?"

Bodhi is looking down at her toenails. She nods her head belligerently.

Leo adopts the stance she'd use with a recalcitrant undergrad. "Would you tell me about those purchases in your own words?"

"Chaz was an idiot. He was playing high-stakes poker and bet past what he could liquidate. To get himself out of debt, he promised to purchase some properties for one of the men at above the asking price."

Jake speaks up. "Quite a game."

Bodhi nods, voice soft and reflective for the first time. "He said it made him feel alive."

Jake responds, "When was that?"

"May 2017."

Leo's turn. She feels a thrill in tag-teaming so effortlessly with Jake. "The properties weren't bought till July."

Bodhi's laugh is humorless. "Following through was not his strong suit. He told me some men showed up at his house and held him at gunpoint until he made those purchases. I'd let him handle several of the real estate deals on my end, so he roped me into those transactions too. I'll be honest, I have a decent amount of money, but not enough that I could afford to lose millions for him."

Leo's voice is focused. "Okay, Ellis, when was that post?"

"August 15, 2017."

"Bodhi, did you break up because your astrologer suggested—forgive me for paraphrasing here—that your journey would be stronger without him?"

Ellis clears her throat and raises her phone. "Bodhi's astrologer said, and I quote, 'My soul gleaned what it could from the fields that Chaz has to offer and I will be more thoroughly nourished by taking my sickle to harvest other pastures.'"

"Thank you, Ellis." Leo turns back to Bodhi. "Was that the real reason you took your . . . sickle to other pastures? Or was it really because of financial entanglements?"

Bodhi juts her chin out. "It *was* my astrologer." She sighs.

"But it was also the gambling and drinking. He was never violent, he never hit me or anything, but he was just a real jerk when he drank. He couldn't remember the things he did or said and it scared me. Then he lost millions of dollars I had worked so hard for—I get up every morning at five thirty a.m. and hit the socials immediately after my thirty minutes of meditation and a green smoothie. I dare you to name anyone who works harder than me."

Leo nods placatingly, thinking that everyone she knows works harder than Bodhi. Bodhi continues. "And Chaz was willing to throw it all away."

"So you broke up with him and bought him out?" Leo confirms.

"Exactly. It took some time, but I got my name off of every single one of those transactions or paid him for them in cash. My lawyer was able to show that I had no knowledge of the three from July. The rest I bought when I could."

"What about the times that fall when you got together on social media?"

Bodhi rolls her eyes. "He thought it was because of the sex. It wasn't *not* because of the sex, but I was happily using him too—every time I posted a picture of us, my engagement went through the roof, then Ellis would reach out to sponsors and we'd get five times the money the next day. I'd buy off another property, kick him out, wait a few weeks, and then do it again. It was an effective strategy for a while. He never caught on."

"Why did you finally break it off with him?" When Jake glances up to look at Bodhi, Leo notices that his reading glasses make his eyes appear slightly bigger—it's nerdy and endearing.

"We'd had some really bad fights and then we went to this coffee shop one morning. The girl there almost killed me; onions constipate my chakras." At Bodhi's response, Leo rigidly does not allow herself to roll her eyes. "Some people got a video of me talking to the girl and her manager and they all turned against me. Later that night, Chaz and I were . . . we'd spent the day . . . meditating, and he wanted more . . . meditation supplies, so he called someone to drop something off. It was a friend of a friend Chaz had never met, and when the guy got here, Chaz absolutely freaked out."

"What did the man drop off?" Jake questions.

Ellis speaks up quickly. "Herbal supplements."

Leo glances at Jake, who responds, "I'm not here to find out what kind of . . . tea you're drinking."

Bodhi glares at Ellis. "Yes, it was *tea* to help us *meditate*. Anyway, the man at the door was good-looking, like a young Lenny Kravitz, but Chaz flipped his lid. He was drunk, but afterward he kept saying, 'Don't let Mack get me' and 'Tell him I'm sorry.'"

Leo squirms. Mack? *Her* Mack?

"I eventually went out on the porch with young Lenny, and we were talking until Chaz came out the door holding a beer and threatening to kill the man, who left, obviously. Chaz told me he was leaving too, but I wouldn't let him—he was still slurring his words. It had been a stressful day already, and my cousin's girlfriend was killed by a drunk driver. I don't mess with that. I found his keys and hid them. By the time he woke up, I had everything that belonged to him in a box next to his folded-up clothes. I handed him his keys, told him to get the hell out of my house, and that he was never welcome back. Drunk driving was the limit for me."

Leo wonders if this version of the story is true or a way to save face after Barista-gate. Ellis's expression gives nothing away.

"Was that the last time you saw him?" Jake asks.

"I mean, I ran into him a couple of times at parties or SouthBy. I blocked him on my phone and my socials and haven't had anything to do with him since."

Leo says, "Bodhi, have you ever met Kymber?"

"Absolutely not. When I karmically unattach myself from a person, that includes everyone in their circle. She was not going to bring the kind of energy I require into my orbit."

Ellis interjects, “Kymber was there last summer at a concert at Shady Grove when Bodhi saw Chaz, and Bodhi and Kymber shook hands, so technically they met, but barely.”

“What about a few weeks ago where you got into a fight at Stubb’s?”

“What about it?” Bodhi sounds like a teenager. “Glowe and Abacus decided to be chaos agents and invited both of us to a concert. I chose to remain classy and barely spoke to Chaz or his latest hanger-on.”

Leo responds, “You yelled that she was a bitch loud enough for it to be caught on camera.”

Bodhi shrugs. “Well, she was a bitch. She dropped her drink on me and then smiled and said, ‘Whoops,’ when it clearly wasn’t an accident.”

“You weren’t jealous of Kymber and Chaz?”

“Of course not. I don’t spend much time thinking about him if I can help it. I would call anyone a bitch who dropped a drink on that sundress. It’s Dolce.” She moves to sit up. “Actually, I’ve thought about him more than I want to today and I have to finish packing.”

“Just a couple more questions, Ms. Bruce.” Jake pulls his phone out. “I want to play a video for you and see if you recognize any of the voices.” He presses play on Chaz’s Instagram Live video from the Fourth of July parade where Kay confronts Chaz. Leo finds herself getting emotional as she hears the voices on the video angled away from her.

Kay saying: “This is an outrage! I’ve had enough!”

Grant: “Whoa, *Queen Kay*, back up!”

Kay: “Say it again.”

Grant: “Back. Up.”

Kay: “Not you. Charlie, say the part where you accused me of wanting to hurt my babies.”

Chaz: “Your *babies*, huh? You mean, your daughter and her *wife* and her *wife’s* kids . . . ?”

And then the thud and grunt of Kay punching Chaz and him falling.

Jake stops the video. Bodhi raises her head. "I recognize Chaz's voice, but no one else's."

Ellis has paled. "What about you, Ellis?" Jake's question is low but firm.

Ellis glances at Bodhi. "That's also his best friend, Grant. And I . . . I think that woman's voice on there is the same one from Chaz's last Insta."

Bodhi turns her head sharply, eyes narrowed. "We don't watch Chaz's Insta."

"Not as you, we don't. But I do sometimes from that burner account I made, just to keep tabs."

"We agreed that we're not going to engage."

"Brit, I don't engage. I just . . . he hurt you for so long and I want to know what's happening to him."

Bodhi stands up. "So you've been following him for how long?"

Ellis remains seated, looking up. "My burner account is only pictures of puppies I found online. No one could possibly know it's me."

"I cannot *believe* my own sister would betray me like this!"

Bodhi huffs out of the room. Jake and Leo watch her go. Jake speaks first. "You're Bodhi's sister?"

"Yes, much younger. We share the same mom. We didn't grow up together and no one knows that we're related. Brit offered me a job when my mom kicked me out, and I ended up as her PA. I make more money here than I would elsewhere. Plus I love her." Ellis sighs. "I know how this looks, but I promise she's better most of the time. She's been under a lot of stress."

Leo asks, "She was a digital media major at UT, right?"

"No one is better at it."

Jake takes a turn. "Your face got pale when you heard the voices."

Ellis puts her hands on her cheeks. "Did it? I didn't realize . . . I didn't mean to . . ."

Jake continues. "Do you think your sister could have spliced the video from the other night to produce something that made it sound like the woman whose voice you heard was at the house?"

Ellis shakes her head and then stops. "I mean, yes, technically, she could have done that easily. Anyone with a good phone could. But she would never do that. She'd never say it, but he broke her heart."

Jake presses. "Hurt her enough that she would want to hurt him back?"

"No." Ellis's voice is hard. "Why would she? She strategized to get rid of all ties to him. She's been happier the last six months than I've ever seen her. She has no reason to come after him now." She glances across the room to the archway where Bodhi exited, then leans in and lowers her voice. "Listen, I know she can be a lot and this woo-woo stuff is a load of crap. I also know she's probably a . . ." She mouths the next word: *narcissist*. She hunches her shoulders. "She pays me well and I use a not-insignificant portion of my salary on therapy. Believe me, my eyes are wide open." She shrugs. "But she truly believes in living and letting live. She doesn't kill spiders. And she has nothing to gain from losing Chaz. Honestly, if they ever got back together again, they'd probably break the internet, so even speaking crassly, it was in her best interest to keep him alive."

"Was she upset about the party where she met Kymber a few weeks ago?"

"She was embarrassed. No one likes seeing their ex with someone new. And Kymber really poked at Bodhi. But, you know, these things happen all the time. It was definitely not something she'd hurt Chaz over."

Upstairs, they hear the sound of water being turned on and a bath filling. A door is slammed shut. "Is there anyone else you can think of that could have made that video?"

Ellis shakes her head. "Anyone in this business, which is half of Austin, could have done that. Any teen on TikTok. It's not hard to edit videos on an iPhone. So take your pick. Other than those gambling people he tried to rip off or that guy he was afraid of, I never got the feeling he had real enemies." She bites her lip, considering. "The day they actually broke up, they were both high off their asses. Britt says it's because of young Lenny and the almost drunk driving, but it was, well. Everything. It was for the best. It had become too toxic."

Jake nods. "That's it for now. You have my number if you think of anything else."

"Can Bodhi still go on the trip?" Ellis stands up.

"Yes, but please send me that security footage before you leave. And I'm flagging her passport so she can only go to Costa Rica. They have an extradition relationship with the US."

Ellis looks spooked. "I'll send you that video footage after she's packed; it'll be later tonight."

Jake stands and nods. As they're walking out, Leo says, "Thank you, Ellis."

As they head toward the car, Jake squeezes her elbow twice—a subtle *good job* signal. He beeps open the car, and as Leo is about to open her door, they hear another screech behind them.

Leo smirks. "Guess Bodhi forgot a towel again."

Jake grins and they both get in the car.

28

Text exchange between Laura Esquivel and Macy Johnson, 10:57–11:08 p.m., July 6:

MACY JOHNSON: I have my big reveal ready! Are you coming home soon?

LAURA ESQUIVEL: We talked about texts on my work phone?

MACY JOHNSON: I can delete these texts so fast, Quackers won't know which end is up.

LAURA ESQUIVEL: I hope I'll be home soon.

MACY JOHNSON: I can't wait.

LAURA ESQUIVEL: For me? Or the reveal?

MACY JOHNSON: My love, I'd wait for you till the stars crumble.

MACY JOHNSON: The reveal.

LAURA ESQUIVEL: I love you. OK, I'm here at my desk. Can we do the reveal now?

MACY JOHNSON: OK. Guess how many people from the subreddit are located in Blue Oak?

LAURA ESQUIVEL: Thirty?

MACY JOHNSON: Try 4,812

LAURA ESQUIVEL: That's . . . like the whole town.

MACY JOHNSON: The population is close to 20,000. But it is a quarter of the town.

LAURA ESQUIVEL: That is astronomical.

MACY JOHNSON: I'm telling you.

LAURA ESQUIVEL: Do you have names behind the Reddit handles?

MACY JOHNSON: Names, IP addresses; I can get shoe sizes and online search history if you give me a few minutes.

LAURA ESQUIVEL: If I name some people, will you check?

MACY JOHNSON: Go for it.

LAURA ESQUIVEL: Kay Schneider

MACY JOHNSON: All the Schneiders.

LAURA ESQUIVEL: Grant Ford

MACY JOHNSON: Every single person working at DreamBawd.

LAURA ESQUIVEL: Bodhi Bruce

MACY JOHNSON: And her assistant, whose name is interestingly Ellis Bruce.

LAURA ESQUIVEL: Kymber Owens

MACY JOHNSON: Check

LAURA ESQUIVEL: Mack Garner

MACY JOHNSON: Check

LAURA ESQUIVEL: What was Chaz's ex-wife's name?

MACY JOHNSON: Tiffani. Check. Plus all of her family members. Also, all of Chaz's family members that I found.

LAURA ESQUIVEL: Jake Nguyen?

MACY JOHNSON: I think you and Jake and Quackers are the only people in Blue Oak not in this group. Williams was in it.

LAURA ESQUIVEL: Wow.

MACY JOHNSON: Also, the way some of them use pseudonyms is REALLY interesting. For example, there's one user in there who calls herself u/NanciDrew42. Guess who that really is?

LAURA ESQUIVEL: Who?

MACY JOHNSON: Melody Garner-Aziz, Mack's sister. She's an immigration lawyer in South Austin. Here's her bio on her firm's website: https://llosalawgroup.com/about/melody-garner-aziz

LAURA ESQUIVEL: . . .

LAURA ESQUIVEL: She's a legit lawyer.

MACY JOHNSON: Yup

LAURA ESQUIVEL: Why does she masquerade as Nancy Drew?

MACY JOHNSON: I haven't gotten through all of her stuff yet, but she's revealed pretty in-depth financial stuff about Chaz online. She seemed to be gunning to take him down.

LAURA ESQUIVEL: Oh, that is VERY interesting. I'll tell Nguyen. Speaking of: you got his text about the Facebook page and that deleted photo?

MACY JOHNSON: Yup. In the queue. But first, I have hours of reading to catch up on from my snarky besties. And some popcorn to pop.

MACY JOHNSON: Take your time. Solve the murder. See you soon.

LAURA ESQUIVEL: I'll try to be there soon. Love you

MACY JOHNSON: Love you more.

29

Two hours later, Jake turns his notepad to Leo. "How do you say this one?"

"Glowe. Like 'Chloe' but with a *G*."

"And that guy?"

"Abacus."

"Atticus?"

"No, Abacus. His tagline is, 'My name is Abacus, because I make it count, baby.' "

"Wow." Jake's eyebrows cannot go up higher.

"Right?"

"Why do they all have such odd names?"

"Perennial question." Leo and Jake spent the drive home from Bodhi's house screen-recording the Instagram stories from the people at her most recent party; almost all the influencers had archived their posts, so they were easy to access still. Despite the late hour, Leo is wide-awake after her long nap and still buzzing from the interview. Jake told her after she got in the car she'd done an incredible job, and Leo felt it herself—that sweet spot when she got to speak competently about a subject she is an expert in. The post-interview euphoria was unexpected, but welcome after such a long day. When Jake suggested they grab Whataburger ("It's been *how* long since you've had the best burger in the world, Leo? Not on my watch!") and head back to the sheriff's station, she agreed.

"I think Glowe is my new favorite of the bunch because she only posted still photos with long paragraphs. Though, can anyone read these words?" Jake holds the phone up close to his face, where it lights up his reading glasses.

Leo laughs. "I think that's how they separate the young people from the rest of us online, like those whistles only teens can hear. You know you're too old when you start squinting and complaining about font size in social media stories."

Jake chuckles. "I think I was born old."

"That tracks. You were always a serious kid even when we were young." Leo takes another sip of her watered-down Dr Pepper. "I think that's the last of the influencers at the party."

Jake glances at his watch. "Wow, it's eleven thirty-seven. I'm sorry I kept you so late."

"I'm glad I got to help. Does it feel crass to say I enjoyed asking Bodhi those questions?"

"No. I understand. There's something about having the chance to get to the bottom of something that I find satisfying. It feels like I'm doing my part to make the world less chaotic every time I wrap up a case."

"I never thought of it like that. That's how research has always made me feel, like the world is falling apart around me but at least I tidied up this corner and preserved it forever. Like Wallace Stevens, I'm fascinated by the interplay of order and disorder."

Jake shakes his head and looks down, smiling. "I have no idea what that means. But you were good out there tonight." When he looks up, his gaze is suddenly piercing.

"Let me." He pauses and leans forward hesitantly. "You have . . ."

"What?" Leo wipes her cheeks.

"No, it's not . . . Here." Jake rises across the desk and runs his thumb along the right side of her jaw, ending just below her lip. He watches her lip for a second, eyes impossibly dark, then steps back and reaches for a napkin. "Ketchup."

"Thank you." Leo's voice is quiet. "Is it gone?"

"All gone." Jake clears his throat, and looks back down at his notebook. "I think . . . it looks like everyone in these videos is present and accounted for except for . . . Oh, I meant to ask you about this." He flips through the videos he's been saving on his phone. "I don't have a name for this person yet."

"Who, Wicket?"

"No, we have Wicket and Barley down. And yeah, I don't need to hear any more about them. The woman behind them, here. The one wearing clothes. Her."

Leo takes his phone, her fingers grazing against Jake's as she grasps it. "That's . . . It can't be." She gazes at the still photo, rewinds the video fifteen seconds and watches again, then grabs her own phone. "I can't get a clear view of this woman's face, but do you know who it looks like?"

"Who?"

"Melody."

"Melody Garner?"

"Garner-Aziz, and yes. Look, right there." Leo holds out a still for Jake to look at. "She's out of almost every shot, which is sort of a miracle at a function of social media influencers like this, but here's a shot of her cheek. Doesn't this look like Melody?"

"I mean, maybe." He hands the phone back. "Is Melody friends with Bodhi?"

"Not that I know of. But I haven't been back here in a long time. She's a lawyer, so maybe she's done some legal work for Bodhi?"

"I'll check into it. Speaking of the Garners, did you notice that Bodhi said Chaz was afraid of Mack?"

Leo nods. "Why in the world would Chaz be afraid of him?"

"Do you have any ideas?"

"No, of course not."

"Do you know of any connections between them?"

"Do you? Chaz couldn't have been his Realtor because Mack lives on the Garner property. Maybe Mack goes to Dream-Bawd?"

Jake shrugs. "I'm sure we can find out."

"You know Mack's cousin Dom was Chaz's best friend in high school. They played on the football team together, and we were all there the night when Dom . . ." Leo swallows. "I don't know any reason why that would make Chaz afraid of Mack."

Jake makes a quick annotation in his notebook. "I have some thoughts. I'll find out more about Melody too." He takes his glasses off and stretches. "But for now, we're done. Can I drive you home?"

Leo nods, fatigue beginning to cloud her brain. On the drive, they make small talk about how Jake's mother, Mrs. Nguyen, feels about his sister Becky's impending baby, the family's first grandkid.

It's midnight when Jake pulls up in front of Leo's childhood home. She gets out of the car, and he follows.

"You don't have to walk me to the door. This isn't a high school date."

Jake's face is inscrutable in the dark. "Believe me, I know. You were too cool for me in high school."

"Please, I was a nerdy girl that no one noticed."

"You'd be surprised." He pauses. "And anyway, I'm not in the habit of taking dates to interview potential murder suspects and then buying them Whataburger. But if it weren't for all of this, well . . . if things had been different, I . . ."

He lets the unfinished thought hang there; he is poised at the edge of a decision Leo can't quite see.

They've stopped so that she's at the top of the three steps onto her mother's porch, and Jake is at the bottom. She returns his gaze thoughtfully. Before this week, she hadn't thought of Jake in years, and she certainly never noticed him when he was a few years younger than her in school. But there's something about him that draws her to him—it's not just that he's good-looking, it's also that he's good at what he does. She's always found competence attractive.

With everything that has happened, she hasn't really processed the fact that she's agreed to go to dinner with Mack. Talking with him by the Schneiders' pool, it felt like they hadn't gone years without really speaking—he'd always been one of the easiest people for her to talk to, which is a short list in her life. The puppyish energy from when they were young had transformed into something driven and focused as he helped his family and fulfilled his dreams. She'd gone to sleep last night with a sense of wonder that someone like Mack might still be interested in her.

As Leo looks at Jake, however, she realizes he is exactly the kind of person she was looking for in graduate school for all those years when she dated men whose aesthetic was "blazer with elbow patches over ironic tee." There is something about Jake that is more solid, more grounded, than any of those men. He's serious and determined, and she feels a quieter kind of pull to him that's very different from the one she felt for Mack last night. With his face shadowed by the lone bulb on her mother's porch, Leo registers a vulnerability to him she hadn't noticed before.

Jake seems to arrive at some kind of decision. He takes a firm step back. "I have ironclad ethical boundaries."

"Okay, great? That . . . seems like a good thing."

"Which is why this conversation is over." He twists his mouth in frustration, brow furrowed.

"I'm sorry, are you upset? Did I say something wrong?"

"No, no, it's not you at all." Jake moves back up a step until only a few inches separate them. "I'm frustrated at myself, but I'm just making this more awkward for both of us."

Exhaustion is making Leo unsure. Is she about to get asked out for the second time in two days? "I think I'm going to need you to spell this out since I'm not quite sure what we're talking about."

Jake reaches a hand out to touch her elbow briefly and then

tucks it back at his side. "I can't ask a witness on a date in the middle of a murder investigation."

"Oh." Leo scoots back slightly on the step. Did he think she expected that? "That... Um, I wasn't thinking that at all."

Jake leans his head back and sucks air in. "Sorry, Leo. I am making a mess of this. It's been a long day, and this is my first murder investigation, and you came home unexpectedly, and you..." He closes his eyes briefly, and then opens them again. With him standing on the step beneath Leo, they're almost exactly the same height. "You knew I had a massive crush on you in high school, right? Becky told you?"

Leo thinks back—she can picture Jake on the edges of sleepovers, stealing popcorn while they watched movies, letting them paint his toenails. He was a sweet younger brother, and he and Becky had mostly been close, with occasional bouts of sibling bickering, but Becky never once mentioned that he might like Leo. She thinks about it for too long, so it's weird when she finally shakes her head no.

Even in the low light, Leo sees his ears redden. "Let's just... Forget I..." He hooks his thumb over his shoulder and takes two steps down to the sidewalk. "I'm going to go. I'll..."

"Where would you take me?" Leo blurts. She'd made the exact same cartoonish thumb-over-the-shoulder move with Mack yesterday, and she feels a kinship with Jake's awkwardness in that moment.

"What?" He glances up.

"Hypothetically speaking, where would you take me on a date?"

He takes a deep breath. "Well, I'd start with my favorite Thai food truck in Austin."

"I love Thai."

"Me too. Then a concert, obviously. Depends on who is in town, but since it's all make-believe anyway . . . maybe Boygenius?" He shrugs his shoulders slightly, looking more like the boy she knew than she'd seen him all day. Maybe she's not the only one who feels out of her depth right now.

"Wow, I feel stereotyped but also seen." She smiles, and he returns it, relief on the edges. "And then?"

"I'd take you back to your house and drop you off at the door. I wouldn't want to come on too strong for the first date."

"That sounds fun." She smiles.

"I bet it would be. Hypothetically." Jake takes another step back, still looking up at her. "But you're a murder witness who has had a helluva day that I've probably just made worse by being awkward."

"Actually, I'm the one who has been awkward."

He shakes his head. "I haven't seen you be awkward all day."

"Thanks." She takes one more step back, and immediately trips on the welcome mat.

He chuckles. "Until now."

"Shut up." But she laughs too.

"Good night, Leo." As she opens the screen door, he speaks again. "Oh, just in case: I want you taking extra precautions right now. Do you have Mace or some kind of protection?"

"Of course, I'm a woman who has lived on my own for years, Jake. I promise, I'll be careful."

"Okay. I'll text or call in the morning if we can get an interview with Tiffani."

"Okay." They stand there for a beat too long.

"Night, Leo."

Leo's voice is a whisper. "Good night, Jake."

Jake stands there until he hears the dead bolt, then walks toward his truck. The wind blows and he hears a rustle in the bushes. He pauses. Silence. He keeps going.

He is about to open the door, alone on the deserted street, when a voice whispers just behind his ear: "Jake!"

30

Jake jumps and whirls around. Karina's face pops up out of the truck bed. "I'm sorry to scare you, but I didn't want Leo to see me."

"Mrs. Holloway, what in the world?"

"Please, it's Karina. And I need you to come with me, Jake. No time to explain." In one smooth movement, she stands, hand on the truck bed, and leaps to the ground. He reaches to help her, but she's already dusting her hands off and walking around the truck. "I'll ride with you."

For the next three minutes, Karina tells Jake a story so wild he barely registers where she tells him to drive. When they arrive behind the parking lot at DreamBawd, he is still gripping the steering wheel when he realizes she's already out of the truck.

"Wait," he says to an empty cab. He unbuckles, opens his door, and steps out. "Wait."

She is kneeling down on the sidewalk. "You'll want your evidence kit."

"I'm sorry, I-I-" Jake stammers. She puts a hand up to silence him.

"I get it. It's a lot to take in. Later, you'll find an email corroborating what I just told you."

"I just . . ."

"But for now . . ."

"No." Jake's voice is firm. "I appreciate that, if this story is true, you need to keep this quiet, but this has been a very long day and I'm going to take two minutes and confirm what you're saying. If that's okay. Ma'am."

Karina stills. "I understand."

"Thank you."

Karina notices that, for the first time, Jake sounds young. His voice is a little petulant.

"In my email, you said?"

"Yes." She waits, watching him. In the glow of his phone on his face, she can see that there are deep circles under his eyes. He types with both thumbs, goes back to the cab of his truck to pull out some reading glasses, then peers closely at the email that is waiting for him.

"This day has been one of the weirdest of my life." Jake looks up sheepishly. "Thanks for letting me confirm. I did not expect . . ."

"I know, she's an old friend, and I thought it would be easier if you didn't just have to take my word for it. I called her while Quackenbush was questioning Kay, and she's had her staff working overtime since then."

"Are they going to pull Quackenbush from the case? Can they do that?"

"No, because we're going to solve the murder before it comes to that."

"And Leo doesn't know?"

Karina's face pulls taut. "No."

"Are you going to tell her?"

"I've gone almost thirty years without her knowing."

"I . . . This conversation is above my pay grade. I'll keep your secret for now. But I'm going to get Quackenbush to sign off on Leo as a social media expert tomorrow . . ."

"Leo's not on social media. She got off social media for the job market."

Jake raises both hands. "You two obviously need to talk.

But right now, Leo is also going to be working with me in an official capacity."

"I'd rather she not. It's dangerous."

"With all due respect, I don't think that's your decision. I can work with you, obviously, with this . . . new information."

"But I cannot be official in any way."

"That's fine. But you're right, we need to investigate this murder, and Leo's going to be critical to getting some of the information we need quickly."

"I still don't see how . . ."

"I'll keep your secret and hers. Again: y'all need to talk." He says each word deliberately. "But now, we'd better get going if you want to take care of this while Quackenbush sleeps, before he wakes up with fresh ideas about how to implicate Kay."

Karina sighs heavily. "Fine. But this is not over."

"Let me get my kit." Jake heads over to the truck, grabs a small toolbox, puts his reading glasses on top of his head, and comes back. "Show me what we came for."

Karina turns on her heel and walks toward the parking lot behind the gym. Like most of the businesses downtown, the storefront is built right up against its next-door neighbor, with the entrance open to the front sidewalk and parking behind.

DreamBawd—housed inside a redbrick building that dates back to the late 1800s—stands on the corner of the cross street that begins the downtown square. All downtown Blue Oak businesses are required to have punny names, though no one is quite sure exactly what pun Chaz was making from the spelling "bawd." It was the subject of debate for three council sessions before they agreed to let the name stand; they all assumed it was a joke they didn't get. On the side of the red brick, a few yards from where Jake parked, is a huge mural with a preening pinup girl in a barely there string bikini and who bears more than a passing resemblance to Kymber Owens. The slogan in cartoon letters above her head reads *Are you ready for your DREAM BAWD?*

The mural has been the subject of numerous complaints filed to the city council, prompting even more debates.

The small parking lot is lit by a yellowed streetlamp. There are ten parking spaces, five facing the back of the building and five opposite them, with entrances into the lot from the street and the alley behind it. A strip of scrabbly lawn lies between the building and the edge of the pavement, and a small shed huddles against the back of the building in the corner next to the fence that separates this lot from its neighbor's.

"There." Karina points to the shadows beside the shed. "But walk on this part of the asphalt." She gestures with her flashlight. "We don't want to disturb the scene."

The last two parking spaces, right in front of the shed door, bear metal signs on poles—the one by the shed reads BOSS MAN and the one closer to the door says BOSS MANAGER.

"Under the door of the shed, there's a half-inch hole, and there's a glove sticking out. Do you see it? Here." Karina indicates the object with her small but strong flashlight. "Then there are blood droplets on the grass here, here, and here." Karina moves her flashlight in an arc across the grass. She then clicks something and the light changes to blue, revealing purple splotches on the ground. "And there is blood on the sidewalk and the door handle here." She shines her flashlight farther, to the small strip of sidewalk leading to the gym's back door, and finally to the silver handle.

Jake turns on his phone flashlight and squats down from a short distance to examine the shed door and the half-visible flowered gardening glove shoved under it. Then he walks around to the other areas Karina indicated. After a minute, he turns. "Thanks, Karina. We need to check this out. I'm calling for backup now."

"I'll secure the perimeter." Karina is already moving, flashlight held low.

Jake raises the phone to his ear. Without thinking, he reaches into his kit and hands her the caution tape. "Hey, I need you. We've found something . . . back of DreamBawd. And bring two DPS officers . . . Good. Thanks."

He hangs up. Hiring Esquivel was one of the best decisions he's ever made. He pockets his phone and watches Karina efficiently cordoning off the crime scene with the yellow caution tape in the amber glow of the streetlight. He can barely see the resemblance between this woman and the boisterous stylist whose wild hair and wilder clothes are a staple in Blue Oak.

He shakes his head. How many mysteries can one small town hold?

31

At 2:47 a.m., Karina opens her daughter's bedroom door and slips inside; Derrida raises his head from his mat but lies back down when he registers Karina. She stands with her back against the wall and watches her daughter sleep in her old bed. As she sighs, Karina sees the apple-cheeked four-year-old she and Richard brought to safety in Blue Oak in the dead of night.

One night in September 1994, with no warning, the Holloways knocked on the Schneiders' sliding glass door leading to the back porch. Phil had jumped a mile when he saw two faces staring in at him through the window. Karina had put her face close to the glass so he could see her features in the light, and only then did he open it. He called as quietly as he could for Kay, who was in their room getting ready for bed. Seven-year-old Beth and three-year-old Emily were already asleep.

When Kay finally came to the living room and saw Karina and Richard with little Leonora, she'd just stood there for a minute, washcloth in hand, half of her face still covered in soap. Then she'd rushed to Karina, and neither woman said a word as they hugged for several minutes. When Karina pulled back, she was surprised to feel tears on her face; she had not cried in years, not even on the most horrific days. Only Kay could reduce her to tears in an instant.

Kay's voice broke. "So it really was that bad, then?"

"Worse, Kay. It's . . ."

Phil's voice was kind. "What if we talk about all of this tomorrow?"

Richard stepped forward, shifting tiny sleeping Leo to his other shoulder to hug Kay. "I agree. Kay, it's so good to see you again. Sorry to surprise you like this, but we didn't want to give anything away."

"No, of course, absolutely." Kay gave him a one-armed hug, and then placed a hand on Leo's back. "And here she is. Oh, Karina. She's beautiful."

Leo stirred but then snuggled deeper into her father's shoulder. Karina laughed lightly. "She is beautiful. She's why we're . . . well."

Phil interrupted, hugging them all and gesturing at Kay's face; in the hubbub, she'd forgotten to finish washing it, so she scrubbed off the soap tracked by her own tears, and then moved into the kitchen to set the washcloth down by the kitchen sink. "Are you hungry? Want water? A beer?"

Richard smiled that warm smile—the one Karina sees every time she looks at their daughter now, though Leo's is more burdened than her father's ever was—and said, "Kay, I would murder for a beer and one of your tomato sandwiches."

"From you, I know that's not an idle threat. Good news for you—our garden harvest was great, and we have some big tomatoes fresh off the vine." For the next several minutes, they kept it light, shuffling Emily into Beth's room, blowing up the air mattress with its agonizingly slow foot pump for the Holloways, and placing the still-sleeping Leo into Emily's little toddler bed.

Karina remembers watching Leo wake up the next morning at Kay's house. Richard had been on a run, the way he worked out his stress—the same way Leo does now. And the Schneiders were at work and school. But Karina couldn't bear to be far from her daughter.

Karina waited with legs crossed on the slightly deflated air mattress, cradling a coffee that was not nearly as good as the coffee they'd left behind, but still tasted fantastic because it meant they were home. She was breathing in and out, the almost-forgotten sensations of air-conditioned air in an insulated house and the deep joy of safety.

When Leo finally blinked her startlingly green eyes open, she looked around curiously at the unfamiliar room—at Emily's purple Princess Jasmine curtains and sheets, at the green plush Baby Bop watching over her while she slept. Leo stretched and then sat up in the bed. Her hair—lighter and thinner then—was matted on the side, the imprint of the pillowcase on her right cheek. When her eyes lighted on her mother, her face broke into a grin. "Hola, mami. Donde estamos?"

Karina's heart had burst open in that instant. The road behind them had been so treacherous. She'd questioned over and over again whether it was worth it, whether they were doing what was best. There was one choice she should absolutely have made for her career, and another for her family, and those choices were diametrically opposed to each other.

But in that moment, watching her daughter wake up safe and happy and loved, she knew they'd made the right decision.

"Mi amor," she responded. Then she switched to only English like she and Richard had agreed, even though it broke her heart. "I know it might not look like it yet. But we're home. This is Blue Oak. And you're going to love it here."

• • • • •

As she hasn't in years, Karina watches her daughter sleep for a long time. Leo shifts and turns. Her right cheek is, once again, indented by the sheets; she has always favored that side when she sleeps. Karina knows Leo will not look at her with love if she wakes up now, so Karina keeps her body in the shadows away from the window. In the morning, she will again become the person she has been for nearly thirty years—the wackadoodle hairstylist, hiding in plain sight under the caricatured disguise she has created for herself. But for the span of seventeen minutes, she allows herself the luxury of gazing at her daughter.

She would do anything for Leo. Has done many things for Leo. And if she has to keep on lying, she will. Indefinitely. Even if it means Leo hates this version of her—the paranoid, inept, hair-sprayed version that has always made Leo bristle. Karina knows it well; she has studied her daughter, tried to find the exact point of irritation to keep her daughter frustrated enough to stay away. She probably should push her away even further, should do something to make the two of them much more estranged. She probably should have prevented Emily from convincing Kay to help bring Leo back.

When Leo is away, Karina worries less. Only here, back in the town she once naively thought was safe, does Karina feel the familiar panic creeping up. She will have to find a way to prevent Leo from getting any more involved in this murder investigation.

But that can wait for tomorrow. For two more minutes, Karina watches Leo hungrily. Then she slips out the door. She has to curl and spray her hair again before bed.

As the door closes silently, Leo turns over once, then settles deeper into the bed.

32

It feels like Leo's been asleep for just a few minutes when she's awakened by the raucous sound of Derrida barking. "Derr! *Derr!* Hush!" Leo stumbles out of bed wearing only her T-shirt.

Derrida is standing on his hind legs by the front door, barking in his deepest tones. The doorbell is ringing incessantly. It's early morning; the sky through the windows at the top of the door is streaked with pink.

Leo stops cold. A man she's never seen before has cupped his face against the glass. He looks around the room and then stops.

He sees Leo and grins maliciously.

"What in the sam hill is that fool dog making such a fuss about?" Karina bursts into the room, sleep mask askew on her head, face vulnerable without its normal layered makeup.

"Derrida. *Down. Quiet.*" Leo's voice finally breaks through Derrida's panicked barking, and he immediately drops, every muscle quivering but obedient to her commands.

The doorbell rings again.

"Who is it?" Karina's voice is sharp through the door.

"Anthony Mueller." His voice is muffled.

"Oh, *no*, sir. This is ridiculous. What time is it?"

"Six fifteen a.m."

"Anthony, go away, we're not talking to you."

"But Miss Karina, I need a statement before we go to press . . ."

"You do not need a statement."

"Is it true that Kay Schneider has been arrested in the murder of Chaz Nickolson?"

Karina opens the door. Derrida startles, but Leo says to him quietly, "Stay."

"Seriously, Anthony. What the hell are you blatherin' on about?" Leo's impressed that her mother's hair looks as styled as it does this early in the morning. Aqua Net should use her in a commercial.

"Deputy Williams told his mother, who called her church prayer chain, which includes my aunt Doris, who called me this morning at five a.m. and told me that the sheriff had arrested Kay Schneider and that Chaz Nickolson has been murdered. Care to comment?"

Karina rolls her eyes so far back in her head, Leo almost giggles. Karina's kimono quivers with indignation.

"Anthony Mueller, you must know better than to trust that prayer chain. Remember last year when you published that report about a boy who rescued kittens because the prayer chain said to pray for them, only to find out the boy stole those kittens in the first place? Did you forget about the retraction article you had to write? Or the donation to the Blue Oak County Animal Shelter the paper had to make?"

"No." Leo is standing by Derrida, just out of sight of the door, but she grins at his chastened tone.

"So do you think you've learned by now that it's not a good idea to trust the prayer chain? Especially when it's the *Baptists*?"

"Fine."

"So that means you won't print anything until you've actually reported the story?"

"That's what I'm trying to do!"

"Oh, well, good luck with that. And what did Kay and Phil say when you asked them about Kay being arrested?"

“They didn’t answer the door. But there was caution tape all around the house.”

Karina hits her forehead with her hand. “Well, of course. If you hadn’t woken me at such an ungodly hour, I would have remembered that they’re in Wimberley tonight on a little getaway. Phil was pulling some kind of romantic joke on Kay. What did he say, Leo?”

Leo shrugs, eyes wide, as her mom glances over at her. Is she supposed to be in on this story her mother is concocting?

“Oh, I remember,” Karina continues. “ ‘I love you so much, it should be illegal.’ He surprised her with a weekend getaway after she worked so hard on pulling off the parade. You know how those two are—he loves her more than grits love butter. Want me to give you the address for their hotel so you can wake them up on their day off?”

“No, of course not . . .”

“Then can we just assume that Deputy Williams’s mother and your aunt Doris—who, by the way, is a client of mine and has never remembered an appointment correctly a day in her life—might not be the *best* sources for this big scoop about . . . what did you say? A *murder*? In *Blue Oak*?” Karina’s vowels make the words that much more patronizing.

“Yes, ma’am.”

“Bless your heart,” Karina says with the kindly-sounding venom only a Southern woman can pull off. “You’re all kinds of twisted up. I’m done talking about this. I need my beauty sleep. So kindly get off my porch. ’Mkay? Thanks. Bye.” The door is locked and dead-bolted by the time she finishes her sentence. She pulls closed the fluorescent-chicken-print curtains that were open over the glass and reties her kimono indignantly.

“Good Lord, this is gonna be a day.” She looks Leo up and down. “Sweet pea, wanna think about some pants?”

“Sorry, I just didn’t have time,” Leo says sheepishly.

As Karina heads to bed, Leo turns on the coffeepot, then quickly dresses and walks her bouncing dog out to the backyard to do his business before slipping on his leash. As she opens the back gate to the street, she slips her earbuds in and queues up her favorite running playlist. The heat feels like a physical force she has to move through.

The reporter is sitting on the curb, camera slung around his neck, texting someone. When she opens the gate, he perks up. “Hey, miss! Hey! I just have a few questions!”

Leo can’t get to the sidewalk without talking to him, so she decides the best approach is a direct one. She pulls her earbud out impatiently. “Can I help you?”

“I’m sure you can! I’m a reporter at the *Blue Oak Gazette*. Well, I’m *the* reporter right now. Hopefully we’ll sell enough ads to hire someone in the near future. Anyway, how do you know Karina and Kay?”

Leo narrows her eyes and considers him for a minute. “I’m not going to answer any of your questions.”

“I just need someone to give me the information that I need!”

“Not me.” She puts her earbud in and sets out in a jog.

Anthony follows, shouting questions. “Did Kay murder Chaz to get back at him? What was her motive?”

Leo whips her earbud out and turns. Her face is stone, her tone low. “What did you just say?”

He repeats the question slowly as if she really didn’t hear him. “Did. Kay. Murder. Chaz . . . ?”

“Derr, *attack*.”

Immediately, Derrida explodes into aggressive barking. What Anthony doesn’t know is that Derrida does not realize that “attack” means anything other than barking.

Anthony almost jumps out of his skin. “Geez, lady! I’m sorry! Call that dog off!”

“Derrida, down. Quiet.” Derrida immediately drops down, but he keeps a low growl in his throat, his ruff bristling. “He won’t attack as long as he’s on a leash, but he doesn’t particularly like men, and I don’t like people who accuse the nicest woman I know of murder. Seems like he and I are both inclined for you to leave us alone.”

"Yeah, yeah."

"As in, get off this property and away from this family. Or I accidentally let him off leash and say it snapped. Your choice."

"I hear you." Anthony holds up his hands and backs up toward his car. He pauses, watching them.

Leo mutters, "Derr, up." Derrida rises, his hackles raising. "If I were you, I wouldn't print anything in the paper today either. Sounds like you have a lot of bad information right now." Derrida's growl intensifies at Leo's tone.

Anthony hustles the last few feet to his car. "It's okay, I can take the time I need. We go to press twice a week, so my next print deadline is Monday."

"You better not print anything Monday either!" Derrida lunges again, not liking Leo's angry voice.

Anthony abandons all pretense of being cool and scrambles into his car. "*You* better keep that dog away from me!"

"Not my fault he doesn't like you! Bye!" Leo crosses her arms until Anthony pulls away in a rust-and-silver sedan.

Once he turns the corner, Leo pops her earbud in. "Derrida, heel." She taps on the earbud to start the music and begins at a slow jog as Japanese Breakfast's "Be Sweet" fills her ears.

The run is just what she needs. Despite the ridiculous heat—literally, how does anyone function?—she finds her rhythm quickly. Leo learned a long time ago that the thunk of tennis shoes on pavement, the controlled environment of music in her ears, and the constant forward motion of running allow her to focus.

She does not try to force it—that, too, will backfire. How many years has she spent working out research problems or teaching dilemmas by running? Like Dorothy heading to Oz in the center of a tornado, images whirl around her: Chaz's dead body. Kay being arrested. Emily's tear-streaked face. Mack lying down, lit in the glow from the pool lights, asking her to dinner. Chaz's apparent fear of Mack. Bodhi shrieking and smirking, barely covering her body. Harassed, overworked Ellis—Bodhi's actual sister. Kymber fiddling with the wires on the float. Hattie alone in the street, wailing in smoke. Grant's sour expression at the parade. Confessing to Jake she's the snark subreddit moderator. Jake standing at the foot of her steps, hypothetically asking her out. Mack's slow dimple-infused grin as they lay with their feet in the pool, blatantly asking her out for dinner. Two men, in two days, showing interest in her after years of mediocre nothing dates. Her mother grabbing Derrida's leash with a barb about Leo not having children. Her mother cutting the woman's hair on the float. Her mother's flamboyant chicken art. Her mother, annoyed and distant, her elevated hair a shellacked shield preventing her daughter from reaching her heart. Her father's absence everywhere, in every crevice of their house, in the air she breathes in their hometown.

She stops, hands on her knees, catching her breath. Derrida sprawls in the shade, mouth open. She's been sprinting without meaning to. She starts again, her pace slower and more deliberate.

She allows the wind tunnel in her mind to continue until it dies down. She intentionally hits her feet to the pavement to the beat of her music. So far since she returned to Blue Oak, she has felt overwhelmed—which is understandable, she thinks, with uncharacteristic self-forgiveness. It's one thing to beat herself up for her failing career, or the list of academic articles she should be working on to stay current in her field, or even her complicated relationship with her mother. She's spent the last several weeks in therapy preparing to deal with those major life hurdles.

But how could she have predicted any of this? The trauma of finding Chaz murdered? The fear that Kay might be falsely accused by an out-of-control sheriff? The worry that, even now, things might be moving too fast for her to stop, and the lives of her loved ones will be irrevocably changed?

That's it—that's what is stirring up the vortex in her mind. She hates the feeling of being out of control. She has hated it her entire adult life, since her dad died and she moved away.

Up to this point, her adult life felt orderly and disciplined—Emily would say sterile and lonely—in part because that was a way to retain control.

Since coming to Blue Oak, absolutely nothing has been under control, starting with Cutout Kay's head exploding. Except when she was interviewing Bodhi. She has a depth of knowledge about this situation that no one else near this investigation can muster, not even Emily.

Leo's breathing evens out, her pace regulated and smooth. Her brain finally settles, the way it does when she's untangling a problem. Normally, it's a research quandary, but really, isn't writing a literary analysis essentially solving a mystery? A scholar approaches a work with theories that become claims that she then proves with evidence. That's exactly what she needs to do now.

"What are the central problems here?" Derrida doesn't even glance up. He's used to Leo muttering to herself while they run.

Leo lays the situation out like she would a piece of scholarship. The first problem is timing, she thinks. Someone went to a lot of trouble to make it appear that Chaz was killed on the morning of July 6, but the cloying smell in the house when she took pictures the night of July 5 makes it clear he'd been murdered several hours before. This isn't new for her—Jake was asking Bodhi about her whereabouts starting at 11 p.m. on July 4, so Leo can assume the cops suspected that's the timeframe when the murder actually happened.

Leo is not an expert on body decomposition, and the sheriff's deputies know much more on that front than she does, but less than twenty-four hours has to be pretty fast for a body to begin to smell. She holds that thought in her mind until a memory surfaces that has been niggling at her brain since last night.

It's a lecture from her ninth-grade biology teacher; he had been angry because a couple of the boys hid their dissected frog in the cabinet rather than putting it in the fridge at the back of the room, and the room reeked the next morning. She remembers the teacher teaching them about how heat speeds up body decomposition. For his body to smell on the evening of July 5, Chaz must have died soon after Cutout Kay's head exploded. And then his body must have been outside, in the apocalyptic July heat.

That feels like important information, then—someone not only killed him much earlier, but either the murder scene or the place where the body was stored was outside.

The questions continue: Who would murder Chaz, leave him out in the heat, move his body, and then frame Kay Schneider for the murder? Someone who wants to hurt Kay as much as Chaz.

Bodhi has the video capability and the digital savviness to understand that the snark group would pay attention to such an odd video. The murder was perfectly designed for the subreddit. Would Bodhi have known enough about the tension in Blue Oak for her to target Kay? Were the financial entanglements enough to provide a solid motive? What would she have to gain from framing Kay?

Now she's arriving at the more important question: Who has the most to gain from Chaz's death?

Leo frowns to keep sweat from pooling in her eyes. Grant does, if he gains control of the company. But he also loses, since Chaz was the driving force behind advertising and marketing. Grant definitely seemed angry and withdrawn at the parade. Leo wonders if Jake has interviewed him yet.

Would Kymber benefit in some way? There were occasional rumors that there was trouble in paradise—Chaz was noticeably smarter than Kymber. Truly, the number of times she posted *TGIF* on a Thursday was astounding. Leo dismisses Kymber immediately; Kymber was likely too busy coordinating her outfits with her gum flavor to plot a murder.

And what about Mack? Jake's questions last night about Mack were pointed. Does he know something he isn't sharing with Leo? Was that really Melody at the party? How are the

Garners involved in this situation? Is there more that Leo doesn't know?

She has too many questions to even try to form a central claim right now. And there could be many more suspects—after all, *thousands* of people were in the snark group. Did some of them hate Chaz enough to kill him?

Her fingers itch to get home and list out her problems, to write it all on the page. For the first time since the parade, Leo really feels like herself, the version she is outside of her hometown—smart, poised, competent. Except there's a new element she tests as she turns back toward her mother's house: In her scholarship, her capability has always been in service of contributing to literary knowledge—a worthy, but admittedly vague, goal. Right now, the need is immediate: Kay is in jail. And Leo's knowledge could be a critical part of getting her out.

In spite of her fear and her worries, Leo feels—she takes five steps before she admits the word to herself—*purposeful.*

She turns the corner from a smaller path to the main one through the greenbelt that will get her back to her mother's. Ahead about ten yards, Leo notices another runner. She is wearing an all-white ensemble—white leggings, white top—that perfectly sets off her fit, tan shoulders.

It's the hydration pack that gives it away—it's fuchsia with a sparkling *K* in the middle of it. It was part of a brand deal a few months ago, and Leo knows the woman has taken hours' worth of footage to show people how much stuff she can fit in her Jackalope backpack while running. She has on matching fuchsia Beats headphones and fuchsia shoes; around her arm she has reflective bands that she doesn't need in the daylight but that show off her arm muscles to perfection. Leo's willing to bet she put on the special glitter glide gel someone sent her for marathons.

But that's Kymber for you. More focused on her outfit than good fitness techniques. She looks sleek despite the heat.

Between Leo and Kymber, the greenbelt path crosses a road. As Leo watches, a navy-blue truck pulls up and then stops on the side of the road, right on the crosswalk. The driver rolls down the window and says something to Kymber, who pulls the fuchsia Beats off her ears and walks up to the truck.

Leo speeds up slightly, grabbing her own earbud out of her right ear as she makes her way toward the truck. She tries to be surreptitious so that it doesn't look like she's listening in. She slows to a walk, then stops to tie a shoe that is perfectly tied. She tugs the other earbud out of her ear.

Leo only catches a few words from the driver in the truck, who is shadowed. All she can see is his cowboy hat. ". . . I'm so sorry, but you know I think you're too good for that douche."

Kymber is coquettish. "You're too sweet, Mack."

Leo stands up instantly, head cocked, as Kymber continues. "I'll get those mock-ups for you. And then maybe we could look at them over drinks like we did the other day? But it'll take a little longer than usual. It's been . . . a difficult couple of days."

The other day? Leo tries not to gawk, but glances over as she walks in front of the truck. She registers that Kymber is wearing lipstick (while running!) that perfectly matches her fuchsia accents.

And then she hears her name. "Leo, is that you?"

Kymber is still leaning with one hand on the truck, but gazes at Leo through the windshield. Inside the truck, Mack rolls his window down and leans out the other side, impossibly good-looking in a crisp white shirt and sunglasses, hat tipped back. Young Lenny, indeed.

"What the hell are you doing here, girl?"

33

Karina sits with Phil in the hard pleather chairs at the courthouse for exactly thirty-seven minutes. Apparently, Esquivel had taken pity on Phil last night. After Quackenbush left, Esquivel went to her car and came back laden with camping gear. She gave both Kay and Phil inflatable camping mattresses, pillows, and a couple of blankets.

This morning, Karina brought them breakfast tacos and coffee. Karina has already told Phil that the telegraph equipment has to be part of his hobby and not Kay's. ("Of course, we've been planning that for years. I have a couple of books on telegraphing in my study to pull out whenever I need to," Phil says, absolutely unfazed.) Karina paces, wishing she could trade these stupid snakeskin wedges for her black tennis shoes from last night, but she can't blow her cover now, arches be damned.

After she has walked the length of the room eight times, she sighs. "Quackenbush isn't going to get here soon, is he?"

"Of course not. You know him. That sharp young lieutenant practically slept here, but he probably passes out in front of the TV with a whiskey while he lets his deputies do all the work and then rolls in and starts calling the shots." Phil's normally kind voice is pitched low, his tone scathing. "Our lawyer has already called. She's excellent and will be on her way soon; Beth got in last night and should be up here in a minute."

"Great. I like the new lawyer, and I'm glad Beth will be with you."

He smirks. "Pays to have friends in high places who can pull strings."

She smiles slightly; the phone calls she made while Kay was being questioned yesterday are already yielding results—including the senator's email to Jake Nguyen last night—but she's still worried. Karina gives Phil a considering look. He stands up straight and turns toward her. His voice when he speaks is barely above a whisper, even though the DPS officer standing behind the metal detector is on his phone. "Karina, the rest of us can be here and support her. Her lawyer can outthwart Quackenbush, who wouldn't see the slowest ball coming toward him. But you can *do* something. Go. I give you permission."

She sighs and gives him a hug. "Thanks, Phil. I'll be back later."

"I'll text if anything comes up," Phil says.

Karina is already out the door. She thinks Jake is a good officer, but she's not trusting anyone right now. So today, she's starting with Grant Ford. Grant lives above DreamBawd in a third-story apartment. As she walks the two blocks to her salon, she puts together a plan. It's not ideal, but it'll do on the fly.

Clearly, the evidence in Grant's shed was left by an inept killer; whether it was Grant or someone else, she's not sure. Karina hopes she can have the case wrapped up soon—maybe even before Quackenbush makes it in, maybe in time for Phil and Kay to go out to lunch and dispel the rumors that stupid reporter is starting. That Baptist prayer chain will be the death of her.

She schools her face and walks with swaying hips. She won't wait for the sheriff's department to catch up; they're woefully out of their depth. And she doesn't want Leo involved at all.

She opens her Find My app, which Leo still doesn't know her mom set up years ago—she's on the greenbelt behind their house, hopefully still on her run.

Karina's hopeful that the evidence she found last night for the officers will keep them busy all morning and Jake won't go anywhere near Leo. She still has no idea what her English-professor daughter can offer the sheriff's department, but she'll watch Leo like a hawk to keep her from getting anywhere near this situation.

The best plan of attack is to solve the murder herself. She'll have to stop at the house first; there's a disguise that, in Blue Oak, has never ceased to work for her.

The murderer in Blue Oak has no idea who is on their tail.

34

It's too hot for a Yankee like you, isn't it?"

Leo walks up to the truck. "We have summers in the north too, you know."

"Yeah, still, running in this heat is no joke. Leo, have you met Kymber?"

Leo holds her hand out, then thinks better of it. She is wearing old high school clothes, not glitter glide and a runway-worthy outfit. "Sorry, I'm really sweaty. I saw you at the parade. I just moved back to town for the summer."

"Oh, hi. Happy . . . Welcome back?" The fuchsia sunglasses hide the expression on Kymber's face. Leo thinks through options in her mind. Does she bring up Chaz? At some point soon, Kymber will learn that Leo was one of the people who found his body. Should she offer condolences? While her mind is racing, her mouth speaks the niceties she's supposed to offer.

"Thank you. It's weird to be back, but good to see so many people." She hooks her thumb at Mack. "Some people look exactly the same."

"So Mack always looked this good?" Kymber's tone is flirty. Leo narrows her eyes. What in the world is going on here?

Mack chuckles, answering the question before she can voice it as if he can read her mind. "Leo, Kymber's been putting together a social media campaign for Garner Ranch as we try to reach a younger audience."

"Oh, are you a social media manager?" Leo turns to Kymber.

"I do some freelance work. For a few companies." Kymber has pulled her elbows in, her body tight. So she doesn't flirt with just anyone.

Leo switches tack. "Well, I might ask for some help at some point—I'm just starting that work myself, for . . . another local business."

Kymber seems to pull even more into herself, crossing her arms across her body. "I don't know how much I can help."

For one moment, Mack looks tense, then his features relax into his characteristic ease. "Ladies, I need to get back to get a horse ready for a trail ride later. Here." He reaches into his glove box and hands a card to Leo. "This is Kymber's card. I have all her info now, so I might as well get her a new client out of this." He almost, but not quite, gives Kymber a wink. His eye twitches like he's not sure what to do.

Leo takes the baby-pink card without looking at it and then steps back. She puts it in the back of her phone case. Kymber stays put by Mack's truck.

"I'm going to get this guy home." Leo raises Derrida's leash in her left hand; he's panting dramatically.

Mack touches his hat brim. "I'll text you in a little bit about tonight."

"Sounds good." Leo adds a little more sparkle to her smile than she normally would, then glances at Kymber. She is holding her thin body in her own arms, as if she's giving herself a hug. Her brow is furrowed—no small feat, considering how much Botox Leo knows is injected in Kymber's forehead. "It was nice to see you again, Kymber. Take care."

Kymber nods in acknowledgment, then turns back to Mack, frigid posture melting immediately. "Just one more quick question about that campaign."

Leo has no choice but to start jogging; she can't hear much as she moves away. Twenty strides in, Kymber's characteristic pealing laugh rings out, the one designed to make her seem adorable and approachable.

Leo feels a surge of jealousy. Was Mack flirting with Kymber? Had Leo misread the entire conversation by the Schneiders' pool? Were the memories crowding her mind in her hometown making her read something into his question that wasn't there?

After the first football game of their senior year, her relationship with Mack changed. Their group of friends had all been over at the Garners', but everyone left until she was the only one remaining. She was reading a book in the living room lit only by a soft side lamp, waiting while Mack took his after-game shower; he'd come in wearing sweatpants and a T-shirt, hair damp, skin warmed by the shower. Without a word, he'd pulled the book out of her hands, placed it gently on the side table so she wouldn't lose her place, and held his hand out. When she grasped it, he pulled her up off the couch. With one hand on her lower back and the other hand cradling her jaw, he tugged her close and said in a rough voice, "If you don't want me to kiss you, tell me now."

She looked at him and realized her friend was very, very good-looking. He tipped her face up a little more and nodded slightly, lips parting. That was all it took. He kissed her like he'd been dreaming of it for ages.

It was not her first kiss, but it was the first kiss that really counted for her. She felt it to her toes, the joy and thrill of kissing the boy she'd been friends with forever but was suddenly getting to know in a wholly new way. They'd been inseparable for the rest of the school year—until her father died the following May. In a haze of grief, she'd left for NYU and he'd gone to UT that August, and they'd faded back into a friendship that became more and more distant with time. But on Leo's end, at least, that love had never really gone away. And she'd never found anyone she shared a spark with like Mack.

As she runs toward her mother's house, Leo tries to bring herself back to the task at hand. Seeing Kymber and Mack had distracted her from the important questions she was heading home to write down in the investigation of who was framing Kay. But instead of reviewing those, a new one rises to the surface:

What in the world is happening with her high school boyfriend and Chaz's problematic, performative girlfriend? Because whatever it is, Leo has to admit to herself, she doesn't like it.

35

Fifteen minutes later, a sweating Leo and panting Derrida arrive at Karina's. After mulling it over, Leo decides she doesn't want to tell Jake about bumping into Mack and Kymber. There's something about Jake's response to what Bodhi said about Mack last night that sets her teeth on edge. She decides she's reading too much into the interaction with Kymber. Mack's always been charming and a little flirty; she may not have seen him much over the years, but she knows him to his core. He's a good person.

She gets Derrida some water in his bowl and leaves him in the laundry room to cool off. She takes a cold shower, quickly dries her bangs, then twists her hair into a bun; she throws on some shorts, a T-shirt, and a pair of flip-flops she finds in the back of her childhood closet. On the front door is a bright-pink sticky note with a message from her mom, like she used to leave for Leo in high school: *Gone to check on Kay. Love you.* Leo puts it in her pocket, then locks the door before walking four doors down to the Schneiders' to get her car. She checks to see if the officers are still there, but the place looks empty, the caution tape around the front porch flapping faintly in the hot breeze.

She calls Tess as she pulls away from the curb.

"Hey." Tess's voice is a whisper. Leo glances at her watch—it's 7:34 a.m.

"Sorry, didn't mean to wake you."

"No, it's fine. Hold on." She hears the sound of Tess walking, then the sliding glass door opening and closing. "Okay, I'm on the back porch. I made Em take a melatonin XR last night and she's still out."

"Good. I was hoping she'd sleep. Did I wake you?"

"No, I was in bed texting with Phil. No word yet on Kay. Quackenbush isn't in yet. Their lawyer is already at it. Phil said your mom is there."

"Good, glad they're together. Can I bring you doughnuts?"

"Of course. I'll have coffee ready. Come meet me on the back porch."

"See you soon."

Leo hangs up and drives through Glazed and Confused, making sure there are several blueberry bear claws in her mixed dozen. As she pulls away, her phone pings.

Mom: *Good morning, sweetheart. I'm up at the courthouse today. What are your plans? Can you sleep in and rest from your long trip?*

Leo shakes her head. How can her mother think she can rest when she just found a dead body yesterday? After parking her car at Emily's, she texts her mom back.

Leo: *Brought Em her favorite bear claws. We'll chill here. Give Phil and Kay my love. I'll check in later to see how they're doing.*

Karina sends back one yellow thumbs-up emoji.

Leo takes the doughnuts around to the back, where Tess is sitting in a T-shirt and cotton shorts on the porch with the fans on. It's not cool exactly, but it's bearable in the early morning. Tess has a carafe of coffee, some mugs, and some paper plates on the small coffee table. Her long brown hair is pulled back by a cloth headband. One of Leo's favorite things about her friends' relationship has been watching Emily fall more in love with her wife over their years of being parents together.

Tess looks up from her phone when she hears the back gate latch. "Lifesaver. I was just thinking I needed some sugar."

"Back at you. I need a vat of coffee." Tess immediately grabs a blueberry bear claw while Leo pours coffee and settles in the navy-blue patio chair facing Tess's couch. "How's our girl doing?"

"Whew, this really hit her hard." Tess pauses for a moment, clearing her throat. "Other than that miscarriage in between Hudson and Hattie, I have never seen her this upset. I think it really scared her."

"I bet. I also think . . ." Leo pauses.

Tess takes a big bite of a bear claw, and says around her mouthful, "Em's feeling guilty?"

"Exactly."

"I think that's it too. This can't be easy, after all the things she said about Chaz." Tess chews thoughtfully and looks over the green yard strewn with a bat and Wiffle ball, a cornhole set, and a small soccer goal with a sagging net. "The cops had to put off interviewing her last night since they had to search my in-laws' place. I told her after her therapy session that she's going to have to come clean."

Leo squirms and buys herself a second by picking out a cake doughnut covered in cinnamon. "About that."

Tess looks at Leo sharply. Behind her, the sliding glass door opens. Emily walks outside in her holey softball team T-shirt from high school and a pair of tie-dyed cotton shorts. Her short blond hair is sticking straight up on the right side and her eyes are squinting against the sun.

"Y'all do know it's summer, right? And we have a whole air-conditioned house to sit in?"

"Morning, sunshine. Trying to let you sleep. I see we're still sporting sexy lingerie for the wifey." Leo points at the tee.

"Screw you, it's comfortable and she loves it," Emily retorts cheerfully, walking up to perch on the arm of Tess's chair. Tess puts an arm around her wife and leans her head onto Emily's hip.

Leo smiles. "I brought you sustenance, Em."

"Blueberry?"

"Do I know you?"

"I knew I was smart to convince you to come back here. Now I just need to get Beth to move back, and then my master plan will be complete."

"Your sister lives three hours away; I think you're doing pretty great."

"I'm going to pee and brush my teeth, then I'll come sit with you weirdos outside for exactly thirty minutes until the swamp ass sets in."

"Did you sleep okay, sweetheart?" Tess taps Emily's booty affectionately when she gets up.

"Yes, but we have *got* to fix that headboard; it almost fell in on me again last night."

"Write it on the whiteboard in the kitchen and I'll get to it later today. I just need more staples for the staple gun." Emily nods and yawns as she shuffles back inside.

Tess looks at Leo as soon as the door closes. Leo sighs and says, "I had to tell Jake. I'll tell her everything, I promise. I'm first and foremost on Em's side. You know that."

"Of course you are." Tess takes a sip of coffee.

They make small talk for a few minutes about the kids' schools and Hudson's latest food obsession. ("Quesadillas with avocados smashed on top covered in heaps of salt; I swear that kid is either going to be a chef or have a sodium overdose by age twenty.")

Emily comes out with her hair damp and combed down, grabs a bear claw and a cup of coffee from the carafe, and then curls up on the couch next to her wife. "Thanks, Lee. This really helps. Beth says hi and she'll see you later today."

"How much did you talk to the deputies yesterday?" Leo asks.

"I mostly cried and told them about being at the house and discovering Chaz. They said they were going to interview me, but Jake called to say they had to put it off till later."

"Did you tell them why we went to the house?"

Emily shakes her head and then sips her coffee. "It's a Schneider Realty house we were working on, so that's all I said, that I was there to take pictures with you."

"Okay." Leo nods, then looks down at her thumb, gathering her thoughts. "I . . . Em, I told them everything."

"What do you mean, you 'told them everything'?" Emily sits forward, startled. "You told them about the subreddit?"

"Emily, I had to. It's for our own good."

36

Macy Johnson takes the last sip of her Red Bull and cracks her knuckles. She doesn't need a ton of sleep, but this is pushing it, even for her. She's been babysitting the Reddit group (which is frankly the most fun she's had on a job in a while). She's also been catching up on the two Facebook neighborhood groups; she hacked their admins immediately. Honestly, why suburbanites post so damn much about lost cats is the real mystery to Macy. And Macy's a cat person. But truly—the number of cat posts is mind-boggling.

Macy dug into the metadata of that gory garage door post that Leo as Bertha Rosenhaus deleted from the Facebook group. She found that it was from a *New York Post* article in 2017. Definitely not a crime scene photo; Macy told Jake and Esquivel that it was a dead end. The other post about the truck driving around seemed to be someone looking for a house—another dead end.

Setting the Red Bull down, Macy sits up: a new message is coming into the Facebook group DMs. And then another, and another. It's a series from Assam Dawood, the office manager of Schneider Realty, to Emily's Facebook account and Leo as Bertha Rosenhaus:

Assam Dawood: Hey, Emily and Leo. I talked to Phil last night. I'm so sorry to hear Kay is still in custody. What an awful situation. Let me know when we're storming the jail.

Three things this morning: I think Schneider Realty needs to release a statement about Chaz's death once we've heard from the deputies that his next of kin have been notified. Leo, would you be on that as our new communications person? From a branding perspective, making sure Kay Schneider remains the classy Queen of Blue Oak Real Estate feels more important than ever. If this situation with the sheriff remains in place in the next day or two, we'll think through how to state that (in a way that makes Quackenbush look bad and Kay look like she's being persecuted, which I sincerely think is true).

Second, we reached out to the owners of the Zora Neale Hurston house the sheriff's department asked us about. They're on week three of a monthlong Icelandic adventure with very little cell service. I know the sheriff's department wants to speak with them, but I've left a message and emailed and I'm not sure how else to get ahold of them. Will you tell the cops they were out of the country and definitely nowhere near the house when Chaz died?

Third, I've had a running theory for a few weeks about how Chaz was getting into the Schneider Realty houses that I decided it's time to go ahead and tell you; I'll let you decide whether it's worth taking to the cops. Sorry I didn't tell you before now; I wanted to wait until I was sure. But now that things have changed, I don't want to wait any more.

Emily, it was a comment you made the other day that made me think about it: you said that the only way that Chaz would be able to get into the houses is if he had access to our lockbox combos. That info is only available in Slack, and obviously we haven't been letting Chaz into our Slack, but I suspected he'd gotten access somehow.

I started noticing a pattern: a day or two after a lockbox combo was uploaded to our agency Slack channel, that house would be sabotaged. Without read receipts, it's impossible to tell who read the messages, so I started to send the lockbox combos to individual agents one at a time so I could control who had them.

It became clear the only houses that were being sabotaged were ones that Sofia Cortez had access to. I didn't want to tell you because I didn't want to accuse Sofia of being some kind of real estate spy (which I suspected at first). I don't think she is. I think she was duped.

I went back to Sofia's Instagram page and compared it to our employee records. Sofia was hired on March 9 of this year. On March 23, she posted a picture in the bluebonnets in Salado.

Interestingly, that same weekend, Grant Ford showed a series of soft launch photos in the bluebonnets, also in Salado. Here's a screenshot: <There's a screenshot of a couple holding hands above their tennis shoes in a field of bluebonnets.>

See that rose tattoo on her right wrist? And the red tennis shoes? Those are definitely Sofia's. Grant never tagged her, but I think they must have had some kind of relationship. I would have asked her, but that doesn't really feel professional and, as office manager, I didn't want to step on any toes. I was going to try to gather more info, but honestly, things have been so busy I didn't get around to it.

The house on Zora Neale Hurston was definitely Sofia's listing. She's the only one who had the lockbox code besides you and whoever else you texted because I sent it to her via DM. That means, somehow, Grant or Chaz have been accessing Sofia's Slack.

I truly believe she's innocent and probably would be horrified; she's a nice person and a good Realtor. But after what Phil told me about how you discovered Chaz, I couldn't in good conscience keep this info from you any longer. Sorry not to tell you before now. Hope it helps. Sending all you Schneiders and Holloways love.

Macy looks up. This is an interesting twist. She'd been planning to dig into the question of how Chaz was getting into Schneider Realty houses; Esquivel came home with that question top of mind very late last night.

Now Macy sends Assam a silent thank-you; she loves it when other people do her work for her. She wheels to the kitchen for another Red Bull, puts her riot grrrl playlist on, and gets to work. It takes her twenty-three minutes to prove that Assam is right: Chaz, and possibly others, have been spying on the Schneider Realty Slack channel through the account of one of their newest Realtors, Sofia Cortez.

Macy picks up the phone to call Esquivel, who needs to bring Grant in as soon as possible. This is the kind of damning evidence that can break open a case.

37

Blue Oak County Sheriff's Department
1904 Phillis Wheatley St.
Blue Oak, TX 00130
(555) 512-6523

July 6

MEMO TO FILE

FORENSIC EXAMINER PROCESSING NOTES: Lt. Laura Esquivel (4132)

FORENSIC CASE NUMBER: 95613

EVIDENCE DESCRIPTION: Screenshot taken at 10:37 a.m., wiki page from the Chaz Nickolson Snark subreddit

Grant Ford: Quickly dubbed LeFou to Chaz's Gaston, Grant is Chaz's business partner and sometime Insta-guest. In general, we find that LeFou doesn't really gather as much snarking as he does puzzlement—why would a seemingly nice guy who is cute in a less "obviously obsessed with his own image" kind of way spend so much time with Chaz? There's been a lot of speculation over the years. One anonymous friend of the sub gave us a full report in late 2021 about what's really going on at DreamBawd Gym in scenic Blue Oak (though again, WE DO NOT GO AND HARASS THE BUSINESS; this was a longtime customer dishing on the drama). In a nutshell, it's mostly just a normal CrossFit gym doing normal gym things—people working out in an environment that smells like ripe socks and disinfectant. And then, occasionally, Chaz comes through and loudly proclaims his aphorisms for the day, or corrects people's form . . . incorrectly.

The one good thing seems to be that even if Chaz has no idea what he's doing, most of the people around him do; his small army of ex-girlfriends and wannabe Bodhis seem pretty competent. Grant feels like a normal manager of a small-town gym, who occasionally ends up in awkward videos like this one where his job seems to be to soothe Chaz's often wounded ego. You can almost hear him sing, "Gosh, it disturbs us to see you, Gaston, looking so down in the dumps." #LeFou4Eva

Lily Ferrero: The intern who works with Chaz, LeFou, and the Bodhi-Lites at DreamBawd Gym. Other than our Gal Pal Tiff, there's no one we love more than Lily. She's just trying to make ends meet till she graduates with a shiny kinesiology degree. Lily, when you quit, call us—we want to hear EVERYTHING. And we will all write you letters of rec. You have 17,000 huge fans over here. Keep up the good work, girlfriend.

38

A driver in a dark-blue Amazon van that has seen better days makes her rounds that morning. If anyone peers closely through the windshield, they might see a small, trim woman in an Amazon vest wearing an Amazon-branded baseball cap pulled low over her face and hair above large aviator sunglasses. But no one is paying much attention.

Karina is banking on that fact. For the last three years, she has rented a parking space at a storage unit nearby and kept a van covered with a tarp nestled between the RVs and fifth-wheels of some of her neighbors. Today she had one of her colleagues who is helping behind the scenes call the front attendant—he is the sleepy sort of attendant she prefers, but she never takes chances—to distract him while she uncovers the van, changes outfits in the back, and pulls out. Later, with a quick couple of texts, she'll have another phone call made to distract the attendant while she parks and covers it up again. And then her colleague will ensure that all video evidence of her arrival and departure is erased.

Karina has spent the last hour since leaving the courthouse traveling around Blue Oak looking for evidence like the glove she found last night at the shed behind DreamBawd. The glove looked like the kind of gardening glove Kay prefers, though they're common enough at almost any gardening store. But still, it seems like someone is definitely planting evidence to make it look like Kay—or another woman who likes to garden—stashed the murder accessories around town.

Or it was poorly hidden by someone who really did use it. But she shakes her head; that doesn't seem right. Something about the placement of that glove is bothering her; it was too neat, the blood splotches too measured. There was no—she tries to think of a better way to say it, and can't—there was no passion behind it.

For an hour, she's just been perusing, keeping an eye out, following her instincts. She learned long ago that going in with an overly rigid plan is a great way to be thwarted in an investigation. The best way, she's often found, is to be in the right place at the right time with her eyes open. She leaves her van several times, standing in front of doors while looking confused, like she's in the middle of a delivery gone wrong. The boxes are dummies, filled with trash or rocks or old books. She's had them waiting in the back of the truck for years. But when she's holding a box, dressed as a delivery person, she becomes part of the scenery. She can look around her and examine the ground, the fences, the road, the windows, the dumpsters, and the fields without anyone taking notice.

After an hour, however, she decides to switch tactics; she hasn't found anything and she wants to know more about Chaz and his business.

In a moment of complete audacity, she parks five doors down the street from her own salon and walks toward DreamBawd—in full view of the woman who should have been her own first client of the day at Hair Today, Dye Tomorrow, but whose hair is being cut by Trina. She'd hoped to make it to the salon this morning, but the investigation isn't progressing as fast as she'd hoped—which is fine. Unlike Quackenbush, she knows not to rush this.

The dim coolness of the gym is a big change from the bright heat. Behind the desk, alone in the gym, is Lily the intern, trying to tie an overfilled garbage sack.

"We're closed for the day. You caught me right as I'm about to close up."

"I have a package." Karina holds up a box that contains three old towels and two rocks. Her voice is deeper and holds a hint of a Midwestern accent.

"Oh, thanks. You can just leave it by the door."

"Just to make sure, the name on the package is a bit odd. It says 'Grant Ford, Personal Only'?"

"Yeah, that's my boss. Normally he gets his packages with the business stuff since he lives upstairs. It has our address?"

Karina and Lily approach each other. Karina holds out the package for her to see the label she printed—from the custom label maker she keeps with the truck—a few minutes ago.

Lily sets the garbage sack down, wipes her hands on her leggings, then takes the package. "I don't know, maybe he doesn't want it down here. Give me a minute and I'll call him." She lifts the garbage sack up to set it by the door, and it splits down the side. "Dadgum, I hate these sacks."

Karina puts the package down and holds the edges of the trash sack. "You go get another one, I've got this."

"Thank you so much."

Lily reaches behind the front desk and gets two more green trash sacks from under the counter. She brings them back to Karina, who keeps her hands on the sides while Lily opens the sack and stuffs the split one into the new one. "They're absolute trash, pun intended. We used to use those big black industrial ones that, you know, businesses use, but then my boss's girlfriend made him change to these because they're biodegradable. I want to support the environment, I just wish they wouldn't degrade mid-use . . . Thank you." She ties the sack up, then turns to put the new one in the trash can. "I'm sorry, I don't mean to speak ill of the dead."

"Oh . . . what?" Karina makes a confused face.

"The owner of this gym just died. The one whose girlfriend switched . . . never mind. That's why we're closed. My other boss, Grant, is in his apartment upstairs. He hasn't left his apartment since we got the news." She holds the sack up. "Let me just put this down and I'll call him, hold on."

"You can take that out if you want to first. I'm ahead of schedule." Karina's hoping for an unguarded minute at the computer.

"No, it's okay, I'll just. . . ." Lily takes a step toward the desk, and then reconsiders. "Would you mind just running it upstairs? I would normally never ask this but, well, I've been doing everything around here. With all the extra work I've had to take on this week, I just . . ." She swallows and appears very young to Karina in that moment.

Karina interrupts quietly. "Say no more. I have a daughter about your age, and I can only imagine how hard this has been." She tries to make her face as sympathetic as possible, and doesn't mention that her daughter is at least ten years older than this young woman. She had been thinking fast about how to get to the office upstairs; she didn't anticipate this would be so easy.

"Thanks." Lily's eyes fill with tears. "This has all been pretty overwhelming. It's up the stairs back there, and then two stories up. Grant has the third-floor apartment."

"I can drop this off and then be gone."

"Thanks so much. Just pull the front door closed when you leave. I'm going to take out this trash and then I have to wipe down the bathrooms and the downstairs before I go."

Karina nods and heads up the stairs while Lily walks out the front door. On the second floor, Karina opens the first door to find a classroom space with some equipment and a water stand beside the door. She silently dismantles the box and stuffs it flat behind weight racks and adds the old towels to the rolled-up white towels on the shelves beside the door, with the rocks shoved in the folds. She has no intention of going up to Grant's apartment. R.E.M. music drifts down the stairwell.

Without another sound, she opens two more doors before locating the DreamBawd office. The doors are all open, so she doesn't even have to pick the locks, though she does lock the office door behind her. Lily leaves soon after that, which Karina confirms by watching the front-door security camera. She hears nothing from Grant upstairs; Karina assumes he's either depressed or self-medicating.

She checks in on Leo's location. Good, still at Emily's. She sends off another text.

KARINA: Hey, sweetheart. Just checking in: how's it going with Emily and Tess? Are they doing OK? What are your plans for the day? I think resting is exactly what you need!

After a minute with no response, she puts her phone down and gets started. It takes Karina less than two hours to find what she's looking for, with the help of a colleague cracking their passwords. Karina could probably do it herself, but she'd rather maximize her time since she can't guarantee Grant won't come down at any point.

One thing has been bothering her the whole time: She's not an avid member of the snark subreddit, like several of her neighbors. And she knew the Chaz Challenge video that ended with Leo and Emily storming into the house was faked, but she wants to confirm. With a few keystrokes, she finds Chaz's shared DreamBawd calendar, which Lily manages. Sure enough, there was no Chaz Challenge scheduled for the morning of July 6 at 7:30 a.m. An email was sent out, requesting the meeting, from Chaz's email at 2:39 a.m. on July 5.

Either Chaz was still alive then, or whoever sent it had access to his email.

She hangs up with her colleague while she digs into Chaz's financial situation; one of her mentors once told her the key to any investigation is following the money, and it has held true in almost every case she's worked since.

The computer is mostly filled with selfies of Chaz in various positions. She feels a pang of sympathy at the first and second photo; by the forty-first, she's tired of seeing him flex his pecs in front of a mirror. And she learns the nature of Chaz's business dealings—namely, that DreamBawd is in Grant's name, and the gym itself is doing fine financially. But Chaz is mortgaged to the hilt both personally and through his realty dealings. And he owes a lot of money to online gambling sites.

No one killed Chaz to get his money, that's for sure, though they might have killed him to get their own money back.

As she's getting close to the two-hour mark, she closes everything up in the DreamBawd office and texts her colleague to erase the security footage of her leaving after she's gone. Then she tiptoes downstairs. She almost leaves the door unlocked, but feels a pang at the thought of Lily getting in trouble—she takes a few extra seconds to use her lock-picking kit to *lock* the door.

As she peels off her black gloves, she moves with certainty toward her Amazon truck; she has a few more errands to run before her day is through, and she might need to chase down Jake to extricate Leo.

She calls the salon as she walks within full view of it. Trina answers and tells her of course they understand. What with Kay in jail—they're all talking about it, the Baptist prayer chain now having spread to the Methodists and Presbyterians—they assumed Karina wouldn't be coming in at all today. The other stylists have already divvied up her customers. She should take the rest of the day to be with Kay. Karina says she still might make it in later today, but she'll stay in touch.

Karina hangs up and, from her perch in the truck, watches Trina do the same at the salon. She turns the corner an instant after Esquivel pulls into the now-freed parking space in front of DreamBawd.

She's leaving just in time, and feeling pleased. Grant needs to come in for questioning.

39

I can't believe you told them, Leo." Emily's voice is angry. "This could seriously damage my professional and personal reputation in town. Did you think of that?"

Leo nods. "I've thought of nothing else. I feel guilty too; I feel guilty that Chaz is dead after years of us publicly shaming him." She breathes in and breathes out. "But they were absolutely going to find out no matter what, and I thought it was better if they heard it up front from me. They have an outside consultant working with them, Emily, and she's very good. I was telling her things yesterday that I could tell she was finding out in real time; it would probably take her five minutes to know every detail of your online history since you bought your first iPad. This wasn't a secret I could keep."

"There are . . . consequences for this kind of thing. And you might not face them, but I definitely will."

"Why wouldn't I face them?"

"Because you're determined to be a *tourist*, Lee. You tell everyone you can that this is just for the summer, that you can't wait to be gone again . . ."

"That's because this is just for the summer, Em." Leo's voice is rising.

"Yeah, yeah, I get it, you're bigger and better than this place. But while you're determined not to get the *taint* of Blue

Oak on you, the rest of us live here. We actually *like* living here. And that means we're in community with these people. It's not enough that my mother is under arrest for murdering that absolute douche-canoe whose *body we found yesterday* . . ." Emily pauses and puts her hand to her mouth like she's going to throw up. "But you just told Becky's brother that I'm the one who led thousands of people in making fun of Chaz for years. Thanks a lot, Lee. You win. You get to come in with your camera and take some pictures and move on. Just like you've been doing for years, in grad school and all those postdocs, showing up for a year and never putting down roots, distant and cool. No relationships, no friendships, nothing but cordial professional acquaintances and then on to the next place. Always removed, so you can't *ever be hurt*. Well, the rest of us get hurt. And you've hurt me. That *sucks*." She stands up, her face red, her voice shaking. "I'm going inside to take a shower."

Leo watches her, stunned.

Emily opens the sliding glass door and turns back to say, "Also, Assam messaged us on Facebook. Did you see it?"

"No."

"Well, you should look at it and probably tell your boyfriend Jake what he found."

She slams the sliding door behind her. Tess calmly takes a sip of coffee.

Leo tears up. "I hate when she does this."

"Oh, me too."

"I didn't do anything wrong."

"You didn't. And I am not going to mediate this for y'all; I assume you're not asking that of me."

"No, I'm not. I just . . ." Leo chokes on her words and stops. Emily knows her better than anyone, so it shouldn't have surprised Leo that Emily identified the very thing that worried Leo yesterday. Emily called her a tourist, Leo remembered her dad saying she could be an island, but either metaphor is apt: she's been isolated, distant, and removed. This whole time, she thought only of protecting herself. But now she can see how much she's hurt Emily. Not about the snark group, though that didn't help. But it's clear Emily's been holding deeper resentment for a while.

Leo has always assumed Emily would come to her, and she has, but Leo realizes now that she's rarely returned the favor. Leo's been nursing wounds that she allowed Emily to attend to while barely giving space to what Emily was going through over the years. Emily always seemed fine, but Leo can see now, she should have known better. Leo wonders: When did her self-protection sour into self-centeredness? She sniffles. "What she said wouldn't hurt so much if it weren't true."

"I know. That insightful bitch. It's so irritating that she's both lethally angry and often right. *Don't* tell her I said that." Tess gets up and grabs the carafe. "Stay for a minute and see if she calms down if you want to. Or go on with your day. But if you want to stay, I'm going to brew more coffee."

"I won't turn down more coffee."

"Good. Sit for a second. She might feel better after her shower." Tess pauses at the door. "You're the only one who can decide whether what she said was her lashing out or whether she saw some real things, but for what it's worth, from where I'm standing, you're not to blame for telling the cops about the sub. The rest of it is between y'all. But that was going to come out anyway, and it's better this way. That part, at least, was Em taking her own guilt and shame out on you."

Leo nods, her breath stuttering around a barely controlled sob. Her voice cracks when she speaks again, changing the subject so she can calm herself. "Did Em tell you what Assam found?"

"No, I usually stay out of real estate business; it's everywhere and I get sick of it. Read the messages and give me a recap when I get back."

Leo pulls her phone out and catches up in the time it takes for Tess to refill the carafe with hot coffee, occasionally wiping angry tears away with the back of her hand. When Tess gets back, she pours a cupful for Leo, who fills her in.

Leo can tell Tess is trying to lighten the tone. "Ooh, I love that the tell was Sofia's red shoes. She wears them all the time."

"I am going to have to tell the sheriff's deputies about this."

"Don't let my wife keep you from doing what you need to do, Leo." Tess plucks a strawberry-glazed doughnut out of the box. "You're her safe person, you know." Tess sighs deeply. "You know the best thing you can do right now? Give her space, and do what you can to get Kay out of jail."

"I mean, sure, that would be great."

"No, I mean it, Leo. You're the smartest person either of us knows." Tess leans over and pierces Leo with a look. "Jake obviously doesn't trust Quackenbush, and right now, Kay's fate is in his hands. No pressure, Leo, but I believe in you. Even if Em's being a jerk right now, she does too. I think that you should trust your instincts, and do whatever you need to do to solve this murder. Soon, before Quackers pins it on Kay."

Leo's phone vibrates and she looks at the screen.

JAKE NGUYEN: Good morning. Can you be ready in an hour? I'm on my way to interview Tiffani Miller. I want you with me.

40

Voice memo on the phone of Mack Garner, 9:17 a.m., July 7: "Do not keep this message. Listen, I have to be quick. You and I are about to be suspects in Chaz's murder. I haven't been as careful as I should have been about looking into his finances; tons of people saw me at Bodhi's party, and I'm betting it'll come out that I was there. I need you to clear your phone right now. Here's how."

He tries to call her twice, but she doesn't return his calls. An hour later, Mack's phone has been reset to factory settings, with many of his messages deleted, including the voice memo from his sister. He's scoured his emails as well.

Something spooked his sister, who is never scared. And if Melody is scared, then Mack definitely is. He has very good reason to be. After all, Jake Nguyen already knows more than Mack wishes he did.

Mack tries to focus on the work at hand, but it's impossible. Every single thing that comes up tests his patience enormously. He's distracted and worried and short-fused. It feels like it's just a matter of time before red-and-blue lights start flashing outside Garner Ranch.

41

Esquivel stands up. "Grant, would you like water? Soda? Coffee?" After almost twenty minutes of pointless conversation with Grant, she needs one minute to breathe and change tack. She plays a game with herself on especially dumb days on the force, or when she's exhausted like she is today: she gives herself mental gold stars. She's already up to ninety-two today. She's probably going to hit a new record. If she gets to two hundred, she's bringing Macy pizza, ice cream, and beer tonight. At the excruciating pace Grant Ford keeps answering questions, she might hit that number within the next thirty minutes.

Grant is sitting on the other side of a white IKEA table in the closet-turned-conference-room at the sheriff's station. Despite copious amounts of gel in his slicked-back hair, she can clearly see his bald spot. He is wearing a Dri-FIT black shirt with gray workout shorts. He is short—only an inch or two taller than Esquivel, who is five foot four—and stocky. His arm muscles stretch his T-shirt seams in a way that he is clearly aware of; he watches Esquivel slyly to see if she is paying attention to the way his body moves. She is definitely not attracted to Grant, but he clearly hopes she is.

"Coffee."

"Great choice. The sheriff recently switched from Folgers

that I swear had been sitting in the cabinet since 1964 to slightly better coffee. Cream? Sugar?"

"I don't do additives. Black is fine."

"Perfect. Be right back." This is the first interview she's ever conducted alone. She felt confident this morning, but that feeling has begun to slip away as she's failed to get Grant to open up.

Grant is Esquivel's top suspect for now. The bloody glove half hidden in the shed points toward him, and he has a lot to gain from Chaz's death if ownership of the gym falls squarely to him. Plus Macy called her at the office an hour ago, her hoarse voice hyped up on Red Bull, and told her what Assam had messaged to Leo and Emily. Esquivel wishes her girlfriend could illegally hack into all the communication for every case she's in. But unfortunately, that information is off the table in terms of building a legal case against Grant. It would be better for her if he offered it to her freely, but she's stymied about how to get him to say it out loud.

She watches the pot brew and thinks, *You can lead a horse to bad coffee, but you can't make him drink.* She shakes her head; no, that was terrible. Minus a gold star. Ninety-one.

But something about the bad pun reminds her of her first college roommate, Daphne, a girl who had been her opposite in every way; despite that, they'd gotten along like a house on fire. Daphne's sense of humor was truly atrocious in the most endearing way. As she used to joke, her spiritual gift was the fact she could charm the pants off a pig.

Esquivel stills. That's it. She just needs to channel her inner Daphne. Grant hopes he's attractive, and if she can charm him, he might open up.

Three minutes later, with two foam cups in hand, Esquivel sits back down at the table. *I'm giving myself up to 110 for this,* she tells herself, taking in a deep breath as she turns the recorder on. Showtime.

"Grant, here's the coffee. Thanks so much for being here; it really helps us out. We're just trying to understand, you know, who Chaz Nickolson really *was*. Since you were his best friend, we wanted to start with you." Her voice is almost an octave higher. She pats his arm sweetly. "I'm so sorry if I've been a little tough. I'm really stressed. It's my first big murder investigation, after all, and, well, I just want to do what's right for *Chaz*, do you know what I mean?"

"No problem," Grant says, sitting up a little straighter. "It's been a hard few days for me too. The police shut down our business and roped off the parking lot and shed. I've just been in my apartment, listening to music. It's been awful."

"I'm sure. I'm so sorry for your loss. Can we start over?" Esquivel practically bats her eyelashes while resisting the urge to throw up.

"Yeah, of course. And thank you." Grant sips his coffee. "How can I help?"

Definitely 110 gold stars.

42

Of the 26,851 members of the r/ChazNickolsonSnark page, 486 are active at 11:32 a.m. CST on July 7 when u/NanciDrew42 shares a screenshot of a text conversation with the caption *Sharing this from a teacher friend.* The names of the texters had been obscured by a black line across the top of each name, as if someone had edited the screenshot with their thumb on an iPhone.

[REDACTED 1]:
OMG, I finally found out what happened to Chaz.

[REDACTED 2]:
WHAT??

[REDACTED 1]:
He died.

[REDACTED 2]:
NOOOOO! What happened?

[REDACTED 1]:
According to my grandmother's Baptist prayer chain, it was mysterious circumstances.

[REDACTED 2]:
Meaning what?

[REDACTED 1]:
The Blue Oak Sheriff's Department is investigating it as a homicide.

[REDACTED 2]:
Who in the world wanted Chaz Nickolson dead?

The post's hottest reply has 2.5k likes:

U/ALOHAALOHA765 • 23 MIN. AGO: Alright, snarkers, our duty here is clear. Until the mods stop us or shut it down, we have to solve this murder. I vote to suspend the sub's rules about excess speculation. We'll call them all "theories," so it's not libel, but have at it. Who killed Chaz Nickolson?

The sub's moderators, of course, will not be shutting the post down since they no longer have access to the sub. But Macy is watching the anarchy unfold while gleefully downing a grape Slurpee. This was exactly what she hoped would happen.

She's the "teacher friend" who sent the screenshot to u/NanciDrew42. She used one of her burner Reddit accounts from another case, one in which she got to expose educators abusing kids with a badass paralegal. She decided an anonymous teacher was just right to reach out to Melody Garner-Aziz as u/NanciDrew42.

U/MOPAY4TEACHERS: Hey, Nanci, longtime lurker, first time DMer here. I'm a teacher who works in San Marcos, not far from Blue Oak, and my team lead just sent me this text. Her friend teaches at Blue Oak Elementary and the whole town has been buzzing because apparently Chaz was murdered?? Anyway, I want to tell the sub but I'm scared of it getting back to me. I know you're our resident investigator: would you mind sharing this with the sub? And just say it's from a teacher friend? Thank you!!

And now she gets to watch for the rest of the morning as the subreddit does a large chunk of her work for her.

Macy's fingers fly, keeping one step ahead of them over the next few hours. She's betting her girlfriend will bring her pizza and beer for dinner tonight. If she's lucky, she'll get ice cream too.

Of the 27,136 members of the r/ChazNickolsonSnark page, 4,921 are active at 12:07 CST on July 7 when the group seems to reach a consensus (with a handful of naysayers, because Reddit):

U/MONICALEWINSKYLOVE • JUST NOW: Y'all have convinced me. His murderer was the person with the most to gain: It had to be Grant Ford.

43

It takes thirty-eight minutes for Grant to break down in tears. "Hard to imagine he's not gonna just walk into a room anymore."

"Take your time." Esquivel infuses her tone with warmth and reaches forward to grab Grant's forearm. Being Daphne is horrendous. "This is *so* hard."

"It's so *hard*. Yeah." Grant blinks for several breaths. "He . . . uh . . . he really changed people, you know? It wasn't just the name of the business. It was . . . He made their dreams come true. Dream bod. Dream house. Dream life. Oh, no." Grant leans his head forward onto the table and sobs.

She glances at her watch. It's time.

"He changed your life, didn't he?" Her voice is syrupy.

Grant nods, not speaking.

"You'd have done anything for him."

"Yeah. Anything."

"He was your best friend."

"The best friend I'll ever have." Grant sits up and looks at the ceiling, cheeks tracked with tears.

"He asked you to start a business and you said yes."

"Absolutely."

"He told you he wanted to start a church in your gym and you agreed."

"DreamSoul in the heart of DreamBawd. Bodies and souls for Jesus."

"And when he asked you to help him with the rival real estate agency, you agreed. There was nothing you wouldn't do for him." Grant has his eyes closed and is nodding along. "Including dating the girl he tells you to, getting access to the Schneider Realty Slack channel, and helping him commit ongoing fraud."

"That's . . . Wait, what?" Grant looks at Esquivel, stunned.

"The night of the Fourth of July, when you were here with Chaz and Kymber and the Schneiders, Kay Schneider told me that her real estate company suspected that Chaz Your Dreams Realty—particularly Chaz, Kymber, and maybe you—had intentionally been damaging houses that she was listing. She told us she intended to file charges. So the night that Chaz died, I'd already begun to investigate him." She pauses and gives him what she hopes is a sympathetic look. "We just want to hear your side of the story. I'm going to highly suggest that you tell me everything you know right now."

Grant blinks at Esquivel, lips a thin line.

Esquivel chirps, "If I remember right, Sofia Cortez gets here in about fifteen minutes, and if I hear the whole story from her first, it'll look much worse for you. But up to you!" She starts to stand up, face bright and friendly the whole time.

"Wait!" Grant plants both hands on the table to get her attention. "It wasn't my idea! None of it was!"

"Oh, good. Want to tell me about it?" Esquivel sits down. Within twelve minutes, Grant has told her every detail: How Chaz stalked Sofia Cortez at Top Shelf, the bookstore and bar in the downtown square, when she was a new Realtor for Schneider Realty. How Chaz approached her and started "negging." (Esquivel gives herself ten extra stars for never having used the word *negging* in her real life, and then another ten just for being queer.) How Chaz's first line was "Girls like you aren't usually my type, but there's just something about you." How shocked Chaz was when she almost threw a drink his face.

Esquivel asks, "Did negging usually work for him?"

"He insulted the hell out of girls and they were usually begging for more. Not Sofia. Chaz came back absolutely beat down. I asked if I could take a shot with her, and he was like, 'Your funeral.' So I went to go talk to her. Turns out, she's really nice. She thought he was being racist, which maybe he was. He'd made her so angry, she appreciated a comforting shoulder." He pats his own broad shoulder.

Grant had walked Sofia home that night and asked her out. "I really liked her. I wasn't doing it because Chaz wanted me to, we just got along. I didn't know what Chaz had in mind until it was too late."

Five dates later, Grant mentioned to Chaz that he and Sofia were going to get away for the weekend. "We went to Salado, stayed in one of those little cabins in the woods. And Chaaaaz . . ." Grant pauses again. "He followed us and, when she was in the shower, he came in the room. Scared me to death. It was the worst fight we ever had. We had to whisper so she wouldn't know he was there. She'd left her phone on the nightstand, and it was still open because she'd been showing me funny TikToks; he got on to the company Slack channel and figured out her email and password. By the time she was done with the shower, he was gone. And that's how he did it."

"How he did what?" Esquivel widens her eyes like she's glued to his story.

"He would log in as Sofia Cortez to the Schneider Realty Slack and get information about the houses they were listing."

"And what did he do with that information?" Esquivel leans forward.

"He . . . used it to sabotage their listings and to get a better deal for his own buyers. He . . . tore out cabinets one time. He pulled apart electric wires. He"—Grant swallows—"one time he peed in the living room."

"Wow." Esquivel doesn't have to pretend that she's grossed out. "And did you participate in this . . . in the peeing?"

"I didn't pee, no. I thought that was a step too far. I didn't commit any of the vandalism. At first, it didn't bother me that much. By then, Sofia had already broken up with me; we didn't make it past that Salado weekend, partly because I felt so weird about what Chaz did that I didn't know how to be around her. So for a while, I convinced myself that I was happy to get revenge on her. But Chaz just took it way too far." Grant pauses, takes another sip of his coffee. "What did he think, there wouldn't be other people here doing real estate before him? I mean, it's a pretty basic job."

"Absolutely." Esquivel nods like he's convincing her, expression riveted. Grant picks up steam.

"He just... Chaz *lost* it, man. He went nuts. I asked him once, WWJD, you know? Like, Jesus wouldn't pee on the living room floor of his rival Realtors' house. But Chaz said Jesus wanted him to be happy, and if I didn't support him, I could get out. It wasn't like him." He finishes off the coffee. "Kymber made him worse."

"In what way?"

"Chaz met Kymber in Austin. We used to go and drink nonalcoholic beer at this one bar we liked. It was a Saturday night. And then this girl just like *squeals* out of nowhere, absolutely *loses* it. She runs up to Chaz, squeezes his arm, and is like, '*Excuse* me, are *you* Chaz *Nickolson*?'" Grant's voice takes on a high-pitched mimicky tone. "Then she blew smoke up Chaz's ass for the rest of the night. 'Chaz, you're amazing, Chaz, you're the best, Chaz, Chaz, *Chaz*.'"

Esquivel wonders if he means to sound exactly like Jan Brady saying "Marcia, Marcia, Marcia!" "Is that when they started dating?"

"Oh, yeah. It wasn't two months before Kymber moved to Blue Oak. She has her own place because Chaz likes his space sometimes, but she was mostly at Chaz's house. He started changing faster after that. The . . . worst parts of him came out. He was drinking again, which I was totally against. It hurt our relationship, honestly. I told him I didn't want to be around that shit. I went to rehab—we *met* at rehab—just to get away from all of that. Then Kymber came along and she became his drug."

"What do you mean?"

"Kymber thought Chaz destroying property was hilarious. She'd go with him. She started reading the Slacks and coming up with ideas herself."

"So she knew how to get into houses that Schneider Realty was about to list?"

"Yeah, absolutely."

"You didn't like her much."

Grant is emphatic. "I did not. He was . . . he could be . . . sometimes he was a tiny bit self-centered. But with Kymber telling him all day every day how amazing he was, how much better he was than anyone around him, that side of him grew." He leans forward, as if about to deliver a secret. "That day he got punched after the parade?"

Esquivel leans forward too, listening intently.

"I think he deserved what he got. I can't believe he started a fire on Kay's float. It was a shitty thing to do."

"He did it for sure, then?"

"Oh, yeah. It was all his plan. After the parade, he and Kymber went back to his house. I was going to go with them, but I was kind of disgusted by them, to tell the truth. There were *kids* on that float, man. I was pissed. And I never talked to him again. They say 'Don't let the sun go down on your anger,' but I did—and he died with me mad at him."

Grant begins to weep quietly again. Once he takes a deep breath, she asks, "You went back home after the parade?"

"Yeah, to my apartment. I watched TV for a while, then fell asleep early. I open the gym every morning, so I have a strict ten p.m. bedtime."

"Can anyone verify that?"

"Our Ring doorbell shows every time I enter and leave."

"And no one else was there."

"No, just me." He gives her a doe-eyed look. "I live all alone in that big ol' apartment."

Esquivel decides her Daphne alter ego has done enough for today. “Great, we’ll follow up to get that info.” She nods as if she’s satisfied. “Thank you so much for sharing with me.” She leans over, infusing as much kumbaya in her voice as she can. “I have just one more question. Do you have any work gloves?”

“Sure, I think there’s a pair in the shed out back at the gym.”

“What color are they?”

“Gray? Bluish sort of gray?”

“Did you ever see another pair at the gym?”

“I mean, Chaz has his own gloves that he special ordered because he said his hands were too big for regular gloves.” He smirks sadly. “That jerk was always making penis jokes.”

“What did those gloves look like?”

“They were leather. They had these really long, like, cuffs or something. They looked like what you’d use if you had hawks. I made fun of him for them, but he loved them.”

“What color were they?”

Grant rolls his eyes affectionately. “I would have said brown. Chaz called them ‘cognac.’ ”

“Did either of you ever use flowered gloves?”

“I didn’t. I doubt he did.”

“Thank you, Grant. Can you write out a statement for me? To help convince my bosses not to charge you?”

Grant nods. “Of course. Anything to help.”

She beams at him. “I’ll be right back with some paper, okay? Thank you, Grant!”

Esquivel grimaces as soon as she’s turned her back and shakes her shoulders like she’s shedding a costume. She heads to the supply room for a fresh legal pad for Grant, and then to the kitchen to get water and coffee for him. She awards herself two hundred gold stars for her first-ever interview lead.

She’s upping her game and bringing home whiskey for Macy instead of beer with their pizza and ice cream.

44

Half an hour after she left Tess and Emily's, Leo is riding with Jake to see Chaz's ex-wife, Tiffani Miller, and ignoring her mother's increasingly frantic texts that she *stay home and rest*. In the pool house she'd changed into something she hoped was both professional and cool, but she didn't have time to fix her hair. And no amount of makeup (that Leo would wear, at least) could cover the fact she'd been crying. Jake didn't say anything; they caught up on the case while they drove.

As they pull into the neighborhood, Leo turns. "Wait, which of us is going to be the bad cop?"

"What?" Jake glances at her with amusement.

"Good cop / bad cop?" She points between them.

"You know that's only the movies, right?"

"Whatever, Quackers is *always* the bad cop."

Jake gives a neither-confirm-nor-deny smile. Two minutes later, Jake and Leo pull up to a small house in South Austin with whitewashed bricks, black shutters, and a white door with a magnolia-leaf wreath. Leo tucks her notebook into her backpack and wipes her hand down the front of her trousers. Linen felt fresh and resort-like earlier; now she looks like a wrinkled paper bag. Her lit-prof wardrobe was not intended for being a law enforcement consultant at the height of the summer apocalypse.

Jake is already ringing the doorbell, Leo behind him. Immediately, a deep bark rings out. While they wait, Leo notices the magnolia leaves on the wreath are dusty and faded. After a few minutes, the door swings open.

"Can I help you?" It's a shock for Leo to see Tiffani—who she always envisions as being very put together—in grubby sweatpants and an oversize tee, her obviously dirty hair pulled into a high ponytail. Her face is makeup-free and her nose is red. She pulls on the collar of a big black Lab. "Tiger, calm down."

"Hi, Ms. Miller?" Tiffani nods. Jake pulls out his badge. "I'm Detective Jake Nguyen, and this is my consultant, Leonora. You spoke on the phone with Lieutenant Esquivel earlier?"

She clears her throat. "You're here to interview me about Chaz?" Her eyes immediately fill with tears.

Jake's voice is tender. "I think 'interview' is probably too strong a word. We have some questions that we hope you can help us with. Can we come in?"

Tiffani nods and steps back. Jake and Leo follow her into the house, letting Tiger sniff them first. The house is a cookie-cutter suburban home and, despite the farmhouse-chic feel on the outside, Leo notes that very little has been done to the inside in at least a decade.

Tiffani drops onto a gray sectional couch with lumpy geometric throw pillows. Tiger jumps beside her, then picks his way across the couch to sniff Leo's face.

"I forgot to ask if you're okay with dogs."

Leo is already rubbing behind his ears, letting him nuzzle her shoulder. "More than okay, who couldn't love this big guy?" Tiger turns over, presenting his belly, which Leo scratches appreciatively.

Tiffani smiles at him wanly. "He's the worst guard dog ever, he'd just lick a burglar to death, but he's been with me since . . . well, since right before Charlie and I split. I kept him in the divorce."

Jake pulls his recorder out of his breast pocket. "Ms. Miller . . . or is it Ms. Nickolson?"

"Please, Tiffani. No one calls me Ms. Miller. And I never took Charlie's name. Should have told me something, as young as I was." She takes a sip of her Coke Zero.

"Tiffani, thank you. Do you mind if I record this?"

"That's fine, I don't have anything to hide." She takes another swallow of her drink. "I'm sorry, do y'all want something to drink? Soda? Water? Coffee?"

Jake nods. "I'd love a glass of water."

Tiffani gets up off the couch and walks into the kitchen, Tiger trailing behind her. The living room and kitchen are open concept; a small island with a beige Formica countertop and four cheap metal stools separates the rooms. The cabinets are faux wood. This is not how Leo imagined Tiffani's life—low-key, undecorated, smelling of wet dog.

Tiffani brings two glasses of ice water to them. "Here you go. And can I say, am I wrong that both of you look familiar?"

Jake turns the recorder on and makes sure the red light is lit before placing it in the middle of the coffee table. "Leo and I both went to Blue Oak High School, though a few years after you."

"Oh, Leo." Tiffani narrows her eyes briefly. "Your dad taught photography, didn't he? You were Beth's younger cousin?"

Leo nods. "Yes, he did. And sort of—not really cousins, but friends who are like cousins."

Tiffani nods. "I'm so sorry about your loss. I loved your dad's classes. I was on yearbook junior and senior year and thought briefly about being a journalist. Not that you can tell now . . ." She waves her arms at her blank walls. "But I loved photography once upon a time. He was a great teacher."

Leo swallows. "Thank you."

Tiffani turns to Jake. "Did I know you?"

"I doubt it. You'd been gone a few years before I got to Blue Oak. My sister, Becky, was a freshman when you were a senior."

Tiffani is shaking her head. "No, I do remember you. Were you a soccer player?"

"I'm impressed, yeah."

Tiffani smiles. "Ha, thank you. My little sister had a huge crush on you. Karlie Miller, remember her?"

Jake chuckles. "I do! But she never talked to me!"

"No, she was shy as all get-out. She's married now with two adorable kids. She'll never believe that you were here. And a detective! I thought you'd go play soccer in Europe or something."

"Ah, my knee blew out in college. Tell Karlie I said hi, though."

"Will do." There's a slight lull. Tiffani sips her Coke Zero and Tiger sighs beside her.

Jake begins. "Tiffani, we have some questions about Chaz . . . do you call him Charlie?"

"Yeah, it was so funny to me that he changed his name after the divorce. It went hand in hand with his whole . . . makeover or whatever."

"When was the divorce?"

"In 2012."

"He divorced you?"

"No, I'm the one who filed."

"After how many years of marriage?"

"We were together for seven years, married for three. Less than three, if you count when I left."

"So y'all were together from high school up until you got married?"

"Well, it was on and off throughout college, but we always ended up back together and I never dated anyone else, so I count it as seven years. I should have known then it was unhealthy. It was long-distance, which was hard. He was at Tech and I was at A&M. We didn't spend a ton of time together during the school year, but on breaks we were both back in Blue Oak like nothing had changed. I think that's probably why we stayed together so long. I don't really like change. And Charlie could be sweet—he was mostly sweet for a long time."

"What changed?"

Tiffani absently pats Tiger's head on her thigh. "It's an old, clichéd story. We got married too young. We wanted different things. We moved to Elgin the first year because I was an assistant coach, and the next year, we moved here. I got the assistant job at the high school where I work now. I took over the program four years ago. Once he realized that this was it, this was my plan, there wasn't some mysterious other path I wanted, he got really unhappy."

"Unhappy how?" Jake leans back like he's settling in.

"Well, we argued. A lot. He started working out all the time. He'd gotten a job as a trainer at the local Orangetheory, and he always wanted me to go out with his friends on the weekend. But I didn't like them. I went a couple times, but it was irritating—we'd go watch games at Dave and Buster's and eat wings and I'd watch them get drunk on cheap beer. I hated it."

"Was Charlie upset about that?"

Tiffani considers. "He was upset, but not because he wanted me to get to know his friends. I've dated some other people since then, and I'm in a serious relationship now. I've learned some things."

Leo feels herself flushing even though she hasn't said a word: she's embarrassed at how excited she is to find out that Tiffani is in a healthy relationship, something the Chazzercisers in the subreddit have speculated about for a long time. There is no way that Tiffani can suspect that Leo is behind the snark group, or the level of investment Leo has in the idea of our Gal Pal Tiff, who Leo is quickly realizing is a character that has little to do with the woman in front of her. She wonders if she'll feel this complex mix of nostalgia, regret, and guilt every time she thinks of the subreddit from now on.

Tiffani continues. "Allen, my current boyfriend, invites me to hang out with his friends—he's a music producer and he's also in a band, they're pretty great. Allen wants me to come because he likes me and he likes his friends and he enjoys it when we're all together. If I showed up like this—post-workout, spent the day sorting out cheer stuff—he probably wouldn't even notice, or he'd notice it like, 'Hey, did you have a hard day? Wanna stay home?'" She pauses again. "In our marriage, Charlie only wanted his hot girlfriend from high school. It took me a long time to realize he loved the idea of me, head cheerleader to his football star, a love story that looked good on paper but wasn't real life."

Jake's mouth twists in concern. "It must have been hard when you figured that out."

Tiffani nods. "It was. I can't believe it took me so long to realize we wanted such different things. I was never going to be . . . well, have you met Kymber yet?"

"We have, have you? Did you and Charlie stay in touch?" Jake leans forward, drawing Tiffani in. Leo observes his tactics, taking mental note of his body language and demeanor. As she follows the conversation, a small part of her registers surprise—is she collecting information about how to be a better detective?

Tiffani nods. "Yeah, of course, it took a little time after our divorce, but eventually we became friends of a sort. I mean, our parents have known each other since we started preschool together. It's hard to completely let go of someone when they've been there your whole . . ." She stops suddenly. Tiger shoves his head onto her lap, looking at her with adoring eyes.

Jake speaks softly. "Leo and I know better than most people that small-town relationships are less like friendships and more like . . . part of your DNA."

"Yes, exactly. Sorry." They wait quietly for a minute while she collects herself. Eventually, Leo gets up and pulls a few paper towels off the roll in the kitchen and walks back to the couch to hand them to Tiffani. "Thank you," she murmurs.

Leo speaks for the first time in the interview. "If you don't mind my saying so, you don't seem much like Kymber at all. I think you were going to maybe talk about how Charlie's relationship with her showed you something about who he was or what he wanted."

Tiffani sips her Coke Zero again. "Yes, thank you." Her voice rasps as she speaks. "Kymber and I met last Christmas, and

I think that was the only time . . ." She stops to think. "Honestly, I sort of hate to admit this, but I watched them on his social media a lot. So I don't really know her, but I feel like I do. There's this whole Reddit group committed to making fun of Charlie—do you know about that?"

Leo carefully keeps her face neutral. Jake nods solemnly. "It has come up in our interviews, yes, but tell me about it in your words."

"Oh my word, I love it so much. I never comment but I read it all the time. They're so freaking funny! And they love me, which is such an ego boost, though they think I'm more badass than I am. Karlie sent it to me a few years ago and was like, 'Do you know tens of thousands of women think Chaz is a douche and you're amazing?' It was healing for me, honestly. Someday maybe I'll jump on and tell them how much it means to me, but it just felt like it would get public fast and, you know, I'm a teacher. I didn't need that kind of press."

Jake says, "That makes sense. What was it like when you met Kymber?"

"I ran into them at the H-E-B in Blue Oak while I was shopping with my mom. Kymber was fine. She mostly just looked at Charlie with these heart-emoji eyes like he poops gold. That's how she looked at him online too, but I thought maybe it was an act for the camera. It seemed genuine, I don't know. It was wild. But it was also . . . I was never going to be that way. I liked Charlie a lot, loved him even, for a long time. But I would never have fangirled at him like that."

Jake continues. "Did you ever meet Bodhi?"

Tiffani's laugh is full-throated. "Oh, yeah, one time at Charlie's parents' after Easter or something. It was a disaster. She was awful, it was clear his parents hated her, she hated them, and that she especially hated me. She said exactly one thing to me: 'Oh, are you Stephanie? I've heard about you. You're shorter than I pictured.' It pissed me off; she definitely knew my real name. So I said, 'Oh, that's so funny, you're pimplier than I pictured.' She had this one huge zit on her chin. It was petty, but so satisfying. My sister and I laughed about it for weeks afterwards. Seeing them together was really clarifying for me."

"In what way?" Jake asks.

"I saw him for who he really was. For what he really wanted. I felt guilty about the divorce sometimes. It was hard, after I found out he cheated and all of his secrets, to think straight, and I just jumped right to divorce."

Leo clears her throat. "He cheated on you?"

"Oh, yeah, probably the whole time. With other trainers at work, with a nanny he met somewhere, who knows who else. I'm not sure he was ever faithful to me. I went to the doctor and found out I had an STD, and when I confronted Charlie, it took him almost two days to confess, and then it all came out." She blows her nose in the paper towel. "But I still sometimes felt bad, especially when I think back to who he was and how we'd grown up together. How, for a long time, he was really just a hurting boy. But then I found out about everything . . ."

Jake picks up the questioning. "What is 'everything'? The cheating? Or was there something else?"

Tiffani swallows. With no warning, she shakes her head, glances ostentatiously at her watch, and stands up. "I'm so sorry, but I was supposed to open the gym today to let my assistant coach in and I just completely forgot. It's . . . what with all the . . . now that Charlie . . ." She breaks off. "Can we finish this another time?"

Jake rises. Leo digs around in her backpack and finds her sunglasses case. Jake turns off the recorder and slips it into his pocket. She watches him the whole time as she carefully slips her sunglasses case behind her, wedges it slightly between the couch cushions, and stands.

Jake's voice is reassuring. "Of course. I'm sure this must be so hard for you."

"Thank you, it really is." She walks determinedly toward the door.

"When's the next time you'll be in Blue Oak?"

"Um, right after lunch, actually. It's my nephew's birthday and . . ." She pauses. "I don't feel much like celebrating, but he's three and my parents are hosting the family for a pool party and I wouldn't miss it. But I'm not sure I'll be up for talking today. We'll see."

Jake nods. "Thank you so much. We'll be in touch. We're so sorry for your loss."

"Thank you."

"Truly sorry, Tiffani." Leo reaches her hand out to shake Tiffani's, holding it with both hands for a second before they leave.

They wait to talk until they get in the car. At the end of the block, Jake turns to her. "She was certainly in a hurry for us to get out of there at the end."

"Seems like we hit a nerve."

"I think she was hiding something."

"Absolutely." Leo looks out Jake's truck window as they drive down the suburban streets. She squints against the bright sunlight.

45

Three hours later, Karina has driven all over Blue Oak and feels a sense of satisfaction that she's found several pieces of evidence. She can feel a mind at work behind what might appear to be random, disparate things.

The items were left around town roughly near the area of the greenbelt, all within easy access for someone traversing Blue Oak down the walkable path that winds through town.

To follow the pattern, she walks briskly in her Amazon uniform with a box in her hand and sunglasses on her face. But twice, checking to make sure she's not being observed, she reaches into a hole in the box, and pulls out caution tape to mark off two areas.

One is on the corner of Winnifred Eaton Street and James Baldwin Drive, in a lot behind DreamBawd gym. That cordoned section holds the remnants of what looks like a bonfire; one small scrap of white canvas remains behind, with a brown dot of what might be blood on it, though of course Karina can't be sure until the lab tests the material.

The second is on the next street over, Ella Baker Avenue, close to where it crosses Phillis Wheatley Street. Near some industrial dumpsters behind a tasteful twelve-unit set of condos, she finds a wadded-up blue tarp with a distinct, coppery odor. She leaves the tarp where she finds it, puts up the caution tape, then sits in her Amazon truck with the air-conditioning on and sends three emails from her phone.

She watches over the spot where the tarp is marked until a sheriff's department car pulls up and Esquivel and Williams get out. As soon as she sees them, she casually puts the van in gear and drives away. She hopes these two finds are enough to keep the sheriff's deputies and DPS officers in town occupied while she checks out Chaz's house.

Beneath her calm professional demeanor, she's increasingly worried for her daughter. Leo has been in South Austin, where Karina's colleague—monitoring the Blue Oak SD communication—says she's working with Jake on an interview. Neither Karina nor the colleague can work out why Leo is of special help to the case; therefore, in Karina's opinion, it has to be because Jake Nguyen is interested in her daughter.

If that crush is stronger than his common sense, especially after what Karina told him, Jake's not as competent as he presents himself to be. As she drives away, Karina calls two unlisted numbers that only a few people have.

• • • • •

Esquivel lifts her phone to her ear and says, "Hey, boss, you were right. I'm not sure what's going on right now . . . And I'm assuming you're going to tell me why an email from . . . Well, yes, they were marked just like it . . . Yes, I'm sending DPS to the other location now. Yes, sir. No, sir. I'm as confused as you are, but we'll check it out." She looks down at the lumpy blue mass in the center of a small circle of caution tape. "While I have you, did you see that email from Johnson? No need to look at it now, just tell Leo it looks like that photo of the garage door was a dead end. But this one might not be—Williams, put on gloves!—I have to go, sir."

She hangs up the phone and makes Williams step back before he ruins the pristinely marked crime scene. Whoever found and marked this evidence moved their case forward tremendously. They still don't know where the murder was committed—even though they're certain, with forensic evidence, that it didn't happen in the morning of July 6 at Kay's real estate house, as the murderer would like them to assume. Esquivel spent several hours the day before, after dusting for fingerprints and gathering evidence at the Zora Neale Hurston Street house, over at Chaz's. But there was nothing they could find; the fingerprints all belonged to Chaz and Kymber and a few other people, including the cleaning lady Kymber said had been there on July 3, which was why the house was sparkingly, bleachedly clean. Esquivel had gotten the fingerprints and statement of the house cleaner already; she had, indeed, cleaned the house the day before the holiday.

But as Esquivel bags the blue tarp covered in dried blood—before driving to a fire circle guarded by the DPS officers bagging a corner of burnt-up painters' cloth that matches what Chaz was wrapped in—she wonders: Was the blood on the tarp and cloths the reason there was no blood at Chaz's house?

Were they seeking a meticulous killer who murdered Chaz in his own home, or possibly at another location, using tarps and cloths to contain the fluids? Or had they just not yet found the spot where Chaz Nickolson took his final breath?

46

Sheriff Quackenbush is on his third cup of coffee of the day. The younger officers had complained about the coffee in the break room relentlessly, despite the fact that Folgers had been good enough for generations of deputies. And as he sips that third cup appreciatively, he admits to himself: he'd made a good call in finally switching the department coffee to Dunkin's.

He's just finished a call with Esquivel, who'd logged the bloody glove from outside Chaz's gym and wrapped an interview with Grant Ford. Quackenbush knows the glove doesn't implicate Grant; men that run gyms don't use flowery gloves. Kay probably stashed it there hoping to make Grant look guilty. But he'll let his young bucks chase the lead down. They need the practice.

Nguyen checked in earlier this morning and told him he'd hired some outside consultants for the electronic business. They'd brought on Esquivel in part because of her abilities with electronics; he'd tried to get her to take over all his computer mail when she started, but she threatened to quit on the spot—said she wasn't a secretary, as if that wasn't a great way for a young lady to spend her working hours. Honestly.

Quackenbush suggested Esquivel help Nguyen instead of this other consultant, but apparently Esquivel was needed to help the *other* outside consultant. (How many consultants did one department need? Back in the day, there was no crime in Blue Oak and only one sheriff and one deputy.) That second consultant was already digging through what Nguyen called a "sub," along with some financial information, and they needed someone else with knowledge of the "influencer world" to help with other aspects of the investigation into Chaz's life.

Quackenbush takes another sip of coffee: Is there a submarine involved somehow? Was Chaz or someone else working as a substitute teacher? He was not one to look the fool, so he replied gruffly, "Absolutely, digging into subs is an excellent idea. No stone unturned. Have Esquivel print up everything for the files. The prosecutor is going to want the case against Kay Schneider to be airtight when it goes to court." Nguyen had been silent for a moment—no doubt overcome with gratitude over his effusive words—and then said goodbye.

Quackenbush sits back and puts his feet up on his desk. Being a good mentor and empowering young deputies is a critical part of a sheriff's job, one he takes very seriously. Someday, they'll be ready to solve cases on their own—after years of learning from his expertise, of course.

When his cell phone rings, he picks it up without looking at who is calling.

"Quackenbush here."

"Sheriff, this is Mike Garner."

"Garner, how are you, man?"

"Can't complain, Sheriff. How are you?" They make small talk for a minute. Quackenbush has known the owner of Garner Ranch, a Blue Oak institution, since the family bought the property in the 1960s. Mike and his wife, Mikayla, are passing it down to their son, Mack, now. Quackenbush asks after Mike's kids and his grandson, and the pride in Mike's hoarse voice is evident.

Mike clears his throat. "Forgive me, Sheriff, my voice has been going a lot lately. But I'm calling for a reason. I was wondering if you'd mind coming out here."

Quackenbush is already pulling his feet off his desk and taking one final sip of coffee. "To the ranch?"

"Yes, I'm here out by the barn with Mack. One of the kitchen staff found something I thought you should see."

"Sounds good. I'll be there in five."

Quackenbush grabs his keys, hops in his old Silverado, and, two minutes later, parks next to the restaurant. He walks around the beautiful path lined with lavender and rosemary, past the white archway leading to the restaurant's patio seating—empty in the direct sunlight—to the back of the main building. The original ranch buildings had been torn down and, in their place, the Garners had built a beautiful barn, the natural wood gleaming, along with some other buildings. Near the back of the barn, Mack Garner stands with his dad, both men sporting cowboy hats and grimy working Wranglers, next to a couple of men dressed in khaki pants and black polos with the Garners' logo.

Mike waves, hand trembling. "Sheriff . . ." His voice breaks.

Mack glances at his dad, then calls out. "Hey, Sheriff. Thanks for coming."

Quackenbush ambles over. He has on the polarized sunglasses his wife got him for Father's Day a few years ago to help him fish better. When he gets to the shaded part behind the barn, he slides them onto his head and holds his hand out to shake with Mike and Mack Garner. "What can I do for you folks today?"

Mack looks to Mike, who nods. Mack takes a step forward. "Sheriff, you know Enrique, our restaurant manager."

"Good to see you again, Enrique. Hope you're keeping my spot warm later—I'll be bringing the missus for my steak."

"Of course, Sheriff. Always good to see you."

Quackenbush nods and turns to the last man, who is younger than the others. Mack continues. "Logan here is one of our bussers. This morning he was taking the trash out of the restaurant when he noticed this large green trash bag open by the barn door. He took the bag . . ."

Quackenbush holds up his hand. "I'd like to hear it from Logan. Logan, how're you doin' today?"

Logan nods, obviously nervous. "Okay, sir."

"Glad to hear it, son. Tell me what happened, if you don't mind."

Logan looks up at Enrique, who smiles kindly at him to go on. Logan wipes the sweat off his forehead with the back of his arm. "Um, well . . . sir. Today I was taking out the trash like I do every morning shift. And I saw this bag."

"It looks like a trash bag to me. What made you think it was unusual?"

Logan glances at Enrique again, who nods for him to continue. "Um, it's a different color than the bags we use here? We use those big black ones and this was green."

"Good eye. Where was the bag?"

Logan warms under the sheriff's praise. "Over by the front of the barn. It was by itself. By the barn door."

"Where by the barn door?"

"Over in the middle."

"Show me, would ya?"

Logan nods once and points to the middle of the dirt path leading into the barn. "It was sitting right here."

"And it was open, you said?" Quackenbush squats in the grass at the edge of the walkway, squinting at the ground.

"Yeah, the sides were kind of folded down. I left it the way it was."

Logan gestures to the back of the barn and leads Quackenbush to the trash area. There are twelve large trash cans lining the back of the barn—four green, four blue, and four brown—and, several hundred feet away, a big green dumpster at the edge of the driveway that is behind the barn. Besides the brown cans, six large, very full black trash sacks lean against the back of the barn. And then, by itself, the smaller green trash sack, the top folded down carefully with a rip in the side. Just visible out of the torn side is the bloodied finger of a gray work glove.

"Who moved this sack?"

Logan raises his hand. "Me, sir. My first thought was that a guest left it by the barn because they didn't want to take it to the dumpster. I know Enrique likes the barn view to be nice, so I took it around back. When I moved it, it came apart slightly. I saw all this bloody . . . stuff." He gestures at the sack. "So I told Enrique."

Enrique speaks up. "And I called Mack as soon as I saw what it was, and we haven't touched it since."

The sheriff scratches his head. "Why are there so many sacks out here?"

Enrique responds. "The city guys pick up the dumpster tomorrow, and they won't get us more brown cans, so we often leave kitchen trash here till the end of the day. It's already overflowing for the week, like it usually is."

"Do you use these kinds of trash sacks around here?"

Enrique shakes his head. "No, we buy everything in bulk and only use the industrial black ones. The hotel staff use small white ones for the guest spaces and the black ones for their cleaning."

"Wouldn't a trash sack in the middle of the path get in the way of the horses going out of the barn?"

Mack speaks. "No, the ranch hands use the back entrance. The front is really just for show; the only people who use it are the guests when they wander in."

"How long was the sack out here?"

The men look at each other, and Mack answers. "I'm not sure. It could have been all day. The ground is sort of hidden from the main part of the house by those bushes in the front, and if you look out of the restaurant windows or off the back patio, it might not have been noticeable."

"Did anyone else touch it?"

Enrique raises his hand. "I kind of poked around in there, and once we confirmed it was a glove and towels soaked in blood, we called you. I wore my plastic gloves, though." He pulls a pair of transparent food-worker gloves out of his back pocket.

Logan holds up a pair of crumpled gloves from his apron. "Me too."

"So none of you touched this bag without gloves?"

"No." Mack's voice is definitive.

"Good." Quackenbush moves forward, squatting by the bag. He pulls a pen out of his breast pocket. He gently pokes at the bag and his face briefly breaks into a grin. It looks like the fuchsia flowered glove is a perfect match for the one found at Grant's shed.

"Well done, son." He turns to Logan. "Your instincts were spot-on." He almost tells them that this is the clue that will break the case against Kay Schneider wide open, but he stops himself—no need to put the cart before the horse. At this rate, though, he'll be heading home soon. Maybe he'll bring the missus to the Garner Restaurant early this week, as a little reward for solving the case so quickly. "We'll rope off the barn and surrounding land for now."

Mack groans. "Do we have to?"

Mike gives him a stern look. "The sheriff said this might have something to do with the death of that young man. Of course we have to."

Mack whispers tensely: "His death already put a damper on numbers. This morning a few guests heard about the murder and checked out early."

Mike shoots him a warning look, then turns. "Sheriff, let us know what you need."

"Fine, thank you, Garner. I'll get my yellow tape out of the car and call in Williams. Could y'all get us samples of the trash sacks, hotel towels, and work gloves used around here?"

Enrique nods. "Absolutely. I'll get on that right now. But when you say samples of the gloves, what do you mean? Because all of us in the kitchen use these non-latex ones, and we throw them away after each shift."

"What about the ranch hands? I'm thinking more like work gloves."

Mack shrugs. "Everyone has their own. But I can ask them to show you."

"That would be great. Mike, can you watch this sack and the front of the barn while I get my yella tape?"

Mike nods and crosses his arms, studiously ignoring his son, who is clearly unhappy about the caution tape.

Quackenbush understands the young man, he really does. Though Mack Garner was never as good as his cousin, he was a very solid football player who came back to Blue Oak to help out his folks after college. He's clearly feeling the death of his cousin's best friend very deeply. First The Boss, now The Bear. What is Blue Oak coming to?

Quackenbush stops in the middle of the path, staring out over the property. Near the main house, which holds the bed-and-breakfast and restaurant, the lawn has been well tended, but closer to the barn, where the horses graze, the grass is sun scorched. Quackenbush detours suddenly to pluck a long stalk of dead grass—it helps a man think better. He chews it thoughtfully as he considers: Is someone gunning for the members of the football team? Quackenbush pulls his phone out and sends a long text to young Nguyen and Esquivel, shifting the stalk from side to side in his mouth. He wants them following up some leads. His gut is telling him that, while he doesn't know how she did this, Kay Schneider is the mastermind behind this whole thing.

Hell, she all but admitted it when he brought her in. Hadn't she said she'd spent the morning gardening? Those gloves are clearly a woman's. He loves it when the evidence is so dadgum clear. Obviously, Kay killed Chaz to remove him as business competition once and for all.

But she's not getting away with it. Not on Quackenbush's watch. The stalk of grass quivers as he clenches his jaw in determination.

47

Back in the Blue Oak County Courthouse, Kay Schneider looks up from her white take-out box. "I didn't believe you that the eggs benny would be as good to go, but you were right."

"Of course I was right." Phil is wiping his take-out box clean.

"Man, you really were." Deputy Williams has already finished his food and is now throwing everything away. Sheriff Quackenbush radioed him just a minute ago to come to the Garner Ranch, and he will be going over there, but at his pace, not Quackenbush's.

As soon as Quackenbush left for the Garners', Williams let Phil come visit Kay again. He'd worked up quite an appetite gathering evidence with Esquivel, who is so persnickety about crime scenes. When the Schneiders asked if he'd mind picking up their order from the Wild Brunch, and told him they'd order something for him, he jumped at the chance.

He gets tired of everyone only remembering he's around when they need something. He appreciates the kind gesture by the Schneiders, who clearly noticed that he was really hungry. They suggested he order the Wild Brunch specialty: Benedict Cassidy and the Sunnydance Kid with Doc Hollandaise sauce.

Kay watches him in amusement. "Young man, I'm so glad you enjoyed that. It's one of our favorite pick-me-ups when we're feeling blue, and it's extra fun to have brunch in the afternoon. Phil, darlin', would you mind . . . ?" She wipes her mouth and hands the wadded-up napkin through the bars.

"Of course. Are you still hungry?"

"Oh, no, that was perfect. Though, is there any more coffee? I'll take a teensy bit more."

"Absolutely." Phil takes her paper cup and fills it halfway from the to-go carton that the young deputy brought with their breakfast. He adds a packet of sugar and one small creamer, stirs it well, and hands it back.

"Thank you, darlin'. Have you finished the crossword puzzle yet?"

"Not yet. Want to take a crack at it?"

"I do, thank you. I might knit later, but my arms are feeling a bit sore after sleeping on that inflatable mattress last night."

"I wish I could give you a massage." Phil lays on the cringe factor, hoping to get a smile from his wife; it works.

Williams blushes slightly, gathering all his things, preparing to leave. "Um, I'm supposed to make sure you're not here when I go, Mr. Schneider."

"Oh, son, what do you think I'm going to do? I'm a retired accountant in his sixties. We're going to do the crossword puzzle together, not dig Kay an escape route with plastic spoons."

"Um."

"Honestly, Deputy Williams." Kay's voice is winsome. "I'm about to take a nap. We'll just finish our crossword and then Phil will be on his way, I promise."

"Well, okay. Just be gone before Quackenbush comes back."

"Will do." Phil pulls the book of crossword puzzles out, lifts his reading glasses off his head, and takes Kay's out of her purse and hands them to her. They sit on the floor so they can share their book through the bars.

"Y'all be good." Williams waves at them. They look like his grandparents. He feels an unexpected surge of anger. Quackenbush has definitely lost it this time.

"Always," Kay chirps.

Williams leaves the room, and instantly, Kay pulls out a small packet of tools from the back of the crossword puzzle book and discreetly slips them into the top of her bra.

"That boy's corn bread ain't done in the middle," Kay says.

"You remember how to use those?" Phil's face is concerned, so Kay pats his hand through the bars.

"Of course. Karina's made me practice thousands of times over the years. What's the point of having a clandestine best friend if you don't learn a few tricks of the trade? Speaking of, what did she say?"

Phil pulls out his phone. "She says she's making real progress and to stay tuned."

"Of course she is."

"She said not to use that kit for now but keep it in case you need it."

"I'm not going to break out of jail. But I admit, it does make me feel better to have it. Just in case."

Phil's phone pings with a text. "Oh, good, Beth's bringing up reinforcements."

"Now, Phil"—Kay pulls her glasses off—"I told both of you that she doesn't need to come."

"Please, Kay. Beth isn't going to just stay in Dallas while you're sitting in jail. We raised her better than that."

"Well, I don't like to make a fuss."

"No one is making a fuss."

Kay smiles softly. "We have good girls."

They spend the next few minutes solving the crossword puzzle. Kay correctly fills in the last word she suspects Phil left for her on purpose: *devotion*.

48

At a stoplight just outside Blue Oak, Jake reads some texts on his phone, including a long one from Quackenbush. Two other texts make him shake his head in frustration.

Leo checks her own texts—just Karina, who has *got* to learn that Leo is not a teenager and therefore will not be responding to her mother's insistent texts and voicemails that she rest. Leo takes advantage of Jake's distraction to rummage around in her backpack.

"Oh, shoot." She lifts the bag off the floor of the truck, bending to look under the seat. "Dang it."

"What?" Jake glances over. "Everything okay?"

"My sunglasses." Leo paws through the backpack again.

"Did you lose them?"

"No, I had them on our way up, but just realized I hadn't put them on . . ." She opens the front part of the backpack, then pats her head, making a show of looking everywhere. She sighs resignedly. "I think I must have left them at Tiffani's."

Jake shoots her a side-eye. "Are you sure?"

She returns his gaze innocently. "No, I'm not sure. But it seems likely. They're prescription and I don't have vision insurance till my health insurance kicks in in a few weeks at

Schneider Realty. Would you mind calling her? Or giving me her phone number?"

"I'll call her." Jake's tone is wry. He reaches for his phone on the holder attached to his windshield, scrolls back through his calls, and presses a number. He leaves it on speaker while the light changes and they drive. It rings twice, and then Tiffani answers.

"Hello?"

"Hi, Tiffani? This is Detective Nguyen."

"Hi, Detective. Do you have more questions?"

"I do, but not for now. I know you're at the gym right now, but when you get home . . ." He hears Tiger bark. "Sorry, aren't you at the gym?"

"Uh, I went to the gym but just for a second to let . . . My assistant coach needed to get in? Just got back home. For a second."

Leo leans over the console. "Hi, Tiffani. This is Leo. Did I leave my sunglasses there? They're in a jade-green case."

"Let me look." They hear her footsteps. "Yep! Found them. They were on the couch."

"Thank you, whew! They're prescription and I don't want to get a migraine."

"Oh, I get migraines too; say no more. I'll bring them with me to the pool party; I'm leaving in thirty minutes. Do you want me to text you? What's the best way to hand them off?"

"I'll have Jake give me your phone number if that's okay, and we can text?"

"Totally! Bringing them soon!"

"Thank you, Tiffani! You're the best!"

"No problem!"

A visibly irritated Jake taps the red button to end the call. "Did you know she gets migraines?"

"Everyone who follows her knows that."

"Do you get migraines?" Jake glances over at her.

Leo gives him a neither-confirm-nor-deny smile.

"So, you what, planted your sunglasses and gave an excuse you knew she wouldn't wait on just to see her again?"

"I can't help that they fell out of my bag."

Jake is silent for the last few minutes into town, but Leo swears she can hear him humming softly under his breath, and she's pretty sure the song is "Witchy Woman."

49

Esquivel calls Macy from the car on the way back to the sheriff's station. "Hey, Mace."

"Hi, how's your day going?"

"You would not believe what we're finding." Esquivel catches her up on the trail of evidence she and Williams just finished bagging with the DPS officers, and the interview with Grant. "That tip about Sofia was perfect."

"We make such a good team."

"I know. Who knew solving murders was so good for relationships?" Esquivel chuckles. "Listen, I wanted to run something past you. Quackenbush just texted; it sounds like they found the match to the glove that was at Grant's over at Garner Ranch."

"Wait, what?" Esquivel hears the sound of a can popping open—she doubts even Macy knows how many Red Bulls she's had today. "Let me review this. You found one glove at DreamBawd, and another one at the Garners'? Do you have a picture?"

"I'll get one . . . hold on." Esquivel's voice fades while she texts Williams and gets him to send her photos of the new evidence and its location.

"It sounds like you're finding stuff all over town. Want a map?"

"Great idea." Esquivel is parking. "I'll send you photos and addresses where I found them."

"While you're at it, there is a Facebook post you might want to check out; we know that garage door and the guy driving around that Leo sent us were duds, but I found one I think might be interesting."

"Okay, text me the info and then add everything to the map just to see if we can find a pattern."

"I'll have to pull out the red string so we can make it accurate." Macy's mouth is half full of her perennial favorite, Lucky Charms cereal.

"I wish I thought you were joking right now."

"Does Quackenbush think Kay somehow planted evidence all over town despite the fact that he put her in jail?"

Esquivel scoffs. "I'll read you a short part of his text from not long ago. And I quote: 'Shoot for the moon, team; even if you miss, you'll land among the stars! A murder investigation is about stamina and focus and determination. We got new evidence pointing us toward Kay Schneider. I don't know how she's running this con, but clearly she is. I want all hands on deck getting this wrapped up, hopefully in the next couple of hours.' He then goes on for . . . five more paragraphs."

"Wait, I'm sorry, 'shoot for the moon'?" Macy cackles.

"You can land among the stars, Mace. Clearly you don't get it."

"Are the stars . . . the other suspects? Other murders? What stars are we looking at in this metaphor?"

"Macy, you're thinking way too hard about this. We don't treat these sayings as accurate depictions of life, we are just *inspired*."

"Mmmmm. Sorry, I get it now."

"Do you? Are *you* among the stars? Somehow, I doubt it."

"I might not be shooting far enough."

Esquivel laughs quietly. "Okay, we need to focus. I called you to ask about Melody Garner."

"What are you thinking?"

"That I, unlike Quackenbush, do not think that Kay is running some kind of crime ring from the jail, but I *am* curious about the Garners."

"Would Melody have planted evidence on her family's property?"

"I doubt it, but maybe she was interrupted as she was taking it somewhere? Or maybe she and her brother are working together? I don't know. I have questions. Has she said anything as Nanci Drew on Reddit?"

"Mostly responding to comments after she shared the post."

"Should we shake things up even more?"

"You know how I feel about chaos." Macy's mouth is full of cereal again.

"I think it's time I pick Melody Garner-Aziz up to ask some questions. And if she gets back on the sub, call me immediately."

"We come at her from both sides?"

"Exactly."

"Gah, you're hot when you're scheming."

"Love you."

"Love you more."

50

Blue Oak County Sheriff's Department
1904 Phillis Wheatley St.
Blue Oak, TX 00130
(555) 512-6523

July 6

MEMO TO FILE

FORENSIC EXAMINER PROCESSING NOTES: Lt. Laura Esquivel (4132)

FORENSIC CASE NUMBER: 95613

EVIDENCE DESCRIPTION: Screenshot taken at 10:39 a.m., wiki page from the Chaz Nickolson Snark subreddit

> **Kymber Owens:** We wish we knew more about the tornado that is Kymber, but despite all of our best efforts (and this sub can RESEARCH), we know very little about Kymber's past before she came into Chaz's life. Her middle name is Dawn, or at least, that's what she wants us to think, because her social media handle is Kymber Dawn. She's somewhere around the age of 30, but her exact age is anyone's guess. She could be 75 for all we know, and

just very “well preserved” for her age (they still use formaldehyde in some beauty products, y’all—check your labels).

She clearly does not have family, or they’re estranged, because she never mentions them and no evidence of them can be found. We suspect that “Kymber Dawn” is not her original name, and there have been a number of rabbit-hole threads with theories about who she used to be, but so far, they’re all just theories. Kymber’s current hair color, evident nose job, filler, and capped teeth make any kind of identification speculation at best.

She’s a mystery to us. But what’s not a mystery: the amount of chaos she brings into Chaz’s world.

51

Karina parks the Amazon truck two streets over from Chaz's house near an abandoned lot beside the park. Leo is heading back into Blue Oak, according to the icon on Find My, so she's as safe as she can be for a few minutes—the sooner Karina wraps up the case, the sooner she can formulate a plan to get her daughter out of town.

She trades her Amazon hat for a trendy black baseball cap with a white logo from Lamppost Coffee. She hopes anyone who sees her will assume it's not her because Karina would normally never be caught dead in a cap.

She thinks about approaching the house from the back but decides at the last minute that, if for any reason she's wrong, it would be easier to pretend to be someone at the wrong house than to get caught trying to break in like a cat burglar.

She walks to the front of the large tan-and-gray ranch-style house overlooking the park, a small investigative kit tucked into a discreet black backpack. It's a beautiful house, with picture windows dominating the front. The landscaping is tasteful and elegant. The front door is wooden with a brass handle. She knocks on the door once, perfunctorily, and is about to pull out her lock-picking kit when she hears something unexpected.

A voice inside yells, "Coming!"

A minute later, Kymber is unlocking the door. She is wearing a pink-leggings-and-sports-bra ensemble, with white tennis shoes and rose-gold Beats headphones around her neck.

"Are you a reporter?"

"Of course not," Karina says, thinking fast.

"Are you from the studio?" Kymber squeals delightedly.

Karina's training takes over before she even has time to think. "Yes." Her nod is curt.

"I can't believe I didn't . . . of course, you must be Paula. Henry said you'd be in touch, but I thought he meant by phone. Please, come in." Kymber opens the door and Karina-as-Paula nods a thank-you. She has already decided Paula will be a reticent person of few words, but she has little else to go on. What studio is she supposed to be from? Dance studio? Workout studio?

"When I talked to the producers the other day, they said you were still making decisions." Kymber talks while leading Karina into the living room and sinking dramatically onto a couch. Karina follows suit, sitting pertly at the other end. "But then . . . but then . . ." Kymber tears up and waves her hands dramatically in the air. "I assume y'all heard about my Chaz?"

Karina nods her head sympathetically. "That's why I'm here. Henry wanted me to check in on you."

"Oh, that is so *nice.*" Kymber starts sobbing now. She bends over, the sobs pouring out of her loudly. Karina looks around the room and grabs a tissue from a side table, holding it out when Kymber looks up. "I just . . . My heart is *broken*, you know? He was the captain of my destiny. I mean, I'm a strong woman, so I'm my own captain, but we were . . . navigating together. As we manifested. Our shared destiny."

Karina hates this woman already. "Oh, Henry knows. He really gets it."

"I knew he and I were on the same wavelength when we talked last week."

"Totally." Karina clears her throat. "Henry felt the resonance."

"I told Chaz, I said, 'Babe, Henry is our kind of people. And he knows that we're just right for something big. It's time. The time is *ripe.*' "

"Absolutely ripe."

"Which is why . . . excuse me." Kymber starts sobbing again. "It's so sad, I can hardly bear it."

Karina tuts sympathetically, but her eyes roam the room rapidly while Kymber is sobbing. She walked into the living room through an arched entrance, and the wall surrounding that entrance is filled with mirrors, repeatedly reflecting Karina and Kymber and, behind them, the far wall's floor-to-ceiling windows. To the right of the entrance, the living room is open to a large, sterile kitchen. To the left of the entrance, a wall of shelves is lined with books, though their spines are turned inside and the pages are out. Karina almost smiles—Leo would have something to say about those books. There are a few other vases, plus—she counts—four pictures of Chaz by himself. One photo of him and Kymber is stuck to the outside of a frame like someone added it. Other than the photos, the room is catalog ready and completely impersonal.

Kymber looks up and Karina whips her head back, nodding like a bobble-head. "I just feel the weight of his *absence*, you know?"

"Absence, yes. Henry understands that too."

"Henry told me that he was hoping for a big bump in numbers from an event and, well . . ." A fresh outbreak of sobbing. Karina waits. "We were . . . He had . . . Chaz asked me to marry him two nights ago! While the fireworks went off around us! Out here in the back . . . yard . . ." She hiccups and sobs some more.

"Oh, you were his fiancée?"

"I know. He was going to take me to Tiffany's this weekend. Like in *Sweet Home Alabama*. He wanted me to pick out any ring I wanted."

"Oh, I'm so sorry." Karina suppresses a sigh—the lie is not even a good one. Austin doesn't have a Tiffany's. If Chaz did say that, he'd probably meant Jared's.

"I hope . . . Do you think Henry . . . Will Henry understand?"

"Understand that you need some time to grieve?"

"Oh, no, my work is everything and I want to keep busy. Do you think Henry is still considering me for the show?"

"Why do you think I'm here?" Karina bluffs.

Kymber squeals. Karina's ears ring. "I knew it!"

"Sure did!" Karina finger-guns at Kymber.

"When I messaged him the other day, I told him a hot grieving widow would play even better for reality TV audiences than a new bride."

"Henry got your message. And agrees!" Karina is nodding.

"Does this mean I'm in?"

"There are still some details to work out, but it's looking likely."

"I can't believe I get to be on *Real Housewives of Austin*!"

Ah, Karina thinks. This is critical information. "It's the chance of a lifetime."

"What do you need from me?"

"Henry just wanted to confirm that this is something you're still interested in."

"Oh, I *am*." Kymber beams.

"Considering the loss you just endured."

Kymber's face falls into somber lines. "It'll give me purpose, Paula. Something to look forward to. After . . . after the funeral." She wails, grabbing for Karina's hands.

Karina pats Kymber's outstretched hands once and decides that Paula is not touchy-feely.

"I'm so glad to hear it. And Henry says he's so sorry for your loss. We'll be in touch soon."

Tears glisten becomingly on Kymber's face as she raises it to the light. "Do you . . . do you think we should start shooting before the funeral? I'd love for the storyline to honor my dear Chaz."

"I'm sorry?" Decades into her career, and Karina's instincts briefly fail her.

"Well, Henry said if I did get the role, the cameras would

come almost immediately. And I thought, well, it would be such a good way to document the *love* Chaz and I shared."

"Oh, I mean . . . uh, maybe. Let me ask Henry?"

"Of course. I'm here and ready whenever you want to start."

"Thank you. I'll pass it along."

"Thank you, Paula. I manifested this future for myself, and you've proven yourself to be a beacon from a karmic cosmos that cares about my happiness."

Karina opens her mouth and closes it. "I'll see myself out."

Kymber nods soberly, leaning her head onto the couch as if she can't bear the weight of it, limbs in elegant lines around her.

Karina walks out without looking back and closes the door behind her. When she's sure no one is watching her, she clambers in the back of her Amazon truck, slips her earbud in, and calls her colleague.

"Hey, could you look into a Kymber Dawn Owens?" She listens briefly. "Yes, top priority. I just talked to her. She's either a coldhearted murderer, or a wildly shallow narcissist who is using her boyfriend's death for her own personal gain." She turns the truck back toward the storage facility. "Right now, the jury is out."

52

As Jake pulls up outside the pool house, Leo fires off a quick text to Tiffani. Jake stops by the curb and pulls his sunglasses off. "What's your plan now?"

"Well, I'm at least going to change out of these clothes that I've somehow already sweated through."

"Welcome to Texas."

"Do you need anything else?" Leo puts her phone down to glance at Jake. She feels rumpled and sweaty and he still looks crisp and professional; in the shadowed cab, his face is all sharp angles, his dark hair falling slightly into his eyes.

"I might, I'm not sure yet. I'm heading back to the sheriff's station to check in with Esquivel and Johnson."

"I'll probably let the dog out and check on Kay and make sure my mom's okay. I've been getting texts and messages all morning." For a reason she does not want to examine, Leo does not mention that some of those texts have been from Mack.

"Is everything all right?"

"She seems frantic about my need to rest, like I'm Beth March with scarlet fever and not just sort of tired from a long drive."

"Beth March?" Jake pulls his sunglasses off.

Leo waves her hand impatiently, not wanting to explain. "At least she has no idea I'm with you. She'd pee her pants."

Jake bites his bottom lip for a second, then switches subjects. "Please wait for me before you go see Tiffani. This is a tricky case. I appreciate your help, but we've brought you on as a consultant, not to investigate anything on your own."

Leo squints slightly, annoyed at his tone. "I'm just grabbing my sunglasses."

"That wasn't a yes." His voice is firm.

"Do you want me to salute and say 'yes, sir'?" She is affronted.

"No, Leo. I have enough pressure right now without worrying that you're somehow going to interfere with my investigation when I've already told you how complicated it is just trying to hold Quackenbush off. I want to work *with* you, not against you."

Leo's expression is wary. "I'm not trying to make your life more difficult."

"I'm not sure you're making it easier. But you're definitely making it more interesting." He taps the steering wheel twice while he watches her, as if debating whether he should say more. Then he grips it. "I have to go. I'll call you to check in or if I think of something else we could use help with."

"Okay. Thanks, Jake, for believing in Kay."

"Well, it's not for you." For one instant, the intense look he gives her belies his words, but it's gone so fast she thinks she imagined it. "It's just the right thing to do."

Inside the pool house, she takes a minute to change into some jean shorts—her third outfit of the day. She has got to figure this job situation out soon and get away from Blue Oak; she can't live in a place where she goes through clothes at this rate. She lets Derrida into the backyard and dips her feet briefly into the pool. While Derrida sniffs around the yard, she checks her messages—nine new ones.

The first three are from her mother, which she ignores completely. The next three are from Emily:

EMILY: What's the best way to say I'm sorry for being a complete jerk earlier?

EMILY: I'm just a girl, standing in front of another girl (who she loves as a platonic best friend, in case her wife reads this message), asking her to forgive that... first girl for being a complete ass. A daft prick, if you will.

EMILY: Did that work? Will you forgive me? I'm so sorry, Lee. I feel awful.

The next two are from Mack.

MACK GARNER: Hey. How's your day going?

MACK GARNER: Been thinking about you. You looked good out there today, Holloway.

She glances up. It sure seems like he's interested in her, but is his flirtiness directed at her, or merely Mack's charming way of being in the world? This feels like more than she can parse out right now.

The most recent text is from Tiffani.

TIFFANI MILLER: Hey, Leo. I'm headed to my parents' house right now; I have your glasses. Feel free to grab them whenever, and I'll save you some cake! We're at 1408 Rachel Carson Ave.

Leo gives Tiffani's text a heart, then texts Emily back:

You are often a daft prick, but I am too. Of course I forgive you. This week is impossible for all of us. How are you? How's Kay? How's my mom?

Emily texts back almost immediately that Beth and her lawyer friends have descended on the jail "like a biblical swarm of locusts" and that Quackenbush has "almost been reduced to tears" by the number of appeals that either have been filed or the lawyers are threatening to file. But Quackenbush seems determined to keep Kay in jail the full forty-eight hours. Kay seems in good spirits, though she looks tired and her hair is slightly greasy. Leo almost gasps when she reads that; she's only seen Kay two or three times in her life without her "face," as she calls her makeup—and then, only in the middle of the night. Greasy hair does not suit the Queen of Blue Oak.

As for Karina, she's been gone for most of the day, probably at the salon, Emily says. When Leo tries to call her mother, it goes straight to voicemail. She decides she'll eat a late lunch and then run by Tiffani's before she heads downtown to check on everyone.

She'll be fast. No need to call Jake. He's busy enough. What Jake doesn't know won't hurt him.

• • • • •

Tiffani's parents' house sits against the greenbelt in Blue Oak, just a few blocks east of DreamBawd, and four blocks south of the Schneiders'. All Leo has to do is cut across the tree-lined trail, and even though it's currently 102 degrees and climbing, she decides to walk.

Coming from the back, she can't see the house numbers, but it's clear which house is Tiffani's parents'—the sound of the loud pool party and the large Spider-Man piñata give it away. Their yard is fenced, but their neighbor's is not, so Leo walks beside their fence to get to the gate in the front.

She plans on coming in the gate from the road like a normal person. But then she stops. Over the din of the children and the music, she hears someone ask: "Is Jake Nguyen as hot as I remember?"

She hears a laugh and a muffled response that she thinks is Tiffani's voice. She looks around, but everyone at the party is on the other side of the tall privacy fence and no one else is out in this heat. She creeps under a crepe myrtle large enough to hide her from the street, and leans in next to a hole in the fence.

"That must have been so stressful for you."

"It really was." That's Tiffani. The other voice sounds similar, but slightly higher—probably Tiffani's sister, Karlie?

"What did they ask you?"

"Just some basic stuff. About our marriage, our past. If I met Bodhi and Kymber. If Charlie and I still talk. Talked."

"What did you say?"

"The truth: that I left because he cheated, that I met both women briefly, that Charlie and I ran into each other occasionally but that I've moved on and am happy."

"Could you tell if they were, like, suspicious of you or something?"

Tiffani laughs wryly. "You watch too much TV. I don't think so. Even if they were, I was at the cheer competition that whole day. And then I came to your house, remember?"

"We were watching fireworks in the park."

"Where in the park?"

"I don't know, by the lake on a picnic blanket."

"Did you stay the whole time?"

"No, just for the first few minutes. The kids started melting down."

"Which is why Auntie Tiff and Tiger came to help out and drink a glass of wine before bedtime. And then we spent the night because we'd had a couple glasses. But then I had to leave for early-morning practice the next day. Remember?"

Karlie pauses. "Is there something I should know?"

Tiffani sighs. "No, really, there's not. I'm just . . . probably being paranoid. It was hard enough being married to Chaz, and I don't know yet how he died, but I know the ex-wife is probably a pretty good person to look at suspiciously."

"Super-glad you were at my house, then."

Leo hears the chink of glass, like bottles clinking together in a toast.

"Did you tell them the rest of it?"

"About Charlie's past?"

"Yeah." Their voices get low, as if they're huddling together.

Leo gets closer to the fence. As she moves, her shoulder bumps the crepe myrtle, and the branches sway above the fence. She doesn't breathe, but no one seems to notice. She hears splashing and laughing by the pool.

"I didn't." Tiffani pauses. "Do you think I should?"

"You know how I feel about it." Karlie is harsh.

"I know. I don't know why I protect him still."

"He's literally dead, Tiff."

"Yeah." Tiffani sounds teary.

"And he broke your heart."

"He did."

"And yet you've kept his secret for all these years."

"I know." Leo realizes that she has not really viewed Tiffani with suspicion, first because she was invested in the idea of our Gal Pal Tiff, and then because she liked the real, grounded version of Tiffani more. But meeting the real Tiffani had also shown Leo that her read on Chaz's ex was not accurate. Now, listening to her confess to her sister that she has covered up a secret for Chaz, Leo wonders if her positive impressions of Tiffani biased her against viewing Tiffani as a potential suspect. She and Jake had both felt like their questions had hit close to the bone with Tiffani, and this conversation confirms it.

"Why do you feel such loyalty to him?"

"I don't know." Leo can tell by the snuffling sounds on the other side of the fence that Tiffani is crying.

"I think it's time. And if suspicion does fall on you, then telling the cops first is going to only look good. Don't you think?"

Tiffani murmurs something Leo can't hear, so she leans in. Is Tiffani about to admit to murdering Chaz? She presses her ear against the board.

Suddenly she hears a sharp creaking sound and a thud as a loose board hits her leg.

"What was that?"

She thinks fast. She steps back a few paces and then says, "Ow!" in a loud voice.

Seconds later, the gate in the front opens and she limps in what she hopes is a convincing manner. Tiffani and her younger sister, Karlie, come out of the backyard. "Leo, are you okay?"

"Hi, yes, I'm fine, just clumsy! I walked over here from my house across the greenbelt and got my foot caught in your neighbors' sprinkler, then I tripped and hit the fence."

"Bless your heart!" Karlie's voice is sympathetic. "I'm Karlie. I remember you from school. Did you hurt something?"

"My pride! Thank you, no, I'm fine. It's good to see you again, Karlie."

"Would you like some cake and soda? Jetson won't mind sharing."

"I don't want to interrupt your party."

Tiffani pipes up. "Please! There's a huge cake."

"Well, thank you. Sounds great!"

Leo follows Tiffani into the backyard but can't think of any good reason to stay. So five minutes later, balancing a Spider-Man plate with cake and a Dr Pepper can with one hand and her recovered glasses case in the other, Leo closes the gate carefully behind her. She slips her regular glasses off and her sunglasses on, and tucks the case into her backpack. She's distracted, so she does not look up until she hears a car door open.

Parked at the curb, Jake's sleek black truck gleams in the sun. He watches her walk toward him, his aviator glasses hiding his gaze. Stepping out of the driver's seat, he stands, arms crossed, waiting for her to reach him.

"Leo." He nods curtly. "I asked you not to come without me. I've been watching you for a while." He points with his chin toward the crepe myrtle Leo had hid behind. "Want to get in the truck while you tell me what you found out?"

Leo is opening her mouth to answer when she hears the gate.

"Hey, Leo?" Tiffani steps out. "Oh, Jake! I mean, Detective Nguyen."

"Jake is fine."

"I was going to . . . I have something . . . I lied when you talked to me earlier. I'm sorry I kicked you out," Tiffani blurts. "I just wasn't sure how to say what I . . ." She looks on the verge of tears. "Years ago, Charlie told me a secret. And it might have something to do with why he was killed."

53

Lieutenant Esquivel hangs up the phone at her desk in frustration. It's been hours since Macy sent Melody Garner-Aziz the faked screenshot about Chaz's murder. The subreddit erupted like a yellow jackets' nest stirred with a stick. But she's no closer to being able to speak with Melody.

Melody's assistant at Llosa Law Firm answered Esquivel's third phone call of the day in a bored voice.

"Lllosa Law Firm, Nicole speaking."

"Nicole, this is Lieutenant Esquivel from the Blue Oak Sheriff's Department again."

"Hi, Lieutenant. Ms. Garner-Aziz is still in court."

Esquivel can practically hear Nicole filing her nails. "Do you think she'll be in recess anytime soon?"

"Like I said before, when she's in recess, she has paperwork and phone calls to make for her immigration case."

"This really is urgent, Nicole."

"Of course." Nicole's voice is completely flat. "That's why I emailed her your last two messages."

"And you told her it was urgent?"

"I put 'urgent' in the subject line." Esquivel can hear the air quotes around the word; clearly, Nicole is unimpressed by Esquivel's title or the idea of a murder investigation. If Macy had not called to say u/NanciDrew42 had suddenly started posting in the snark group—five times in the last hour—Esquivel might be less suspicious. But if Melody has time to post in the sub, she has time to talk to Esquivel, whose next move will be to show up at the courthouse and bring Melody in for questioning, even if that means arresting her.

"Do me a favor. I want you to write this down verbatim. You ready?"

"Verbatim. Got it." Esquivel can almost hear Nicole rolling her eyes.

"Tell her Lieutenant Esquivel has a special message for Nanci Drew. That's Nanci with an *i*. Then give her my phone number. Can you do that?"

"As in . . . the fictional detective?"

"With an *i*."

"I mean, sure. You want to tell me what this is about?" Nicole clearly feels that Esquivel has lost her mind.

"Nope! I really don't. Thank you, Nicole. I hope we won't have to talk again today."

"Oh, hard same. Bye." Nicole hangs up.

Four minutes later, Esquivel's phone rings. It's a blocked number.

54

Tiffani agrees to go with Jake and Leo. She goes back briefly to say her goodbyes to her family, and Leo takes the opportunity to tell Jake that she's joining the conversation: "You need me."

"No argument."

"And we shouldn't go back to the station. It's too intimidating and impersonal."

"Where else are we going to go? Not a coffee shop or restaurant." Leo realizes that Jake is asking, not informing her, and she sees again a level of vulnerability in him that surprises her. He seems so poised and contained most of the time, but she knows better than anyone that what looks to outsiders like assuredness can often be a way of pulling back till you know what to do. She suspects she and Jake are a lot alike, and it touches her that he asks her opinion even when he's frustrated with her.

"The pool house." Her voice is confident.

"Will that be okay with your devil dog?" His voice is teasing.

"He's literally the nicest dog ever, you just met him when he was overstimulated. He'll probably help Tiffani."

"Good point." He indicates she should ride with him, so she clambers in the passenger side of his truck while they wait for Tiffani.

As the AC blows out hot, and then cools, she says, "Jake, I'm sorry for coming without you."

"Thank you." His mouth is a thin line.

There is a beat where neither of them talks. Finally, emboldened by his show of vulnerability, Leo wants to extend an olive branch. "So you're a cat person, you said? Do you have one?"

"First of all, she's not my cat, I'm her human. Get the ownership straight. And her name is Peanut. Here." He pulls his phone out, thumbs through it for a second, and hands it to Leo. It's open to an album called "Cat." She flips through his photos of an adorable gray-and-black cat. Most of them feature close-ups of Peanut, but a few are selfies of Peanut and Jake. One of them is Peanut's forehead smushed against Jake's cheek while he's lying in bed; Jake wears black-rimmed glasses, his normally tidy hair mussed from sleep. His toned bare shoulders and chest are visible at the bottom of the frame.

Tiffani knocks on the truck window. Leo feels her cheeks heat. She almost drops the phone, then hands it to Jake while she rolls down the passenger window.

"Are you okay following me back to the Schneiders' pool house, where I'm staying?"

Tiffani nods, holding her arms around herself despite the heat. "That sounds great, honestly. This is . . . this story is hard for me to tell. I'd rather be someplace quiet."

• • • • •

Less than ten minutes later, they're settled onto the beige couches while coffee brews in the kitchenette. While riding back, Leo sent one text to her mother, telling her only that the officers let her back into the pool house and she and Derrida were planning on a quiet afternoon there. Not technically a lie. She got another yellow thumbs-up emoji, so she assumes that's what her mother wants her to do. They will be having the boundaries conversation soon.

She almost ignored Mack's text but, at the last second, sent him a quick *Busy day. How's yours?* He responded immediately, but she hasn't opened it. Jake had already pulled up to the pool house and, with Jake's level of tension about her following Tiffani, she doubted he'd respond kindly to her texting Mack as well. She tucked her phone in her bag, then hustled to get the coffee going.

Now, watching Leo across the room finish getting coffee mugs down, Tiffani sighs. "I really don't want to do this."

Jake leans forward. "Take your time. You're here of your own free will bringing us information. That counts for a lot in my book."

"Okay." Tiffani sits forward, putting her hands on her knees.

"Do you mind if I record?" Jake asks.

She nods. When the recorder is down on the table, she takes a deep breath. "Do y'all remember Dominic Garner?"

Leo, who is bringing over the mugs of coffee and beige containers of cream and sugar Phil filled before she came, sucks in her breath. "What about Dom?"

Tiffani stalls, mixing in cream and sugar, murmuring, "Thank you." For a moment, she cradles her mug with two hands and then begins again: "It was our last big party before the end of high school. May 13, 2005. I'll never forget the date. It was a Friday night, and we were at the Deep Hollows."

"I was there that night," Leo says. Jake glances at her but does not stop her, so she continues. "It was my first high school party. Beth let me tag along, even though I was a ninth grader."

"Oh, I'm sorry. I'm sure I didn't talk to you."

"Please. You were so cool. I was a lowly freshman."

"Was the party at the firepit? That's where our high school parties always started." Jake is picking up on the vibe Leo thinks will work best to make Tiffani comfortable—friends reminiscing, not a cop interviewing.

"Yeah, exactly."

"I just remember someone playing the guitar," Leo says.

"I'd forgotten that. It was Cole Riley, playing the same songs he played all year. Every time I hear 'Travelin' Soldier' or 'Such Great Heights' or 'Your Body Is a Wonderland,' I think of Cole at that party."

"Did Chaz . . . Charlie . . . sing that song to you?" Leo scrunches up her face like she's trying to remember. Her back is ramrod straight and she works consciously to relax it, to keep her stress from souring the conversation.

Tiffani laughs. "Yeah, I'd forgotten. It was awful. He was . . . well, he wanted to convince me to sleep with him, but I grew up Evangelical, so, you know. Purity ring and all." She makes a rueful face. "I had no idea till later how many people he'd slept with, how many he probably was sleeping with at the time. I was so naive."

"What else do you remember about that night?" Jake asks.

"We sat on logs around the fire with all of our friends. We were all kind of mushy. We grew up together, you know? Most of us started at Blue Oak Elementary in kindergarten and it felt . . . almost impossible to think we wouldn't always be together all the time." A tear spills and Tiffani lets it fall. Leo grabs a box of tissues and hands it to her. "Then Charlie left with the guys for a while. They were headed down to the Hollows." She grabs a tissue. "The next thing I knew, he ran up to the fire circle."

"I remember that." Leo's voice is quiet but steady. "I was on the outside of the circle, listening to the guitar half asleep, waiting for Beth to take us home. I saw Charlie come up. He kept opening and closing his mouth, but nothing came out."

"It was like . . . he'd seen a ghost." Tiffani is talking only to Leo now.

"And then he yelled. He roared, actually."

"It's what he used to do in football. I called him 'Charlie Bear' and they started calling him 'The Bear,' and he would roar loudly to get them to move fast. It was almost instinct, his teammates following their leader."

"Mack was there. He was also a ninth grader, but he played second-string varsity that year."

"Those Garner boys were always killer football players." Tiffani smiles nostalgically through her tears, and then gasps. "Oh, Leo. I didn't realize . . . He saw?"

Leo feels what Emily calls her Teflon skin falling into place—an almost robotic ability to be objective when she's stressed. Before her dad's heart attack, the night Dom died had been the hardest of her young life, and she'd been there with Mack through all of it. Playing detective with Bodhi had made her confident; this only makes her upset. Later, she knows the emotions will catch up with her, but for now, she withdraws, becomes observant and objective.

"He was there that night through the whole thing." Leo's voice is quiet. "Mack saw it all."

"What did he see?" Jake asks gently.

"The fence was ripped back." Tiffani turns to him.

"Which fence?"

"The one at Deep Hollows, the section around the Deep itself," Leo supplies. "My mom said it used to not be fenced when she was a kid, just a hole in the ground filled with really deep water you tried not to fall into, back in the sixties and seventies. Back then, people would go swimming in the Hollows, then run over to the Deep and see how far down they could go, then run back to the creek. But we never did that. By the time we arrived, the Deep was always kept fenced and locked. That night, someone had ripped the entire gate out from the hinges; the lock was still there. The rest of it had been torn apart." Leo pauses, waiting for Tiffani to pick up the story.

"Can you finish telling him what happened?" Tiffani chokes out, dabbing her eyes.

"Yes." Leo's voice remains steady. "By the time I got there, I saw two seniors on cell phones calling the cops. Charlie watched from inside the fence. His eyes were like . . ." She gestures at her own eyes, trying to come up with the words. "I don't know, dark shadows. I saw . . . what was his name, Jason?"

"Yes, the team's star kicker," Tiffani says. "Jason jumped in the Deep."

"I thought the thing in the water was a bunch of blankets or something. I didn't . . . It took me a while to realize it was Dominic." Leo is watching this memory from a safe distance. "Mack started running, and the team held him back. A junior girl was straddling Dom, performing CPR."

"That was Ashley. She's a nurse now."

"That makes sense. Then the paramedics got there. Some of the team held on to Mack, and the rest ripped the fence off the poles completely so they could get to Dom."

"But it was too late," Tiffani pipes up tearfully.

"It was too late," Leo echoes. "A few days later, instead of having the senior baccalaureate service, they had Dom's funeral."

Tiffani openly sobs. Leo holds the square pillow in her lap. She traces one side with a finger and inhales: *I breathe in*, she thinks. Her finger moves up the next side: *I breathe out. I breathe in. I breathe out.* Slowly, she calms her body, brings herself back into the moment. She hopes she never has to have a conversation like this again; today, she's deeply grateful not to be a detective like Jake. At least that's one choice in her career she got right. Literary analysis is, blissfully, free of this kind of grief.

Tiffani holds on to the coffee mug like it is anchoring her to the couch. Eventually she wipes her eyes and nose with a damp tissue and continues. "After Dom died, Charlie and I only got closer. I'm not entirely sure I would have married him without that experience. But it was just so awful, and we knew what we'd both been through, and well . . ." She waves her hand to fast-forward through the story. "After college, we got married. And it was almost three years later—three roller-coaster years—that he came home absolutely wasted one night."

She takes a shaky sip of coffee. Her voice wobbles but she goes on. "He was totally off his rocker. I know now he probably combined drugs and hard liquor, but I was so young. All I knew is that I couldn't even lift him when his friends dropped him on our porch. I finally got him on the couch, and he kept saying, 'I didn't mean to, I didn't mean to' and 'After, I threw it away from me as far as I could.'"

Leo bites her bottom lip to keep from interrupting with more questions. Jake sits forward slightly. "What do you think he meant by that?"

"Oh, I know. He told me outright." She puts her coffee mug down and doesn't take her eyes off it. "Charlie was jealous of Dominic in some weird, twisted way. Dom was deeply loved by a close-knit family. He was good-looking, but he was also truly kind. He didn't mess around with girls. He made straight As and had a full football scholarship to Notre Dame. He was getting out of town in a big way. From what people said later, he probably would have played in the NFL. He was just the very best person." Tiffani pauses, sucks in air, her eyes unfocused. "I think something in Charlie snapped that night. They were goofing around, or he said they were; maybe they weren't even throwing rocks, maybe it was just him."

She pauses and looks up—straight at Leo. "We may never know now exactly what happened, but when it was just the two of them, Dominic turned away from Charlie, and Charlie grabbed a big rock and hurled it at him."

Leo clutches the pillow, holding her breath. Jake is silent. Tiffani continues.

"He said he thought Dom would move after he got hit, or that it would bruise him but not really injure him. I don't know if I believed him. All I know is he killed Dominic Garner."

For a moment, the only sound in the room is Derrida's panting and the faint whirring of the fan.

"I don't know much more than that. Somehow, he got Dom's body to the Deep so it would look like he fell in and hit his head on the way down. Then he, I don't know, ran up to the party. The rest of the stuff I told you. And then he just"—she clenches her jaw—"went to the hospital and lied through his teeth, all 'Yes, Officer, he was a good friend. No, sir, I have no idea what happened.' He was Dom's *pallbearer.* He spoke at the funeral. He called Dom 'The Boss' and told funny stories, and the whole time . . ." Tiffani cannot speak for several minutes. When she does, her voice is deep and hoarse. "Anyway, after he told me, our marriage was over. Tiger and I were gone by the time he woke up the next day. I filed the paperwork so fast he didn't even have time to argue with me."

"And you never told anyone?" Leo's voice is small.

"I told Karlie. And now I'm telling you."

"Thank you, Tiffani. This is going to be really helpful." Jake reaches over from his couch and grabs her hand. "It means a lot that you'd share it with us." He squeezes her hand. "Can I ask a couple more questions?"

Tiffani nods.

"Did Charlie tell anyone else?"

"I'm not sure. He was on a lot of substances in those years, really up till he went to rehab. Possibly after. I have no idea who he told."

"Did he ever say anything about Mack Garner?"

"I doubt it, why?"

"Just curious if he and Mack ever talked."

"Not that I know of."

"Do you think Mack knew Charlie killed Dominic?"

"I have no idea. Truly, after I left that night, Charlie was almost completely gone from my life. He became Chaz, and Chaz was someone I hardly knew."

Jake nods. He grabs the recorder and turns it off. "Let's be done for now. If I have other questions, I'll let you know."

Tiffani's face is swollen and red as she leaves. She shakes

Jake's hand, gives Derrida a pat on the head, and then stops at the door to hug Leo tightly. "I'm so sorry. I should have said something earlier. Will you tell Mack I'm sorry?"

Leo pulls back and looks at the person the entire subreddit has been putting on a pedestal for years; in that moment, Leo sees she is not a character in a story, but a real, messy, complex person.

Leo crosses her arms. "I don't think I can do that."

55

Lieutenant Esquivel shakes her head as she knocks on the door. Of all the things that need to be done today, this is the silliest. She's supposed to meet Melody Garner-Aziz in forty-five minutes at a coffee shop near the Travis County Courthouse, but Macy felt she needed to make one other stop first. She tries not to roll her eyes.

"Hi," she says when the faded tan door opens. "I'm Lieutenant Laura Esquivel. I spoke with someone on the phone a few minutes ago?"

"Oh!" The woman's dyed brown hair has half an inch of white roots. In the hottest month of the year, she's wearing a green velour tracksuit. "Are you a police officer?"

"Hello, ma'am. I'm Lieutenant Esquivel from the Blue Oak Sheriff's Department. You're Mrs. O'Malley?"

"Of course! Do you need my ID? You can't be too sure these days, you know. There are all kinds of people out there."

"No, no, that's fine. I heard you found something you think we should investigate?"

"You could say that! Actually, I found all kinds of things you should know about." She turns and leads the way down a hallway that has not been updated in thirty years, lined with family photos.

"Why don't we start with the yard and go from there?"

"First, what do you want to drink? Iced tea? Water? Dr Pepper?"

"No, thank you." Mrs. O'Malley's face falls, so Esquivel continues quickly. "It feels too important to wait any longer. We're in the middle of a murder investigation, and my boss sent me out here on a priority mission."

She perks right up. "Of course. Say no more. Don't mind this kitchen; it's such a mess," she says, leading the way through a kitchen so clean the counters gleam. Esquivel feels a pang missing her own abuela, a few hundred miles away in South Texas. Mrs. O'Malley walks through a screen door that thwacks when it closes behind them.

"It's over here in the side yard. I saw it two days ago and I thought to myself, who would mess with a flower-bed border? I called and left a message on the non-emergency line; I would *never* clog up the emergency line. But I knew—someone had stolen my rock. What in the world is this town coming to? I tell you . . ."

Esquivel interrupts when Mrs. O'Malley takes a breath. "Did you move this rock at all?" The white stone is muddied with a rusty stain.

"No, not at all. In fact, I always feel that—"

"Actually, I am kind of thirsty." Esquivel shades her eyes. "Could you bring me something to drink? Would you mind?"

Mrs. O'Malley stands straight and almost salutes. "Absolutely."

"Do you have sweet tea?"

"Of course, coming right up, Lieutenant!" Mrs. O'Malley is clearly delighted.

Esquivel shoots several pictures of the rock, then takes it to her car and opens her trunk to get to her small crime scene kit. Though she knows it won't be conclusive, she performs a luminol test anyway, using her sheriff's department jacket and the lid of the car's trunk to make a sort of darkroom tent so she can see the results. She is not an expert, and she's confident someone higher up than her will have something to say. But she's also in love with a huge nerd who loves trivia, which means she knows that Central Texas limestone quarry rocks like this one have very little iron, making them creamy white instead of pink or orange. The low levels of iron also mean there's less of a chance for a false positive.

Even in the imperfect shade of her jacket-formed tent, the blue glow across the surface of the rock seems bright.

Pulling the jacket off her sweaty back, she bags the rock and returns to the garden to retrieve the two on either side, and places the evidence in a box in her trunk. She takes off the nitrile-barrier gloves and puts them into the box, then closes her trunk. She'll have to take this back to the station before meeting up with Melody.

She walks back up to the screen door and knocks before opening it. "Ma'am?"

"Oh, Lieutenant, what did you find?" Mrs. O'Malley hands Esquivel a glass of sweet tea with a mint leaf in it. Esquivel downs it gratefully; she really does love mint sweet tea.

Esquivel nods. "Thank you, that was perfect." She hands the glass back. "I'm so glad you called us. Your hunch was spot-on. I can't say any more, but I'm afraid I'm going to have to go right away."

56

When Tiffani leaves, Jake starts packing up his recorder and notebook and Leo checks her phone. She has three texts.

MACK GARNER: Mine has been busy too, and kinda weird, tbh. I'll catch you up tonight.

MACK GARNER: Any requests for dinner? I was thinking Nacho Daddy's at 8:30? I'll meet you on the patio so you can bring that cute dog?

MOM: Leonora, I realize you are ignoring me. But I also know you're not just at the pool house resting. I'm not sure how to say this more clearly: you have to promise me you won't help the sheriff's department any more.

She almost throws her phone down in frustration at her mom's text, but ignores it instead. She hearts Mack's text, and writes back that she'll meet him at Nacho Daddy's. She looks up to find Jake watching her.

"Everything okay?"

"Yeah, fine."

"You ran through quite a mix of emotions there."

"What do you mean?" She glances up self-consciously.

"Your face lit up, then got so angry, then you smiled again."

"Oh. Yeah. Um. Texting with different people, one of whom is my mom who is borderline harassing me about helping you."

"What is she saying?"

"That I have no idea what I'm getting into. Like she's the expert or something. And I have no idea how she even knows I'm with you; I told her I was at the pool house resting. This town is something else. Probably the Baptist prayer chain again."

"And the other one?"

Leo puts her phone face down. "Nothing to do with the case. What's next?"

Jake's lips thin into a line for a beat. "I need to head back. Just a few more questions. Would you say Mack has always been obsessed with his cousin's death?"

"Not 'obsessed.'" Leo is instantly defensive. She doesn't like Jake's tone. She doesn't want to admit to herself that Bodhi's story of Chaz thinking Mack was after him, combined with this news that Chaz had actually killed Dominic, made her wonder briefly during Tiffani's story whether Mack actually might have hurt Chaz.

She tries to dismiss that thought; she might not have talked to him for a few years, but she still knows Mack. She flashes back to Mack's sultry grin at Kymber. Doesn't she?

"But he never let it go, did he? The idea that Charlie might have killed Dominic?" Jake's shoulders hunch as he sets his elbows on his knees and leans toward Leo.

"No, it wasn't like that at all." Leo's voice rises. "Sometimes in high school, I went back with him to the Deep. A few times, we were looking for more information. He never got past the idea that Dom hitting his head didn't make sense; Dominic didn't drink or do drugs and everyone knew it. There was no reason he would have fallen into the water on his own. But..." Leo thinks back, and then nods decisively. "I never heard him say that Charlie killed Dom. Mack just—he knew that Charlie was the last one to see him alive, that's all."

"How often have you talked to Mack in the last few years?"

"I mean, not often, but I know him." She hates that this

echoes her own thoughts, so her voice is sharp. “What are you getting at?”

“Something I saw firsthand that lines up with what Brittni told us yesterday. A reason Chaz might have been afraid of Mack.”

“What was it?”

Jake had just told Leo she’d run through a mix of emotions checking her texts, and now she sees the same thing on his face. He hesitates, then comes to a decision, his mouth tightening. He also, she thinks, watches her for her reaction when he says: “Last year, Chaz got drunk at the Garners’ restaurant, and the manager called the sheriff’s department when he and Mack got in each other’s faces. I was on duty, so Esquivel and I went to break it up. Chaz kept yelling, ‘All you Garners always thought you were God’s gift to the world. You’re all so stuck-up.’ We ran up to stop them. Chaz tried to punch Mack, but he was too drunk to do much. Before we could get there, Mack caught Chaz’s fist and folded his arm behind him to incapacitate him. He held him till Esquivel and I took over and started to walk him out. As we left, Mack whispered in Chaz’s face, ‘I know you killed him. And when you least expect it, I will come for you.’ That’s what I mean when I say, Mack’s obsessed.”

Leo sits silently, but now a couple of things click into place for her—Mack’s almost glee at hitting Chaz and his antagonism toward Jake after being questioned that first time in the sheriff’s station on the Fourth of July, as well as Jake’s cryptic comments about Mack. She also realizes that, just like she had with Tiffani, she’d allowed a sympathetic view of Mack to prevent her from seeing him as a viable suspect. The truth is clearly more complex than she knew.

Still, she is confident that Mack is essentially the person she knew him to be. Except for him flirting with Kymber. Which was odd, at the very least. She sighs in frustration. Is the thread of doubt she’s feeling because of the facts, or because of jealousy?

“Call it obsession if you want.” Whatever doubts Leo is harboring about Mack, she's not going to share them with Jake. "But it turns out, Mack was right. So is that obsession? Or intuition?" She doesn't want to talk about this anymore. "The weird part of this to me is Tiffani. Why didn't she tell anyone?"

"I don't know. People do strange things when they've loved someone."

"Did this fact eat at her?"

"I don't know. Are you thinking she's our killer?"

"I overheard her telling her sister, Karlie, to pretend she spent the night at her place on July Fourth." Leo sits back, arms crossed, with the air of someone laying down a winning hand of cards.

"And you were going to tell me this when?" Jake barks.

"Immediately, except Tiffani followed me out of the yard, and here we are."

"We had a minute in the car."

"You were showing me pictures of your cat."

"Leo, that was important information to lead with!" Briefly, Jake's irritation takes over. She notes for the first time that there are dark circles under his eyes. "You just . . ." He stops, pulls out his phone, and swallows. His tone is professional when he speaks again. "I might have handled that whole conversation differently. I'll get Johnson and Esquivel on it immediately . . . as soon as they can follow up some other leads." He closes his eyes for a brief second, and she feels remorse and frustration in equal measure.

She waits quietly while he finishes texting. Then he peers up. "I know you're not trained in this. But I need you to tell me anything important like that. I feel like we're walking a knife's edge right now. We don't have enough people as it is. I would never . . . Normally . . ." For just a moment, Jake appears terribly young. He takes a deep breath. "Is there anything else I'm missing?"

"Not anything I'm keeping from you. I wasn't trying to keep *that* from you." He did tell her it was difficult to be a cop in his hometown, and she can see it—how hard it must be to be forced to view the people he's known most of his life as suspects. "Want to talk it through? That always helps me when I'm writing, and if there's anything I haven't said, I'll let you know."

"Okay, sure," he admits. "That probably would be helpful. Esquivel and I've been too busy to talk anything through, and I'm afraid I'm missing things." He reads his notes for a few seconds. "Why did Tiffani ask her sister for an alibi? What else can you tell me about that?"

"Karlie seemed to think it was odd too, and Tiffani said she was just being paranoid because cops always suspect the ex."

"She's not wrong, it's an easy place to start. Maybe that was just misplaced paranoia."

"Do you think she did it?" Leo sits forward.

"I mean, maybe. But it feels far-fetched. Why now? Unless there's something we don't know, it's odd timing. They weren't even in each other's lives. There's no urgency to this for Tiffani."

"Maybe she was planning to tell someone that he killed Dom?"

"Does that sound right to you?" Jake's voice is earnest.

Leo warms to the conversation. It feels like when she and her grad school friends used to talk through ideas for papers, pushing each other to examine an argument from every side. It's a relief after the emotional conversation with Tiffani to be able to analyze. She shakes her head. "No, when she talked to her sister and didn't know I was listening, it seemed clear she'd only ever told Karlie, who *really* wanted her to tell us. Unless she was aware I was behind the fence, there's no reason to think she was making that up."

"Well, no offense, you were not *exactly* clandestine, so we'll just keep that tab open for now."

Leo glares at him without heat. "Sorry, I must have missed that part in my training—oh, wait."

"Well, I *did* tell you to wait for me, so . . ." Jake smiles to take the sting out of his words. "However, I'll be the first to admit, if you hadn't been there, she might not have confessed to holding Chaz's secret, so even if I disapprove of the method, and I wish you'd shared it immediately, I can appreciate the results." Jake sits back, tapping his pen on his notebook, thinking. "Actually, if she did know you were there, she probably wouldn't have made it so clear she was asking her sister for an alibi." Leo gives him space to formulate his thoughts. "If she did murder Chaz, there are a lot more questions: Could she have moved his body to a house that Kay represents? Pulled together an elaborate digital stunt to make it look like Kay was the murderer? And if so, why? It feels likelier that it was someone who knows much more about Chaz's personal life and his daily dealings in Blue Oak."

"Or anyone who follows the subreddit. Which Tiffani said she did."

"As does, apparently, most of Blue Oak."

"Wait, what?" Leo blanches.

"Macy said more than four thousand people from Blue Oak are in it."

"You have got to be . . ." She swallows. "And here we thought it was our little secret."

"Apparently not." He makes a note on a page. "So Tiffani could have known more about his daily life from the subreddit or, honestly, Chaz's oversharing on social media. But still, that doesn't address why now."

"Or how." Leo sits forward, her brain moving rapidly through possibilities. "The video framing Kay seems like it came from someone with online experience. Which sounds more like Bodhi. Or Grant. Or even Kymber. We haven't talked much about Kymber, but we can't discount her."

"She's on my list too. But you have to admit, Mack might be a better fit. He knows a lot about what's going on in Blue Oak; he was in the subreddit."

"Mack was?"

"And Melody."

"No!"

Jake gazes at her, weighing his choices. Finally he says, "Leo, Melody is NanciDrew42."

Leo immediately stands up and begins pacing, like she does when she's stuck on an article and she needs to think, except her movements are jagged and upset. Both Garners were in the subreddit, and *Melody* was the snarker who had been so viciously gunning for Chaz's financial records. She'd used *Melody's* thread to grill Bodhi. Leo had told Jake Nanci Drew was probably a lawyer or journalist, but there's no satisfaction to learning she was right.

It's now instantly clear to Leo why Jake is so suspicious of Mack. Everyone knows the Garner siblings are very close, so she dismisses immediately the idea that Melody was doing something Mack didn't know about. They had always been like her and Emily—wherever you found one, the other was inevitably nearby.

She sighs. Was the entire subreddit really just her small town, interacting with each other anonymously? Once again, she has to reframe everything about what had seemed like a harmless hobby for so long.

She feels doubt creep up in her mind. Jake must see something on her face, because he pushes quietly, "Maybe Melody and Mack worked together. They could have figured out that Chaz was targeting Kay and decided enough was enough. And Mack's a big guy. It would have been easier for him to kill Chaz, and then move and arrange his body."

She shakes her head. She doesn't want to betray Mack by even considering Jake's line of reasoning. Except, is Jake the person she's betraying by not talking through his suspicions of Mack with any seriousness? This is a mess, and she is suddenly exhausted. It's been . . . all of this . . . the whole thing has been too much.

Her next words are clipped. "Any of these very fit women could also have killed him and moved the body."

He nods for a second, and then says, "You're right. It's possible. Moving the body is going to have to be a consideration for whomever killed him, and it could have been one of these women, or a couple of people working together. But Mack alone could easily have handled it—that's all I'm saying."

"It was definitely moved after he died?"

He nods. "Absolutely, there's no way he was killed in the Zora Neale Hurston Street house. There's just no physical evidence for that."

"So someone killed him, placed his body to make it look like he died in a Kay Schneider listing, then staged an elaborate Instagram Live with Kay's voice to frame her. And the body was kept outside at some point because of the accelerated rate of decomposition."

He lifts an eyebrow. "Exactly. But how did you know—?"

She interrupts him impatiently. "The rapid increase in smell. You haven't found a murder site?"

"No, but we have found evidence all over town of someone planting things that we think are associated with the murder."

"Like what?" Her voice is now professional, with a hard edge. She's back to the side of herself she found in interviewing Bodhi.

Jake rubs his hand across his face and says, "Might as well tell you everything. We found two separate gloves, some towels, a tarp, what looks like burnt material that has blood on it. It's all being tested, but it seems likely that someone is planting evidence in various spots in Blue Oak. And at least some of it was found at Garner Ranch." He does not tell her how they were uncovering that evidence.

"Which is even better reason not to think it's Mack." Leo sits forward triumphantly. "Why would he leave evidence on his own property?"

"Which is even *more* reason to think it's Mack," Jake counters. "Because that's exactly what he wants us to think; it could be to throw us off. And now that we know about Chaz's secret, it seems clearer than ever. There are just too many coincidences."

"What do you mean by that?"

Jake breathes deeply. His eyes are entreating. "Leo, if I tell you this, I have to know I can trust you. And that you won't say anything to Mack."

Leo hesitates, her loyalties wavering. "I won't . . ." She pauses and finds her words. "How about this: I'm going to dinner tonight with Mack, but I won't say anything about the investigation at all. I wouldn't have anyway, because he has no reason to think I'm helping out. And I'll promise not to say anything about your suspicions until the real killer is caught. Because there is another killer, and it's definitely not Mack."

Jake stands, his face deathly serious. "Leo, you *cannot* go to dinner with Mack."

Leo stands, crossing her arms. "Excuse me?" Her normal levels of reserve have been burned off. She and Jake have been teetering on the edge of anger since she followed Tiffani, and this tips her over. Her mom has been telling her what to do, and now Jake is telling her what to do, and she will not lose control of herself—not to them, not to anyone.

"Was that who was texting you earlier?" His voice is angry.

"So what if it was?"

"Where and when are you supposed to meet him?"

"Why do you care?"

"Leo, I'm in the middle of a murder investigation and you're going to dinner with my lead suspect. What time and *where*?" His voice rises.

"Nacho Daddy's at eight thirty. But it's ridiculous to think I'm in danger from Mack. He—"

Jake interrupts, moving even closer. Leo hates that she notices how his tight mouth makes his cheekbones more stark. "Chaz was killed by a blunt-force blow to the back of the head." He spits the words out, enunciating each syllable. "It was not a clean blow, like a big pipe or a baseball bat."

Leo winces.

"I'm still waiting on the full report." Jake clenches his jaw.

"But, Leo, I'm willing to bet my professional reputation on the fact that a tall person took a large rock and struck Chaz from behind, killing him instantly."

Leo sucks in air. Finally she breathes. "Like Dom."

Jake nods tersely. "Exactly like Dominic."

57

Esquivel doesn't like to speed, but this time she makes an exception; it takes her longer to log the rocks than she wants, and by the time she leaves the sheriff's station, she has to leadfoot it all the way to the coffee shop in South Austin. She even puts the lights on for a bit on the highway, and enjoys the feeling of watching cars scurry out of the way, worried she's after them. Melody's been so skittish; she doesn't want to lose her. Something shady is clearly going on, and Esquivel isn't taking any chances.

She gets to Medici café three minutes before she's supposed to, and she takes two of those minutes to catch her breath. By the time she walks inside, she's gotten herself under control.

Melody arrives five minutes later. Her gray suit is impeccably tailored, and her hair is straightened and pulled back into a bun at the nape of her neck. Her fingernails are a tasteful crimson that perfectly matches her lipstick. Her black heels show pops of red when she walks. Everything about her outfit is designed to show tasteful elegance. But the shadows underneath her eyes are dark, and the lines around her mouth are deep.

"Ms. Aziz." Esquivel stands.

"Garner-Aziz, but call me Melody. You're Lieutenant Esquivel?"

"That's me." She intentionally does not tell the other woman to call her Laura. "Can I get you something?"

"Chai latte, please."

Esquivel orders for Melody and gets herself a small black coffee. Melody fiddles with her phone while she waits, and then tucks it into her leather bag when Esquivel brings the drinks to the table.

"That was clever, getting Nicole to take a message for Nanci Drew."

"I couldn't get you to call me back." Esquivel's reproof is mild. The coffee is scalding. She takes the lid off to let it cool.

"I was in court. And I'm going to be honest, I didn't really want to talk. I haven't done anything wrong, but I'm also concerned about the implications of this discussion."

"Right now, I'm just filling in some gaps in my investigation. Do you want a lawyer?"

"I am a lawyer, and I haven't done anything that breaks the law."

"Then why are you nervous?"

"Because . . ." Melody fiddles with the edge of the corrugated cardboard sleeve around her chai. "Even if what I've done is technically legal, it's ethically dubious."

"And that concerns you?"

"Not enough not to do it." Melody looks up and smiles without humor. "But enough to be worried about how you're going to handle this."

"I can't guarantee that this won't come out."

"Yeah, I know." Melody sighs.

"But I can tell you, this probably isn't even the biggest secret we've heard today." Jake had left Esquivel a long voice memo and given her permission to reveal to Melody what Tiffani had told them about Chaz murdering Dominic, if she felt it would serve the investigation. It's Esquivel's ace card. She wants to get a better sense of Melody's hand before she plays it. "How about I just ask you some questions, and if you don't want to answer them, you don't have to? Plead the fifth and get a lawyer, whatever you want."

Melody nods.

"Tell me about being Nanci Drew."

"Well, it started as a whim after Chaz moved back to Blue Oak. He was just so . . . *everywhere.* One night we had a girls' night out at one of those paint-your-own pottery places. My son was a few months old and was finally taking a bottle, so I was free to drink and I'd probably had a few too many. Heaven knows my pottery looked like a mound of dog crap. Anyway, one of my girlfriends told me about the subreddit."

"Who was it?"

"Honestly, I can't remember. It could have been anyone. We were all joking and we decided to sign up then and there; I picked Nanci Drew because I loved those books and I wanted to dig into Chaz's life. Chaz had been around town for weeks, just showing his stupid smug face with his stupid selfie stick, and it drove Mack and me *nuts.* We knew he killed Dominic; it was so obviously him. The sheriff hadn't even bothered investigating at the time because Chaz said it was an accident. Did you know that?"

"And that frustrated you?"

"You have no idea. I became a lawyer because of it. When I was a baby undergrad, I thought I'd prosecute bad guys and put them away. Turns out, I hated criminal law, so I ended up in immigration by the time I actually finished law school, but Dom's death was my main motivator when I was young."

"And Mack thought Chaz killed Dominic too?"

"Yes, and my parents, though they'd never admit it now. They're of the 'toe the line and trust that the arc of history is bending toward justice' generation."

"Do they hate Quackenbush? Wasn't he the sheriff when Dominic died?"

"He was, and no, for whatever reason, they don't hate him. He and my dad are friends of a sort. I know the city council is all a bit much, but Blue Oak has been really good to my family.

My dad especially didn't want to rock the boat after Dominic died. There was no evidence, he said; the cops had cleared everyone. Over the years, we stopped talking about it. My aunt and uncle, Dom's parents, moved away; he was their only child, and the few times a year we see them, they look like they've aged decades. The only way Mack and I could bring it up was with each other."

"But you were convinced Dominic was killed?"

"Murdered, yes, by Chaz."

"So you joined the snark subreddit group to prove that?"

"No. I joined because it was funny at first, and then I realized I could find out information in the public record that . . . embarrassed Chaz. My goal wasn't to prove he killed Dominic, though I would absolutely have done that if I could have." Her voice catches, but she forges on. "My goal was to make his life miserable."

"Did you do that?"

"Yes. After one of the other users outed him at rehab, it became sort of a thing to dig into his past. It took me a couple of weeks of filing Freedom of Information Act requests, and looking at real estate holdings and LLC names and all kinds of other stuff, but then I figured out the truth: Chaz was up to his eyeballs in debt. He'd gambled online, he'd participated in questionable business dealings. It was probably drug related, but I didn't dig far enough into that part to find out the answers. As Nanci Drew, I put together a massive thread and released the financial aspects to the group, and they took care of it from there."

"Did you confront Chaz? Or, what do you all say, touch the poop?"

"No, I didn't have to say a word. Based on my conversations with people in town, it seems like a number of them were in the Reddit group. There were real-life consequences for Chaz. One of my friends works at the bank in downtown Blue Oak, and she told me Chaz didn't get a business loan he needed. I already knew that Chaz's house was about to be foreclosed on, and I think—though I don't know for sure—that my thread sped up that process. He was weeks away from losing everything he'd built."

"What else did you do besides uncovering his financial transactions?"

Melody sighs, and tugs the cardboard sleeve off her chai. "I know a leading question when I see one." She rolls the edges of the cardboard, takes a sip of her drink, and seems to come to a decision. "Fine, I went to Bodhi's party this week. I was hoping to find out more information about their involvement together."

"Did you?"

"No, it was awful, really. A bunch of shallow, pretty people talking about themselves all night. I tried to sneak around her house, but her assistant, Ellis, was all over me. We were the only people who were sober, and it was like she and I were playing hide-and-seek with the lights on while everyone else was blindfolded. She never let me out of her sight. I drank a fruit punch, stayed for two hours, and eventually went home."

"What about Mack?"

"What about him?" Melody's tone is defensive. She sets her cup down firmly on the table.

"Did he help you . . . bend the arc of justice?"

"If you're asking me, did Mack hurt Chaz? Absolutely not. Mack and I both hated him. We never made a secret of that fact. But neither of us is a . . ." She looks earnestly at Esquivel, eye contact unwavering. "I didn't kill Chaz, Lieutenant. Mack didn't either. Our dad has Parkinson's; our aunt and uncle almost died from the grief of losing Dom. Neither of us would ever do anything to hurt them any more." She unclenches and then clenches her fist again. Esquivel appreciates the show of sincerity, but she also knows a lawyer knows how to coach witnesses to appear to be telling the truth, so she takes all the small gestures and the eye contact with a grain of salt. "The things I revealed about Chaz in the group were childish, and probably immature. But I promise you on the life of my son, I didn't kill Chaz."

Esquivel leans her elbows on the table, signaling to Melody she's conceding without saying it. She's studied gestures all her life, and can employ them effectively too. For now, she wants Melody to think she's buying her story. Which, to be fair, she actually is. "I'll need to see everything. All of your financial searches, all of your texts and emails. Any records you found."

"I can do that. You can look, but there aren't any texts; we only ever talked on the phone about Chaz, and even then, it was rare."

"You only ever talked on the phone about Chaz?" Esquivel sits back, disbelieving.

Melody's face is wide open. "Believe it or not, he didn't occupy that much of my life." It is the first time in the interview that Esquivel can tell unequivocally that Melody is lying.

Esquivel decides to ratchet up the tension. "I'll need your laptop and phone and any other electronic devices you might have used."

Melody is stunned. "I only have a company laptop. I'm in the middle of a case."

Esquivel shrugs her shoulders regretfully. "That really sucks. But surely you know that a murder investigation trumps that."

"Only if you have a warrant." Melody's emotional voice has taken on a professional edge.

Esquivel wants her a little bit off-kilter again. She pitches her voice low. "It will take me no time at all to get that warrant, Melody. I'm so sorry to be the one who tells you this. But you and Mack were right: all those years ago, Chaz Nickolson did kill Dominic."

"*What?*"

"Tiffani told Detective Nguyen an hour ago that Chaz confessed his secret to her. That's why she divorced him."

"And she never told anyone?" Melody's voice is fire. She pulls her hand away from Esquivel's and wipes angrily at sudden tears.

"Not till today."

"She didn't . . . She never thought we'd want to *know*?"

"I can't speak for her motives. All I know is what she said. We'll investigate it more fully, of course, but with Chaz dead, there seems little reason to doubt Tiffani's story. Does it make you feel better to know that you were right?"

"You think it changes anything to know that I was *right*?" Melody's tone could strip paint.

"It doesn't?" Esquivel asks innocently.

"Not. One. Damn. Thing." She spits each word. "That bastard killed Dominic and got away with it for *years*. He ruined our family's lives." The tears continue unbidden down her face; the shadows under her eyes deepen. "This is how you know I didn't kill him—because if I'd had even a *hint* . . . if I'd ever heard Tiffani say *anything*, I would have stopped at *nothing* until he was behind bars. A swift blow to the back of the head would've been too kind a fate for him."

Esquivel stills. "Melody, how do you know how Chaz was killed?"

58

As soon as Jake leaves, Leo checks her phone: sixteen more texts from her mother. She doesn't stop to think; if she pauses, she'll have to face what Jake said about Mack, and that thought makes her feel like she's drowning. This murder investigation is spiraling out of control, with first Kay and now Mack as the sheriff's department's prime suspects. She realizes she never really felt fear for Kay; Quackenbush is so inept, and who could truly view Kay as a murderer? But she has nothing but respect for Jake; she can see how his mind works, and it makes her very afraid that he's already putting together a case against Mack. She's not sure how to stop him.

But she can, at least, stop her mother from this incessant, unreasonable texting.

Ten minutes later, when she arrives overheated and raging at the salon, Karina is at her usual station. She looks manic, her makeup hastily applied, her hair . . . Leo stops in the door. Her mother's hair is *unkempt*.

"Leonora Jane, shut the door! Don't let out the bought air!" Accent thick as ever, Karina barely acknowledges her and turns back to her client.

Leo walks to her mother's station. "Mom, we need to talk."

"I just need to finish . . ."

"Hello, Mrs. B," Leo acknowledges her client. "It's good to

see you. I'm so sorry, but I need to talk to my mom right now."

"Oh, honey, it's good to see you too! Your mama was just telling me—"

Leo interrupts. "Mom. *Now.*" Leo stares at her mother in the mirror. She has never spoken to her mother in this tone.

Karina looks over her shoulder. "Trina, would you mind handling this shampoo? Mrs. B, I'll be right back."

"But I—"

Without looking behind her, Leo spins on her heel and slams through the front door, feeling for once like Karina—taking up space and causing a ruckus. The pressure of the last few days has finally exploded. She wheels around on the sidewalk.

Inevitably, her mother beats her to the punch. "What in the ever-lovin' world, Leonora?"

"Are you *serious* right now? You've done nothing but text and call me all day."

"Is it a crime to care about my daughter? To want her to rest?"

"To *rest*? You sent me sixteen texts in the last hour, Mom. This is ridiculous! What is really going on?"

"What are you talking about? What else would it be?"

"I don't know, Mom. I just . . . I don't get how you can be so worried about me that you text me all day but hate me enough to do everything in your power to keep me from ever, ever coming home."

"I don't *hate* you."

"Could've fooled me." Leo's voice catches.

"I just want what's best for you."

"Which is what, in your opinion?"

"Not work with the sheriff's office."

"How do you even know I was helping Jake?"

"It's a small town, Leo."

"I know, I know, the Baptist prayer chain."

"Yes, among other things, though they've been on fire. You've forgotten what it's like in a place where we all know everything about each other. That's part of why I didn't want you to end up stuck here." Karina's hand flutters toward Leo, then falters. She puts it down at her side.

"Fine, you and I can agree that neither of us wants me to be here in Blue Oak. And this time, when I leave, I can promise that I won't be coming back. You've made it very, very clear that there's nothing in this town for me."

"Honey, listen—"

"No, *you* listen. Coming home is a short-term necessity. And while I'm here, this business of you texting and calling and telling me what to do will *not* work. I'm not a child."

"But I don't understand—why do the deputies even need you?"

"You don't *need* to understand. That's what I'm telling you. You're not involved in this decision in any way. I am in my thirties."

"All I want to do is protect you." Karina's face is anguished, and it tugs at Leo's heart—it feels, in some way, like the first real emotion she's seen from her mother. She's not sure what to make of that thought.

"I get it, Mom." Leo has just enough wherewithal to realize she's probably channeling the rage and fear from the last two days into this confrontation with her mother. When Emily yelled at Leo—was that only this morning?—Tess said it was because Leo was Emily's safe person. The phrase echoes in her mind now. After all this time, is her mother still her safe person? The thought brings her closer to tears than she's been all day. She changes tack. "The day I found Dad after his heart attack, my world tore in two. His death destroyed me. And I know it destroyed you too. We both became different people. I know that somehow, in your mind, preventing me from coming home to Blue Oak feels like you're protecting me."

"No, Leo. It *is* protecting you . . ." Karina's voice deepens; she stands straighter.

Leo talks over her. "It's *paranoia*, Mom. I don't know what kind of paranoia—my therapists won't diagnose you, and I have no idea if you go to therapy, but I'm not *doing* this anymore. I just . . ." She pauses, trying to put the storm in her mind into words. "E. M. Forster wrote, 'Life is easy to chronicle, but bewildering to practice,' and I thought of you the first time I read that—you're the most bewildering of all."

Karina visibly swallows, and Leo pauses to see what she will say. After a moment of silence, Leo continues. "I'm an adult, and my choices are my own. You have pushed me away for years. And that means you've lost the right to have any say, even a suggestion, in what I do."

Karina's eyes fill with tears. "Mi amor . . ."

Leo steps back as if she's been slapped. *"Don't."* "Mi amor" is what her father always called her, the phrase a last vestige of their years in El Salvador. It's what he called her that last morning when he dropped her off at school like normal and gave her a kiss on the forehead, then walked to the photography classroom, where, a few hours later, he would suffer a heart attack that killed him instantly. Where he lay on the floor until Leo walked in after school and found his body. Her voice cracks but she barrels on. "I know you probably mean well, Mom, and you're working through a mountain of your own stuff. But Dad would be horrified if he saw who we've become to each other." She looks at the sidewalk, the sun so intense she can feel the headache behind her eyes. "Don't text me. Don't call. I just need to finish tying up some loose ends, then this whole case will be over, and we can deal with . . . whatever this relationship is. And I can leave this town." She furrows her brow and pushes her bangs out of her eyes. "I love you. But I cannot deal with you anymore."

Without another word, without looking back, Leo walks away under the searingly hot afternoon sun. Behind her, she hears a muffled sob, but she squares her shoulders—she will hold this boundary. The resolve is clarifying.

That feeling applies to solving the case too, she realizes. Her mother's desire for her to stop investigating has made it clear that's exactly what she has to do. She's allowed Karina's behavior to keep her from other people she loves for too long.

No, she thinks as she walks, it's not just Karina's behavior—it was her own choices too. Emily is right—she *has* been a tourist. But no longer.

As she walks, her resolve deepens. She has not been there for Emily nearly enough over the years; she's going to make up for it now by doing what Tess asked and proving that Kay didn't murder Chaz.

And she's going to do it for Mack. The intense sun and her blazing anger burn off the last of her doubts. She might not know all of Mack's secrets, but she still knows *him*.

Jake suspects Mack. Quackenbush is gunning for Kay. The murder investigation is threatening to rip this small town apart. She might have complex feelings about Blue Oak, but it is the home of the people she loves most in the world. She cannot allow Chaz's death to destroy this community.

As she walks back to the pool house, she decides: she's going to solve this murder before it's too late.

59

As soon as he drives away from the pool house, Jake calls Esquivel, who doesn't answer, so he calls Macy.

"*Proceed*," she purrs.

"Johnson?" He coughs.

"Oh, sir, hi! I didn't look at who was calling and I . . . What's up? How can I help you?"

"I'm heading back to the station. Have you heard from Esquivel?"

"She's still with Melody Garner-Aziz right now. I've been working on a map to see if there's a pattern with all the evidence that's been found. Sending it to you now."

Jake hears a few clicks. "And the footage?"

"We're pulling as much security footage as we can to corroborate alibis."

"Footage that's obtained legally?"

"It will be legally obtained by the time we go to trial."

Jake pinches the bridge of his nose. "I'm going to pretend you didn't say that. We need search warrants for all of this."

"Way ahead of you. This report will tell you what search warrants you need."

"So what have you found, hypothetically speaking?"

"Hypothetically, there might be footage from Tiffani Miller's across-the-street neighbors' Ring camera showing her on a walk on her street in South Austin with the dog around nine thirty p.m., then going into her house and staying there for the rest of the night when Chaz was murdered. She could have slipped out back or worked with an accomplice, but she didn't pull out of her driveway and drive to Blue Oak that night."

"Okay, that's helpful."

"Also, you'll want to pull DreamBawd security info. A federal agent sent me a file with all of Grant Ford's data. It looks like he was in his apartment all night; he didn't leave by the front or back door. But it's an old building, and there are only two entrances on the security feed. There could easily be other entrances that are unrecorded. I don't feel like that tells us much."

"Anything on Chaz's house?"

"No, just that his home security system hadn't been working for months; he hadn't paid them and they disconnected everything."

"Any updates on his financials?"

"Again, thanks to the feds, we have a full workup. It looks like he owed a lot of people money. There's a very good chance this case is financial."

"I'll take that into account. Anything else?"

"Yes, following the hunch you texted us about earlier, I found a gas station near Garner Ranch that had footage at two eighteen a.m. on July fifth of someone who looks an awful lot like Mack Garner on a walk."

"Do you see any evidence of him elsewhere?"

"No, and the ranch also doesn't have security footage. I can't swear it's Mack, but it's a reasonable assumption that it might have been him. Definitely enough for you to ask him."

"Send it to me. And thanks for the map. Will you send the map to Leo too?" His voice is grim as he puts his truck in gear. "I'm going to visit the sites on this map now. I think I know who is behind all of this and I need to confirm."

60

Leo walks into the pool house in a huff, dumping her tote bags and pillow by the door. The walk has only made her angrier and sweatier, which she wasn't sure was possible after the conversation with her mother.

Luckily, she has plenty of time before her dinner with Mack. She contemplates a nap, but she's too wired. Instead, she takes a long, cool shower and throws on some Dri-FIT shorts and a tee. She plays with the idea of canceling her dinner with Mack, but with all the new information, she decides she wants to see Mack for herself—and she doesn't want Jake to think she canceled because of him. She digs through her suitcase, pulling out item after item that doesn't work for seeing her former high school boyfriend who is currently a suspect in a murder investigation.

She sighs. Virginia Woolf would be so ashamed of her, sitting here in a room of her own, wishing for prettier clothes to look good for a man. She grabs a blue sundress that she doesn't hate and sprays it with water to take out the worst of the wrinkles. That's enough.

She grabs her notebook and her phone and takes them into the bathroom; she often gets her best ideas while she's drying her hair, and she wants to put together a timeline of what she knows to see what she's missing. But first, as she flips the hair dryer on, she checks her email. She has a message from an anonymous sender (the email address is only a random collection of letters and numbers) with the subject line *Nguyen said to send this*. Inside it only says *See attached.—MJ* which she assumes is Macy Johnson. She clicks on the attachment.

It's a map. She zooms in for several minutes, but finds it difficult to read on her phone. She wants to print it out, so she turns the hair dryer off and glances in the mirror: the left side of her hair is half dry and the right is dripping wet. Her bangs make her look like a sheepdog. She reaches the hand holding her phone up to fluff her bangs. She'll just get the printer out of the box, get herself a copy of the map, and come back and fix her hair—

In the mirror, she sees the card tucked into the back of her phone case. It's Kymber's, from the day Mack handed it to Leo from his truck's glove compartment. Leo opens her phone case and takes it out. She stares at it for a minute, then rushes to her laptop.

• • • • •

Minutes or hours later—she has lost all track of time—her hair is a ridiculous mess she has pulled up into a bun, and the blond-wood table is covered in papers from the printer she dug out of a box; she found tape and Post-it notes too. She's hung papers haphazardly over the black-and-white-photo collage wall that Kay decorated the room with. Leo learned a long time ago that she makes the best progress on her research when she can stand back and see patterns. She already knows what Emily would call this, the same thing she's called Leo's research process for years: "conspiracy-theory chic."

But Leo knows in her bones that everything is in its place. It's the same way she felt in the years of researching E. M. Forster and his circle, the influences and ideas that informed his writing. The way she could find one line in a letter to a lover and another line in another writer's poem and bring them together—this idea informed this other idea, and both of them worked together to lead to this scene in *A Passage to India* or *Where Angels Fear to Tread* or—her favorite still—*A Room with a View.*

Leo is not a trained detective, but she is a hell of a researcher. The feeling she had interviewing Bodhi, or even Tiffani despite the heartbreaking subject, rushes back to her—not joy, exactly, but earned confidence. She knows this material, this world, these lives, these . . . writers, in the sense that their online content is a narrative they write and perform for others. In the years when she was turning into one of the best E. M. Forster scholars alive today, she was, unknowingly, honing skills to allow her to investigate this crime.

She puts her fists on her hips and surveys her handiwork. The truth is bleak and ugly. But before she faces the emotions of that, she allows herself one small moment for her favorite part of research: the deep appreciation of good craft. Because she's done it.

Leo has solved the murder.

61

At 8:29 p.m., Mack Garner—in a crisply ironed blue button-up shirt, tan shorts, and brown sandals—walks into Nacho Daddy's. The outdoor space is shaded by plants and a large roof, and the misting fans keep the area relatively cool even on the hottest days. He wonders if Leo's already there. The hostess leads him, holding two menus, and they turn the corner onto the patio—where Jake Nguyen rises, pulling his sunglasses off.

"Mack."

Mack greets him. "Jake." They shake hands briskly.

Jake indicates the table. "Do you mind if I join you?"

"Actually, tonight's not a good night for it. I'm meeting Leo in a minute."

"I'll wait with you till she gets here, then."

"Um, I'd rather not."

Jake's smile is tight. "It'll just be a few minutes."

Mack looks at him as if unsure what to do. "Let me just text Leo."

"I'll check on her. Hold on." Jake pulls his phone out and shoots off a text. His phone buzzes with another call, but he ignores it and places it down on the table.

Mack scowls, then presses send on his own text. "You know what, I *really* don't mind texting my ex to see if she's here for our date."

Jake sits back, nonchalant. "Leo's been helping us on the case, and I want to make sure she's okay. With a murderer around and all."

"What do you mean, Leo's been helping you on the case?" Mack's voice is sharp. The waitress comes by to ask what they'd like to drink, and Mack asks for a margarita. Jake asks for a water. Mack's scowl deepens.

Jake puts his forearms on the table and leans in, taking up space like he's in charge of this conversation. "The case to find Chaz's murderer has moved faster than any of us expected. I know Quackenbush came out to the ranch today; I was at the station when Williams logged the evidence and sent it off to the lab. I was there when Esquivel came back from talking to your sister. And I know so many other things you don't. We picked up lots of evidence planted around town, all within a mile of your family business."

"I'm sorry, what? What evidence?"

"Painters' cloth. More work gloves. Towels. A tarp. All kinds of things you easily have access to at the ranch."

"Those are things anyone who has ever done any work on their house or has a garden also has access to. I mean, Blue Oak just had a hailstorm not long ago; everyone's been painting their houses and fixing their roofs. Those are hardly damning pieces of evidence."

"But the placement of them shows the work of someone who wants to turn attention elsewhere. We found the match to the glove from in front of your barn stuck in the door of Grant Ford's shed behind DreamBawd."

"Are you . . ." Mack sits up, matching Jake's posture. "Are you accusing me of something, Jake?"

"I'm not accusing you." Jake's voice is low and steady. "Not yet, anyway. I'm just asking you: Where were you between eleven p.m. on July fourth and three a.m. on July fifth?"

"Seriously?"

"Seriously."

"Asleep."

"Alone?"

"Of course alone."

"And you didn't leave the house that night?"

Mack sighs and wipes his face. "Hold up, Jake. I need to catch up. My dad and I called the sheriff today because we found what clearly seems to be evidence that was . . . I don't know—planted? placed?—at the barn. It was stuck in the entrance right where guests could see it, as if someone wanted to make sure we found the bag, which one of our bussers did. Think about it . . . are you trying to imply I killed Chaz, then planted evidence in my own family's business?"

"You might have done it to throw us off the scent."

"Are you serious right now, man?" Mack's voice is loud. Around them, heads turn to stare. Jake keeps his shoulders down and his voice level.

"I'm going to need you to calm down."

"Jake, you are a cop of color implying that I, a Black man who has feared his entire life that the cops will falsely accuse him of something, might have murdered a white business owner." Mack's voice breaks. "I'm not upset because I'm guilty. I'm upset because this shit scares me to death. As it should."

Jake sighs. "I get it and I'm not—" The waitress brings Jake's water and Mack's margarita and sets them down with a basket of chips and a bowl of salsa, then hovers for a minute watching them. Mack turns and shakes his head, and she walks into the corner, but she stays nearby, glowering at Jake.

Jake drinks some water and holds his hand up. "I'm putting my cards on the table, okay?" He waits for Mack to nod tersely. "You have to see how it looks to me. On the fourth, you pushed Grant and punched Chaz. And several months ago, when there was an altercation between you and Chaz at your restaurant that we had to break up, you threatened Chaz."

"You did not *break up* an altercation at the restaurant. Yet again, *we* called *you* because he was being belligerent. I restrained him when he got aggressive. It's sounding more and more like we can't trust the sheriff's department in Blue Oak.

But yeah, no joke, it's not a secret that I hated Chaz. Literally the entire town knows."

"Why did you hate him?"

"I'm going to text Leo again. She's . . . ten minutes late." Mack pauses and fires off another text.

Jake watches him, sipping his water. When Mack sets his phone down, Jake asks again, "Why did you hate Chaz, Mack?"

"Because Mel and I think he killed my cousin and got away with it." Mack's voice is quiet and raw. He picks up a chip and breaks off a corner with his fingernail.

"Why do you think that? Did he ever tell you that?"

"He didn't have to. I knew that night. I've known ever since. I don't know exactly what happened, but I know it was Chaz. He was always jealous of Dom."

"The night you kicked him out of your restaurant when he was drunk, did you follow him to Bodhi Bruce's house?"

"Who?"

"The woman he was dating a few years ago."

"Of course not. I knew Tiffani, and I've met Kymber, but I never met his other girlfriends. Why would I follow Chaz?"

"He thought you did. He told Bodhi you'd come after him."

"Dude was probably wasted. And he wasn't really scared of me, he was scared of his *conscience*." He leans across the table. "Jake, I swear to you, I have never threatened Chaz or even touched him, other than that one night when I restrained him at the restaurant, and when he came after Kay at the parade." Mack sighs and puts both hands on the table. "Listen, I'm telling the truth and I'm also trying to convince you I'm telling you the truth, and that is frustrating." He looks Jake in the eyes. "Even that night at the restaurant, when I told him I'd come after him, I didn't mean it. I saw what Dom's death did to my family. It's not worth putting them through more pain just for the momentary satisfaction of making Chaz pay for what he did. Even if he deserved it." He leans in, holding Jake's gaze. "I'm not going to act like I cared about the man, but I swear on everything my family has built that I did not physically hurt him."

"Other than punching him on the fourth."

Mack concedes. "Other than that one time, when it looked like he was going to come after Kay Schneider, yes."

"So . . . did you find other ways of hurting him?" Jake gazes at Mack consideringly.

"I . . . yes." Mack sits back.

"Like what?"

"Like, Melody went after his finances. And I . . ." Mack takes a gulp of his margarita. When he speaks again, Jake has to lean in to hear him. "I flirted with Kymber. And tried to convince her to tell me Chaz's secrets."

"Did it work?"

"I was just getting started. I asked her to help us with social media. Punching Chaz definitely didn't make me go up in her eyes, but I was trying to convince her I did that because I was jealous of Chaz." He grimaces. "It wasn't my finest plan."

"So you were planning to seduce—or were actively seducing?—his girlfriend?"

Mack sits forward. "I wasn't *seducing* anyone. I didn't have some kind of big dastardly plan I was following, I was just . . . I don't know, using what the good Lord gave me to try to see if I could find out more about Chaz. Flirting is not illegal, Jake."

"Were you with Kymber on the night of the fourth? Or early the morning of the fifth?"

"No!" Mack smacks the table in anger. "I've never been *with* Kymber. Nor was I ever going to be. She's not my type."

"Which is . . . ?"

Mack narrows his eyes. "Are we talking about the investigation right now?"

Jake narrows his back. "Again, where were you?"

"What are you asking?"

"I think you know, but I'd like to give you a chance to tell me."

Mack's sigh is explosive. "Fine, I left to go on a walk. I do that sometimes when I can't sleep. But you already know this, don't you?"

Jake nods. "Where did you go?"

"Nowhere, Jake. I left my casita, walked for a bit on the sidewalk, where I'm assuming you saw some security footage of me or something, then I swung back to one of the ranch trails and walked it for a while."

"Away from cameras?"

"Away from everything."

"Did you go to Chaz's house that night?"

"No."

"The Garner Ranch butts up against Deep Hollows, and Chaz's house is right across the street from the park."

"I didn't go to Chaz's house."

"What time did you come back?"

"I don't know, three or something? We have those Schlage security systems on all the doors, the ones you have to punch the numbers into when you enter and exit. There's a record of when I go into my house and when I leave every time. I can get that for you, and you can see when I came and went."

"All that will show is that someone went into the house, not that it was you." Jake's voice is considering. "Do you have a doorbell camera?"

"No, we don't want the guests feeling watched or like the place is unsafe."

"And you just . . . went for a walk? In the middle of the night?"

Mack leans in. "My high school girlfriend just came home, and I realized while I was walking her to her car after the sheriff's station that I've probably been in love with her half my life, and I almost asked her out within a couple hours of seeing her even though I know that the fastest way to make her withdraw is to force her to face an emotion before she's ready. So yeah, I stayed up for hours overthinking and finally left my house and *went on a walk*."

Jake's face is opaque. He watches Mack for several minutes, considering. "I will be looking into everything you've said."

"I expect you to." Mack holds out his hands to indicate he's an open book.

"If what you're saying is true—" Jake raises his hands to ward off Mack's protest. "Listen, I know how that sounds. But I have to follow every lead all the way through, and a lot of the circumstantial evidence was pointing to you." He thumbs the moisture on his glass. "Even in a small town like Blue Oak, we can't cut corners or jump to conclusions. Especially in a small town like Blue Oak. It's too easy for grievances to take over the department." He holds Mack's eyes. "At the end of the day, I'm doing my job to the best of my ability."

"Well, your job sucks." Mack gets up and pulls several bills out of his wallet, tossing them on the table.

"Tell me about it." Jake's voice is grim.

"I'm leaving. I'm going to find Leo. I'll see you around."

Jake stands as soon as Mack rounds the corner. He's not completely convinced Mack is innocent, but Jake is less sure that he's guilty than he was before he sat down. The questions in front of him are urgent: If Mack didn't kill Chaz, then who did?

And where in the world is Leo?

62

Kymber's card unlocked it all. Baby pink with embossed gold, it advertised the content strategy and consulting services of Kymber Dawn. But the email to book one of her "consultation's" (Leo spent twenty minutes twitching at the extraneous apostrophe) was one that the sub, or at least Leo, had never seen before: kimberlyogn14@angelo.edu.

Kymber was always the subreddit's biggest unsolved mystery. She burst onto the scene when she started dating Chaz, and try as they might, they couldn't find any definitive background information about her. But with the email from Angelo State University, Leo has unlocked the mystery that is Kymber Owens within the hour.

She looks at the narrative taped on her wall: Kymber was born Kimberly Ogniewski in 1992 in Las Cruces, New Mexico. She attended Angelo State University in San Angelo, Texas, graduating with honors in 2014 with a dual degree in computer science and business. She worked as an administrative assistant briefly in her hometown before coming to Austin sometime in 2016 or 2017. Over the years—on a defunct Facebook page and in friends' photos on various social media platforms—Kimberly's transformation into Kymber becomes clearer. Leo's fingers itch to share her research with the subreddit; they would gobble it up like piranhas.

The write-up from Angelo State when Kimberly Ogniewski graduated with honors is glowing. Kymber's persona of "dingbat chewing gum" is clearly an act.

Leo gazes at the middle of her conspiracy collage: comments she found less than a month ago on a fan site for the hit reality TV show *Real Housewives* written by someone with the username kimberlyog2014. Under a post speculating about an Austin show: *Anyone know how to get cast on this season? I'm a RH in Austin and I'd love to be considered. I'm like Lisa and Ramona, but younger and cuter.*

There are other comments by kimberlyog2014, mostly in response to users' conversations—asking about fillers or makeup routines, in one case talking about a love triangle that Leo doesn't fully understand. Leo printed up the pages so she could tape them to the wall, and added questions scribbled on yellow Post-its:

Was Kymber trying to be a real housewife?

Wouldn't that make her LESS likely to be a suspect in Chaz's murder, since supposedly he was the "husband" or partner she would be housewife-ing for?

But at the bottom, the clincher, a comment less than a week old, circled several times by Leo's favorite highlighter. Kimberlyog2014 asks: *Does anyone know if there's been a RH widow? I know Bethany was divorced, but wouldn't a widow be sad?? And sad in a good way??* One user wrote back: *Carole,* followed by kimberlyog2014's *Thx.*

To the right, Leo has taped the map that Macy sent, marking all of the sites where the law enforcement officers found possible evidence. Something about it is stirring a memory for her.

As Leo always does when she researches, she intentionally quiets her mind. She feels her anger at her mother fade, her nerves about dinner tonight with Mack dissipate.

And it comes to her: this map looks just like the running app that Kymber uses, the one where she shares her public routes.

Minutes later, Leo locates her phone under piles of paper, ignores all the notifications, and prints up nine more pieces of paper: eight maps from Kymber's profile, including dates and times from early in the morning on July 5 through July 6, from the archived data on the Runsafe app where she publicly shares her runs. They coincide exactly with the map Macy made, including a 3:57 a.m. stop at the Zora Neale Hurston Street house on July 5.

Underneath it, Leo tapes an image of the Jackalope fuchsia hydration pack Kymber promoted, bragging about how roomy it is and how much you can fit into it without the pack looking full. The one where, Leo suspects, Kymber hid the evidence of her murder of Chaz and, after deciding to frame Kay, hedged her bets by distributing bloody towels and gloves and other items all over town to cast suspicion on almost anyone who had reason to hate Chaz.

Leo glances down as the screen on her phone changes. Emily is calling but it's still on silent. She puts Emily on speakerphone.

"I was calling to leave you a suggestive voicemail; I can't believe you're answering in the middle of your *date*!"

"What?" Leo looks at the time. It's 8:50. She flips to the notifications she's been ignoring: several missed texts from both Mack and Jake. "Oh, no, Em, I need to go."

"You're not on your date?"

Leo's looking for her shoes so she can go tell the deputies, but stops as the truth hits her—it wasn't Mack. She was right all along. Maybe she'll call Jake and then drive to the restaurant to go find Mack. After all, now that she's solved the murder, the rest should be in the hands of the sheriff's department.

"Leo?"

"Oh, sorry, I've just got a lot . . . What's that noise? Are you at a *party* while your mom is in jail?"

"Lee, I'm *at* the jail. Beth has been here all afternoon with some of her lawyer friends. Turns out Mom's lawyer went to law school with one of Beth's friends and they called a few other people to come up here. Everyone thinks that Mom has good reason to sue Quackers, so they're plotting to take him down. And apparently even the Baptist prayer chain is now saying that Anthony Mueller heard from the medical examiner's sister that Chaz died from a blow to the back of the head. It's all over town. There's no way it could have been my mom; even Quackers has to admit that eventually."

"Is he there?"

"No, the bastard left early. Apparently having dinner at the Garners' restaurant. Mom's rotting in jail and he's eating *steak*."

"Sounds like she's hardly rotting, but point taken."

"An hour ago, Deputy Williams showed up with some boxed wine the cops confiscated in a raid. Then, well, you know how law students can drink; apparently, they're worse once they pass the bar. Mom made some of the officers go out for crudités."

"Of course Kay Schneider is hosting a party in the jail. Is my mom there?"

"She was. She left five minutes ago."

"Did she say anything about our fight?"

"What fight? Oh, Lee, I'm so sorry. First, I was horrible—I'm still sorry, by the way—and now you had a fight with your mom?"

"Yeah, it's not worth getting into right now. Where did my mom go?"

"I don't know. Williams returned from the lab and announced to a roomful of tipsy lawyers that they got results back from the lab in record time; he's having a great time. Your mom asked to see the evidence, and Williams showed it to her—which, between us, I don't think he's supposed to do, but also, my family's throwing a kegger in jail, so we're not judging. Anyway, he made some comment to your mom, and she took off."

Leo grips her phone. "What did he say?"

"Something about how he recognized the green eco trash sacks from DreamBawd."

"Which green sacks?"

"I think they found a sack with some evidence in it. At the Garners'."

"At the Garners'? And it was in a trash sack like the ones they use at DreamBawd?"

"Sounds like it. I didn't see the pictures, but your mom booked it. She just waved at my mom, who waved back, and walked out the door."

"Do you know where she was going?"

"No. Lee, what's going on?"

"Call Jake and tell him what you told me."

"Okay, I will, but can you tell me why?"

"No time. My mom might be in danger."

"Whatever you're planning, be careful, okay?"

"Call Jake. Give him this exact message: tell Macy to follow Kymber's Runsafe app. Can you tell him that?"

"Macy, Kymber, Runsafe. Got it. But why don't you call him?"

"Because I need to go." And, Leo doesn't say it, but because Jake will certainly tell her to wait at home. "Call Jake. And, um . . . Mack too? Tell him I'm sorry and I'll call him later. See you soon."

Leo opens up her Runsafe app and finds Kymber's profile: Kymber's on a run right now. Her red dot is moving; she's only a few blocks away from Leo, on the greenbelt running trail. Kymber's running home.

Leo checks her mother's location on her iPhone and suddenly her hands start to shake: Karina is at Kymber's house.

Without thinking, Leo grabs her keys and—at the last second—her can of Mace, then runs out the door.

Leo's going to have to hustle if she wants to catch Kymber before she hurts Leo's mother.

63

Leo's feet smack the pavement as she runs. It seems best to act as if she's out for a normal run on the well-lit path in the greenbelt. There are still several people out, some ambling with dogs, others running or biking. She hopes no one will suspect that she's following Kymber.

After sprinting for several minutes, she spots Kymber's bleached-blond ponytail, like a beacon. She's wearing black biker shorts and a black sports bra and gold Beats, which shine iridescently in the fading sun.

To make her "I just happened to be behind you" vibe authentic, Leo has stuck her earbuds in, and she glances down to her iPhone to see her mother's location: still at Kymber's. Her mother is well-meaning, but she has no idea what is about to come at her.

What is she going to do, blind Kymber with Aqua Net? Leo increases her pace.

64

Kymber's house is small, a rental probably around a thousand square feet. In the dim light from the single-bulb porch light, Karina notes the rotting vinyl siding, the cracked pavement. This house saw better days a couple of decades ago. Karina knows: Kymber is a social climber. And she is desperate.

Which means Karina needs to stop Kymber before she gets to Leo.

She stays in the shadows to the side of the house, tugging black gloves on, then—when the wind picks up and the shadows shift—charges in a swift burst to the back door. It takes three seconds for her to pick the lock and slip inside without a sound.

The house carries the stale smell of years of used frying oil. Karina closes the door behind her silently. The kitchen is tiny; Karina notes the sticky linoleum with peeling corners and cabinets thick with too many coats of paint. The table in the corner looks like a garage sale find.

She glides through the rest of the house: a living room with a TV and an innocuous brown love seat but nothing else; an empty room with some weights; a bedroom with a mattress on the floor. No pictures, no books, few personal items. One room seems to be the storage place for the various products Kymber places in videos; a pile of half-opened boxes of supplements, protein powder, and running and yoga gear comes up to Karina's waist. A ring light camera is set up in a corner of the room facing a green velvet chair next to a brass lamp, white marble table, and some tasteful plants: a studio area, where Kymber films.

Only in the bathroom does Karina see evidence that Kymber lives there—the hunter-green-and-white-tiled countertop is stuffed with skin care products and herbal supplements. Karina picks up various pill bottles and moisturizers and serums. By these, more than anything else, she confirms she's on the right track: Karina knows better than anyone how to camouflage in plain sight, how to craft an illusion so thorough that few see a cunning mind beneath the glitter and ditziness.

Karina checks her Find My app. Leo was at the pool house, but now the little yellow circle that says *LH* is moving slowly. Is she in the car? No, the dot is on the greenbelt. Is she . . . running at this time of night?

Karina watches the dot for a minute. It's moving toward her own location.

Then she realizes: Leo might be following Kymber toward Kymber's house. She shakes her head; Leo is not prepared for this confrontation. She has no idea how dangerous Kymber is. Karina moves through the house quickly and finds a hiding place in the back of the front coat closet.

Leo is running right toward her.

65

Leo is behind Kymber as they enter the wooded section of the greenbelt. The noise is hushed by the trees, the highway a distant thrum behind them. The birds still trill sleepily, and occasional bats ping in the air above them. It's too late in the season for fireflies; the lights along the path are more sporadic here.

Leo is wary, slowing down a bit. The path curves and she loses sight of Kymber for a minute before seeing a flash of blond through the trees. Leo keeps running.

They pass beneath the walking bridge where Sandra Cisneros Avenue turns into a bike path above them. Kymber doesn't turn around once, the gold trim on her Beats gleaming in the yellow lights beneath the bridge.

Leo's heart is beating much faster than it normally does by the time they follow the slow turn of the path to the left. Leo knows they're coming to a crossroads. From several yards behind Kymber, she forks to the right. She assumes she'll see Kymber moving along that path.

She sees nothing.

She slows down. The wind in the trees picks up, throwing shadows as the branches block and reveal the lights.

Still nothing.

She takes her earbuds out and bends down like she is worn out, panting. She listens hard.

The silence is broken only by the sounds of cars on nearby roads. No footsteps. No voices. Nothing.

Where in the world is Kymber?

66

Nestled behind two winter coats and a vacuum cleaner in the back of Kymber's coat closet, Karina hears her breath loud in her ears. She watches the yellow *LH* dot on her screen: Leo's agonizingly slow progress toward Kymber's house, where Karina sits and waits.

The dot pauses, then stops.

Karina sits forward, cupping the phone in her hands, willing her daughter to move.

67

Leo turns in a circle, listening with every fiber of her being. Suddenly she hears a scrape ahead to the left, a shoe on pavement. She starts up again, a slow jog. She keeps her earbuds in but the music off. If she runs into Kymber, she wants to appear as innocent as possible.

There is movement through the trees, and then Leo spots her. Kymber is running again. Leo surges quietly ahead.

68

Karina breathes a sigh of relief when the dot that is her daughter starts moving again. But less than ten seconds later, Karina is opening the door and racing to her car, which is five houses away, banging open doors and not bothering to close them behind her.

Leo's dot did not turn right along the fork in the running path toward Kymber's house. She turned left.

Toward Chaz's.

69

Jake hangs up the phone with Emily. He could barely hear her over the noise. Was she at a party? While her mother was in jail? She just kept repeating, "Leo said to tell Macy: check the map and Kymber's Runsafe." Jake's not sure what that means, but he texts Macy anyway.

He drives to the pool house. Leo's car is there, and Derrida is inside the cottage—barking repeatedly in response to Jake's knock—but Leo doesn't answer.

The door is unlocked. He walks inside and holds his fist out for Derrida to smell. The two of them had been doing better together, but Derrida's ears remain back, so Jake quickly opens the fridge and grabs some lunch meat.

Jake throws the meat to the dog, then turns on the light—has the room been ransacked? Is Leo a serial killer? He walks around the paper-covered walls, reading her writing, following the progression of ideas. Occasionally he throws more meat at the dog to keep him happy.

Jake stops at a map and reads what she wrote. He stands back, mouth open. It's all here.

He pulls out his phone and dials.

70

Leo's phone vibrates from the pocket in the waistband of her shorts. It's Jake. She presses ignore. She's already ignored several calls from Mack. She'll have to make it up to them both later.

It rings again. Her mother. She ignores that call too.

She followed Kymber left at the fork, and now they're headed toward Chaz's house.

She runs until the path ends at a curb. She cannot see Kymber for a minute, and she pants with her hands on her knees again, buying herself time to look surreptitiously to the left and the right . . . there.

She has a flash of inspiration. She pulls out her phone and fires off an Instagram message.

A flick of Kymber's ponytail shows her where she's headed. Leo starts walking slowly, like she's cooling off, to the north. These houses are nestled between the greenbelt and the park; just a few hundred yards away, hidden by trees and hills, is the Deep. She had seen so many pictures of Chaz's home, but seeing it now, in the shadow of night, after the story she heard from Tiffani, the full implications of the location he chose hit Leo.

Chaz had been living within sight of the place where he killed his best friend in high school.

Leo is so busy looking toward the Deep on her left that she misses the motion on her right.

Suddenly she feels the cold edge of steel right behind her ear, and hears the voice she's heard so many times before on videos, this time without the gum and the giggling.

"Who the hell are you and why are you following me?" Kymber asks.

71

Karina's Nissan Altima races around the greenbelt as she curses the city planners. The roundabout a quarter of a mile north of where Leo has stopped is equipped with six separate speed bumps, all of which Karina attacks as if they are specifically responsible for keeping her from her daughter.

As she whips past the twenty-five-mile-per-hour speed limit, Karina makes another call.

72

Jake answers his phone as he gets back into his truck.

"Yes. Where? Are you sure?" He starts the car and puts it into gear. "Gotcha. Thanks, Macy."

He heads around the greenbelt to the south, then swings up north.

73

Leo yelps.

"Hush." Kymber's voice is low, cold.

"Kymber! Did you . . . are you pulling a gun on me? I met you the other day!"

"Oh, I remember you. You're Mack's friend."

"I'm Leo, yes, I grew up with Mack. Can you put the gun down?"

"No. You've been following me."

"I'm so sorry, I didn't mean to be a creeper. I just saw you, and, well, I messaged you on Instagram."

"No, you didn't."

"Truly, I did. It's probably in your hidden requests. I wanted to get some advice about social media, since Mack says you've been helping at the ranch? I think this is all just a big misunderstanding."

"Cute. You're trying to act like you don't know what's going on. Start moving."

Leo tries to turn her head, but Kymber shoves the gun deeper behind her ear. "Don't you dare turn around. I'm going to drop my gun to my waist, but trust me, I know exactly what I'm doing."

"What are you . . . Where are you taking me?"

"Walk." Kymber shoves Leo slightly and she stumbles over

the curb. She feels her can of Mace fall out of her waistband pocket, into the lush grass of Chaz's front yard. She thinks about trying to grab it, but doesn't want to risk Kymber shooting. She stands up, pulling her shirt down slightly to hide her phone. At least she still has that. Not that it will do her much good; no one knows she has come here. If only she'd answered Jake's call and kept the phone on so he could hear this.

It's too late now. She's completely alone. The only thing she feels glad about is that her mother is nowhere nearby. At least Leo doesn't have to save Karina while trying to save herself.

Kymber walks Leo into Chaz's home. The walls just inside of the front door are lined with mirrors and the decor in the open-concept main area is beautiful but impersonal. "Sit right there and don't move." Kymber keeps her gun on Leo while making sure the front and back doors are locked and electronically lowering the blinds on the floor-to-ceiling windows lining the back wall with the flip of a switch.

The blinds are still buzzing shut when Kymber turns on Leo. "Tell me what you know, or I'll kill you."

Leo lifts her hands. "Kymber, I swear . . ."

"Shut up!" Kymber screams. "I'm giving you one last try: Who are you and why are you following me? The truth, or you're done for."

"You're right, I'm sorry. I should have known you'd be too smart for me." Leo sighs, like she's caught. "Let's start over. My name is Leo. And I'm . . . well." She puts her hands down, rubbing them against her bare thighs twice. "Kymber, you don't know me yet, but I know all about you. I've been following you for a while."

She looks down, and then up intentionally, past the gun and straight into Kymber's eyes. She slowly turns her lips up into a wide, maniacal grin. "Kymber Owens, I'm your biggest fan."

74

Kymber! Sheriff's department! Open up!" Jake pounds on the front door, gun held aloft. He has already called backup, and Esquivel should be there shortly with the DPS officers. But he's not going to wait. He doesn't want to play around with Leo's life.

He hears a scuffle around the side of the house and rushes through the back gate.

A cat scurries over the fence. The back door is open, yellow light spilling into the night.

"Leo!" Jake runs in the back door, gun drawn. He checks every room, throwing each door open. Nothing.

He returns to the backyard just in time to see the flashing lights and hear two sets of tires screech. He pulls out his radio. "Esquivel, it's Nguyen. Stand down."

He gazes out across Kymber's desolate backyard. "They're not here."

75

In position, Karina hits a button on a discreet black box on her belt and then taps once on her earpiece. The tech really has gotten so much better in recent decades. She'd called in a favor earlier this morning, and then activated that favor in the car on the way over. Everything happening inside the house is being recorded.

She prepares to go inside, but then her daughter says: "I'm your biggest fan."

Is Leo . . . trying to get information out of a suspect? Karina's smile is slight; the many agents she has trained over the years know that that almost-smirk—so different from her wide-open, boisterous-hairdresser grin—is the highest compliment Karina Holloway ever pays.

"Hold on. Stay in position. Let me see where she's taking this."

"Are you sure?" a disembodied voice asks in her ear.

"Be ready. But let's give it a second." The evidence against Kymber for the murder, for now, is all circumstantial. Karina had to restrain her scoff when Williams showed her that the sheriff's office had performed a luminol test on a rock and retained screenshots of the Reddit group. She has never worked in any official domestic law enforcement role, and even she knows that kind of evidence would never hold up in court. But if they could get a confession on tape? It could make all the difference.

She hears Leo clear her throat, and she leans in to hear what happens next.

She is gambling with her only daughter's life. She holds her breath, hoping it will pay off. Trusting—for the first time ever—in her daughter's ability to get out of this situation alive.

76

Kymber cocks her head but the gun doesn't lower.

"Seriously, Kymber, I was following you because I saw you were running. Check your Instagram DMs. You'll have a message from Flowers4Life4Ever—that's me."

"If you were just out running, where's your dog?" Kymber keeps her gun trained on Leo while she pulls out her phone.

"I decided to give him a break tonight." Leo looks down coyly, then up with what she hopes is an eager expression. "Look, I'm really sorry, yesterday when I saw you, of course I knew who you were. I've followed your every move for the last two years. I just didn't want to come on too strong. It must be hard to be a celebrity."

She worries she's laying it on too thick, but Kymber's gun drops just a notch. Kymber scoffs. "Well, hardly a celebrity."

"Are you kidding me? I'm a massive fan of your work. I've told everyone about it. My friends and I trade your posts with each other almost every day." It helps that she's not lying at all, though "fan" might be a slight misdirection. "That post you did last week, about the noble paths of Buddhism? I mean, honestly, I can't stop thinking about it. It's made me more, I don't know, spiritual."

Kymber narrows her eyes. "Really?"

"Yes!" Leo makes her voice lighter. "I, too, have been seeking the middle path!"

"Oh, wow, I'm so glad!" Kymber lowers the gun a few inches more. "That tea company, SaniTea? They sent me an *amazing* pamphlet about the noble paths of Buddhism with their Busy Hibiscus blend. Everything about right understanding and right . . . all the other stuff they said . . . I could *feel* the zen, you know? I just want to make a difference in the world. I've always been spiritual." She looks back at her phone. "I'm looking through my messages. I don't see you."

"Try the hidden requests. The algorithm probably thinks I'm scamming you."

Kymber gets distracted reading other messages. Leo needs her to find that DM. She keeps talking. "Your spiritual influence is making a difference to me. I've been meditating after I watch your workout videos, and I can tell you, it's really changed my life."

Kymber hoists the gun back up. "Are you pulling my leg?"

"Kymber, three weeks ago, you did a video about how to adjust your chakras through mindful body positions to get rid of unwholesome destructive thoughts, and I have been doing those body positions every day since."

"Show me." Kymber gestures with the gun. Leo turns her head questioningly, then—when Kymber nods—she moves.

Her voice is muffled because she's upside down as she narrates the move back to Kymber. "Down dog into flip your dog into whole body stretch, then reaching up for an everything breath and . . ." She jumps up and breathes out hard. "Exiting destruction." She breathes in, pulling her hands toward her heart. "So I can inhale the good."

"Wow, you weren't lying." Kymber lays her gun down on the counter beside her, beaming at Leo. "I found your message." She reads aloud. " 'Kymber, your spiritual posts about the noble paths have changed my life. I'm Mack's friend who got your card while we were running the other day and I'm looking for a mentor to help me with content creation. Could we meet for coffee so I can gush about how much I love your work? I'm excited to learn anything you can teach me!' " She puts the phone down, beaming. "I guess you really are a fan!"

"You have no idea, Kymber." Leo makes herself look Kymber in the eye. "I think about you every single day."

Kymber tucks her chin down. "Aw, that makes my day!" she says, as if she had not just held Leo at gunpoint a second before. "Would you like a hug?"

"I'd love nothing more!" Kymber opens her arms. Leo steps into them.

77

Are you at the ready?" Karina's whisper is tense.

"Say the word. Do you want to move?"

"Not quite . . ." Karina is watching now through a gap in one of the blinds, where she can barely see Leo, who steps back.

Every muscle in her body is tense. She has not prayed much since Richard died, but now she sends up a quick one—please let her be making the right decision.

"Roger. Ready when you are." The voice in her ears is surprised.

Karina squints. Kymber indicates a stool, and Leo settles in—like they're about to gab.

78

Please forgive me for earlier." As she waves dismissively toward the discarded gun, Kymber's voice is much brighter now, the chipper performance voice she uses on the internet and with fans. "Stalkers, you know."

"Totally!" Leo's voice sounds overly loud to her. She takes a deep breath. It's all she can do not to say *Pshaw*! She's not good at being in character; she hated theater class as a kid.

"Can I tell you a secret, Leah?"

"Of course." Leo wouldn't dream of correcting her name right now.

"Wait." Kymber squints at her. "I saw you with Mack, but weren't you also at the parade the other day?"

Leo looks down in what she hopes is a bashful way. "Honestly? I was just there to try to see you in real life."

"Not Chaz?"

"Of course not. I never really loved Chaz. I thought you could do so much better."

"Oh, that is so sweet to say. I'm so sad, of course, about him dying. It's just so awful." Kymber looks off into the distance, lips pursed. "But—please keep this between us—things weren't going great."

"Oh, we could tell."

"What do you mean?" Kymber's expression is quizzical.

"It was obvious that Chaz knew you were better than him and that he was going to lose you. He was desperate to keep you. But he was also rude and condescending sometimes. You're such a strong woman. But you're also so compassionate and kind! You didn't want to suffer, but you didn't want *him* to suffer. You were looking for a middle path to *end* the suffering."

"That's it, exactly!" Kymber's face is suffused with joy. "That came through in my videos?"

"Oh, you have no idea. So much more came through than I think you can really understand. We could all see the real you."

"I'm so glad. I've been . . . I really feel bad about almost shooting you!" Kymber breaks into a hearty cackle and Leo joins in a beat later. She glances down at the gun: it's still pointed toward her, a good foot from Kymber's relaxed hand on the counter. She looks away, still laughing—haha, best joke ever, you almost shot me. What a night!

"Oh, man, you know what I always say about laughter, right?"

"That it's the . . ."

". . . *best medicine!*" They finish together, as if it's some spectacularly insightful phrase Kymber thought of herself.

"But I feel like you were going to tell me something important, and I really want to hear it." Leo puts her chin in her hand on the counter, listening attentively.

"Leah, it's been a hard few days. And that's saying a lot, for me. My life hasn't been easy, you know."

"I don't know. You're like this . . . mysterious goddess who just showed up one day."

"Aw, you are *so* sweet! Hardly a goddess. Try Angelo State grad trying to make a new life."

"Really?"

"Yeah. You might not realize, but 'Kymber' isn't my full name."

"No!"

"It's Kimberly. And it's not Owens, it was Ogniewski. I grew up in New Mexico. In college, I saw all these influencers making bank and thought, they don't have anything that I don't have!"

"Exactly! You knew you could be one of them. As you are!"

"Thank you! I couldn't do it without my fans!"

Leo nods, leaning her body fully on the counter now, as if she's cuddling up and raptly listening to Kymber's story, her arm within six inches of the gun. She is still afraid, but Kymber confirming that her research was right solidifies her certainty. She has an idea, a tricky one, but it just might work—like pretending to be Kymber's stalker evidently has.

"But it was harder than I thought. I care so much—I just want my fans to have a better life, you know? To work out and feel great and know that they're full of love and light?"

"That is so inspiring!"

"Thank you! But it started . . . I don't know, the universe was teaching me some hard lessons, you know? I was suffering. And there is an end to suffering, Buddha teaches. I found it in that pamphlet. When SaniTea sent it, I realized it was clear the universe wanted me to have it. The universe wanted my suffering to end."

Leo nods, face enthralled, mind whirring rapidly.

"That's why I started dating Chaz. At first, I didn't suffer anymore with him, you know? I was so happy!"

"You really were." Leo sighs jealously.

"But then . . . I stopped being as happy. I encouraged good thoughts, you know? I tried to have compassion for him. But he was so . . ."

"Can I say it? He was greedy. And the *cause* of suffering is greed, Kymber. He *caused* your suffering." Kymber's eating out of her hand, Leo realizes. All these years of snarking have given her all the information she needs to appeal to Kymber in a personalized way.

"Okay, so. This new opportunity came along. A producer in Austin was looking at my portfolio to maybe cast me in a reality TV show."

"Are you serious?" Leo sits up animatedly.

"I know, right?"

"That would be . . . gah, that would be life-changing, Kymber. The universe is really blessing you." Leo leans on the counter again, even closer to the gun. Maybe she won't need to pull her plan off. Maybe she'll just be able to grab the gun while Kymber's talking.

"Thank you." Kymber puts two hands together at her heart. "All I needed was something big from Chaz. A big public statement."

"Like a wedding?" Leo's eyes are wide.

"Precisely." Kymber leans in, like Chaz isn't dead. But then her face falls in a carefully curated version of grief. "But he wouldn't hear of it. He said he'd never marry again after his first wife, that she was his great love, and if he wouldn't marry Bodhi, he definitely wouldn't marry me."

"No." Leo suffuses her voice with indignation. "What a pig!"

"Thank you!"

"And your big opportunity! He didn't even have to really marry you, he could have . . . I don't know, green-card married you or something. Social media married you."

"You should be my publicist!" Kymber's laughter peals out.

"Compassion over selfishness, right?"

"No." Kymber shakes her head. "Chaz never got Buddhism. Leah, he *caused* suffering." She looks at Leo meaningfully. "It took me weeks of meditation, but finally I realized what I had to do. He stood between me and my happiness."

"Meditation leads to nirvana. What did you find?"

"That I had to eradicate every obstacle. *Every* obstacle."

"Of course you did." Leo nods decidedly, as if they're in complete agreement.

"I met with the producer, and they told me without a big jump in numbers, like from a wedding or a funeral, I didn't have enough followers to warrant getting on the reality show."

"Did you say"—Leo grins slyly, hoping she's reeling Kymber in—"a funeral?"

"I did." Kymber tips conspiratorially toward Leo.

"So you did what you had to do."

"I did something to end my suffering, Leah. With a calm mind, which is how I know it's right."

Leo breathes in and out as if she's in such awe. "Wow. You killed Chaz . . . to end his suffering and to open the door to your happiness."

Kymber leans back triumphantly. "I did."

"You took the initiative to find your happy!" Leo tries to keep her voice enthused, even as her stomach turns. She didn't like Chaz, but to kill him in order to be on a TV show—she'd suspected that was the reason, but to hear Kymber admit it makes Leo's blood run cold. And yet part of her mind is working fast. She's been right about everything up till this point. Even if it's risky, she thinks her plan just might work.

"I did. And honestly, I know Buddha says not to cause suffering in others, but doesn't *ending* suffering count? Because Chaz was really suffering. He felt so guilty about some things he'd done in the past. It was eating him up. He was gambling away all the money he got."

"But he should have been sharing it with you!"

"*Exactly.* I thought we were partners in business and in life. It turns out his only partner was his own ego."

"The love you had to give to so many should not have been squandered, Kymber. I'm so sorry he didn't see your truth."

"Me too, Leah. I manifested a future for both of us. He was the obstacle that stood in the way of our happiness."

"How did you . . ." Leo pauses, like she's about to ask for a secret.

"What?" Kymber raises one eyebrow.

"I mean, I heard the sheriff's office already arrested someone else, so clearly you took care of everything you needed to. But can I ask . . . how did you break the cycle of selfishness that was Chaz's daily existence?"

Kymber cackles again. "I truly need to hire you as my publicist. Listen, this doesn't leave this room, okay?"

"I would *never.* I'm just in awe of your mental strength and courage."

"Meditation, Leah. That's the key. At least thirty minutes a day. It's *so hard,* but enlightenment is worth the hard!" She pauses and looks around her. Leo shifts slightly, her face eager, keeping Kymber's attention on her and not the gun.

"I realized that my big break would only come if I took action, so after the parade, Chaz and I came back here. We had a huge fight. He was just such a . . . Did you know he'd set up a Tinder account?"

"No! Kymber!" Leo sits up in outrage. Two inches from the gun.

"I know! We argued for over an hour. I was so excited to tell him about the conversation with the producer. This could have changed his life too! We'd already had that big success with exploding the float . . . Well." She gives Leo a side-eye, as if she's let loose a little secret. "His online engagement has been in the tank lately, and he hoped an explosion like the one at the parade would help. Then he got punched by Mack, so his numbers *did* jump, but not the way he wanted. He was *pissed* by the time he got home. I kept telling him, being on a reality TV show was the answer. Those kinds of numbers could've sent him into the stratosphere. He wouldn't see it. We were sitting on the chairs on the grass watching the fireworks in the park and he was just being *so stubborn.*" Her hands ball into fists. "I went inside to get him a beer, and I just . . . I realized I was done allowing a man to be the arbiter of my happy, you know?"

"Hell yeah, sister!" Leo winces internally. *Sister?*

"So I took my destiny into my own hands."

"Yeah, you did."

"I grabbed one of the big rocks near his deck."

"You're the queen of your own fate."

"And I hit him on the back of the head. Like he . . ." She grimaces. Leo wills her to continue. "He did something like that a long time ago. He told me about it one night when he was drunk.

Hit someone on the back of his head. And I thought . . . you know what? Time to suffer like you've made others suffer."

"Like he'd made *you* suffer, Kymber." Leo suffuses her voice with sympathy.

"Exactly. So I . . . well, I changed the course of my destiny." Kymber swallows, looking away—the most human moment Leo has seen from her all night. "And then . . . after, I put the rock down, but I realized I couldn't just leave him there. The fireworks had finished at the park, but they were going off all over the neighborhood, and it was so loud, which was *very convenient* for me. I didn't know about this crazy town and the obsession with fireworks. The whole neighborhood was yelling and there were people moving around all night. I took advantage."

"Of course you did."

"I used Chaz's truck. I put him in some old cloths from the shed and drove him up the street to the house he had been planning to sabotage next."

"What house?"

"The one being sold by that old hag who threatened his business. The one whose float exploded. Those people aren't your friends, are they?"

"Oh, no. I mean, I've talked to them, but you know this town, everyone knows everyone." Leo lies seamlessly.

"Well, that lady is terrible. She takes all of Chaz's business. He and I used to go into the houses she listed to do things. I moved Chaz onto that back porch." Leo notices she doesn't say *body*. "I did all the moving at night so no one could see me."

"So he was outside all night?"

"So?" Her voice is defensive.

Leo hurries to smooth it over. "No, just that . . . honestly, Kymber, that's genius. The heat would have made it harder for the cops to know when he was actually killed."

"That was the plan." Kymber's mask slips, briefly, and Leo sees the conniving mind behind the dingbat persona. "And then I loaded everything else I needed to get rid of into my

Jackalope pack and I went for a few runs that night and the next day. The hydration pack has extra storage for water and for life." She quotes the tagline.

"Kymber, that is *so* smart of you! You're always running anyway!"

"Thank you! I left little clues around town to confuse people."

"What did you leave?"

"Oh." Kymber stops to think, like she's remembering some menu items from a dinner a few days ago. She grabs the gun, which is right by Leo's elbow, and pulls it back toward her absent-mindedly. "I'd grabbed some gloves at one of that Realtor's houses a few weeks ago. They were on the ground in the front yard and I wanted to piss that lady off. I used them . . . when I took control of my own destiny. I left one at Grant's, and one at Mack's. I even changed out the rock I used to . . . you know. I traded it for another one in someone's yard. And then, when it was light, I went on another run, and I brought Chaz into the house for someone to find. That was the hardest part, but I managed to pull it off." Her voice is smug. "And then you'll never believe what I did!" She giggles, pushing the handle of the gun until it twirls on the counter like a fidget spinner.

"What?" Leo tries to make her face look like she's delighted, while trying not to flinch as the gun, with the safety off, spins nearer to the edge of the counter.

"I made a video to make it seem like that woman, *Queen Kay*, whose head exploded on the float, was yelling at him so that no one would know it was me." She sits back triumphantly, cradling the gun in her lap. Her hands are relaxed around it, but Leo nods to herself internally: grabbing the gun is obviously out. She'll have to implement her riskier plan, then.

Kymber continues. "I'd emailed the Chaz Challengers the night before, and then I set up the computer for the Chaz Challenge. I logged in to his Zoom with his camera up, but I Instagram Lived it from his phone, which I put on my tripod. Then I held *my* phone and played an edited video with her voice and stomped around, so it sounded like that other Realtor came into the house and killed Chaz. Then I put *his* phone down on the counter, left out the back door, and ran home. It turns out some potential buyers or someone came into the house soon after I left. It all went perfectly." She sits back, waiting for praise. "No one could possibly know it was me!"

Leo, who has glanced around the room, takes a second before she remembers she's supposed to respond. "That is truly incredible, Kymber. The forethought! And the genius-level cover-up! Honestly, I'm just blown away!"

"And you'll never believe the best part!" Kymber sits forward eagerly.

Leo mimics her stance. "Tell me!"

"That video went viral and my follower count tripled. The producer saw my post yesterday after Chaz's death. He sent his assistant Paula over here. She said I'm basically a widow and the one thing audiences like best is a hot widow. So guess what?" She squeals. "I got on the show! *Real Housewives of Austin*, here I come!"

"You've got to be kidding me!" Leo jumps up and claps. "Kymber, that's *amazing*!"

She opens her arms as if for a hug, and Kymber stands up and hugs her tightly. The gun handle digs into Leo's back and she tenses, but Kymber lets go.

Leo gestures toward the large sectional couch, a few yards from the kitchen in the open-concept living room. "Do you care if we move into the living room? I'm sore from running but I want to hear. Every. Single. Detail. Don't leave out a *thing*."

"I mean, the wardrobe *alone*, Leah . . ."

"You're getting *new clothes*!" Leo squeals, eyes riveted . . . there.

As Kymber walks in front of the wall of mirrors in the living room, she catches her own reflection and stops, tipping her hip out and pursing her lips—just as Leo knew she would. Kymber has never passed a mirror without body checking.

Three things happen at once.

Mid-squeal, Leo lunges for the gun. She grabs it and points it at Kymber's chest before Kymber even lifts her eyes from the mirror.

A fist pounds at the door. "Sheriff's department! Let us in right now!" Leo recognizes Jake's voice.

And a voice from the back door says calmly, "Kymber Owens, I'm armed and I'm a stellar shot. Back away from my daughter. Now."

79

Fifteen minutes later, Leo, for the second time this week, sits on the curb across the street from where the cops are securing a crime scene.

Except this time her mother is in the building with them. After running in on Leo and Kymber, holding a gun. Leo shakes her head. Did she really just see her mother—devoid of the makeup and the Aqua Net and the ferociously bright colors and everything that made her mother her mother—point a gun at Kymber?

She feels shaky, but not like she did after finding Chaz's body. Something came alive in her when she thwarted Kymber. It's like she was firing on all cylinders, mind and body alert and active. She's never really felt that way before.

Esquivel comes out and stands over Leo. "Macy says thank you. For the Runsafe info. That's how we found Kymber—and you."

"Tell Macy thank you for locating me."

"Well, we didn't. That was the feds. Jake went to Kymber's house. I was entering evidence at the station after interviewing Melody in Austin. The Runsafe app hides your location within five hundred yards, and Kymber turned it off before coming here instead of her house. Macy got us close, just not close enough."

"What do you mean, it was the feds?"

"They're the ones who told us where you were. They were running the show. We just followed their orders."

Leo shakes her head. "I don't understand."

"I'm sure there's a lot to—actually, I have to go inside." Esquivel takes a step back. "Nice to meet you, Leo. Hope we get to work together again sometime soon."

"No offense, but I hope we never work together again."

"Fair enough." Esquivel chuckles and walks away.

Karina is coming up behind Leo. She sits down on the curb. Mother and daughter look at each other for a long time. Leo feels the tension in the moment. This is a before; an after is coming. She knows her life will never be the same.

"Mom."

Karina sighs deeply. "I should have told you. Kay tried to convince me to tell you over the years. Even your dad wanted you to know. But I thought . . ." Karina glances down before looking up again, her eyes full. "I thought I could keep you safe. And that's all . . ." She grasps Leo's hands. Leo is relieved, in some small part of her mind, to realize her mom's riotous nails have not changed. "That's all I ever wanted to do."

"So the whole argument today . . ."

"The reason my actions haven't made sense to you is because I've been lying to you for years. For most of your life, in fact." Karina closes her eyes, her expression defeated. "It's going to take us a long time to talk this through. I know you'll be mad. I'd love to say my motives have all been pure, but if I'm truly being honest, I've been afraid to tell you some of this because"—her voice breaks—"you're going to hate me. And you'll never trust me again."

Leo looks at her mother, sees the fear in her eyes.

"Can you tell me the truth now?"

"Yes. It's time." She leaves her hand on Leo's and looks around, then turns back. "Leo, I'm—"

"Get your *filthy* hands off my *body*!" Kymber screeches. Leo and Karina turn; Karina still holds her hand.

Jake leads a handcuffed Kymber out of the house with the help of two of the uniformed DPS officers. "Ms. Owens, you have the right to remain silent . . ."

"Silent? Do you think I'm going to be *silent* while you manhandle me? *Ow!*"

Jake lifts his hands, not touching her, but still speaking. "Anything you say can and will be used against you in a court of law—"

Tires squeal. Williams pulls up in a car with flashing lights. He parks in the middle of the street.

Sheriff Quackenbush bursts out of the passenger side. "And furthermore, when I tell you to pick me up, I mean pick me up *right then* . . ." He stops as he takes in Jake beside a handcuffed Kymber. "Who told you fools to . . ." Williams clears his throat and nods discreetly to the neighbors lining the street, especially one with her cell phone out recording. Quackenbush blusters. "Who told you *fellows* to . . . move forward without me while I . . . finished up with the paperwork back at the office?"

He walks determinedly toward Jake, muttering. The edges of the paper napkin tucked into his uniform shirt like a bib flutter in the blustering breeze he makes. He does not notice. No one tells him.

Jake's voice is loud enough for neighbors several houses away to hear him. "Sheriff, you'd be proud of your crackerjack team that coordinated with the *feds* in a raid that went off seamlessly. Your training made all the difference, sir."

Quackenbush's eyebrows are high. "The feds, huh?"

"Yes, sir. Do you mind if I finish Mirandizing her? Now that we have her confession recorded?"

"Good, good, of course. Make sure the tape of her confession is on my desk by morning. Carry on, son." Quackenbush's spine straightens as he walks into the house, breaking through the caution tape Esquivel just secured. Esquivel sighs, then gets to work rehanging it.

Kymber is silent while Quackenbush arrives, but begins her

protests as soon as he walks into Chaz's house. Jake tucks her into the back of a waiting squad car, making sure her head doesn't hit the ceiling despite her squirming: ". . . if you cannot afford an attorney, one will be appointed for you before any questions are asked." He closes the door and taps on the roof. The squad car, driven by one of the DPS officers, pulls away.

Jake turns to Karina and nods. "Ma'am. Can we talk for a moment?" He walks down the street to his truck.

"That is one excellent officer." Karina squeezes Leo's hand. "I'll be right back."

Karina walks down the street. Leo suddenly hears footsteps beside her.

"Leo." Mack's voice is husky. She is standing before she realizes it, and they're hugging. When he tucks his head down, his cowboy hat blocks out the light. She breathes him in deeply. "Oh, Mack, I'm so sorry I missed dinner."

"Are you serious? I don't care about dinner." She can feel his deep voice through his chest. "I'm just glad you're okay." He strokes her hair and gathers her against his chest. "Emily called me from the jail—apparently there's some kind of party there, and they were all listening to the police scanner? The feds are involved? And it sounds like you solved Chaz's murder?"

"It was Kymber, Mack. She killed him with a rock. Like . . ." She stops and gazes up at him. He pulls back, his hands grazing her arms.

"Like Chaz killed Dom." His voice is quiet, resigned.

"You know?"

"Mel called. Apparently Lieutenant Esquivel told her. It sounds like Tiffani finally confessed Chaz's secret to you and Jake today?"

Leo nods, overcome.

"That prick could have told me, at least," Mack mutters.

"Jake? He was solving a murder!"

"Um, sounds like *you* were doing that. *He* was coming after me and my family."

Leo leans back tensely but Mack pulls her to him. “Forget it, Leo. It’s been a devastating day. Just . . . finally learning the truth about Dom, and then Chaz and Kymber . . . I don’t think I’m rational right now.”

She snuggles in and he wraps his arms around her. “Me neither.” Nothing, in all the years since they broke up in high school, has felt as good as this hug.

He holds her for several minutes, his cheek on top of her head. Finally, with a prolonged sigh, he says, “You’re going to have to give me a rain check for dinner, though.”

She laughs dryly. “Can’t wait.”

“Leo, I thought I’d lost you right as I . . .” He lifts his head but does not pull away. His big hands cradle her face, thumbs beside her ears, hands digging into her hair, tipping her chin up. His warm brown eyes are anguished.

Leo thinks of the hours spent wondering if Mack could have committed murder. The relief she feels that she was correct all along floods her; she can trust her intuition, she thinks. She knew Mack was a good man, and he is. There are certainly things about each other they don’t know, but who he is inside—none of that has changed.

“Shhhh. I get it. I really do.” She tugs on his shirt, pulling him down to her level.

“Are you . . . ?” His mouth is a breath away from hers. “Is this okay?”

“Yes,” she breathes where only he can hear, and before the word finishes, his mouth is on hers.

The kiss lasts for seconds, or an eternity, Leo’s not sure. Finally he rests his forehead against hers. “We have an audience,” he whispers, “so I can’t show you how much I’ve missed you, but, Leo . . .” He kisses her lightly, like he’s sipping at her lips, then again. And again, like he can’t get enough. His hat creates a dark little space only for them. His stubble is rough against her skin. “I have really, really missed you.” He brushes his thumbs down the sides of her cheeks, then steps back.

She feels hot all over. In three of the most stressful,

exhausting days of her life, when it feels like everything is changing around her, Leo wonders if this kiss might be the most seismic change of all.

She slowly registers her surroundings again—the cops bustling in and out of the house, the neighbors watching, her mother and Jake nearby.

Her mother.

And Jake.

Mack seems to come to himself at the same time. He steps into her space one more time, kissing the top of her head and squeezing her shoulders with one arm. He says into her hair, "Go, get a citizens' badge or whatever you're supposed to do. I'll call you later. Okay?"

She clears her throat. "Sounds good."

He walks away, boots clicking on the asphalt. He turns to look back at her once and grins, before he crosses Deep Hollows park—past the Deep, where Dominic died, through the woods to his home.

When she finally turns toward her mother and Jake, they are standing beside each other, watching her watch Mack.

Jake's dark eyes are unreadable, his posture stiff. He looks from Leo to her mother, then back to Leo. He holds Leo's gaze for a long, long moment. His arms are crossed and his clenched teeth heighten the razor edge of his jaw. Leo feels a tug of regret—for what, she's not sure.

"Thank you for all your help, Leo." His expression is raw for one instant, so fast she thinks she imagined it. No, she tells herself. She can trust her instincts. She steps toward him.

"Jake, I—"

He backs up swiftly. "You'll need to . . . You must be so . . . We'll debrief soon." He turns and walks up the sidewalk toward the house, ducking under Esquivel's tape. He doesn't glance back at her.

Karina sits down on the curb. Leo drops, boneless, beside her. The warmth from the pavement seeps through her running shorts. "Mom, I just . . . I need the truth. Now."

Karina turns her knees toward Leo. She stares at her daughter for one long moment. "Okay. Here it is." She swallows. "Leonora, in those years when your father and I lived in El Salvador, when we fell in love and had you, we weren't humanitarian workers like we've always said. We weren't there to teach, or work on the farm." Leo breathes in. "I was a CIA officer. I still am. Your father was too."

Leo opens her mouth and then closes it. She thought everything changed a moment ago? The entire world shifts beneath her now. Her mom reaches a hand out.

Leo suddenly moves. *"Don't touch me!"*

Her mother holds her hands up like Leo's a skittish horse. "I'm sorry. I know it's a lot."

"You know *nothing.*" At Leo's exclamation, Karina looks as if her breath has been knocked out of her. "You're telling me, all of this"—Leo gestures up and down at Karina's body—"the clothes and the hair and the language and the *ridiculous flamboyant chickens* and, I don't know, a bubble-gum-pink shop called Hair Today, Dye Tomorrow . . . all of it is, what, a lie?"

"It's a cover." Karina reaches for her daughter's hand and stops herself.

"*You* were the federal agent?"

Karina nods miserably.

"So that whole holding the gun . . . you know how to do . . . all that?"

"I'm an excellent shot." There is that half smile again. "Since your father died . . . For the past fifteen years, I've gone on a few missions, but I'm semiretired for . . . several reasons I should explain when I have more time. Mostly I train other agents; that's when I travel—you know those cruises I take. Which is how I know that your tactics tonight were not just stellar, they were—"

Leo interrupts her. She does not want a single compliment from her mother. This stranger. "Who else is in on your secret?"

"Kay and Phil, of course."

"And Jake?"

Karina nods again.

Leo continues. "You told him, but you couldn't tell me?"

"*No*, I couldn't tell you." Karina's voice bursts out more harshly than she evidently means it to, because she modulates it, pulls it back. "I'm so sorry I've hidden this from you all your life. I'm sure you'll have questions, and we can spend the next several days, or probably years, answering them. I realize now that trying to protect you hasn't actually protected you. You were almost killed tonight, and *you're* the one who got yourself out. I should have trusted you long before this, and I'm sorry." Karina stares at her feet.

"Mom, are you telling me that this . . . all of this . . . our entire relationship, all of the tension of my adult life, everything we've ever fought about, the distance, the pushing me out of Blue Oak, keeping me from this community, all of it was . . . what, fake? A lie?" Leo can tell she's repeating herself, but it feels like her brain is swirling in circles, unable to accept what Karina has said.

"A . . ."

"I know, a *cover*." Leo spits the word out. "I could probably . . ." She trails off. "But you've been *awful* to me. For years. Since Dad died."

Karina nods numbly.

"What in the actual hell were you thinking?"

Karina swallows. "Leo, I had no choice . . ."

"Please, stop." Leo looks at her mother—really looks at her. It's as if she's gotten glimpses her whole life of the face behind her mother's mask, and now that she sees the full thing, she wonders how in the world she could have been fooled. The betrayal of it is a white searing poker, shoved into her stomach. Leo has no idea who her mother is, and, in this moment, she feels that she has no idea who *she* really is. The adrenaline and confidence from solving the murder—that wild rush to save her mother from nothing, her mother the *federal agent*, she thinks ruefully to herself—of carefully manipulating Kymber, of grabbing the gun, of kissing Mack . . . it's seeping out of her body. She begins to shake.

Her mother looks sick. "Leo, I'm so sorry. I'll probably spend the rest of my life saying it, but I really am."

"You have lied to me all of my life, and you think *sorry* is going to cut it?"

Karina turns to her now, her face and her stance completely open. "I don't, actually. You might never forgive me. It's the greatest fear I've faced, the one I've carried with me for years. But it was worth it, even if it hurt you, because it kept you *safe*." Karina breathes in a shuddering breath. "Leo, there's more I have to tell you."

"What more can you possibly say?"

Karina gazes at her, as if gauging her ability to handle what's about to come. "All these years, I've let you believe your father died of a heart attack."

Leo thinks, for one awful second, that if she can just silence her mother, she'll never have to know this thing. But she is frozen from stress and grief and exhaustion. She cannot open her mouth to stop what's coming.

"Mi amor, your father's death all those years ago . . ." She closes her eyes, bracing herself. "Leo, your father was murdered."

"What?" It's a harsh, guttural whisper. Karina reaches for her hand and finally, finally, Leo lets her take it.

"And you were their next target."

Leo shakes her head, trying to rid herself of this information.

"Yes, Leo," her mother insists. "I lied to you for all those years and drove you away on purpose because I really *was* trying to protect you the best way I knew how. As long as you're in Blue Oak . . . you're in grave, grave danger."

Acknowledgments

My writing career began with two narrative nonfiction books and numerous articles about displacement, genocide, and immigration. After I realized (thanks to my excellent therapist) that I developed secondary trauma from that reporting, I started reading murder mysteries and romance at night to calm my brain and escape to a world where the good people always won, the community was protected, and everything ended up okay. To the authors who provide us with joy and help us envision a better world, I can never thank you enough—your work is more important than you know. And you inspired me.

When I told my extraordinary agent, Mackenzie Brady Watson, that I wanted to shift from nonfiction to murder mysteries next, she didn't bat an eye; she just got to work reading, making connections, and learning what she needed to about the genre. She edited multiple drafts before this book went to auction, got deep in the weeds on murder and romance (I know who you're rooting for in this love triangle!), and made this book a thousand times better. Believe me, I know I'm the luckiest writer in the world to call her both my agent and my dear friend. Thank you also to Aemilia Philips for excellent notes on an early draft, Stuart Krichevsky for the poignant advice on parenting, and everyone else at SKLA for being such wonderful people.

Grace Layer is an exceptional editor. At every turn, she has pushed and challenged and tightened this book, helping me to shape it into something that exceeds anything I could have imagined. As I write this, I'm in the middle of finishing the second manuscript, and I already hear Grace's voice in my head clarifying and strengthening my writing—she's the editor every writer dreams of. (And I know who *you're* rooting for in this love triangle!)

Thank you to everyone at Dutton. The exquisite cover of Leo pointing her camera at Blue Oak (which has *just* the right amount of blood) is illustrated by Nathan Burton, with Kaitlin Kall as cover director. Chandra Wohleber's eagle copyediting eye made the mystery elements and my grammar so much sharper—thank you! Special thanks to Alice Dalrymple, Lorie Pagnozzi, Melissa Solis, John Parsley, and Maya Ziv. And, of course, to Diamond Bridges and Sarah Thegeby, whose tireless efforts to get the word out about this book mean the world to me.

Thanks always to Authors Unbound, especially Christie Hinrichs and Amy Loomis. Every time I tell them I'm adding one more aspect to my career, they respond with enthusiastic efficiency, and I'm so grateful for the whole team of fierce women and all of the communities I get to know through speaking.

Terry Dwyer read several sections of this book and gave me great edits as a retired detective and now incredible author—I can't wait to celebrate your book soon! Other people in law enforcement who do not want to be named helped me understand procedural aspects that were especially critical in writing about a small-town sheriff's department. I'm so appreciative of Brad Livsey for his insights as a firefighter. Any mistakes are my own.

I won't name all of them (because the FBI is probably already monitoring my internet search history), but thank you to the many, many friends who have plotted murder with me over the last few years. Especially to my friends who continue to send me unhinged neighborhood Facebook group posts—I will love you forever. (Yes, the two rival Facebook groups are based on my real neighborhood. Yes, they debate fireworks twice a year. Yes, I make popcorn and settle in every New Year's Eve and Fourth of July.)

Special thanks to Aili Ashford, whose knowledge of running gear opened up this mystery for me; I miss our conversations. To my friends at SoulStrong Yoga, thank you for keeping me functioning and grounded—sorry for scheming about murder during shavasana.

My community in the Maslow Family Graduate Program in Creative Writing at Wilkes University is life-giving; getting to teach and learn with such incredible writers in the very best low-res MFA program is one of the highlights of my life, and I love too many to name them all. Thank you to Christine Renee Miller for being my podcast co-host on *The Beautiful and Banned*, my twice-a-year roomie, and always my friend—I love chatting and adventuring with you the most. And special thanks to Maureen Corrigan, who is as lovely and brilliant in person as she is on NPR.

Thank you to all my writing friends. To the group of (mostly) journalists in Austin: our conversations are the highlight of my month. Alejandra Oliva and Lauren Pinkston: thank you for partnering with me on the "Injustice Report"—I learned so much from you. Victoria Blanco and Carrie R. Moore: conversations with each of you recently reminded me why I love writing. Christiana Peterson and Amy Peterson: you're always there and I'm so grateful. Allison Hunter and our book club of amazing women: thank you for so many good discussions. Nisha Sharma, Nia Davenport, Ehigbor Okosun, Susan Lee, Ali Hazelwood, Lindsey Kelk, Destinee Hodge, Alyssa Moore, and so many others: thank you for letting me hang out with the romance crew—I love being the crocodile among you capybaras.

Naina Kumar: thank you for everything, always. Pivoting together from serious careers into fun writing has been so joyful, and I love that one of my favorite friends is now one of my favorite writers.

I'm especially grateful for the friendship of Caren George, Lindsay Wilkerson, Chez Dishman, Ashley Luksys, Kim Pollard, Constance Dykhuizen, Ann Reese, Amy Carder, Holly Mock, Kameryn McCain, Amy Sullivan, Claire Shoop, and Sam and Sarah Donohoe—I love you all and I'm so happy to be writing fun books for you to read next.

I can never thank my incredible family members enough for all the love and support. I love each of you dearly. Jay, thanks for letting me borrow your name.

My thanks always to Jonathan for being the love of my life and for making all of this possible, and for our kids who are so wonderful. On a road trip last year while I was working on edits, I read this book out loud for the first time—and listening to my husband and kids laugh and gasp at just the right moments will always be one of my favorite memories.

To the people in my community, which looks a whole lot more like Blue Oak than anything I ever see on the news, who are tired of explaining "why we stay"—I hope I caught at least some of the spirit of this state we love. I'll see y'all at H-E-B.

And finally, to the booksellers and librarians and teachers and literature professors who create and protect our reading spaces, and to my fellow readers who love nothing more than to escape into a good book—from my nerdy heart to yours, thank you.

About the Author

Jess Cannon is the pseudonym of a failed academic who never made tenure but still sleeps great at night. She spends her days writing award-winning journalism and her nights plotting fictional murders. She lives with her family and an irascible blue heeler in Austin, Texas, where her funky community is a constant source of joy (and writing material). She has a PhD in literature from the University of Texas, teaches fiction and nonfiction at Wilkes University, and has written for *The New York Times*, *The Atlantic*, *The Washington Post*, and *Teen Vogue*, among others. She also co-hosts *The Beautiful and Banned* podcast with Christine Renee Miller.